Undying

ZOMBURBIA

The first book in the Zombie Apocalypse Series

"*Zomburbia* combines deliciously dark humor with genuine moments of gut-wrenching horror. Adam Gallardo's world building is innovative and fascinating, turning the typical vision of post-zombie survival on its rotting ear. *Zomburbia* is sick and twisted and unexpectedly touching. I only put it down long enough to check that my zombie apocalypse closet was well stocked."
—**Molly Harper White,** author of the Naked Werewolf series

"Meet Courtney, a flawed but spunky teen, and her misfit pals, who are trying to find their places in a world where death lurks around every corner. Readers are guaranteed plenty of mayhem and romance, laughter and heartbreak, in Adam Gallardo's accomplished debut novel."
—**James Patrick Kelly,** winner of the Hugo, Nebula, and Locus awards

"If you haven't read *Zomburbia,* you haven't read about zombies. This is a new take, and it is scary, freaky, and original. Gallardo resets the zombie bar and it's sky-high. Get this book!"
—**Nancy Holder,** *New York Times* best-selling author of *The Wicked Saga*

"Courtney's smart and ambitious, and she makes terrible decisions. Comics author Gallardo nails her voice—likable yet self-absorbed. This rough world lends itself to drug dealing, partying, guns-blazing action sequences, and unvarnished language . . . the interpersonal drama strikes a comfortable balance with undead action. More brains than your average zombie novel . . . and more entrails as well!"
—*Kirkus Reviews*

"With its complicated and believable heroine, exploration of moral dilemmas, and disturbingly mundane vision of life among the undead, this action- and gore-soaked adventure entertains on numerous levels."
—*Publishers Weekly*

"Fans of zombie fiction will devour this book; teens who haven't made the leap (or shuffle) to the genre will be hooked. A gory, campy read."
—*School Library Journal*

"A fresh take on the post-zombie apocalypse. . . . Gallardo develops Courtney with an authentic voice, and she becomes a strong heroine. Teens looking for zombie action with a determined female narrator will enjoy this quick read."
—*Voice of Youth Advocates*

ALSO BY ADAM GALLARDO

Zomburbia

ZOMBIFIED

ADAM GALLARDO

KENSINGTON BOOKS
www.kensingtonbooks.com

KENSINGTON BOOKS are published by

Kensington Publishing Corp.
119 West 40th Street
New York, NY 10018

All Kensington titles, imprints, and distributed lines are available at special quantity discounts for bulk purchases for sales promotions, premiums, fund-raising, educational, or institutional use.

Special book excerpts or customized printings can also be created to fit specific needs. For details, write or phone the office of the Kensington special sales manager: Kensington Publishing Corp., 119 West 40th Street, New York, NY 10018, attn: Special Sales Department; phone 1-800-221-2647.

KENSINGTON and the k logo are Reg. U.S. Pat. & TM Off.

ISBN-13: 978-1-61773-100-6
ISBN-10: 1-61773-100-5

First Trade Paperback Printing: February 2015

10 9 8 7 6 5 4 3 2 1

Printed in the United States of America

First electronic edition: February 2015

ISBN-13: 978-1-61773-101-3
ISBN-10: 1-61773-101-3

ZOMBIFIED

CHAPTER ONE
Do Me a Favor in Return?

From the top of some hill I didn't know the name of, the whole of Salem seemed to spread out before me. I thought I might puke.

The day before my senior year started up and this had been my first time out of the freaking house all summer without my dad in my back pocket—except for some late-night vigilante shenanigans that Dad didn't know about—and where does my buddy Phil decide to bring me? To look out at the town I hate and can't wait to get away from. Needless to say, he is not Casanova. On the plus side, he'd probably have been able to tell me who Casanova was. I think. I decided not to push my luck and ask him.

I closed my eyes and drew a deep breath. Jesus, I was acting like a grade-A bitch, even if it was only in my head. I opened my eyes and tried to see the town in a more positive way. Obviously Phil liked this, and I wanted to get in sync with him.

The Willamette River glittered in the sun, cutting Salem off from West Salem. The one surviving bridge was covered in traffic—the other bridge had been blown up years ago in the first days after the dead came back. There was the downtown dominated by the capitol building and the Gold Man shining on top. The courthouse, a few churches, a big bank or two; all of it dotted with parks and clumps of trees.

I wanted to barf. The smell of old cigarettes didn't help much. Whoever owned this car before Phil had been a heavy smoker and we'd been unable to get rid of the stench. If Phil noticed my deep dislike of this little excursion, he didn't let on. But then Phil seemed not to catch too many social cues. It was simultaneously cute and infuriating.

"Why did you bring me out here?" I asked.

Phil turned slowly to look at me and blinked his eyes. A tic of his. He had brown hair that fell into his eyes, also brown. A sharp chin. Good lips and nose, too. I used to think he was plain-looking. When I caught myself thinking that, I blushed and mentally backed away from the thought the same way I might back away from a dog that might be dangerous. Again, he didn't seem to notice.

"I thought you'd like it," he said. He shrugged. "I like it."

Someone who hadn't been socialized by feral cats might ask what it was exactly that he liked about the town.

"How's the movie theater?" I asked.

"Good," he said. "I like running the projector. It's old and needs to be constantly repaired just so it runs, but that's fun." He smiled and I wondered again at ever thinking he was plain.

"That reminds me," he said. "Have you been by the Bully Burger lately?" The Bully Burger is the local fast-food joint where we worked together before he left to work at the theater. I didn't work there anymore, either, but my departure was a little more complicated.

"Nope," I said. "I haven't been back since I quit. What's up?"

"I was in there a few days ago," he said. "I heard that someone had been in looking for you."

"Oh, shit," I said. "It wasn't Brandon, was it?" I asked. Brandon was a boy I had been falling for at the end of last school year. Before everything went to hell, that is.

"I don't think so. They would have said it was him, but they didn't seem to know this guy's name."

"Did they say what he looked like?" I asked. "Who told you this, one of the Olsen twins?" The twins weren't really named Olsen, but they were for real named Mary-Kate and Ashley. No, seriously.

"No," said Phil. "It was Chacho, and I didn't ask what the guy looked like."

"Ah, how was Chacho?" I asked. He was the security guard at the Bully Burger, and the only cool adult I knew.

"He was okay, I guess," said Phil with another shrug.

My mind raced for a while wondering who might have been looking for me. Listen, I had just turned seventeen, and you wouldn't know it to look at me, but there was a good chance that a number of unsavory characters might want to find me.

"Can I ask you something?" Phil asked.

"Well, you can ask."

"What's up with you and Brandon?" he asked.

This threw me. I wasn't expecting Phil to really be aware of what was going on between me and Brandon.

"How do you mean?"

"You two seemed to be an item last year," he said. *An item?* Was Phil a character in a Sweet Valley High novel? I let it slide. "And then you weren't, and now you act weird whenever his name comes up."

I slid down in the front seat of the horrible old Ford Taurus Phil had bought over the summer, and the cracked leather upholstery creaked and made fart noises. I knew that I'd have to talk about all of this with Phil at some point. I was just lucky that he hadn't asked me before now.

"Can we get out of the car?" I asked. "Get some fresh air?"

"Is this some sort of stall tactic?" he asked.

"Only sort of," I said. "Mostly I want some fresh air." The stale cigarette smell really was getting to me.

Rather than answer, Phil opened his door and climbed out. I did the same, but as I got out, I grabbed my bag and started rummaging through it.

"What are you looking for?" he asked as he squinted in at me through the windshield.

"My gun," I said. Technically, it's a revolver.

"Are you planning to shoot me?" he asked. It took me a second to realize he'd made a joke. They were pretty rare coming from him.

"Ha," I deadpanned. "I just don't want any uninvited guests." I grabbed the pistol and stood, tucking it into my waistband.

He looked around us. We'd parked at the end of a dead-end street. There were a few houses on either side of the street, all of them surrounded by chain-link fencing, and a few trees.

"I don't think there are gonna be any zombies around here," he said.

"Yeah, well," I said, "the last time I thought I'd have a zombie-free evening with a group of friends, I had to deal with a whole army of the damned things." At Brandon's end-of-the-school-year party a couple months ago, we'd been attacked by the zombie equivalent of the Golden Horde. That was one of the reasons I'd stopped seeing him. But just one reason.

Phil sat on the bumper of the car and I did the same. I waited for him to ask me again, but I realized he wasn't going to. He seemed happy just to look out over that city I wanted to get out of so badly. I considered not talking, not bringing it up again, but I worried what the consequences of that might be. I couldn't figure out how Phil was doing such a number on my head, but I thought it might have been sorcery.

I noticed that he was sort of gesturing in the air with his hands, another tic. Little movements like he was conducting a symphony or something. I thought about his hands and what they'd feel like on my skin, then put that thought away where it had come from.

"As preface to this whole story," I said, and I kept my eyes forward, definitely not looking at him, "I just want to say that I don't do it anymore."

"Ominous," Phil said. "Do what?"

"I used to sell drugs," I said. "For, like, the last year that I worked at the Bully, I was selling Vitamin Z out of the drive-through window."

I waited for a response, but Phil stayed silent. I weighed his particular silence and it didn't feel judge-y. Believe me, as a girl raised in the American school system, I know judgmental. I decided I'd be able to go on.

"I never tried it myself," I said, "until I did. Just once." I glanced at Phil and he nodded slowly. "Brandon was with me. And Sherri." Sherri had been my best friend since birth, and she'd worked at the Bully Burger with Phil and me. "While we were high, we got separated from Sherri. The next time I saw her, she was a zombie.

"The whole episode freaked my shit something fierce. I decided to stop selling, and I definitely decided I'd never do Z again."

"But Brandon," Phil said.

"But Brandon," I agreed. "He kept on going with it. He had some at his end-of-year shindig last year and wanted me to smoke it with him. That was right before the zombies made their grand entrance."

Phil nodded. He'd been there for that part. Not as a guest of the party. He'd just shown up in case there was trouble of the undead variety.

"And he'd smoked it once or twice before that night, too."

"Why?" Phil asked.

"He said it made him forget himself," I said. "Not just his troubles, but himself. He liked that, I guess."

Phil cocked his head and looked at me.

"No," he said. "Why did you sell Vitamin Z?"

"Oh, right." Of course he was asking about me. I'd been trying to focus on Brandon because that made things easier. I felt a little ember of resentment start to glow in my chest. My fallback position whenever I'm put on the spot is to get angry and let my inner bitch off her leash, but I knew that wasn't fair to Phil. He deserved some answers. I took a deep breath and did my best to grind out that fire.

"I needed it to fund my plan," I said.

My plan to get the hell out of Salem, to move to New York City—if the Army ever reclaims it from the zombies—attend Columbia University, and find a cure for the zombie plague. Phil knows all about it.

I braced myself for him to be horrified. Or at least mildly grossed out. What I wasn't prepared for was him taking it in stride.

"I'm not surprised you don't want to see him anymore," he said. "Especially after something as scary as Sherri dying, maybe because of you guys taking Vitamin Z."

I took a deep breath.

"That's it?" I asked him. "Nothing about me selling it?" Why the hell was I pushing it? He'd let me off the hook, I should stop picking the scab.

"You stopped selling it after that, right?" he asked. "After you figured out it was bad mojo?" I nodded that this was true. He shrugged. "You want me to judge you for doing something dumb? I don't do that. I've done too many dumb things myself to start judging people."

"Are you Christian?" I blurted out. It was such a good explanation as to why he wouldn't want to judge me. It would also explain why, after months of going out on zombie patrol, he hadn't made one attempt at kissing me. Or even copping a feel. I'd briefly considered that he might be gay, but my sexuality-detecting equipment wasn't picking up any fabulous signals.

He looked confused. "No, I'm not. Would it matter if I was?"

"No," I lied. As much as I like to be open-minded, churchy-Joes rub me the wrong way. It was something I needed to work on, okay? "I'm just trying to figure you out."

"My aunt says that that way leads to madness." He said it without a smile—smiles from him are rare—but he didn't seem sad about it, either.

"Your aunt seems to have you pegged," I said.

A grin played across his lips.

His lips.

Man, I needed to get a grip. I stood up and checked that the pistol was still firmly in place.

"Let's go for a walk."

"Where?" Phil asked.

I pointed past the end of the street. Where the pavement ended, a small foot trail led down into some trees.

"Maybe we can get a better look at this beautiful city of yours," I said.

"Sure," he said. "Let me get my bat out of the trunk."

I thought about that for a moment. His bat is of the ordinary baseball variety—wood and about yea long—except that it had nails pounded through it and it was more than likely covered in the gore of a hundred undead.

It occurred to me I'd never seen it in full light. I didn't think I wanted this to be my first time.

"Why don't you leave it?" I asked. "If we run into trouble, I have this." I lifted up my shirt to show him the pistol, and exposed a good portion of my belly, too. Not that he seemed to notice.

"Okay," he said, barely glancing at me. "You want to go down first, or me?"

"Let me," I said. Maybe I'd at least find a zombie who found my body appealing.

I started picking my way down the path, which was steeper than it had appeared from up on the street. A few times my feet tried to get out from under me, but I never actually fell on my ass. So, points to me, I guess.

Once we got down about six feet or so, the ground flattened out a little and I became less worried about falling off the hill. Then I noticed that the trees were a lot thicker and closer than they'd appeared from up above, and I started worrying about new stuff, i.e., shufflers deciding I looked like a tasty snack.

Phil skidded the last foot or so and he grabbed me to stop himself from falling. His hand snaked around my waist and he left it there for a second after he got himself righted. My heart started to thud in my chest and all thoughts of the undead went right out of my head. I felt like the heroine in a Regency novel that featured monsters, as dumb as that sounds.

"Sorry," Phil said.

"No problem." I looked out at the city. Being a few yards closer to it didn't make it any prettier. So much for my brilliant ideas.

"Let's go down here," Phil said as he started walking. "I think there are some big rocks we can sit on." He paused and grinned at me. "The better to enjoy the incredible view."

"More jokes," I said. "You're like a junior Dane Cook."

"I hope I'm less douchey."

I didn't answer that and just followed him. We found the rocks pretty easily. Big, flat stones that jutted out of the dirt. They were probably part of the mountain we were crawling all over. It felt good to sit in the sun with a boy I was starting to like. I warned myself that this was only the second time I'd been through this, and the first time— with Brandon—hadn't turned out well. It wasn't that I didn't trust Phil; it was that I didn't trust myself.

We sat there without talking for a while and then, as I'm prone to do, I started mentally turning over something Phil had said earlier.

"What dumb things?" I asked.

He stared out at the city and frowned a little.

"Too soon," he said.

"When?" I prodded.

He turned toward me and said, "I'm not sure. But I'll know when it's the time. If it ever is."

"And you expect me to be satisfied with that answer," I said, teasing him.

"You don't have a choice," he said, serious like a heart attack.

"I was joking."

"Okay," he said. "Good."

The sun was behind us, but it must have started to set because we were in shadow by then and the air was getting cooler. I rubbed my arms when goose bumps sprang up on them.

"Let's head back to the car," I said. "I've had enough of this scenic beauty for a while."

"Okay," said Phil. He stood and turned back the way we'd come, and then he froze. "Oh," he said.

A zombie stood right on the path that led back to the car. Of course. She wasn't all chewed up and bloody, but her gray skin and the black slime that oozed out of her mouth were good indicators of what we were dealing with. I took a second to admire her Smiths T-shirt. It was the Meat Is Murder one. How's that for shitty irony? She looked like she was our age, maybe a little younger, and she used to be pretty. I guessed that maybe West Salem High was missing a cheerleader.

We just stood there for a minute. All three of us. She made no attempt to come at us, and we weren't exactly ready to rush her. I started to look around because the last few times I'd had run-ins with some shufflers, they'd sort of been traveling in packs. But if there were others with her, they weren't coming out to play.

"Courtney," Phil shout-whispered at me.

"What?" I said.

"Don't you have a gun in your pants?"

No, I'm just happy to see you, I thought and grinned despite the situation. I was so scared I felt a little giddy. But he was right, I did have a pistol. Making no sudden movements, I slid my right hand across my belly and under my shirt. I found the pistol and wrapped my hand around it— I was careful to keep my finger off the trigger so I didn't shoot myself in the gut when I drew it out. Just as slowly, I moved my left hand up and grabbed my shirt. I took a deep breath, let it out, then simultaneously lifted the shirt and drew the pistol.

Which stuck in my waistband!

I was so confused, I almost did shoot myself. I looked down to see what was going on and I heard the zombie snarl. I felt the gun's sight snag on something, but I wasn't able to tell what.

"Courtney!" Phil shouted.

I looked up to see the dead girl charging me. I yanked the gun free and felt a searing pain on my stomach. Then she hit me like a freaking undead linebacker. We both went over and she landed on top of me. I let go of the gun to grab her arms and keep her off me.

The bitch was inches from my face, snapping her jaws and drooling black shit all over me. I was trying to keep the ooze from getting in my mouth, and my arms were already shaking with the effort to keep her up.

"Philip," I screamed, "grab the gun or something!"

I didn't hear him respond. Where the hell was he? I knew I couldn't last much longer. A whimper escaped my throat and I cursed myself for that. There was no way I wanted to go out crying in front of a goddamn zombie.

Just then something flew across my body and knocked the dead girl off of me. Phil had tackled her and now he wrestled on the ground with her. He'd ended up on top, but I knew that he couldn't let her go or try to get away without risking getting bitten. At least she wasn't leaking zombie tranny fluid all over him.

Despite just wanting to curl up into a ball, I got up on my hands and knees and started searching for the gun. Rocks and other junk dug into my knees and the palms of my hands as I probed under bushes and scanned the area. I didn't see the damn pistol anywhere.

"Courtney!"

Somehow, Phil was now lying flat on his back, the dead girl contorting every way she could to try and get her teeth into him. His eyes bulged, and his face and neck were a scary shade of red. I knew he wasn't going to last much longer. Screw the gun.

I found the biggest rock I was able to palm. It felt good in my hand—jagged and heavy. I stood and walked over to where Phil tangled with the zombie, stopped, and raised the rock high in the air. Phil's eyes turned toward me and something like relief washed over his face. If this were a movie, it's at this point I'd say something ironic, but I couldn't think of anything.

"Do it!" Phil screamed.

The dead chick turned to look at me and hissed through blackened teeth.

I brought the rock down with all my strength right on her nose. I felt more than heard the sickening crunch of her nose caving into her face, and more black ooze squirted from the wound. She screamed and let go of Phil to clutch at it. Then she fell over backward as Phil bucked her off him.

I immediately collapsed onto her chest and, with my free hand, pushed her arms out of the way. She looked up at me with one ruined eye and I almost hesitated because of what I saw there. Almost. Instead, I brought the rock down on her face and felt/heard another crack. Then I did it again, and again. I lost track, but soon the crack was replaced with a sucking, squelching sound.

I felt fingers close around my wrist as I raised the rock one more time. Phil stood over me, his blank expression taking me in, then looking toward the zombie's busted gourd.

"Okay, Courtney," he said. "It's done. She's done."

"I should have let you bring the bat," I said, and the last few words came out strangled because I started to cry. I was only marginally less embarrassed to cry in front of Phil than I had been about squirting a few in front of the shuffler.

Phil pulled me off of her and helped me walk back to the rocks. We sat there for a few minutes while I got my shit together and the last of the sunlight disappeared.

"We need to get out of here," Phil said. "Just in case there are more."

"My gun."

"You can buy a new one," he said. "C'mon."

We made our slow way back to the car. My knees were killing me, and something had happened to my hip that I was just starting to feel. Also, I had a deep gouge in my stomach where the pistol's sight had dug into me. After a lot of tripping and sliding, we made it up the steep embankment and over to the car.

I sank into the seat and tried to ignore all of the flares of pain. Phil flipped on the dome light and we examined each other for gouges and bites. We didn't find any—not that finding any would help out a whole lot at that point. We'd be zombies before we made it to the hospital.

We sat back down and Phil started the car. Elvis Costello, Phil's favorite, came pouring out of the speakers. I sat there thinking about how, earlier, I'd been fantasizing about Phil's hands on me. Well, he'd just been pawing all over me, and I couldn't think of anything less sexy.

"Thanks," he said, "for saving me. I wasn't going to last much longer."

"You bet," I said. "Do me a favor in return?"

"Anything," he said.

"Never bring me to this damn place again."

"Done," he said.

He put the car in reverse and got us turned around. Then we drove off toward home and the start of the school year.

CHAPTER TWO
A Really Crappy First Day of School

Phil picked me up the next day and drove me to school. Over the last couple weeks of summer, he'd undergone an intense screening process conducted by my newly security-conscious father. This included more than one dinner at my house, which featured more questioning than they did eating. Sample query: "Have you ever done Vitamin Z, Philip?" The response was a slow blink followed by a "No, sir." Mr. Subtlety just grunted at that. But I guess Phil passed the screening process because there I was in his car on the way to school. It might have been that Dad was tired of hauling my ass everywhere and wanted to give someone else the pleasure of my company.

An entire flutter of butterflies had taken up residence in my stomach as I thought about facing all my old friends—people I hadn't been allowed to have contact with over the summer. Dad didn't even let me have any friends over for my birthday in June. It was either the saddest or angriest birthday in the world as Dad and I sat by ourselves in our favorite Mexican restaurant—not even the giant Happy Birthday Sombrero was able to make me feel better. I knew my exile had been because my dad had locked me away like a delinquent Rapunzel, but my friends might actually interpret it as me being arrogant and standoffish and generally a douche bag. It wasn't like I was able to tell them the truth—you know, that Dad discovered I was selling drugs that were addicting and killing our classmates so he made me stick close to home. I'd rather have everyone think I was a stuck-up bitch, thanks.

Phil cleared his throat and asked, "Everything okay?"

"What do you mean?" I asked. Maybe "snapped" was a more accurate descriptor.

He took it in stride. "You're usually more talkative than this," he said. "So I thought maybe something was wrong. That's all."

"Just thinking about the first day and all," I said. "Wondering who will still talk to me, who'll want to shiv me in the girls' room."

"There may be some overlap between those two groups," Phil said. I smiled despite my queasiness. I liked when Phil made jokes.

"Har," I said. "My social status was up in the air at the end of last year, and then there was my enforced absence from the scene. You see why I'm a little worried."

Phil nodded. He pulled the car to a stop and looked both ways before moving on. His driving habits were very different from what I was used to. My old friends, Sherri and Willie, both drove like there was no tomorrow, and why not hurry up and get there, for Christ's sake? I guess for them there really was no tomorrow.

The butterflies started doing aerial maneuvers.

"Listen," Phil said. "People will either be cool, or they won't. There's not really much you can do about it either way, so why sweat it? If they're cool, then, you know, cool." I restrained myself from making fun of him, since I recognized he was trying to make me feel better. "If they're not, you've dealt with worse."

He pulled the car into the school's driveway and we waited for the guards to let us in.

"Is that how you deal with it?" I asked. "You just ignore it when people are shitty?"

He pinned me with his gaze; his brown eyes seemed lit up. "Shitty is what I expect from people. If I get anything else, I'm pleasantly surprised. Or suspicious."

He pulled up a space and rolled down his window. We went though the ritual of getting through security—having guns pointed in our faces, displaying our IDs, being polite to men who might very easily shoot us.

We got out of the car once we parked. Phil stood close to me and I was really aware of his presence. "I'll see you later," he said.

"I wish we had lunch the same period this semester," I said. I kept the whine to a minimum.

"Me, too," he said. "But I'll see you at the pep rally."

All I was able to say was "Guh."

Right before we turned to go our separate ways, Phil put his hand on my shoulder and stopped me.

"You're worth ten of anyone else at this school," he said. "They'll only affect you if you let them."

Then he turned and walked off and I wondered if I'd have time for a good cry in the girls' room before homeroom.

I didn't make it to the bathroom. On my way, I ran into Crystal Beals. She and I were friends back in grade school, but we had drifted apart when it became apparent she was destined for the upper reaches of the social hierarchy. But we connected again at the end of last year and we'd been texting all summer. Unfortunately, Dad's Draconian disciplinary methods meant I hadn't actually seen her at all. She's super cute and happy—on the outside, at least—and she didn't make me feel weird about pulling a vanishing act over vacation.

"Hey, Courtney?" she said. She still made most sentences sound like a question. "It's really good to see you."

"You, too," I said. "Look at you with the school spirit."

Crystal had been named captain of the cheerleading squad, and she was decked out in a frighteningly short cheer outfit for the upcoming pep rally. I noticed that she wore long sleeves under her top despite the September heat. One of the things I learned last year was that Crystal either had been or was still a cutter—scars crisscrossed her upper arms. Not so sexy for the cheerleading, I guess.

"I hope we can get together later," she said. "Maybe for coffee?"

"That'd be great," I said. I meant it. I was relieved she was the first person I'd run into on the first day.

"We can talk about it later in Journalism," she said. "I took your advice, and I joined the school paper." She twirled away and ran off to practice making human pyramids and whatever it is that cheerleader types do.

She stopped and twirled back to me.

"Oh, and there's been a boy asking about you?" she said.

"What?" I said. "What boy?"

She turned away again and, over her shoulder, said, "He's *very* good-looking!"

A slightly different tingle erupted in my stomach. Who was this mystery guy? I grinned after her, then I put on my game face and marched off to homeroom to face the day.

Turns out she was the first of four or five people to tell me that a boy had been looking for me, or asking about me. Whenever I asked them who the guy was, or at least what he looked like, they all got weirdly vague. They all said pretty much what Crystal had. "He's good-looking."

Though one person did mention that he was also tall. It was all very annoying.

Whatever. I needed to keep my guard up in case the day took a turn for the crappy.

The day was as bad as I worried it might be. I got the collective stink-eye from both the ruling glitterati—Brandon's friends, who felt like I'd stepped above my station when I'd dated him—and from my usual peer group, the wasters. The only person who was sort of nice to me was Elsa Roberts. But that may have been conditioning more than anything else.

Let's just say that I was happy to see Phil by the time the pep rally happened. I'm usually loathe to attend these things, but I wanted to stay and be supportive of Crystal. I'd have been lying if I said I wasn't curious to catch a glimpse of Brandon. The rally would climax with the introduction of this year's football team, and I already knew he'd been named captain. I wanted to torture myself by seeing how easily he'd moved on from me and how great he looked. Oh, great, the butterflies were back!

The student body endured Principal Ibrahim's welcome-back speech and a painfully unfunny skit put on by the boys' JV football team. Then Coach Amara came out and told us all how great a year it was going to be based on how many games the pumped-up football team were certain to win. Then the lights dimmed and the coaching staff took turns introducing the football team. The entire team, all four thousand of them. The cheerleaders did their thing for each player. I really admired their stamina.

Finally, the mic was handed back to Coach A and he said, "And here is this year's fighting Seagulls quarterback and captain . . ." dramatic pause . . . "Zander Matthews!"

Everyone around us went wild, but Phil and I just exchanged glances. Where the hell was Brandon? Phil shook his head in answer to my unasked question.

I immediately dug my phone out of my pocket and texted Crystal:

Up for that coffee after the assembly?

I knew she wouldn't respond right away, and yet I still fought the urge to check my phone every ten seconds.

Phil shot me a questioning look, but there was no way to shout this conversation over the roar of the mini-circus going on all around us. We waited it out to the bitter end, then hightailed it out of there the moment the fluorescents zapped to life overhead.

As we walked out to Phil's car, my phone chimed. It was a message from Crystal:

GIVE ME A HALF HOUR. STRBX DOWNTOWN. FUN!

"Of course she texts in all caps," I said.

"What?" asked Phil. I ignored him and climbed into the car.

"Help me think of something to tell my dad," I said after he'd gotten in and closed the door.

"Tell him about what?" he asked. He was completely deadpan. With anyone else, I'd think he was mad at me, but I decided it was just his default state.

"I want to meet Crystal for coffee and I want to get my dad to let me."

Phil thought for a moment. "Why don't you tell him you want to meet Crystal for coffee?" he asked.

"What?" I asked. "There's no way he'd . . ." My voice trailed off as I thought about it a little bit. Was Phil right? Maybe my dad wasn't a game I had to figure out—maybe

I could just be straightforward and honest with him. I supposed that stranger shit had happened. I shrugged and hit the speed dial for my dad.

"Hi, Courtney," he said. "Everything okay?"

"Yeah, Dad," I answered, then paused and took a deep breath. "I was wondering if I could get a coffee with Crystal before coming home."

There was silence on the other end and I was ready to start moping, but then he said, "Crystal Beals? I don't see why not. Is she driving you?"

"Um, no," I said. Even I was able to hear the surprise in my voice. "Phil will take me there and then home. I'll go right home after, okay?"

"That's fine," Dad said. "Why don't you turn on the oven when you get home and I'll stop for a pizza on the way home. Maybe Phil will want to join us?"

I started to wonder who was really on the other end of the phone. Obviously my dad had been replaced with a highly agreeable replicant.

"I'll ask him," I said. Then Dad said he loved me, and I couldn't bring myself to say it, too, so I signed off with a lame, "Me, too."

"What'd he say?" Phil asked as I took the phone away from my ear.

"He said it was fine," I said. "He also asked if you'd want to have pizza with us tonight."

"Can't," he said. "I'm having dinner with my family tonight. But tell him thanks."

I was more than a little relieved, actually. Which was weird, since Phil had already had dinner with us a few times. Those had always been my idea, though, and that made it different somehow. I decided I'd ponder this later. Or I'd completely suppress it and never think about it again. One or the other.

"Okay, let's head to Starbucks," I said. "The one on Liberty."

"Which one?" Phil asked. "There are two."

I rolled my eyes. Phil had just said a true thing. My town had two horrid franchise coffee places within *one block* of one another. It was mortifying.

"Just head to Liberty and we'll figure it out," I said. I knew it was petty, since we live in a world with zombies and all, but that felt like reason number 1,000 why I wanted to get out of Salem.

Crystal found us at the first Starbucks she tried. Her smile faltered a little when she entered the place and saw Phil sitting next to me, but she recovered quickly and walked up to give me a hug. I doubt that Phil noticed or cared. I was thankful she'd changed into jeans because I didn't want to imagine her sitting in that cheer skirt. I'm sure that much exposed thigh might grab even Phil's attention.

"I hope you don't mind," I said as we sat down. "Phil gave me a ride . . ."

"I could go sit somewhere else," he said. He said it the way he'd mention he had to go to the bathroom, and not like it would be completely insulting for him to leave the table.

"Don't be silly," Crystal said and she shook his hand. I let out a breath I hadn't realized I was holding. I guess I thought she wouldn't be cool about Phil? "I'm Crystal," she said to him with a megawatt smile.

"I know," Phil answered and introduced himself. He grinned at her. Phil actually grinned. I started to tense up again.

"How have you been, Courtney?" Crystal asked. "I'm sorry I didn't see you over the summer."

"Yeah, well," I said, "it was my fault." And before Crystal could ask what I meant, I pressed on. "Say, do you know why Brandon wasn't introduced as part of the football team?"

Her face clouded over. She sat back and crossed her arms over her chest. My heart beat a little faster. Had something happened to him over the summer and I missed it because I was out of the action?

"Oh, God," she said. She turned her head away a little to look out the window. I realized her hands were way up on her upper arms. I thought about the scars I'd seen there. "It's so *sad,* you know?" she went on.

I exchanged a look with Phil. He looked as clueless as me.

"It's sad because . . ." I said. I left the conversational door open for her to slip through.

"I don't like to think about it," Crystal said and slammed the door shut. She shrugged and turned toward me again. A weak smile played at her lips. "So, what were you up to all summer?"

I cleared my throat and stared at my coffee. This very normal question really stumped me. I felt like I'd grown up in a bomb shelter and knew nothing of the world outside. I opened my mouth to say *something,* when Phil answered for me.

"She was grounded all summer."

I fought for air as my throat constricted. That was true, of course, but I think I might have taken a different tack. Phil sipped his drink and I felt Crystal's gaze fall on me.

"Why was that?" she asked.

I glared at Phil and I hoped that he'd either die instantly or at least keep his stupid piehole zipped tight.

"I just got in some trouble," I said. My cheeks grew hot and I clenched my teeth. Slipping into embarrassment was one of my least favorite things, even though it happened pretty often.

"What sort of . . ." Crystal's voice faltered. She looked from Phil, who was doing his best to pretend he was somewhere far away, to me. Her smile fell away. God, she probably imagined the worst. Was she at the table with a cannibal? Had I been caught selling babies? "What sort of trouble?"

There was really no way to sugarcoat it. I took a deep breath and just dived in.

"I admitted to my dad that I'd been selling drugs."

Crystal was in mid-sip and I thought she was going to choke on her coffee. She coughed and sputtered and set her cup down so hard that foam shot out through the hole in the plastic top. A few of the people in surrounding tables looked over at us.

"What kind of drugs?" Crystal demanded.

The people around us had gone from glancing to staring. Business dudes, moms with little kids, a cute couple on their first date. They'd all gone from living their lives to being cast as extras in an episode of *The Wire*.

"Crystal," I said and got no further.

"What drugs, Courtney?" she said. Her voice was quieter, but now she leaned forward and gritted her teeth. I fought the urge to move away from her. "And did Brandon know?"

"It was Vitamin Z," I whispered. My stomach flopped a couple of times. "And yes, Brandon knew."

Crystal shot up out of her chair, which skidded back and tipped over. The sound was like a gunshot in the now-silent coffee shop. All eyes were on the Crystal and Courtney show.

Phil put his hands on the table and kept his eyes on Crystal. I think he was getting ready to jump in in case she decided to come across the table after me. Instead, she grabbed up her bag.

"See you around, Courtney," she said. Her tone told me

she wasn't going to be seeking me out again anytime soon. She marched to the door. On the way out, she stopped and turned. "And say 'hi' to Brandon when you see him." Then she was gone.

I kept my gaze down at the table, studying the grain on the fake wood like its pattern held some sort of secret. Phil stood and walked away. A second later, I heard him pick up the chair and replace it at the table. Then he came around and put his hand on my arm. I gasped at his touch and almost pulled away, but I let him help me to stand.

"Let's go," he said.

I nodded. The light in the shop looked funny, and I realized it was because tears were messing with my sight. I blinked and wet trails ran down my cheeks. Great. I knew from experience how shitty I looked after crying.

Phil held on to my upper arm and guided me out onto the street. The sounds of traffic and conversation were a welcome change from the silence we'd just left. Though I did hear more than one person stop talking as they saw me walking past.

"I'm sorry," Phil said.

"Why?" I asked, and my voice barely reached my own ears.

"I just am," he said. "Because that sucked. Because she was shitty to you. Take your pick."

"She was right to be mean to me," I said. Now that I'd been sucked into self-pity, I'd really found my groove.

"Hell, no," Phil said as we reached the car. He unlocked the door and helped me into the passenger seat. I felt like an invalid. Some sort of social leper who was meant to stay away from society. Oh, man, this was going to be a pity party of epic proportions. He climbed in behind the wheel and got us going toward home. At some point, he dug tissues out of the glove box and handed them to me. I blew my nose and wiped gummy mascara away from my eyes—

not with the same tissue. I just hoped my dad would still be gone when I got home. I didn't want to explain to him why I was already an emotional wreck so early in the school year.

Music blared from the radio. I think Phil knew I didn't want to talk.

We finally pulled up to my house and Phil let the car sit idling. I looked up and down the street—no shufflers to be seen on the street—though I might have welcomed a zombie attack at that point. I didn't see my dad's car, either, so that was good.

"Want me to come inside?" Phil asked.

I thought about that. Under other circumstances I'd welcome the chance to get him alone in the house, but not just then.

"No," I said. "I'll be okay."

He nodded and I wasn't sure whether or not he believed me.

"This was a really crappy first day of school," I said.

"Maybe it's all puppies and rainbows after this," he said.

"I seriously doubt that," I said.

He grinned for just a second. "Me, too," he said. "But you'll handle it."

With that I got out of the car and darted through the chain-link fence into my yard. I waved good-bye as he pulled away. Why did he have so much faith in me? Why did he think I'd be able to handle all of this garbage when I wasn't so sure myself? Great, now I felt like I had to bear up to it or I'd disappoint Phil.

"Asshole," I said to no one at all.

Then I went into the house to wash my face before Dad got home.

CHAPTER THREE
A Group of Elite Z Hunters

The next day wasn't much better. If anything, there seemed to be an escalation in hostilities from the Jocktocracy. My books were knocked out of my arms on more than one occasion. People hissed unsavory names in my ear. In general, I felt like a Black Panther at a Republican convention. (We'd just started a unit on the civil rights era in A.P. History . . .) The only thing that salvaged the day was when Phil's friend, and our frequent partner in late-night shenanigans, Cody suggested a zombie hunt.

"I think a ghoul hunt might do our little Courtney a world of good," he said to Phil. Speaking about me as if I wasn't there was a great source of amusement for our boy Cody.

"Our little Courtney," I said. "Keep up that kind of talk and I'm going to use you as bait, pinhead."

His smile faltered.

"But he's right," I said to Phil. Turnabout is fair, right? "Going out tonight and catching some Zs might be what I need."

"Sure," said Phil. "It's been a few nights since we went out. Let's do it."

We agreed to get together well after our parental units went to bed.

I drifted through the rest of my day trying to make myself as small and unnoticeable as possible. Still, lots of glares followed me through the halls. Though, for some reason, it seemed like people from my social phylum were being nicer to me. Maybe they thought I'd been raked over the coals enough already. Or they were trying to get me to lower my defenses so they could properly kick my ass.

At one point, Carol Langworthy sidled up to me as I walked the halls between class.

"Hey, Hart," she said. She smiled at me and exposed braces that I swear she'd been sporting since kindergarten. I'd consider a malpractice suit against her orthodontist if I were her parents.

"Hey," I said warily.

"So, a new guy was asking about you." She said it with a thick layer of amazement in her voice. Like the fact that a boy asked about me was something she wasn't able to wrap her wee brain around.

"Yeah?" I said, trying to play it cool. "Who was he?"

"His name is Warren," Carol said. "He's new to town. Just started school."

Warren! Now I had a name. "Who is he, though? What's he look like?" I asked. "Not that I'm shallow or anything. I just want to be able to spot him."

She frowned and then said, "Oh, you know. He's tall. Kind of good-looking."

"Right," I said. "I'll keep my eyes out for a tall, good-looking guy. That's very helpful, Carol."

"Yeah, well," she said, pointing down a side hall, "I gotta go to Algebra."

Algebra, for God's sake. She was a senior and hadn't even mastered domain and range yet. Enjoy your career in the service industry, Carol!

I waved good-bye and headed off to class feeling only slightly like a bitch.

★　★　★

Waiting for my dad to go to bed that night was like special torture. We had leftovers and watched a TV show about a cop who was trying to catch a serial killer who used zombies to commit murders. Then I did homework while Dad stayed up forever working on something or other for his work. Dad taught psychology at the local community college, so I guess he was grading papers, or building a wire mother, or something? I didn't ask him—I was too busy trying to psychically will him to go to sleep. Finally, after eleven, he stood and stretched and yawned, his potbelly straining against his polo shirt.

"I'm hitting the hay," he said. "Don't stay up too late, okay?"

"I'm going to be right behind you," I said. Which was technically true. I was going to my bed; I just wasn't going to sleep.

Dad went off to his room and closed his door and I did the same. I texted Phil that we were on. As quietly as I could, I dressed for the night—black jeans, my Dr. Martens, and a black sweatshirt. I lay down on top of my covers to wait for Phil and Cody to show.

The next thing I knew, a tapping noise woke me and my heart was beating a million times a minute. I had absolutely no clue where I was. I wiped drool from my chin and squinted at the window above my bed. Phil stood out there, fist raised, ready to knock some more. I climbed up and slid the window open.

"You were really out," Phil said. I looked past him and saw Cody hanging out of the rear passenger window of the car. "I've been knocking for a while."

"Yep," I said. "I guess I passed out. Back up."

He did as I asked and I crawled out the window. I gave him a quick hug and felt his body tense up. He was still getting used to the idea of being touched, I guess. I hoped he'd start to like it.

"Let's go," he said.

We walked through the yard, and Phil held the chain-link gate open for me. Ever the gentleman, I suppose. Cody waved at me, excited. If he was a dog, his body would be shaking with the force of his wagging tail. I gave him a curt beauty queen wave in return.

After we got ourselves in the car and pulled away, Phil asked me, "Were you dreaming?"

"What do you mean?"

"When I looked in at you, you were sort of thrashing around," he said. "I figured you were dreaming."

"How long were you peeping in at me, you perv?" I said.

Cody cackled in the backseat. "Perv!" he repeated.

"Don't change the subject," Phil said.

I sighed. I usually liked how straightforward he was, but every once in a while, it was a pain in the ass.

"Yeah," I said. "I was dreaming."

"What'd you dream?" Cody asked.

"I dreamed about Sherri," I said.

"Oh," said Phil and Cody in unison. They both knew she had been my best friend since forever and that she'd died at the end of the last school year.

"She looked like she did before she died," I said, "but I knew she was still dead. We were at her place, drinking cheap cola. She told me that I wasn't done."

"Done with what?" Cody asked. I knew from the sound of his voice that he was a little freaked out. Well, good, because so was I.

"That's what I asked her," I said. "She said that something big was coming." I paused and swallowed. My mouth was dry and my tongue stuck to the roof of my mouth. After a second I went on. "The funny thing is that I had a few dreams like that last year, before the big zombie attack out at Brandon's. The dreams stopped after that, so I thought that was the thing that was gonna happen. Tonight's the first time I had that kind of dream since last June."

"What do you think it means?" Cody asked.

I shrugged.

"I think it's a dream," Phil said. "You're stressed out about the new school year, and your mind is trying to sort some stuff out."

"Thanks, Dr. Freud," I said. His unwillingness to entertain that bigger forces might be at work annoyed me a little. What, like I wasn't fit to be a conduit for the supernatural? Well, he could suck it.

"I think it means something, Courtney," Cody said.

"Thank you," I said. At least someone believed me.

Phil didn't rise to the bait. He kept on driving in silence. After a while, I got tired of the silence, and I asked, "So, where are we going tonight?"

"Cody and I scoped out what might be a shuffler nest a couple of days ago," he said.

This was something new we'd been seeing over the summer. Evidence that zombies were congregating out in the woods—discarded clothing, matted-down grass, half-eaten body parts. The nests were obviously a real party zone. Normally, the zeroes were solitary, unless they were swarming, but something new was at work and they'd started hanging out—having little undead coffee klatches, probably.

"We'll be there in a minute," Phil said as he pulled onto Cordon Road. Cordon runs along the extreme east side of town. It was all farmland and trees out there. The perfect place to find some Z-heads.

After a bit, he pulled off to the side of the road and shut off the engine. He pointed to a copse of trees off in the distance. It was hard to see out there. It was just a dark clump against a slightly less dark backdrop.

"Let's do this," Cody whispered. Excitement laced his voice. I felt it, too. Since I'd helped repel the zombie attack at Brandon's, I'd really developed a taste for hunting them. I'd started to crave the thrill of stalking the bastards. Even being in a tight spot, surrounded by shufflers and, as was happening more and more often, runners, I felt a tingle of excitement. Mostly because I knew my friends were with me and they'd get my back. Even though we'd been in some hairy situations, I never felt like I was in danger. I knew that Phil or Cody were there for me. I thought they felt the same way about me.

Phil switched off the car's dome light and we crept around to the trunk. Once that was opened, we picked out our weapons. Phil and Cody went with their usual favorites, baseball bats with nails pounded through them. I preferred a little number called—I shit you not—the Dead-On Annihilator Utility and Wrecking Bar. On one end, it had a hammer head and claw; on the other, it came to a nice sharp point. It was forged from a single piece of steel and weighed less than four pounds. Sure, it was only eighteen inches long, which meant I had to get in pretty close, but once I started swinging that baby, the undead started dropping. On sale at a hardware store near you for a mere $39.95.

We'd given up on guns because none of us was able to afford ammunition in the amounts we needed for these patrols. Besides, getting up close and personal with a zombie and splitting its head open felt more satisfying than shooting it from a distance.

I clenched my hand around the shaft, which I'd wrapped in friction tape, and hefted the wrecking bar.

"Let's go mess up some living-impaired humans," I said. The giddiness of the hunt sometimes made me talk like a bad 1980s action hero.

Phil led the way to the outcropping of trees. We all

crept along as silently as possible. Crickets chirped all around us and sometimes I heard the tall grass we walked through rustling in the wind. A sliver of moon hung in the sky and gave us enough light to see by. Just as we were about to enter the trees, Phil paused. We all hefted our weapons. He held up his hand and silently counted off.

One . . . two . . . three . . .

We burst into the trees, no longer interested in being quiet. I gave a war cry as we entered a small clearing in the middle of the trees.

And we came to a dead stop.

Zombies lay all around and they were dead. For-real dead this time. Someone had hacked them to pieces. There were so many body parts I wasn't able to tell how many shufflers had actually bought it. I tried to imagine who had done it, and what they'd used—meat cleaver? Machete? I stopped wondering because I figured it might be best not to know.

"Who the hell is ganking our kills?" Cody demanded. He looked down at the mess in utter disgust, but I guessed he wasn't upset at the carnage, he was cheesed off because it hadn't been him that had caused it. "I'm serious," he went on, gesturing at the dead Zs. "These were ours."

"It's not like we called dibs on them, Cody," Phil said, ever the voice of irritating reason.

"The Gimp has a point," I said, agreeing with Cody.

"Thank you," Cody shouted.

"Who did this if it wasn't us?"

"Yeah," Phil said. "It's a good question." He kicked absently at an unattached arm, then he shrugged. "I have no clue. I think we should keep plugging away like we have been and see if our paths cross with our mystery hunter."

"Or hunters," Cody said. "What if it's a whole, like, elite group of zombie hunters and they want to recruit us?" His voice grew louder as he got more excited.

"I'm sure a group of elite Z hunters would love to have you on their team," I said.

"You think so, Courtney?"

"You," I said and smiled. "I'm sure they have a constant need for bait."

"Har-har-har," Cody said as he made the jerk-off motion with his free hand. "You're funny like cancer, Courtney."

"Let's go," Phil said. He turned and walked away without waiting for us to agree with him. Like, there was no way he thought we might argue with him.

"Man, this sucks!" Cody slumped away, his shoulders rounded and his head hanging down. He looked like Charlie Brown after a particularly awful baseball game. He even had a baseball bat, though it had nails sticking out of it and it was covered in black zombie gore.

"Cheer up," I said to him. "Maybe we'll spot a shuffler on the way home and we can run it over with the car."

"Do you think we might?" he asked, suddenly cheery again. "That'd be awesome!"

"Sure," I said. "Anything is possible."

We all climbed into the car and Phil got us headed toward home.

"Sorry this didn't work out," he said.

I shrugged and didn't say anything right away. I stared out my window at the hills off in the distance and the moon in the sky. All of this maudlin, self-pitying bullshit ran through my head. Thoughts about how nothing worked out for me lately, so why even try? *Et cetera*. It felt exhausting to be so negative all the time. Maybe it made those around me tired, too. Tired of me.

"Thanks for trying, at least," I said. "I appreciate the effort."

"You're welcome," Phil said. "And it doesn't feel like it's an effort."

"Okay," I said.

I went back to looking out the window, but the landscape didn't look quite so bleak anymore.

"Hey," Cody piped up from the backseat. "What'd you mean by calling me a gimp?"

CHAPTER FOUR
Define Ugly

I slouched through the next few days at school in a haze. I decided to keep my head down and keep to myself as much as possible.

As I lay low, I spent a good portion of each day looking for Brandon. I was surprised he wasn't in Journalism class. I didn't want to ask anyone if they'd seen him, mostly because I didn't want to start up the rumor mill, but I had to admit that I was curious about him and how he'd been over the summer.

Trying to remain inconspicuous seemed to work. People started to leave me alone, or to ignore me, which was just as good, if you ask me. But as people began to get out of my face, a funny thing happened—I started to notice *them* more.

As I wandered the halls, I began to really look at my classmates. I mean, sure, I looked at them every day, but I felt like I never really saw them. Now that their ire at me seemed to ebb away, I began to notice them. I was kind of shaken by what I saw. A lot of the kids I considered part of the ruling oligarchy looked different than I remembered them. Sort of gaunt, drawn out. Sunken cheeks; hollow, darkened eye sockets. What was going on here? These were the beautiful people, both figuratively and literally. Now they seemed to be wasting away. It was like

The Picture of Dorian Gray in reverse. Looking at them kept reminding me of something or someone, but I couldn't quite place it. It was goddamned frustrating. I tried not to think about it, hoping the answer might just come to me, but I couldn't *not* think about it. Like when you burn the roof of your mouth and that skin hangs down? If you'd just leave it alone, it would heal, but of course you can't.

In class and out, I studied all of my classmates. I thought that maybe everyone looked slightly uglier than I was used to, but no, it was just the upper crust. All of those in my hierarchical strata and below looked the same as always— which is to say ugly, but no uglier than usual.

One day as Phil drove Cody and me home, I decided to bring up my new finding. Like any good scientist, I wanted to test my theory by subjecting it to peer review.

"Are the jocks looking raggedy-assed to you lately?" I asked.

"All the jocks?" Phil asked. "Like as a collective?"

"Define ugly," Cody said from the backseat. "Because I have to admit that I'd still do about ninety percent of them."

"Cody," I said, "shut up. Phil, no, I guess not all of them. But enough that it's noticeable."

"Okay," said Phil. "Now I'm going to do something unexpected and repeat what Cody asked, 'Define ugly.' "

"Okay," I said, "not ugly. Not like, you know . . ." I hooked my thumb over my shoulder at our compatriot in the backseat. "Just sort of, not as good-looking."

"I have not noticed a significant drop in our classmates' attractiveness," Phil said. He said it in all seriousness, which made me think he was making fun of me. Then I told myself that Phil had joked around with me, but he'd never outright made fun of me. I squelched any bubbling anger I'd felt coming on.

"Well, please keep an eye out for any upticks in cases of butt-face, okay?"

"Done."

"New topic," Cody announced from the backseat.

Phil checked him out in the rearview mirror. "What's that?" he asked.

"This is for Courtney," he said. I turned around in my seat and I didn't like the grin I saw once I got all the way around.

"What?" I asked.

He continued to grin without answering me.

I knew he was trying to be funny, but I felt my anger growing again. I wanted to force-choke him like Darth Vader.

"If you don't want me to slap that stupid-ass grin off your face," I said, "you'll tell me what's up."

A boo-boo lip replaced the grin and I was fine with that.

"Why do you have to be so mean?" Cody asked.

"You haven't seen me mean, jack-off," I said. "What?"

"Someone asked about you today," he said.

I squeezed my eyes shut for a second. Of course. More of this bullshit.

"Who was it?" I asked, even though I knew the answer.

"A guy in my American History class," he said.

That got Phil's attention. "A guy?" he asked into the rearview.

"Yeah," Cody said and nodded.

"What'd he look like?" I asked. Again, I knew the answer.

Cody looked weirdly uncomfortable. He kind of squirmed in his seat. He looked like he was holding in a fart.

"He's, you know, tall," Cody said. "And sort of . . ."

"Good-looking," I said.

"Have you met him?" Cody asked.

"No," I said, "but I've heard about him. What's his name again?"

"Warren," Cody said.

I turned and sat back in my seat.

"Warren," I said. "Right. How did I forget."

"What's this guy's story?" Phil asked.

"I honestly have no idea," I said. I tried to discern any signs of jealousy in Phil's posture, expression, or voice, but didn't find any. Call me crazy, but I sort of hoped to find some there.

"Huh," was his only reply.

We drove on for a little while in silence.

"I have something that might make you feel better," Phil said out of the blue.

"What makes you think I don't feel great?" I asked. Then I realized I was sitting there staring out the window with my arms folded across my chest, my teeth gritted. I had probably been cursing under my breath and not noticed it.

"Fine," I said, "what is it?"

"Let's go out tonight," he said. "Hunt up some of the undead."

I hated when he used that word, "undead," but I was willing to let it go this time.

"Where?" I felt a grin spread across my face.

"No idea," he said. "That's why it's a hunt. Can you get out tonight?"

"Probably," I said. "Tomorrow's Saturday, which means my dad doesn't have to work, so he might stay up later than usual."

"Well," Phil said, "we'll see if we can make it work."

"Yeah," Cody said, "but remember that we want to get there before our mystery slayer."

That was a good point, not that I was going to tell him that.

"I'll do what I can," I said. "It might just mean that we go out later than usual."

"Whenever," Phil said. "Any time is the right time for a monster hunt."

That struck me funny—probably funnier than he meant. "If we ever get corporate sponsorship, that can be on our T-shirts."

"Zombie Squad," said Cody, doing his best imperson-ation of a sports announcer, "brought to you by Axe body spray."

"The only thing that smells worse than undead," I said, making my voice as deep as possible.

"Hey!" Cody sounded hurt. "I wear Axe."

"That's the point, dumb-ass."

We went on like that for a while, exchanging little bon mots until we reached my house. But I did it on autopi-lot. I was already trying to think of ways to get my dad to go to bed early.

Turns out that I didn't need to plan it. Which was good, because I came up with zero things that might actually work. As we sat and ate dinner, Dad said, "I'm going down to Eugene tomorrow to a small conference. Gil was sup-posed to go, but he got sick. Want to come?"

Eugene is a town about an hour south of us, and it's even smaller and has less to do than Salem. Also, it's full of hippies. I tried to imagine myself hanging out there for the day, eating organic tofu and getting a contact high from people's body odor. It took me less than a second to de-cline the invitation.

"Well, if you change your mind," Dad said, "I'll be leaving about seven."

"That's pretty early," I said, trying my best to sound completely innocent.

"Yeah, I'm going to hit the hay pretty quick after we clean up the kitchen," Dad said.

"I'll clean it up," I said. Dad gave me a suspicious look. Had I overplayed my hand in my excitement? I sat back and tried to play it cool. "So you can have some free time before you go to bed. Since I'm not going, I can stay up a little late."

"Sure," Dad said. He looked like he was trying to believe me. "I'd appreciate that. I did want to review some stuff before heading down." One last piercing glance, then, "Thanks, sweetie."

So I made like Snow White, minus the helpful woodland creatures, and cleaned the kitchen by myself. By the time I was done, I heard my dad snoring in his room—on the other side of the house. It was like living in a house with a nuclear test range, I swear to God.

I texted Phil that we were a go for festivities, and then while I waited for him, I got dressed for a night out on the town.

We'd been on the road for about half an hour when I asked, "Where are we going?" We'd headed south, out past the freeway entrance and the end of anything that might be called civilization. Out that far, the strip malls had disappeared and were replaced by run-down houses and overgrown yards.

"It was Cody's idea," Phil said and hooked a thumb toward the backseat. Cody was asleep, sprawled across the bench. His mouth hung open and a thin line of drool fell out of his mouth and onto his jacket. I wrinkled my nose. He looked like the world's biggest, ugliest baby.

"What idea of his might possibly get us to drive all the way out here?"

"Remember that little nest of zappers we took out a few weeks ago out this way?" Phil asked. I looked around. Okay, all of this did look vaguely familiar. I made a non-committal sound. "He thought that maybe zombies gather at spots where they've congregated in the past," Phil said. "That maybe they'd be attracted to the smell of carnage."

"What made him think that?"

"I hesitate to speculate how Cody's mind works," Phil said. "But it seems like it paid off this time." He slowed and turned off the main road. I heard gravel popping beneath the tires. If I remembered this place correctly, there'd be a huge oak tree coming up on our left. Sure enough, it came into view.

"Sometimes Cody skips school and goes scouting for our hunting trips." I wondered what that did for his GPA, and got shudders. Seeing a failing grade on my report card would give me the heebie-jeebies way worse than any zombie ever did. "Long story short, he found some zombies on his last little reconnaissance mission."

"Huh," I said, sort of impressed despite myself. "Cody was right about something. Will wonders never cease?"

Phil killed the headlights and drove by the light of a half moon. We were in the middle of a field of tall grass, so there wasn't really a lot of maneuvering to do.

"Cody's smarter than you give him credit for," Phil said. He stopped the car and set the parking brake.

I didn't have an answer for that. I didn't really think he was necessarily *dumb*; it was just that he made some interesting choices. Choices I wouldn't have made. As important as I felt hunting zombies was, there was no way in hell I'd skip school to do it.

Phil climbed out of the car and I followed suit. I raised my arms above my head, stretching. My spine did its impression of a certain breakfast cereal.

My phone buzzed in my pocket and my heart stopped.

I wrenched it out, expecting to see a message from my dad asking where I was, why I was such a terrible daughter, and wondering if he'd be able to sell me to an organ donation center. Instead there was a message from a number I didn't recognize.

> Heard you were asking about me. We should get together. I've been thinking about you.

I stared at the screen for a few seconds. Who would send me this text? Whom had I been asking about . . . ? Then it hit me. Brandon. My ex-boyfriend-even-though-we-only-went-on-one-date. Oh, man. I'd deleted his number from my contacts; that was why I hadn't recognized who it was from.

"Who is it?" Phil asked. "Your dad?"

"No," I said. "It's just a notification from Facebook." I attempted a smile.

"Okay," Phil said. He looked in the window at Cody sleeping in the backseat. "He's so adorable," he said. "I hate to wake him." With that, he pounded his balled fist against the glass and screamed, "Get up!"

Cody bolted upright, eyes wide and screaming curses. It was pretty funny, but I was in no mood to laugh.

"How about taking it down a few decibels?" I asked.

"They're, like, a long way off," Phil said. "I think we're fine."

"Never do that again, you dick!" Cody screamed as he got out of the car. "I can't be held responsible for my actions next time." His eyes bugged out of his head. Even in the moonlight, I saw his face was bright red and spittle flew out of his mouth. All of this struck me as intensely hilarious just then despite the certainty that my life was about to become complicated to an obnoxious degree. I cackled like an idiot.

Cody fixed me with a glare that made me glad looks truly couldn't kill.

"Did you put him up to that?" he asked me.

"He came up with it all on his own," I gasped between ragged peals of laughter.

Cody crossed his arms against his chest and gave us the evil eye one more time before walking off mumbling threats about payback.

When my laughter had finally subsided into giggles, Phil walked over and stood next to me.

"He's never managed to pull off a gag," he said, "but there's always a first time. You ready?"

"I am," I said.

"Hey, Rip Van Ugly," he called to Cody, "we're ready to go if you're done pouting."

Cody stalked back to us. "Very funny," he said. "If any zombies start to gnaw on your ass, don't count on me to save you."

"I'm officially on my own," Phil said. "Got it." He popped open the trunk. "Choose your weapon."

I grabbed my old standby and swung it once or twice. Phil and Cody did the same. I felt ready to do violence upon some unsuspecting shufflers.

Normally I'd have been creeped out by the walk though the dark field. It was easy to feel lost in the tall grass—cut off from civilization. But we marched along in silence toward the house, which gave me a lot of time to think about the Brandon Situation. Yes, I thought of it in capitals. Technically, I had been asking about him. Asking Crystal and a lot of other people who didn't want to talk to me, sure. It was no surprise that word had gotten back to him. It was also not a shock that he'd reached out to me. But, c'mon, we were both nearly grown-ups, right? I'd just write and let him know that my concern was a more general type and not of the let's-hook-up variety. Honestly, since I had been concerned about him, I should be glad that he'd texted me. At least I knew he was alive.

I decided to drop the capitals; this was no longer a Situation.

"Are you sleeping standing up?" Cody shout-whispered at me.

"What are you talking about?" I asked.

"Phil and I have both been jabbering at you," he said, "and you just stand there like . . . something that just stands there."

"You've painted a picture with your words, Cody," I said. "Sorry, I was just wrapped up in my head for a minute."

"The only thing wrapped around your head is your butt," Cody replied and then grinned. He looked to Phil and raised his hand for a high five. Phil declined.

"That was funny, but nothing's that funny," Phil said. "You know how I feel about high fives."

Cody's arm slowly sank to his side.

Phil looked at me, concerned. "You okay?" he asked. "You up for this?"

I hefted my wrecker. "Let's go, cowboy." It sounded tougher than I felt.

"Wait a minute," Cody said. "Do you hear that?"

A slight breeze rustled the grass all around us, and that sounded like people whispering. The three of us stood absolutely still, straining to hear anything out of the ordinary. I was just about to say I didn't hear a thing, and probably call Cody a dumb-ass to boot. Then something did reach my ears. A grunt, maybe? The house we were approaching, a broken-down place with no doors or windows, sat maybe sixty yards away. I concentrated on it. There was another sound—a thud, like an ax in wood, or like a blade in undead flesh.

"You heard that, right?" I whispered.

"Someone's killing our zombies," Cody said.

"Again," Phil added.

We broke out in a run toward the zombie nest. I wasn't sure if we were bent on joining the fight against the shufflers, or in taking down the A-holes who'd bogarted two of our kills. Either way, we wanted to get there in a hurry.

The tall grass snagged at my clothing as I ran, slowing me down, and I felt a hitch in my side coming along. I really needed to get in better shape. Pretty soon I'd get outrun by even the slow variety of zombies.

Phil was the first to round the corner to the back of the house and he stopped short. Cody was right in front of me and he stopped, too. Unfortunately, there was no way to stop myself in time and I ran into Cody's back at full speed. We both went down with a thud.

I looked up from my perch on top of Cody and couldn't make out what I was seeing at first. It looked more like dancing than fighting. A head fell to the ground and rolled toward us. Cody gave a little scream and pushed me off him. I sat down hard on my tailbone, but I ignored the pain. It was easier to make out what I was seeing now that I was sitting up.

A single guy dressed from head to toe in black, including a balaclava, stood in the middle of four Zs. It took me several seconds to convince myself that what he held in his hands was an honest-to-God sword. Like from King Arthur or some shit. All of the Zs still standing looked relatively fresh, and fast. They hung back like they were trying to pick their moment. That was probably a smart move since the dismembered bodies of several of their buddies littered the ground.

One of the runners broke from the pack and charged the dude. Too fast to see, Ninja Man moved to meet him and did something with his sword. The zombie fell to the ground, his head still attached but split in two lengthwise.

The other zombies moved in then, and the guy danced among them, his sword swinging. Bodies and parts of bodies fell all around him. The last runner, its days of running now a distant memory, fell on its face right in front of us, both arms taken off at the shoulder. It still writhed and snarled and tried to stand up. It stopped snarling just for a second when it saw me and Cody still sitting on our butts. It began to wriggle its way toward us like the world's largest, yuckiest worm.

Then the thing seemed to sprout a two-foot-long length of steel from its head and it stopped moving.

The guy who'd just offed nearly a dozen zombies all by himself stood over us. Even with the balaclava covering his face, I thought I saw a mocking smile.

"Are you Courtney?" the guy asked, and my heart leaped up into my throat. How in the hell did this zombie-killing machine know my name?

He reached up and grabbed the edge of his mask. He pulled it off in one sweeping motion to reveal a really gorgeous black kid who must have been my age. Sweat dripped off his face, and I'm going to restrain myself from saying that he glistened in the moonlight . . .

"Oh," said Cody beside me. "Hi, Warren."

CHAPTER FIVE

Not Racist, Per Se

I felt like my head exploded into a million tiny shards. I'd been hearing the name Warren for days now. Everyone I talked to said that some guy named Warren had been asking about me. Now it turned out that Warren was the ultimate zombie hunter of my dreams. I was going to need a minute to process this. In the meantime, I just needed to not say or do anything stupid.

"You are very pretty," I said. And immediately wished for my death.

"I'm sorry?" Warren said.

"What?" Phil said somewhere behind me.

"I mean," I said, "I mean, yes, I am Courtney."

Warren extended his gloved hand toward me. I took it and he pulled me up onto my feet. Based on that one action I started to calculate his strength and to match it with the evident musculature that lay beneath his very tight black clothing. What was happening to me? Someone must have assumed control of my brain, most likely the heroine of a Regency romance novel.

"Well, it's very nice to meet you, Courtney," he said. "I've heard a lot about you."

"From who?" Phil asked.

"I think you mean 'whom'," Warren said. He gave me a little wink. An honest-to-God wink.

Phil's mouth formed a thin, tight line of unhappiness across his face. He wasn't one to make too many grammatical errors and when he did, I usually called him out on them. He never gave me that look, though . . .

"Yeah," I said to Warren, "so, to *whom* were you speaking when my name came up?"

He flashed me a brilliant smile that worked magic and created dimples where none had been in evidence. I almost looked around to see if the sun had come out because I swear light glinted off his pearly whites.

"Well," he said, "you did save a large percentage of the senior class from an onslaught of the undead last summer, didn't you? Those people mentioned it."

"She had some help," said Cody as he struggled to get himself up off the ground.

"Yeah," Warren said, "I heard she had help."

I waited for Cody, or even Phil, to jump on him for calling them help, but instead, they both just exchanged looks and bristled. Cody decided to air another grievance.

"So, what's up with you bogarting our zombies, man?"

Warren's brow creased in confusion.

"Wait," he said. "Did you want to kill these ones?"

"Yes," said Phil. "And we wanted to kill the nest you beat us to a few nights ago."

Warren started to laugh. A deep, rich sound that rang through the mostly silent night.

"Do you think I was jumping your claim?" he asked. He took in Phil and Cody's faces. "You did, huh?" He raised his hands like he was surrendering. "Listen, it's just coincidence, okay? I didn't mean to poke my nose in where it didn't belong."

"You're saying you didn't follow us around to find zombie nests and then attack them before we had a chance?" Cody asked. Even in the dark of the night I saw that his face was beet red.

"Cody," said Phil in a soothing tone of voice, "when you say it out loud, it sounds kind of crazy."

"Yeah," I said in agreement.

Warren wisely kept his trap shut.

"How else could he have found the exact same nests we were thinking of zeroing?" Cody demanded.

"Great minds think alike?" Warren asked.

Cody glared at him. He opened his mouth to say something and, fearing what awfulness might come out, I jumped in first.

"Listen," I said, "no matter how it happened, the zombies are dead now, right?" The three boys each eyed me, suspicious, then they slowly nodded. "And that's what we want, right? Dead Zs?"

More nods.

"Then what's it matter who got to them?" I asked.

Phil looked more accepting of this than Cody, but I'd take that because Cody would follow Phil's lead on this like on most things. "Also, hey, new zombie killer, right?"

"You did have some pretty sweet moves," said Phil with begrudging respect. At that, I saw Cody relax a bit. If Phil was able to cut this guy some slack, who was he to argue?

"Thanks, mate," said Warren. *Mate?* I almost said something but bit my tongue. Maybe use of the word "mate" was culturally appropriate in this circumstance. I figured I'd better err on the side of caution until I knew for sure I wasn't being a racist asshole for breaking his balls. "Maybe I'll get the chance to check out your moves one of these days."

"Sure," said Phil, but he didn't sound very convincing.

"But it's your skills I'd really like to see in action," Warren said and turned that brilliant smile on me.

"Oh, yeah," I said. "I have mad skills."

Suddenly my mouth and brain didn't work. Dammit.

Cody snickered behind me and I was glad there was so little light that night because I felt my cheeks grow hot.

"I meant it sarcastically," I hissed at him.

"Whatever you say, dawg," he said and then ran away as I kicked at him.

"This is fun and all," Phil said, "but since there's no living dead to make just plain dead, we should be getting back to the real world."

"Yes," I said too eagerly. "Can we go home?" I really felt it was important for me to be somewhere other than Warren's current location.

Warren nodded as if he sensed what was going through my head. "Yeah, well, I hope I can see you again sometime." He grinned without turning on the full wattage of his teeth, then added, "To see all of you."

"Uh-huh," Cody said.

Phil hooked his finger over his shoulder. "We're this way."

"And I'm over there," said Warren as he pointed to the west side of the house, the side closest to a road. With that, he waved, turned his back on us, and strode away. I made a point of not watching his butt as he did this.

"Well, this has been a great night," said Cody. He was staring right at me as he said it, but I refused to rise to the bait.

"Yeah," said Phil, "let's just get home before any other great things happen."

We walked back to the car, Cody griping the whole way. Mostly he didn't like how he and Phil had been relegated to the role of "helpers" in last year's zombie invasion. Phil didn't say anything at all, which worried me a little bit, and since it's easy to tune out Cody, I was once again left alone with my thoughts. I tried to examine my reaction to Warren. I thought there was more to it than just the fact that he was good-looking. *Very* good-looking. I was shallow, but not that shallow. Just about then, I bumped into Phil's shoulder as we walked along and I felt how stiff he was. That was it. Phil was always stiff. In the months we'd been hanging out, he'd barely given me any hints that he liked me. *Liked me* liked me, if you know what I mean. Here I just met a boy who had not only been looking for me since school started, but who'd made eye contact with me, smiled, and made me blush. All within seconds of meeting.

I shook my head. It was wrong to compare the two of them. Wasn't it? Phil was a stand-up guy, considerate, nice, and funny and, admittedly, operating under an impaired set of social skills. Warren, for all his good looks and charm, might be a tool, or a serial killer. I was comparing them again. Crap. Okay, I told myself, I was going to stop comparing them starting now.

We got to the car and all piled in. Phil keyed the ignition and nothing happened. Silence filled the car. The kind of silence you only hear when you're miles from home in a car that won't start.

"Give me a minute," said Phil even though no one had said anything.

He tried it again and the engine chugged, chugged again, and finally caught. It wheezed to life and we all relaxed.

"Know what was wrong?" I asked.

Phil shrugged. "Maybe I flooded it."

He put it in gear and we started to bump along through the grass toward the road. As we went along, I started to blink, then sat forward to peer through the windshield.

"Am I slowly going blind?" I asked.

"No," Phil said, obviously frustrated. "The headlights are dimming."

"The headlights are what–ing?" Cody asked as he leaned against the back of our seats. "Why are they doing that?"

"Something must be wrong with the alternator," Phil said.

I was about to ask how he knew that since I didn't even know what an alternator did. Alternated between two or more things, I guess? But before I was able to ask, the lights faded out completely, then the engine died and the car coasted to a stop just as we reached the road.

Cody started in with a steady stream of curses from the backseat. Phil just sat behind the wheel, staring off into the distance. I wasn't sure why, but I thought his reaction was a lot scarier than Cody's.

A short horn blast came from right in front of us. A sleek black car sat out there. I knew who it was and I felt a mixture of relief and dread wash over me. Relief that I wouldn't be walking home tonight and dread that more interaction with Warren might just push our little group right over the edge.

"You guys need a ride?" Warren called to us.

Cody and I looked to Phil to see how he'd react.

"I guess we'd better," he said. I'd never heard him sound so defeated.

Before I was able to say something to make the situation better, he got out of the car. Considering how often I actually made things better versus how often I made people cry, it was probably for the best. I climbed out of Phil's car and approached Warren's. I don't know a lot about cars and don't really care to know more, but looking at the sleek black thing that he drove, I knew it was either reverse-engineered from an alien spacecraft, or it came from the future. It was so much nicer than Phil's that it seemed doubtful they were even the same species of technology.

For some reason, Phil and Cody both climbed into the

backseat. It was probably a better location from which to pout was my guess. Warren leaned over and opened the passenger door from the inside. This is probably the cool-kid version of getting out and opening the door for a girl. It might fly with the jet set, but it didn't earn any points with a dainty flower such as myself.

But then I planted my butt on the bit of heaven that was the leather bucket seat and I was prepared to forgive everything. It was like having your cheeks cupped by angels.

Warren turned on that smile and I couldn't help but notice the very dimple-ness of his face.

"Who's first?" Warren asked.

"First?" I asked.

"He wants to know who to take home first," Cody called from the backseat. "What the hell did you think he was asking?"

"Of course I knew that's what he was asking," I said. "Screeched" might have been more accurate. "I'm not mentally deficient."

"We'll take your word for it," Cody shot back.

I turned to glare at him, but he'd already forgotten me as he and Phil whispered with their heads together. I sat back in my seat and restrained myself from delivering an audible harrumph.

"From here," I said to Warren, "Phil lives closer than me. Cody does, too . . ." I realized I had no idea where Cody lived.

"Take Courtney first, if you don't mind," Phil said. "I'll have you drop me at Cody's house. Tomorrow he can drive me to the auto parts place for a new alternator."

"When were you gonna let me in on this plan?" Cody whined. "Maybe I had things to do tomorrow."

"*Do* you have things to do tomorrow?" Phil asked.

There was a long pause during which I did not turn to sneer at Cody.

"Yeah," he finally said, "take Courtney home and then take Phil to my house."

Warren did something complicated-looking to the gear shifter. "Okay," he said, "how do we get to your house?"

I gave him basic instructions with lots of unasked-for help from the whisper twins in the backseat. Once we'd gotten it hashed out how to get me home, we settled into an uneasy silence.

After a mile or two, Warren cleared his throat. I recognized this for the conversational gambit that it was.

"So you were probably wondering why I'd been asking about you," he said.

I tried to play it casual. You know, *Oh, had you been asking about* moi? *I simply hadn't noticed.* What I said was, "Hmm?"

He flashed a grin even though he kept his eyes on the road. "One of the first people I met when I moved here was Crystal Beals. She mentioned what happened out at that kid's cabin last year. I thought to myself, *Warren, you've got to meet that girl.*"

"Why?" I asked, skeptical.

"Because I've never known anyone else my age who was great at hunting Zs."

Putting aside the fact that he'd just proclaimed himself great—which seemed sort of grandiose—it was sort of flattering. Then a small, nagging voice told me to come clean about something.

"That night I just did what I had to to save myself and my friends," I said. "Truth is, I never hunted shufflers in an organized way until I hooked up with these two knuckleheads." I hooked my thumb behind me.

"Thank you," Cody said instantly like he'd been waiting for me to give him credit.

"Then I'm happy to meet you guys, too," Warren said. "I hope we can hunt together sometime."

"Crystal didn't mention them?" I asked.

"I don't think so," Warren said and he frowned a little. Good God, he even had dimples when he frowned.

"Typical," Cody said. "We're probably invisible to people in her caste."

Nice vocab word, Cody, I thought.

"Well," said Warren, "the way she tells it, things were pretty confused that night. Lots of gunfire, lots of real fire, zombies everywhere. That sound right?"

"Yeah," said Cody. He sounded suspicious.

"In all that noise, she probably just wasn't aware of you two helping out." Warren fixed Cody in the rearview mirror. "Next time I talk to her, I'll set her straight, okay? Not in a mean way, just lay out the facts, okay?"

"Okay . . ." Sheepish.

"And I was serious about wanting to hang with you all," Warren went on. "We'd probably have a lot to show one another."

"Sure," said Cody. "We could do that, right, Phil?"

"Sure." I wasn't able to read anything in Phil's voice, but I settled back in my magic seat a little more relaxed. Whatever else he might be, Warren wasn't coming off as arrogant. That was good.

Something started tickling my brain. It was that part of me that was unable to allow a peaceful moment to go by without lobbing a shit grenade into the middle of it. I tried to suppress it, I really did.

"Let me ask you something," I said to Warren.

Cody chose that moment to sit forward and offer several instructions on how to get to my house.

I cringed as this obviously rich kid started to steer us past the ugly yards, cheap chain-link fences, and peeling paint that meant we were close to home.

"Shoot," Warren said after Cody got him on track to my house. It took me a moment to figure out he meant I could ask away.

"All this past week, people have been telling me that some guy has been asking about me." I shifted in my seat, hoping it didn't make a fart noise when I did. "And every time I asked who it was, what he looked like. So I could identify him in the halls if I ran across him. You."

"Sure," said Warren, "and so you'd be able to hightail it if I turned out to be a creeper or a bagger."

It took me a second to understand that bagger meant ugly.

"Naw," I said. "Most folks, mostly girls, told me the guy was good-looking." He didn't have anything to say to that—and neither did the audience in the backseat, so I went on. "In all the times I asked what you looked like, no one ever said that you were . . . you know . . ."

"Black?"

"Right."

He chuckled. "White folks," he said like that explained everything. I waited for more of an explanation. "Most white people are raised to think it's bad to notice if someone is a different color. They'd never say I was black. Unless they were describing me to a cop, I guess."

"What?" I asked. "Are you accusing everyone I know of being racist?"

"Not racist, *per se,*" Warren said. "Just overly sensitive. You mostly get it in people who don't see a lot of people of color. Where I'm from, you grow up with all sorts of people, so it's no big deal to say, 'Oh, yeah, Warren's a black kid,' or, 'Tom, he's that Korean guy, right?' "

"Where'd you grow up?" I asked.

"Seattle," he said. I knew that Seattle was one of the first big cities reclaimed from the zombies. I'd never been there.

"Why the hell did you move here from there?" I asked.

"Dad got a new job, the family moves." He gave an eloquent shrug of the shoulders. "I might move back there for college after high school. Or maybe I'll go to Gonzaga. I'm not sure."

"I like your confidence," I said.

"Oh, look." Cody sprang up between the two front seats. "There's your house, Courtney. Have to cut this little jaw session short."

There it was. Thank God clouds were covering the moon just then. For some reason it looked really ugly to me at that moment.

"Yeah," I said. "Well, thanks for the ride," I told Warren.

He gave this sort of two-fingered salute, like he was touching the brim of an invisible hat. But his smile saved it from looking totally douchey.

I turned in my seat. "'Night, you guys. Sorry the Z hunt was a bust. I hope you get your car fixed."

"Thanks," Phil said, his voice flat.

"Yeah, well, good night." I opened the door and started to remove my ass from that amazing seat when I felt a hand on my arm. Warren grinned at me, but the grin was different. There was something else behind it I couldn't read.

"I meant what I said, Courtney," he said. "I'm glad I was finally able to meet you."

"Um, yeah," I said, ever ready with a pithy comeback. "It was good to meet you, too."

I closed the door and as the car's dome light faded, I saw Cody and Phil looking at me. Cody glared, but Phil's expression was blank. He might be thinking anything. I shuddered. Warren put the car in gear and pulled away.

I hugged myself for a second, then I remembered I was on the wrong side of our chain-link fence. I hustled into the yard. I found my bedroom window still open—whenever I sneaked out, I was half-convinced I'd find my dad waiting to bust me, but my room was dad-free.

I stripped down to my delicate underthings—boy shorts and a sports bra—and crawled into bed.

It was a really long time before I fell asleep.

CHAPTER SIX
Zombified

The next few weeks went really well, all things considered. My dad started to let me off the leash more and more. Phil came over to dinner with us every once in a while. I even invited Cody over but he claimed that "family stuff" gave him the heebie-jeebies, whatever that meant. I was acing my classes, including a couple that I had at the community college where my dad worked—by the time I got to Columbia University I'd have enough credits to be considered a sophomore. If the credits transferred.

While we hadn't gone out zombie hunting with Warren, we had all hung out with him a few times. He introduced us to a bunch of people in the upper crust of the school hierarchy. Which was funny when you thought about it. We'd gone to school with most of these people since kindergarten, but it took a new kid to give us access to their world. High school was a weird, shitty world. Like if Philip K. Dick wrote for *Degrassi High*, or something.

Things were going so well in my life, that one Saturday in November, I decided to do something I hadn't done in a long time. I flipped open my laptop and Googled news about the recovery of NYC. I figured that even if there was no news, or even bad news, things were going so well that I would only be laid low for a day or two. A week tops.

I fired up Google, entered the search term, and hit return. Then I closed my eyes and crossed my fingers.

When I opened them again, I nearly crapped my pants. From excitement.

ARMY ANNOUNCES RECLAMATION OF NYC BEGINNING IN NEW YEAR, screamed the headline. Then I screamed.

Dad came running down the hall. He threw open the door and stood there panting from the twenty-foot jog.

"Is everything okay?" he asked.

"They're going to take back New York!" I gushed. I jumped up and hugged him. His body was oddly resistant and he didn't return the hug. In my overhyped state, I ignored it.

"Um, yay?" he said.

"Isn't it great?" I asked. I smiled up at him. Signals began to seep through my bubble of joy. Brow: furrowed. Mouth: frowning. Body: stiff. What the hell? Why wasn't he joining in on my lovefest?

"Um, what gives?" I asked. "I thought you'd be excited, too."

"I'm happy," Dad said, "for the people of New York, a city so nice they named it twice, I might add." He paused for me to laugh, but that wasn't going to happen, so he went on. "Anyway, I'm glad they'll finally get their city back, but I'm not sure why you're so excited."

"Not sure . . . ?" How was he so dense? I almost said that out loud, but a finely honed sense of self-preservation made me swallow it. "Columbia University," I said instead. "The Mailman School."

"Courtney, you know that's not part of the plan right now," he said. Not part of what plan? Whose plan? It sure as hell was a part of my current plan.

"What does that mean?" I demanded.

Dad sat on my bed and patted the place next to him. I

chose to stand, even though I felt bratty doing it. He sighed.

"I thought you'd go to Chemeketa for the first two years," he said and then held up his hand to stop me. Chemeketa was the community college where he taught. "And then we might see about you transferring somewhere."

"There's no way I'd be able to transfer to Columbia after attending community college for two years," I said. Dad frowned. He hated it when I talked down about his place of employment. He didn't understand why I didn't jump for joy at the chance to go to something just a step above vo-tech.

"And how would we afford it?" he asked. "There's no guarantee you'd be able to get enough in scholarships. I know you're brilliant, but that's an awful lot of money."

"Scholarships? Money?" I heard the edge of hysteria in my voice, but I wasn't able to control it. "There's a whole brick of money in your sock drawer that says we can afford it!"

All of the air got sucked out of the room. Dad opened his mouth, then closed it again. He took off his glasses with his right hand and pinched the bridge of his nose with his left.

I knew I'd said the wrong thing, but, dammit, it was true. Last year I earned nearly seventy thousand dollars selling Vitamin Z out of the drive-through window at Bully Burger. Now it just sat in Dad's dresser in a gallon-sized Ziploc.

"Maybe you're not so brilliant after all," he said. He replaced his glasses. "The fact that you might suggest using that money—money you got from selling poison to people—tells me that I may have been granting you too many freedoms. What makes you think it's okay to use that money?"

"Why else haven't you got rid of it?" I asked. "I thought you were keeping it around so that I could use it to go to school."

"I'm keeping it around because I can't figure out how to give it away to a charity in a way that doesn't end with us both going to jail!" His face darkened and the cords on his neck bulged out. Dad almost never got so mad that he raised his voice. I kept all of my rebuttals to this argument firmly inside my big, fat mouth.

"Maybe I should just burn it," he said.

Every scrap of energy and joy I'd felt just a few minutes before drained out of me. I walked across the room and slumped into my desk chair. I put my feet up on the seat so my knees were under my chin, then hugged my legs. I wanted to be as small as possible.

"Sweetie . . ." Dad said, then stopped. He looked around the room like maybe he was seeing everything for the first time. "Your mom didn't cause the zombie invasion, you know?"

"What?" I said. This new tack surprised me so much, it shocked me into speaking to him. Something I didn't think I'd ever do again.

"You heard me," he said. "Your mother dropping out of Columbia did not cause the dead to rise up out of their graves."

"Well, it didn't help keep them in the ground, either." I felt petty even as I said it.

"I guess not," Dad said. "There was a lot going on at that time. She and I had just started dating seriously. She was already questioning whether or not she wanted to be an epidemiologist. She'd also been accepted to the California Institute of the Arts, did you know that?" I shook my head. "She wanted to be a painter. She was a great painter." He lay back on the bed and threw his arm behind his head. What was he doing, and where was this going? And how was this going to make it okay that I wasn't going to New York?

"Her parents wanted her to go into medicine," Dad went on. "So she chose that to make them happy. At the expense of her own happiness. Know what happened next?"

"Yeah, you two fell in love and you got a job teaching out here so you left one of the coolest places on earth to move out to nowhere, Oregon." Jesus, was it possible for me to sound any more like a spoiled child?

Dad chuckled. "That's almost everything that happened. She got pregnant. I got her pregnant." He propped himself up. "With you." He frowned, then got a faraway look in his eye. "I think she saw it as an opportunity to chuck school and get away from her family. I'm sure she thought she'd be happy, but it turned out that a family of her own wasn't what she wanted, either."

He sat up and rubbed his face. "Maybe you can blame me for the zombie invasion. I got her pregnant, after all. Or maybe you can blame yourself. Who knows, maybe if she'd . . . given you up, maybe she'd have stuck with school and concocted a miracle cure for the undead." He stood up. "The point is that it's pointless to assign blame in a situation like this. There's a lot to go around, but assigning it won't make things better. Maybe you can think about no longer blaming her, and maybe you could stop feeling like you need to make up for something you never had any part in."

He walked over to where I sat and put his hands on my shoulders. I didn't shake him off, but I also didn't make any move to hug him or anything.

"I love you," he said. "And I'll support anything you want to do. I just wish you wanted to do it for you and not because you feel you owe it to the world."

I didn't know what to say, so I didn't say anything at all.

"Okay," he said. He bent and kissed the top of my head. "We can talk about this later."

He walked out of the room and left me alone with my shitty mood.

"It is what I want," I said to no one in particular.

After fuming for a long time—a period when I waited for my dad to come back in my room to apologize so that I might either scream at him or ignore him altogether—I got up and climbed into bed without changing out of my street clothes. I switched out the light, lay on my back, and stared up at the ceiling. What the hell did he know about why I was doing what I was doing? Sure, he was a psychologist but that didn't give him any great insight into my inner workings. If he really knew what was going on in my head he wouldn't just give me all of that cash, he'd be on the corner helping me sell more Vitamin Z so I could leave to go to school.

My phone lit up as it received a message. The green light threw long shadows up on the ceiling and made me think of monster movies. I guessed it was a message from Phil asking if I wanted to go out to kill the undead. To which I was going to give a resounding, "Hell, yeah!" Instead, the message was from a number I didn't recognize right away:

You ever gonna call me?

Perfect. It was from Brandon. I stared at the screen until it went black from inactivity, then I thumbed it to life. My thumb hovered over the call button. Any other night, I'd have deleted the dumb message and gone to bed. But that night I was feeling weak and vulnerable, and I was curious about what he was doing with himself. It might have made me a horrible person, but I was also flattered that he kept reaching out to me.

I brought my thumb down on the call button and put the phone to my ear. It rang three times and I started to think it was going to go to voice mail. Maybe he'd turned it off for the night, or maybe he'd gotten another call. Whatever, I was relieved as I started to pull the phone away from my head.

"That you, Courtney?" I heard come from the other end and put the phone back.

"Hi, Brandon," I said.

"It's good to hear from you."

Was it really Brandon? The voice sounded too thick somehow, too slow.

"Nothing to say?" he asked.

"Brandon?"

"Who else?" he asked. He laughed, but it sounded all wrong. The Brandon I knew had a laugh that was light and friendly. This laugh was slow, and thick, and somehow mean.

"You sound different," I said. Stupid, but I couldn't think of anything else to say.

"I'm still me, Courtney," he said. "Want me to say something only I'd know?"

I didn't answer. I grasped for something to say.

"You compared me to John Travolta when you broke up with me," he said and chuckled.

"Not really," I said. "I compared myself to Sandra Dee from *Grease*."

"Right," he said, "but that would make me Danny Zuko in that analogy, right?"

"I guess so," I said.

"See," he said, "I went out and watched the movie after you broke up with me."

I winced. He kept saying that—that I'd broken up with him. It was true but mentioning it again and again seemed like bad manners. Like calling attention to someone with a disability or something.

"I liked it," he went on.

"Good," I said. "I'm glad you did."

"Let's meet up," he said.

I nearly gagged. That statement did not flow logically from what we'd just been talking about. We were supposed to talk about the relative merits of Sid Caesar's performance as Coach Calhoun, the awesomeness of Rizzo's overall aesthetic, and the way "Beauty School Dropout" almost flushes the whole production down the toilet. We weren't supposed to jump nearly context-free to suggesting we get together. I sat up in bed. Even though we were talking on the phone, I felt like I needed to be ready to run away.

"I don't know, Brandon," I said. "I don't think that'd be a good idea."

"I'm not going to force it, Courtney," he said. "I just think it'd be good to see you."

"Yeah, well, I . . ." I started.

"And I think you'd like to see me, too."

"I just wanted to know if you were doing okay," I said. "That's why I was asking folks at school about you. You weren't at the football rally."

He laughed, a genuine Brandon laugh. Somehow it chilled me more than relieved me in that context.

"No more football," he said. "It just doesn't seem worth it."

"What changed?"

"Meet me and I'll tell you," he said. "It doesn't have to be tonight. Whenever you're ready. Listen, I gotta go. An old friend of yours is calling. I'll say hi for you."

"What?" I asked, feeling lame. "Who?"

"I'll talk to you later, Courtney. Thanks for calling."

The line went dead.

I sat on the bed looking at the phone wondering about the last thing he said to me. An old friend of mine was calling him? What the hell was that supposed to mean? Crystal? Were they a thing now? And if they were, why was he suggesting that I meet with him? I had no idea what was going on and it was frustrating the shit out of me.

"I refuse to let you control me," I said to the phone as if it was Brandon I was talking to. "I broke up with you and I refuse to let you manipulate me into changing my mind. Also, I am talking to my cell phone." I needed to go to bed.

This time I got up and changed into my nightclothes. Then I went to the bathroom, did my business, and brushed my teeth.

I climbed into bed and made sure to turn my phone off so any new, incoming messages wouldn't wake me.

I lay on my back and stared at the ceiling again like earlier, but I wasn't angry at my dad anymore, though I guessed that'd come back. This time I replayed my conversation with Brandon. Especially the last part. Who was he talking about?

"Nope," I said out loud. "I'm done with you."

I turned over and closed my eyes. I fell asleep wondering if it was possible that my dad heard how often I talked out loud to myself. I wondered if he thought I was crazy. Then I was asleep.

I sat in one of the hard plastic benches in the Bully Burger and squinted under the too-bright fluorescent lighting. I hadn't been back since I'd quit the place six months before. It hadn't changed. Ashley and Mary-Kate were still behind the counter. Glum customers gave their pathetic orders without making eye contact.

Somewhere I heard a moan.

"Hey, Chacho," I called out to the only decent person who ever worked at Bully Burger besides me and Phil. He was the security guard, and as with most nights, he sat reading the newspaper, his anti-bite armor piled up next to him. "How've you been?" He kept on reading the paper like he hadn't heard me.

"I said, how have you been?" I practically yelled it across the dining room but he just kept on reading the stupid paper. What the F, Chacho? I knew I hadn't come to visit him in half a year, but that was no excuse to give me the cold shoulder.

"He can't hear you, dim bulb."

Sherri threw a tray of paper-wrapped food down on the table. I just gawked at her. Sherri, my best friend from birth, my constant companion, the girl I always trusted to be ready with a snide remark. God, I loved the crap out of her. Too bad I watched a sniper put a bullet through her zombified brains last year.

Now she was sitting across from me munching on a double Bully Burger dripping with Rough Rider sauce. Some of it ran down her chin, and she wiped it off with the sleeve of her faux leather jacket.

"Jesus, this is terrible," she said. "I've missed it so much. I can't get it in my face fast enough!"

"What do you want?" I asked. I wasn't exactly thrilled to see her.

Another low moan, louder this time, filled the room. No one, including Sherri, seemed to notice.

"What is this?" I asked.

"It's the double Bully, you dick," said Sherri with a grin that was full of half-chewed food. "You slung enough of these in your time here. You should be able to recognize it."

"That's not what I meant and you know it." I knew this was a dream. I was huffing in my dream, which annoyed me to no end. "I thought we were done with your little nocturnal visits after the zombie attack last year."

"That was just the beginning," Sherri said just before she took another bite. Why did that burger look so rare? It dripped blood. Bully Burger regulations called for us to cook every last bit of flavor out of the patties. It pooled on the table, candy-apple red and thick.

"I don't want to do this."

"Yeah, there are things we all wish wouldn't happen." With her free hand, Sherri made her finger and thumb into a gun and pointed it at her head. A small, neat hole had appeared in the center of her forehead. I knew that was the hole left behind by the round that ultimately killed her. I imagined the crater left on the back of her head, and I knew I didn't want to see it.

Another moan, louder. I turned to look behind me. It came from the back hallway where the public restrooms were.

"You can ignore it for a while," Sherri said. It sounded like she spoke around a mouthful of food. The smell of rotted meat flooded the room. I breathed through my mouth to keep from gagging. I turned around slowly, trying to prepare myself for what I was about to see.

And there was Sherri as I'd last seen her. Zombified, undead, but still pretty freshly dead. Her mouth and cheeks were shredded and raw from when she tried to get at me through a chain-link fence. She still had the bullet hole—black fluid dripped out of it and ran down her face. It formed into a puddle of black gore on the table.

"Eventually, you'll have to deal with it," Sherri said. I tried to give her the benefit of the doubt, but I swear I heard a hint of glee in her undead voice.

I put my head down. I did not want to deal with this. Or with anything. I thought I finished this last year when I helped hold back a huge zombie attack and saved a good chunk of my high school class. The thought of doing more made me feel exhausted. I was just going to sit here until it all went away.

Then a huge centipede crawled up onto the table and slithered away toward Sherri.

I stood up in disgust. Then anger filled me.

"I'll just deal with this now."

Sherri played with the centipede, letting it slither from hand to hand, never letting it get free of her grasp. After a second, she clutched it in her fist and shoved it in her mouth.

"Atta girl," she said and smiled. She had tiny insect legs stuck in her teeth.

I turned and stalked off toward the bathrooms. I noticed that there was no one else in the store. All of the customers who'd been sitting around us, each of the employees behind the counter, they were all gone. The moaning grew louder. It sounded like more than one voice now. The handle to the bathroom door rattled. Someone was trying to get out and couldn't quite figure out how to work the door.

The anger seeped out of me with every step, but I kept going. I'd deal with this and be done.

I stood in front of the door. It shook so hard I thought the door frame was going to come loose from the wall. I reached out slowly toward the handle.

The door burst open and the thing inside reached for me.

My eyes flew open, my heart beating fast, and I stared off into my darkened bedroom. Whose face had I seen right at the end of the dream? I almost dredged it up, but it kept receding. It seemed important to remember, but the more I struggled, the dimmer it became.

I finally gave up and rolled over to try to go back to sleep.

"It was good to see you again, Sherri," I said to the darkness.

I didn't care if Dad thought I was crazy.

CHAPTER SEVEN
Time to Stomp Some Zs

On Fridays that semester I got off early from school. I had enough credits that I didn't need to carry a full load. That sounded like bragging, didn't it?

Anyway, one of those Fridays a week after the call with Brandon, Phil skipped his last class to come hang out with me at a local coffee shop called The Governor's Cup. Everyone just called it the Gov Cup. I guess politicians used to walk the few blocks from the Capitol to come hang out here. They didn't do that much anymore. I liked it because they roasted their own beans, they had good Wi-Fi, and it wasn't a certain, unnamed corporate coffee joint. It's sort of dark in there, it never gets much sun, and the dark wood furnishings sort of swallow up the available light. Call that a plus.

Phil and I sat in the upper level. I nursed my coffee, which Phil bought for me—I probably needed to start thinking about getting a new part-time job. Maybe if Phil ever decided to stop buying me stuff I'd get serious about that.

"Are we going out tonight?" I asked. Both Phil and I knew that this meant hunting zombies. No dating was implied.

"Can't," said Phil. "I close tonight and open tomorrow."

"That," I said, "sucks."

"Agreed."

"But you still like working at the theater?"

He sipped his drink and nodded. After he quit the Bully Burger, he scrounged up a job at the indie movie theater, Salem Cinema. "I like running the projectors," he said. "They're kind of crotchety and need to be coaxed along. Actually, there's just one thing I don't like about working there."

"The customers," we said in unison.

"The bane of the service industry," Phil said, "is that you have to actually, you know, serve."

"Sure," I said.

"Maybe we can go out tomorrow night," he suggested. "I'll get off early enough."

"That'd be great," I said. I paused for a second, gathering up the courage to say this next bit. "I think we should invite Warren to come along." He fixed me with his gaze without answering. Hey, it wasn't a "no." "We've hung out with him a few times and he isn't a total tool, right?"

"Sure." His face was completely impassive, no emotion, no hint at what he thought. Sometimes his stoic, tough-guy demeanor was okay, but this wasn't one of those times.

"And it'd be nice to have some backup, you know?" I plowed on, hoping to bury Phil under an avalanche of logic. "Last time we went out, there were more shufflers than we originally thought and Cody nearly got his ass bitten by a—"

"I said, 'Sure,' " Phil said in that same flat tone.

"Oh, I thought you were talking about him not being a total tool," I said. "Okay. That's good." I studied his face. "You're not mad, are you? Are you mad? It's just hard to tell sometimes."

"Courtney, I said he could come if he wants to." He

downed the last of his coffee, then stood up. "You can ask him. I've got to get to work."

"Okay," I said. "I'll call you tomorrow."

He turned and left without saying another word.

I sat there wondering if I'd said the wrong thing by asking for Warren to come along, then I got mad. Who the hell was Phil that I had to grovel and ask him for permission for someone I considered a friend to join us on stupid and suicidal zombie hunts? He could blow it out of his unemotional butt if he didn't like it. Damn right I was gonna ask Warren to come along.

I whipped out my phone and did just that.

We're going on a Z hunt tomorrow. You in?

My phone buzzed in my hand almost immediately.

Of course. Just say where and when.

Thank God. I put my phone on the table and popped open the laptop I got as a gift for my last birthday. I planned to start doing research for a paper I had due after Thanksgiving for my AP World History class. I figured if I got it done early, I'd be able to treat myself to worry-free gorging on turkey and starchy foods. But first, I put in my earphones, cranked up The Killers, and drowned out whatever terrible lite jazz the coffee shop saw fit to inflict on its patrons.

It hadn't been very long into my reading about the relationships between George IV of England, Wilhelm I of Germany, and Nicholas I of Russia and how it led to WWI when I started to get the sense that someone was watching. Listen, I'm a girl who hadn't grown up sheltered in a cave, so I was used to boys—and men—staring at me in public. It was unpleasant, but something I just had to put up with, like dealing with my period. I hunkered down and tried to send out a "screw off" vibe and got back to reading.

A few minutes later, a shadow fell across the table and I knew I'd have to deal with someone who had no clear idea about boundaries. More than likely, I'd find some doughy nerdy boy standing there, his lack of experience with the fairer sex more pathetic than irritating, though it would certainly be irritating. I started preparing a speech about how, even though I looked like the girl of their dreams, I was, in fact, a real person with real thoughts and emotions, many of which would probably be off-putting to the average sheltered man-boy.

I looked up to find a junkie standing there. He was painfully thin with long, greasy hair that fell into his sunken eyes. While he stood there, he seemed to jitter or vibrate. Every wiry muscle in his body jumped beneath his skin. How had this guy been allowed into the coffee shop? Like any city, Salem has its share of crazy people and druggies, but most stores have the good graces to keep them away from their customers. That system had obviously failed here.

Then it struck me why this guy had come in here to pester me.

"Listen," I said in a harsh whisper, "I don't know what you may have heard, but if I ever did sell drugs—which I didn't—I certainly don't sell them anymore."

"No kidding, Courtney," the dude said.

I stared at him and he smiled. Even though the guy's teeth were no longer the brilliant white I remembered, there was no mistaking that orthodontia.

"Brandon?" I asked.

His smile broadened and there was no denying it. This

wrung out—looking skeez was somehow the boy I'd started to fall for last year. What the hell had happened?

He sat down across from me despite the lack of an invitation.

"You look good, Courtney," he said. "Just like always."

And you look like the post-apocalyptic version of yourself, I thought. I'd asked myself what had happened to him, but I knew the answer. I'd happened to him. Last year, he, my best friend, Sherri, and I had all smoked Vitamin Z together with my supplier, Buddha. The experience had scared the shit out of me, mostly because Sherri'd OD'd and been turned into a zombie, but Brandon had developed a taste for it. Looking at him, I guessed it was true what they said about there being no such thing as a casual Z user.

Knowing that I was responsible for this train wreck didn't make me want to stick around to study the results. I started to pack up my gear.

"My dad'll be here in a minute to pick me up," I said.

He looked toward the entrance. "Oh, yeah? How's he doing?"

"Fine," I said. Boy, wasn't he in for a surprise when he got a load of the all-new Brandon?

"So," I said, "I didn't see you in the football lineup this year." Mostly I was trying to kill time until Dad came to rescue me.

Brandon started to laugh, and it was that same low, thick sound I'd heard on the phone the other night. It sounded nothing at all like the laugh I remembered. That had been clear and ringing and open. This sounded dark and guarded.

"You mentioned that when we talked on the phone," he said. He shook his head. "Yeah, football. I decided that wasn't as important as I used to think."

"Uh-huh," I said lamely. "And school? I haven't seen you around school lately. Is that unimportant, too?"

"Right," he said with a grin. "I got a job."

I slipped my laptop into my bag and started to gather all of the cords.

"Where are you working?" I asked as I zipped up my bag.

"All over town," he said, and he shrugged.

What did *that* mean? I was just about to ask him when I heard someone call my name.

My dad stood down by the entrance. He looked up at me and his smile faltered a bit.

Brandon waved. Dad hesitated and then returned the wave, his smile gone now.

"I've got to go." I stood up and shouldered my bag.

"We should get together sometime, Courtney," Brandon said. He flashed me that smile again. It was a lot more effective before his teeth had turned gray.

"Uh, maybe," I said. "I'm sort of busy. School and stuff, you know."

"Sure," he said. "Well, say hi to Phil and Cody. And to that new kid you're hanging out with. Don't know his name."

I stared at Brandon for a long time trying to formulate a response. How did he know I was hanging out with Warren? Had he been following me?

"Courtney?" Dad called from downstairs.

"I'm leaving," I said to Brandon.

"I'll see you around," he said back to me.

I rushed down the stairs and joined my dad. He gave me a brief one-armed hug.

"Who's that you were sitting with?" he asked.

"You don't recognize him?" I asked.

"I do not."

Brandon waved down to us again.

"He's just someone I used to know from school. He's not doing too well now." I turned and walked outside.

"Well, it's good to try to help people," Dad said as he walked beside me. "Just don't get mired in whatever trouble he's in."

Too late for that, I thought.

"I'll try not to," I said.

"Anything you want to talk about?" Dad asked. We reached the car and he unlocked the passenger door for me.

"No," I said, "but I reserve the right to talk about it later."

"That works," Dad said as he reversed out onto the street.

As he put the car in drive and headed toward home, I glanced in the side mirror. I noticed that Brandon stood on the sidewalk and watched us drive away.

Not *too* serial killer . . .

I refrained from texting Phil with the news about my little run-in with Brandon. I wanted to have it in my hip pocket as a conversation starter when I saw him and the boys the next night. I occupied my time with homework. Homework that I did in my room. With my curtains drawn in case Brandon was being creepy and following me. I told myself I was being paranoid, but I just didn't like the co-incidence of him showing up at the coffee shop the day after I'd called him. I figured there was no reason to take chances, you know?

I was buried in research about royal cousins when my e-mail chimed that I had a new message. Since I was ready to put aside the various causes of the First World War, I checked to see who it was, even though no one I wanted to communicate with ever actually e-mailed me.

The subject line read "New Mutants?" and all I thought was that someone had sent me a message about a second-tier *X-Men* comic book. There was no way I'd be able to tell you who wrote or drew the book anymore, which mutants were on the team, or if the book was even being published anymore.

Then my eyes skipped over to the sender's name and I almost threw up in my mouth because it was so unexpected. "Rjkeller@ucdavis.edu." Rjkeller was Richard Keller. Richard Keller was a professor at UC Davis I saw on TV last year. He had a theory about communicating with zombies and was doing research to see if it was possible. He was attacked not too long after I saw him on a talk show and was left in a coma. I e-mailed him and kind of poured my heart out one night about my "fast zombie" theory. I seriously never expected him to come out of his coma, let alone contact me.

My hand shook as I moved the mouse over the line and clicked it.

To: AwesomeSauce29@gmail.com [Give me a break, I thought up my addy handle when I was twelve.]
Subject: RE: New mutants?

Dear Miss Hart,
Thank you so much for writing me, and for your concern about my health. I was only in a coma for a short time. I then spent a longer stretch of time in physical therapy. It is indeed disheartening that individuals feel the need to attack—in this case, literally—those with whom they disagree. But it has always been this way, I'm afraid.

Regardless, now that I am once again well enough to return to work, I have been catching up on my backlog of unanswered e-mail. Yours struck me as particularly interesting and I hope you have not experienced any further attacks.

The tl;dr version of the e-mail was that he was interested in the attacks I'd mentioned—he wanted me to describe them in detail—but he really wanted to know about Vitamin Z and my theory that there might be a connection between it and the new, faster zombies. He wondered how he might be able to get a sample. Then he mentioned that he'd be visiting OHSU, Oregon Health & Science University, after the New Year and asked if I might be able to come up and visit him on the campus. The university sat on a huge, heavily-fortified hill on the west side of the river up in Portland. Since they were doing a bunch of research into the zombie virus, it was the one place on that side of the city that the government decided to keep open after the zombies claimed everything else.

I just about messed my pants. I certainly squealed because my dad walked down the hall and came into my room without knocking first to see what was the matter.

He caught me doing an impromptu dance in front of my laptop.

"Is this about a boy?" Dad asked. I knew he was struggling with not being upset at running in here expecting to see me being accosted by an army of the undead only to find me doing a terrible bit of twerking. God, he probably thought I was dancing for someone since I was in front of the computer.

I almost blurted out what had made me so excited, then I remembered his reaction the last time I displayed the slightest bit of joy over New York being reopened.

"Sorry," I said. "I just found the piece of research I needed for my AP History paper. I guess I got a little excited."

"I guess you did," he said. "I'm trying to do some paperwork. Mind keeping it down to a dull roar?"

"I'll keep it below riot levels, yes, sir," I said. A queasy feeling settled into my stomach just like always when I wasn't entirely truthful with my dad. You might say it was a feeling I was used to.

"I'm glad you found what you needed." He leaned in and kissed my forehead. I let him. It seemed like the least I could do. After that, he left my room and closed the door behind him. Guilty stomach be damned, I turned and starting working on a response to the doctor's e-mail. I told him I might know how to get ahold of a sample for him—I was vague on details—and that I'd love to come up and visit him at the OHSU campus. If he wasn't visiting until after the New Year, I knew that gave me plenty of time to figure out a way to convince my dad to let me go up.

For my to-do list: figuring out how to actually get my hands on a sample of Vitamin Z. I'd be able to call up Buddha and ask him for some—I'd even offer to pay—but that seemed fraught with danger. Maybe I could ask around and figure out who was selling it in town since I knew Buddha must have gotten a new mule.

But first, I needed to get ready for my excursion that night. I dug through my drawers and pulled out what I thought of as my "ninja" gear: black jeans, black T-shirt, black hoodie, and black socks. I took a while deciding between my Dr. Martens and my black-on-black Chuck Taylors. I finally chose the Chucks because it was so warm out. I liked the Docs, but after I wear them for a while, it feels like I have bricks tied to my feet. The last item was the new pistol Dad bought me after I finally 'fessed up to losing the old one at the lookout. We'd gone to the gun shop together and made a day of picking out something. It was really sweet when you forgot that I was buying a firearm to fight off undead monsters. The shop owner, a beefy guy with a tattoo of a zombie in the crosshairs of a rifle scope, sold us a .38 Special Smith & Wesson Model 438 Bodyguard. The .38-caliber slug will stop most shufflers in one shot and it's small enough that I can actually wrap my hand around the grip. We got it in matte black.

Also, thinking back on the number of times I needed to dig my pistol out of my bag, I asked about a holster. Bubba (as I came to think of him) sold us on a thing he called a "cross draw pancake holster." It slid on to my belt and rested on my left hip. I had to cross my body with my right hand to draw it. Cross draw, get it? It was a little awkward at first, but I finally got used to it. I certainly liked knowing that it was always handy rather than hiding underneath my organic chemistry textbook or something. With all of those things ready, I went out to spend some time with my dad. I started to formulate ways to gently badger him into going to bed early.

I didn't need to worry about it. I found him sitting in front of the TV, his chin resting on his chest. Little snorts escaped him as I shook his shoulder.

"You're alseep, Dad," I said. "Let's go to bed."

"I'm not asleep," he said, as a line of drool plopped onto his baby blue polo shirt. Real attractive.

"Sure," I said. "You always watch TV with your eyes closed."

He stood and stretched, and his back sounded like small arms fire, which, given my experience with guns and zombies, I knew all too well.

"Think you're so smart," he said and grinned. "Maybe I will get some shut-eye."

He wrapped his arm around my shoulders as we walked down the hall. Well, I walked; he sort of shuffled and lurched. His movements were very zombie-like, but I didn't bring that up. Because I was raised properly.

"'Night, pumpkin," he said.

"Good night, Dad." He closed the door to his room and I went into mine. The moment I flopped onto my bed, I had my phone out and was texting Phil. I told him the Dad-creature was slumbering and that he should come get me. My phone pinged just a few minutes later.

Nearly done here. Give me an hour. We'll come get you.

I got dressed, then killed the hour with the research I'd lied to my dad about. Just as I thought about texting Phil again, Warren's ninja-mobile pulled up outside. I climbed out of my window and jogged across the yard toward the car. The gate into our yard squealed as I opened it and I winced. I looked toward the house, but I doubted Dad had heard it.

As I approached the car, I saw Cody in the backseat sitting next to Phil.

"Ride shotgun," I said and rapped on the glass. He looked to Phil like he was asking permission.

I wasn't able to hear him, but I saw Phil say, "Why are you looking at me?"

Reluctantly, Cody climbed out and got in front next to Warren. I plopped my butt in the seat next to Phil and closed the door. Warren sped away as soon as it was shut.

"Two things," I said to Phil. "What do you want to hear first, the good item or the bad?"

"Hello to you, too, Courtney," Warren said from the front seat. "I'm doing well, thanks for asking."

"Do you need me to come hold your hand up there, Warren?" I asked. "Are you feeling a little less than special?"

Cody laughed. Probably louder than my little joke deserved, but Warren still bugged him and he liked to see the guy taken down a peg or two every once in a while. Not that Cody would do it himself, because he was also more than a little afraid of Warren.

"Charming as ever," Warren said.

"Well?" I asked Phil.

"The bad, I guess. Get it out of the way."

"I like your style," I said. "I think Brandon has been stalking me."

"Your ex?" Cody asked. "The jock?"

"Bingo," I said.

All Phil was able to muster was, "Huh."

" 'Huh'?" I asked. "That's it?"

"Why do you think he's following you?"

"Not following," I said. "Stalking. There's a difference." I ran through the recent events. The texts, the call (though I left out the fact that it had been me dialing Brandon), the surprise appearance at the Gov Cup. It seemed like a rock-solid chain of evidence.

"I've heard he's pretty isolated," Phil said. "He dropped out of school—"

"He dropped out?" I asked. This was news to me and it seemed like it shouldn't be.

"Yeah," he said. "At least, he never actually showed up at the start of the year."

"I thought he just gave up football."

"Nope. What else? His friends don't really hang out with him. Or they don't want to be seen in public with him anyway."

"What does that mean?"

Phil looked at me like he couldn't believe what I was saying. Cody turned in his seat to check me out, and even Warren shot me a glance in the rearview.

"What?" I demanded. "What's the big secret?"

"No one wants to be seen with him because he's selling Vitamin Z," Phil said.

Cody chimed in, "But they all buy from him on the sly."

"When the hell did he start selling Vitamin Z?" I screeched. My life was suddenly spiraling out of control and I had no way of getting a handle on it.

"He started selling after you stopped," Phil said.

Warren nearly lost control of the car. "*You* used to sell Vitamin Z?"

"This isn't the time, Warren," I said. "How long have you known about this, Phil?"

"I don't know. Couple of months."

"And you didn't tell me about it?" I knew I was wearing my harpy face, but I didn't care. Phil had been withholding vital information from me and I was pissed. If I didn't get answers soon, it wasn't zombies I was going to be hunting that night.

"I don't pass every single fact I learn on to you," Phil said. He turned and gave me one of those slow blinks. I hadn't seen one in a while; they were usually an indication that he was retreating emotionally even more than usual. I started to argue back, but he cut me off. "It's not like you share everything all the time, is it? When did I finally learn about you selling Z?"

He had a point and it made me furious, but I refused to keep arguing like that because it might just turn into screaming and name calling, and even as mad as I was, I knew that wouldn't be good for our relationship. Whatever sort of relationship it was. Instead I just sat back and faced forward.

We drove on for a while in silence.

"Are you going to tell us the good news?" Phil asked.

"Go to hell," I spat at him.

"I'll take that as a no."

"This is fun," Cody said up in the front seat without turning around. "We are having fun."

I ignored him.

As we drove, Warren kept glancing back at me in the mirror. Great, was he having second thoughts about going hunting with me because of my past occupation? Every time he looked at me, I got more and more mad. I was just about to yell at him to keep his eyes on the damn road when Cody chimed in.

"Why don't you use this quiet time to fill us in on tonight's hunt?"

"What?" Warren asked. He'd been looking at me and was caught off guard by Cody's question. He recovered. "Sure," he said. "There was a Z attack out this way a couple of days ago. Cops got a couple of them and called it good. But I thought there might be more."

"Sure," Phil said. "The police hardly ever look thoroughly enough."

I wanted to ask since when had he become such an expert on police tactics, but I bit my tongue. I felt an electric pang in my chest. My heart was sending signals that I needed to cool my jets.

The guys talked, but I tuned them out. I didn't need the details. Just point me at the shufflers and I'd do my thing. Easy-peasy, black-brain-squeezy.

Warren drove around the outskirts of town. Of course. All of the hot zombie action these days took place where the fields and woods bumped up against the houses of poorer neighborhoods. Neighborhoods like the ones me and Phil and Cody lived in. Nicer 'hoods, like the ones Warren and Brandon lived in, were safe, and not just because of the gates and fences and walls that contained them.

Shit, did Brandon still live in his old place? Did his dad put up with his new shenanigans? I never met Mr. Ikaros, but from what I saw of Brandon's life, I don't think he was the best parental unit. Of course, folks probably thought that about my dad, too, based on some of my choices. Maybe parents can only carry so much blame; kids have to accept a big portion of the responsibility for their messed-up decisions, right? God, the way I sounded, I could run for a spot on the Salem city council on a "get tough on teens" platform. I'd be elected in a heartbeat.

"You still with us, Courtney?"

"What?"

Warren turned in his seat and grinned at me. "We're here. We've been here for a while now, but you didn't seem to notice."

"Sorry," I said. "I tuned out your delightful banter. I hope I didn't miss anything."

He just laughed and climbed out of the car. The rest of us did the same.

"There's the house," Warren said. He'd parked in front of a little shotgun shack, the front of which was decorated with yellow police tape, like the world's saddest birthday party banners. The chain-link fence in front had been trampled down, the front door busted in. I'd seen fences like that before, but the door was a new one on me. Usually zombies couldn't figure out porch steps, let alone a locked door.

The wind picked up and it cut right through my hoodie. Worse, it felt like rain. I wished I'd brought something heavier. It was just that a down jacket didn't have the ninja effect I had been aiming for.

"The cops zapped the zombies in the field across the road," Warren continued, "but I don't think they went in far enough."

The field was about forty or fifty yards of overgrown grass before a wall of trees sprang up. Big old trees. Maybe oaks. Before people showed up in this part of the world, even before the Indians, this area used to be what they called an "oak savannah"—oaks as far as the eye could see. In the light of a half moon, the old trees looked malicious, like they were just waiting for us to get close.

I shivered and pretended it was because of the wind.

"Saddle up," Warren said. He pressed a button on his key fob and the car's trunk opened slowly. "Choose your weapons."

Cody giggled and rubbed his hands. "Time to stomp some Zs!"

Something felt off. Why were the boys so cheerful? Maybe it was me; maybe I was off-kilter. I drifted to the back of the car and took out my old standby. The wrecking bar glowed dully in the moonlight. I hadn't done a very good job of cleaning it after the last hunt, and black gore caked into the crevices on the nail-ripper head. Seeing it then made me queasy. It just added to the sense that things were off about this.

"Are you okay?" I started. I hadn't realized anyone was standing next to me.

Phil stared at me, concern—or as close to concern as Phil got—evident on his face. Annoyance crept in around the edges of my fear. Good. I'd rather be angry than afraid.

"You don't have to babysit me," I said.

"That's not what this is."

"Then what?" I asked.

"If you're not into it, then you might get yourself hurt," he said. "Or one of us."

He had a good point. I knew he had a good point and that his logic was sound, but I didn't want to hear anything logical just then.

"Why don't you keep it to yourself?" I asked. "Since you seem to be so good at that."

I stormed off, a very dramatic exit, except that I slipped in the wet grass and went facedown. I decided to lie there for a while and hope for the world to disappear all around me. No such luck. Phil kneeled down beside me.

"Let me help you up," he said. "Please."

"Fine," I said, "but don't think this means I forgive you. I just don't want to get too wet."

He hooked his hands under my arms and lifted me up. I didn't think he'd have been strong enough to do that.

"I'm sorry I didn't tell you about Brandon," he said. "The way you talk about him sometimes, it seems like you want to forget he exists."

"That'd be nice."

"I didn't do it out of spite or jealousy or anything," he said.

"I know," I said. I was going to say more, but Warren interrupted us.

"Do you two need to get a room?" He grinned at us and sliced his sword through the air before replacing it in his scabbard. Cody stood beside him and looked at us like he was disgusted by our—or any—display of emotion.

"Really," he said. "If you two want to start dry humping, we can go on alone."

"I'm going to hump your butt with Mr. Annihilator here," I said to Cody and showed him the wrecking tool. He made a disgusted sound. Then to Phil I said, "Let's just go, please."

We all double-checked our gear. I made sure my pistol was in its holster and hefted my weapon. Then we walked across the field and into the trees.

CHAPTER EIGHT

That Mythical Clearing

As we walked through the trees, the feelings of anger and self-doubt melted away and fear and excitement replaced them. My muscles felt taut, my heartbeat raced— I felt alive. It occurred to me that this was the opposite of taking Vitamin Z, this feeling of being alive.

I wondered briefly why that thought had come to me. Then I stamped on it like a bug and put it out of my head. There was no room to think about anything but the job we had in front of us.

Warren walked lead and he held up a fist. He wanted us to stop. Weeks before, he'd tried to teach us more hand signals to use "out in the field" as he said. That lesson devolved pretty quickly to me and Cody making every rude hand gesture we could think of. We decided after that that we'd just whisper when we needed to communicate out on a hunt.

"Smell that?" Warren asked. He was right; there was a definite tinge of spoiled meat and farts in the air. Call it *eau d'shuffler*. "There's a clearing once we get through these trees. Twenty, maybe thirty yards across. That's where most of the zombies are." He swiped his arm across his face to get the sweat out of his eyes—even though it was the end of November and cold, we were all sweating.

"We rush through these trees, and we'll be in the middle of them. Okay?"

We all made agreement noises. My heart beat fast, all thoughts of Brandon and Phil gone from my head.

Warren held up his hand, his index finger extended. "One." Without speaking again, he held up a second finger.

Beside me, Phil hunched down like a sprinter on the starting line.

Warren held up a third finger and we all took off running.

Trees whipped past me and I started looking for a clearing full of shufflers. I cut left around a tree in my way and came face-to-face with a Zipp. I barely had time to register that he was around my age and looked pretty clean before I smashed his face in with my wrecking tool. It happened again with a female zombie and again. After the last one, I had to stop for a second to catch my breath. While I sat there willing my lungs to keep working, I looked around. Where was the damn clearing?

I heard shouts from the boys, but nothing I could make out. Panic started to grip me and I shoved it away. I got a firmer grip on my tool and ran toward where I'd heard the shouting.

Despite the cold air, sweat ran down my face and coated my arms and back.

Two more zombies came into view. They must have been going after the shouting, too, because they had their backs to me. I raised the wrecking tool and brought it down on the head of the one closest to me, a wiry dude with a crappy ponytail.

"Take that." I meant to whisper, but because of my lack of breath, it came out like a sharp barking sound. The guy fell face-first into a tangle of underbrush. The second zombie, a fat girl with half her face missing, whirled around and made a weird chirping noise at me. Her mouth fell open and black drool fell down her chin.

"Come here, sweetheart," I said and gave the tool a yank. "I've got something for you." I pulled on the tool again and it didn't budge. It was stuck in the zombie's skull, and no matter how hard I yanked on it, it wouldn't come out.

The zombie, thank God she was a slow one, was nearly on me. I stood up and started to back slowly away, the picture of Zen-like calm. At the same time, I got my hand on my revolver and made to draw it. Which was when I tripped over some roots or shit. I went down hard on my butt and bit my tongue hard enough that hot, salty blood filled my mouth. I spit and the zombie's eyes went huge as she looked at it shining black in the moonlight. Then she screeched and threw herself at me, moving way faster than she had before.

I barely had time to actually draw my pistol before the monster was on top of me. Her weight trapped my arms against my chest, but with a grunt, I was able to lift her up a little, her jaws snapping inches from my face, and then snake my gun hand up until the revolver rested under her chin.

I pulled the trigger and her head snapped back. The little bit of light that had been in her eyes went out and she went limp. I let her stay on top of me for a minute and rested. I saw a sliver of sky through the trees from where I lay and I was tempted to stay there for the rest of the night.

Then I heard the shouts of my still very much alive friends. I gave another grunt of effort and threw the dead girl off me. I barely managed it—I guess there's a reason they call it dead weight—and staggered to my feet. I holstered my revolver.

"Phil?" I called as loud as I dared. "Warren?"

I crept over to the zombie I'd killed with my wrecking tool. By putting my foot on his neck and wrenching with all my strength, I was able to pry the stupid thing out of his skull, but it made a sucking/tearing noise that nearly made me spew.

"Courtney?" someone called.

"Phil?"

He emerged from some trees right in front of me.

"You're bleeding," he said. He sounded as close to panicked as I'd ever heard.

"I bit my tongue," I said. "I'm fine." I hardly noticed it, actually, but I knew that as soon as my body wasn't flooded with adrenaline, it'd hurt like a bitch.

He relaxed. "Where are the others?"

I felt stupid shrugging, but it was all I had.

"They're probably in the stupid *clearing*," he said. "If Warren gets out of this alive, I might just kill him myself."

"Get in line," I said and the words sounded thick because of my damn tongue. I spit out another mouthful of blood.

"Pleasant," Phil said.

Just then we heard a scream somewhere off to our left. It had a distinct Cody-ness about it so we both took off running.

We only encountered one more zombie, which Phil took care of with his nail-studded bat. As we ran on, we started to hear a steady stream of high-pitched shouting, mostly swearing, definitely Cody. Then I heard someone saying "sorry," but in a way that I knew they were exasperated and annoyed more than sorry. Warren.

The only reason we found them was that Phil nearly tripped over Cody, who was sitting on the ground holding a bloody bandanna against the side of his head. Warren stood over him, his arms crossed over his chest, his sword still in his right hand. He looked disgusted.

"Why'd you sneak up on me, dude?" he asked Cody.

"Sneak?!" Cody screamed. "I was just trying to get through the trees to find that mythical clearing I'd heard so much about, you asshat!"

"I told you about calling me names, little man," Warren said. He gripped his sword more tightly.

"That's the least offensive name I'm going to call you tonight," Cody said.

"Shut up," Phil said and knelt beside his friend. "Move your hand and let me see." Cody complied and Phil gave a low whistle. "That's not a small gash," he said. "What happened?"

"Ninja McDouche here tried to cut my damn head off," Cody said.

Warren bristled at that and uncrossed his arms—a pretty ominous sight since he still had the sword in his hand.

"If I wanted your head off, I'd have taken your head off," he said.

"Do me a favor, Warren," I said. "Go ahead and sheath that sticker before you really do cut off someone's head."

He looked down at his right hand like he was surprised that he still held the sword. Then he put it away.

"Right," he said.

"So there was some confusion and Cody got hurt," Phil said, sounding super reasonable. For some reason, that made me afraid.

"Right," Warren said, obviously relieved.

Phil helped Cody to his feet. "I guess the question we'll have to answer, after we get Cody stitched up, is, what was the confusion?"

"What's that mean?" Warren asked, his voice low, dangerous. I realized he wasn't so handsome when he scowled.

"Where was the clearing full of zombies?" Phil asked.

"Yeah, numb nuts," Cody said. "Where was it?"

"You guys must have run off in the wrong direction," Warren said.

"We ran in the direction you told us to." It took me a second to realize that it had been me that'd said that last bit. *Shit,* I had meant to stay out of this as much as possible.

A hurt look spread across Warren's face as he looked at me.

"Okay, I see how it is," he said. "Yeah, go ahead and blame me for this—I'm the new kid so it must be my fault."

"Who else can we blame?" Cody hissed, then he wobbled and Phil had to steady him.

"Let's worry about assigning blame another time," Phil said. "We need to get Cody to urgent care. He's losing blood here."

"Right, sure," Warren said, but he said it all petulant, like a three-year-old who'd just lost an argument.

"One of you help me with Cody," Phil said. He had one of Cody's arms draped across his shoulders.

I pushed past Warren. "I'll help."

"I can do it," Warren said.

"You can guide us back to the car," I said. I bit back a few choice insults. In a rare display of maturity, I chose not to make the situation worse.

He gave an exasperated sigh and then did just that. We had Cody back to the ninja-mobile in about five minutes.

Warren hesitated before he unlocked the doors with the little key-fob thing.

"What's up?" I asked.

"Is he gonna get blood on my seats?" he asked.

"What?" Phil asked, anger rising in his voice.

"If you're asking if the head wound you gave him is still bleeding," I said, "then the answer is yes."

"Do you have a towel?" Cody asked. "I'd be happy to bleed into a towel."

"Yeah, hold on." Warren popped the trunk and before we all threw our weapons inside, he pulled out an old beach towel. It didn't look like it had been laundered recently. "Let him rest his head against this."

"Well," said Cody, and his voice sounded faraway and dreamy, "if you're nice to me, I'll just start expecting it."

"Let's just get him to urgent care," Phil said. That got Warren to unlock the car.

By the time we got Cody out of the car and under the fluorescent lights of the urgent care parking lot, he was looking pretty pale. The towel was a goner. When the staff saw him, they rushed him right in to be taken care of. They didn't even ask how he was going to pay, so he must have looked bad.

Warren went off to find a vending machine, and Phil and I sat in the too-bright waiting room. The security guy at the door kept giving us looks, which I accepted as our due since we'd brought in a dude with a huge head wound and I had blood all down my front. I chose to ignore him and focused my attention on the religious programming that ran on the TV set bolted to the wall.

"Sorry about the whole Brandon thing," Phil said. He didn't take his eyes off the set.

"Doesn't seem as anger-inducing anymore," I said. My tongue hurt like a mother and it seemed to take up too much space in my mouth. I wasn't able to move it at all without it rubbing painfully against my teeth. "But don't hide things from me anymore."

"I wasn't hiding it," Phil said. This time he turned away from the TV and fixed me in his gaze. I had a hard time not turning away. "I just didn't realize it was something you'd want to know about."

"Okay," I said. "But now you know, right?"

He nodded. "Now I know."

We both went back to watching the televangelist. The sound was off so I had no idea what his wild gestures meant. I pretended he was doing an impromptu interpretive dance.

"What was the good news you had earlier?" Phil asked.

"I'll tell you when my tongue doesn't hurt so much," I answered.

"Fair enough."

He wrinkled his nose and glanced around the room as he sniffed dramatically. I'd noticed that the place smelled weird, too—antiseptic, sure, but kind of rotten, too, like the cleaner wasn't able to cover up the smell of sickness. It wasn't pleasant.

"I've been talking to my aunt and uncle about you," Phil said and the very un-apropos-ness of that statement made my jaw hang open. Then I snapped it shut and caught my tongue again. I stifled a scream and doubled over. The sensation was a lot like what I imagined chewing on red-hot nails might be. I wondered what the security guy was thinking then.

I grabbed a tissue from the table next to me and spit into it. No new blood. So there was that.

I crumpled up the tissue and put it in my pocket.

"Are you okay?" Phil asked.

"I'm sorry, you were saying something about your aunt and uncle?" My heart raced like I was about to run into a nest of shufflers.

"Yeah," Phil said. "They're always asking if I've made any new friends, you know?"

I gritted my teeth and nodded. Of course I knew. That question was a regular part of the nightly interrogation one experienced at the hands of one's parental captors.

"The last time I had an answer for them, it was Cody." He let that fact sink in for a minute. "Yeah, so, the last time they asked, I told them about you. They seemed pretty excited."

I tried to imagine what he might have said to his aunt and uncle that would have elicited *excitement* as a response. The word "lies" popped up into my head, but I squelched it. I was willing to accept that Phil might have given me a completely glowing review that he believed to be true. Rather than stroke my ego and ask him what he told them, I said, "That's nice."

"Yeah," he said. "So they were wondering if you might want to come over to dinner some night." He gave me a sidelong glance. "Thanksgiving dinner may have been mentioned."

"Oh," I said. "I don't know if that'd work. I mean, my dad and I always . . . You know."

"Didn't you say that you and your dad always have a sad Thanksgiving by yourselves?"

"Yeah," I said. Those sad dinners were the closest thing we had to a tradition.

"Well, they thought you *both* might like to come over," he said.

And suddenly I was caught in a relationship-algebra death-spiral. What did it mean that I was being invited to a family dinner, one usually reserved for close family? This was Phil, so I was tempted to take all of this at face value, i.e., he mentioned me favorably and his aunt and uncle were moved to invite me over. But this explanation lacked so much of the delicious and crazy-making drama that my hormone-addled brain desperately craved. What exactly had Phil said? Had he really mentioned me only in response to their questions, or had he brought me up to them? Had he asked them if I could come over? It all boiled down to, what did this new development mean for how Phil felt about me?

I realized that Phil had just been staring at me as I went

through my mental calculations. Jesus, what must he be thinking now?

"I'll have to ask my dad," I said. "But thank them for inviting me."

"Sure," he said. "Even if Thanksgiving doesn't work out, they'd love to have you over some night."

They'd love to, Phil? Not *you*? God, I needed to stop it.

Just then, Cody and Warren came into the waiting room. A huge bandage covered Cody's right ear and a sizable piece of his head beside. But he was grinning, so that was good.

"How you doing?" Phil asked. We both stood as they walked over.

"Seven stitches," Cody said by way of an answer. "And this guy paid for it!"

Warren shrugged. "I did it. Seemed like I should cover it."

"Any way I can get you to spring for some erythromycin?" Cody asked. He was still all grins.

"Did they give you pain meds?" I asked.

"A blue pill about the size of my fist," he said happily. "I can barely feel my feet."

"Right," Phil said. "We should get home before he does anything dumb. Dumber than usual."

"First," said Warren, "I want to apologize. I conducted some bad reconnaissance. I could have got us hurt, or worse. It won't happen again."

We all just stared at him. Humility wasn't an emotion we'd ever seen him display before. Suddenly, Cody swept in and grabbed Warren in a bear hug.

"Love you, man," I heard him whisper.

Warren awkwardly patted Cody's back. "Um, thanks."

"Well," I said. "I'm about to start crying. Or barfing. One or the other. Let's go home."

We left the acrid smells and too-bright lighting of the

urgent care waiting room and stepped out into a night that wasn't nearly as dark as I'd have liked. The eastern horizon was tinged with red. The sun was going to be up soon.

"Oh, man," I said. "I need to get home before my dad wakes up." I didn't think he'd be likely to check on me if he woke up early, but it just seemed safer to actually be in my bed and avoid the possibility.

"We can take you home first," Warren said. "And I meant what I said to you guys in there. I'm sorry."

"Okay," Phil said. "Thanks."

I opened the rear door to his car. "What he said."

Phil and I slumped into the backseat at the same time and bumped shoulders. I just stayed there, too tired to move.

"I will ask my dad about Thanksgiving," I said. "And no matter what he says, I think it was sweet of your aunt and uncle to invite us." My tongue really hurt just then, and I wasn't sure how much Phil was able to understand what was coming out of my mouth.

"I'll tell them you said so," he said. He rested his hand on my leg for a second and I felt an electric thrill rush from the point of contact up to my secret girly places. He moved his hand and I stifled a little moan of displeasure.

"Yeah, tell them." I meant to say more, but I was out, asleep with my head resting on Phil's shoulder. I didn't wake up until we got to my house, and then just long enough to endure a hug from Cody and then to have Phil help me into my room through the window.

I told him good-bye and didn't bother to take off any of my clothes before I threw myself into my bed and a long, dreamless sleep.

CHAPTER NINE
Pretty Smart

I was caught by complete surprise when my dad said that joining Phil's family for Thanksgiving sounded like a neat idea. He actually used that word. "Neat."

So, on the last Thursday in November, I found myself wondering how exactly to dress for dinner with one's potential love interest. Was that what Phil was? Was he just my zombie-slaying buddy? Why were there so many questions when I thought about him? I craved just a single declarative statement where he was concerned.

Really, this was the exact reason I thought school holidays should be outlawed. Give me too much time off from worrying about my GPA, and I filled my head with all this stupid shit.

Not being sure how to dress, I went with my standard uniform: plaid flannel over a black T-shirt, black jeans, and my Dr. Martens. Everything was clean at least. I threw a hoodie on in lieu of a jacket.

Dad frowned when I emerged from my cave. I needed to tell him that it gave him unattractive lines around his mouth when he did that, but I didn't think he'd appreciate it.

"That's what you're wearing?" This from a man who'd chosen a knit sweater vest.

"I like to set the bar of expectation low right from the start," I said.

"Mission accomplished, smart-ass," he said.

A soft but steady rain fell as we drove to dinner. I acted as navigator and read Dad the instructions that Phil had written down. They were very precise directions. Turns out, Phil's place wasn't that far from ours. Maybe a mile away. His neighborhood sported the same depressing little houses and their flimsy chain-link fences. Phil's house was a sun-bleached pink color. Maybe it had been salmon or peach once upon a time, but it had faded long ago.

We parked on the curb and rushed through the rain, Dad opening the gate for me.

As I ran up the front steps, the door swung open and a thin, tall woman stepped out, her face lit up.

"You must be Courtney!" she shrieked at me.

I stopped short because it felt like an accusation. She shrieked again and I realized it was a laugh delivered at full volume.

"Oh, I didn't mean to scare you, sweetie," she said. "Come on in before you melt!"

She got me inside and stripped my hoodie sweatshirt off me. Then she nearly cracked my ribs with a bear hug.

"It's so nice to meet one of Philip's friends," she said right into my ear. She broke the hug and I drew a breath. She held me at arms' length, one hand on each of my shoulders. Very obviously, she looked me up and down. "I can see why he likes you."

By this time, my dad had come up the steps.

"Oh, I can see where Courtney gets her good looks," Phil's aunt said and Dad went an entertaining shade of crimson. He held out a bottle of wine in response. Maybe not the smoothest move, but it did preempt the sort of hug that nearly snapped me in two.

"Jesus, Diane," said a man's voice, "let them come in-side."

"Of course," said Phil's aunt, Diane. "Come in, both of you. Dinner's nearly done."

At the mention of food, I noticed how great the place smelled. I wasn't too used to the aroma of cooking in my house and my mouth immediately started watering.

Diane ushered us out of the little entryway and into the living room. Phil stood awkwardly in the middle of the immaculate room. His carbon copy stood next to him. It took me a second to realize that the man standing next to him was a couple of inches taller and maybe twenty pounds heavier, but the resemblance was uncanny.

Phil half-raised his hand. "Hey."

His uncle stepped forward, grinning, and extended his hand. "We're glad you were able to come, Courtney. I'm Gene." My hand completely disappeared in his as he shook it. It wasn't one of those bone-crushers like he had something to prove, but he let you know he was there. "And this is . . . ?"

I'd been so caught up in the weird and strong genetics at play between him and Phil that I'd forgotten my manners. "Oh, right. This is my dad, Fred."

The two of them shook hands and started to exchange whatever passes for conversation between adults, all against a background of Phil's aunt apologizing for the state of their house. A house that was actually well-suited for receiving the queen of England. As they did their grown-up business, I sidled up to Phil.

"I'm guessing sales of some sort," I said.

"My uncle?" Phil asked. "Sort of, he's a lobbyist for the teachers' union."

"Wow," I said. "That is *so boring.*"

"He's really nice."

"I can tell. I know I'll like him despite myself."

"How long until dinner?" Phil asked in the general direction of his aunt and uncle.

"Just a few minutes," Diane said. "Are you going to take little Courtney to your room?"

Little Courtney?

"Yes, ma'am," Phil said. Diane's smile seemed to falter a little at his use of the word, but she recovered quickly.

"C'mon," Phil said and he turned and led me away.

The hallway was lined with photos. It started with Gene and Diane as kids themselves, then them together when they were younger. Their wedding, Diane pregnant, them with first one kid, then another. Then them alone, both of them looking tense and far away. I guessed what happened. Finally, Phil joined the photos. I got to see him go from a little kid to the hoodlum I knew all in the space of a few steps.

I wondered if I'd ever take up some real estate on those walls someday, then stifled the thought. It was too early for that kind of thinking.

Phil walked into a room at the end of the hall and I followed him. Not one thing in the whole room looked out of place, and the bed was made. That right there separated Phil's room from mine, but there was more. I had never seen a space so well organized. It was, frankly, a little creepy. His bed was up on a loft, underneath it sat a drawing table and chair, and a cabinet stuffed with drawing supplies. I said "stuffed," but really, everything was obviously in its intended place. Pencils, brushes, pens, paints, and inks. Rulers and erasers and a thousand little things I couldn't even have named. Bookshelves lined two of the walls, and I just knew that there was some elaborate system of organization at play that I'd never figure out. I wanted to start reading the titles, but that could wait.

"You have a closet organizer, don't you?" I asked.

"Yes?" he said.

"Of course you do."

As vaguely sterile as I found the room, the art lining the other two walls—and I mean every bit of available wall space—gave me a glimpse of Phil's interior life. It was his own art, of course. Some of it was obvious kid stuff, but still more accomplished than 99 percent of the stuff I'd seen in any art class. Some of it was more recent and so well done, it seemed like it should be in a poster shop. Friends, I'd guess, and family, and people he'd sketched on the street after seeing just once. And zombies. Zombies everywhere, but never really the focus, and never dominant. They were always being slayed by the people in the pictures.

One in particular caught my eye, and I stepped forward to look at it.

A girl dressed in jeans, Chucks, and a hoodie stood with a bloody ax resting on her shoulder. One foot rested on a small pile of zombie corpses. Around the edges of the drawing, Phil had suggested an army of the undead without actually drawing them in. The girl sneered as she looked out at the viewer and said, "Who's next."

"That's me," I said.

"It is." Phil rubbed the thumb of each hand against his forefingers. When he realized he was doing it, he stopped and put his hands in his pockets. "Do you like it?"

"No, dim bulb," I said. "I *love* it. Why didn't you tell me you'd done another of me?"

He shrugged. "I wanted you to see it here."

"It's gorgeous," I said. It drew my eyes in and refused to let them go. It was so weird the way the figure had my face, but it also wasn't my face. *Idealized.* That was the word.

"Are you still working on your comic?" I asked. Since the beginning of the school year, Phil had been drawing a comic about a zombie-slaying girl. He hadn't shown me any of it, but I guessed that the girl in the drawing—me, basically—was the main character.

"Every day," he said.

"Show it to me after dinner?"

"Not yet," Phil said. When I turned to glare at him, he shrugged. A simple raising and lowering of the shoulders that might have meant anything. "It's not ready yet. Soon."

Before I was able to bawl him out, his aunt poked her head into the room. "Phil, will you go help your uncle in the kitchen?" He moved off in that direction and I was left alone with a scary Stepford aunt. She walked toward me and I had to stop myself from stepping backward. She put her hands on my shoulders and then she got a really serious look on her face.

"We are so glad you and your father could join us, Courtney," she said and I thought she might start crying. I was not prepared for this eventuality. "Phil never brings his friends over, so any glimpse into his world is something we really treasure."

Before I could think of something to say, she swept me up in another rib-cracking hug.

"Thank you," she whispered in my ear.

"You're welcome," I finally said when she released me. It seemed best to keep it simple since saying something like, "Well, I've really been hoping your nephew might finally put the moves on me and coming to dinner tonight seemed like a good way to seal that deal," was probably inappropriate. "Thank you for asking Phil to invite me."

She did one of those confused-puppy-head-tilt things. "Is that what Philip told you?"

"Yes?" I said. The question crept into the word and I was powerless to stop it.

"That's odd," she said. "It was his idea to invite you. Of course, we leaped at the chance."

This tidbit of information made me extremely happy.

"Oh," I said. "Maybe I misunderstood." Not that it was a big deal.

"No, of course," she said. "You want to go wash up? We're almost ready."

She headed off to the kitchen and I went into a bathroom clean enough to receive the pope's fanny. I felt like I was defiling a holy site by using it for its intended purpose. When I was done, I joined everyone else in the dining room. Diane and Phil carried load after load of amazing food out of the kitchen. I'm guessing that Gene was playing field marshal in there. Dad and I stood by feeling inadequate since we'd been made to understand that as guests we weren't allowed to help out—without being told so, of course.

When all of the preliminary dishes had been staged, Gene emerged, still wearing an apron, and carrying a Tiny Tim–sized turkey. Or was that a goose? Phil and I sat next to one another, Dad across from us, and Diane and Gene at the head and foot of the table.

"Do you folks say grace?" Gene said, and my dad and I exchanged horrified looks. This caused Gene to burst out laughing.

"Oh, Gene," Diane said, but she was laughing, too. Even Phil smiled.

"Thank God," said Gene. "Neither do we. Let's dig in."

What followed was a scene of such carnage that I'm sure turkeys will sing of its horror for generations to come. I didn't think I'd ever eaten such delicious food and had trouble getting myself to stop. Those beautiful German linguists must have a word for that type of indulgent overeating. I'd have to Google it when I got home. If my guts didn't explode before I was able.

We talked about all sorts of stuff after the first rush of gluttony. Dad and Gene had a lot to say to one another about the state of the education system. My mom came up and was quickly put down again with only the barest raised eyebrow from Diane. Gene was very interested in my plan to go to Columbia to study epidemiology.

"The timing might be right for that," he said. "The latest news is that the Army is scheduled to finish clearing out the city by June."

"Well," said Dad, "we still have to work out a few kinks in the plan." He gave me meaningful eyes and I just smiled.

Phil told Dad that he'd like to study art when he was done with high school.

"He'd be an amazing painter," Diane chimed in.

"I hope to get accepted to a school with a comic book program."

"You need to take a look at the art on his walls," I said quickly when I saw his aunt frowning. Dad promised he'd do that before we left.

Diane let it drop, but I knew it took some effort.

"Ma'am," Phil said. When she looked up at him, he tapped his wrist. He didn't wear a watch.

"Oh, my gosh!" she exclaimed. "Phil and I never miss an episode of *Survival,* and tonight's a special episode." *Survival* was a terrible reality show that re-created stories of people escaping from zombie attacks. It also featured interviews with the survivors. I hated the show. I never understood its appeal, but then maybe most people hadn't had as many run-ins with shufflers as me. She gave Gene a pleading look.

"Go on," he said. "I'll clean up while you watch. Never could stand that show."

"I'll help you," I said. Everyone turned to look at me in shock. My dad's jaw might have fallen open.

"Oh, Courtney, you don't have to . . ." Gene said.

"No, sir," I said. "I don't have to, but I'd like to."

"You should take her up on it," Dad said. "She might never make that offer again."

While the others sat on the couch and watched an hour of shitty reality television, I mostly got in Gene's way as he tried to tidy up. After all the food was put away, we started washing dishes and I was finally able to lend a hand—even I know my way around a dish towel. Gene washed and I dried and stacked.

We chatted as we worked, mostly about school. Given his job, Gene was very interested in what I thought of the school experience. He kept calling it that, an "experience." Like it was the most depressing ride possible at Disneyland.

At one point, there was a lull in the conversation. I heard dramatic music drift in from the living room, and Diane squealed in fear and delight.

"Diane and I are thrilled that you were able to come over tonight, Courtney," Gene said, filling the conversational void. Oh, boy, was he about to get all weepy like Diane had earlier?

"I was wondering if you'd mind me asking about your relationship with Phil."

And with that, I felt a hot ball of lead fall into my stomach. Relationship? Was that what we had?

"What were you wondering, sir?" I asked.

"Oh, God, just Gene, okay?" he said. I nodded.

"I know every parent thinks their child is special," he said, "and Diane and I are no exception. Especially given the way he came into our lives." I wasn't sure if I was supposed to ask how that was, but I let it lie. "We know that he can be . . . distant. But that's a mask, or a shell. He's protecting himself."

"I thought that might be what was happening."

He smiled at me. "Because you're smart." It was so matter-of-fact, the way he said it. I was used to thinking that, but not to hearing others say it. "It's part of why he likes you." He stopped washing for a moment and looked right at me. "You know he likes you, right?"

"I think so," I said.

"Yeah," he said, "pretty smart." He went back to sudsing up some plates. "I just hope you'll be delicate with him. That's all. I know that at your age, everyone believes that they're impervious to harm, physical or emotional, but it's just not true."

"I don't plan on hurting him," I said. I felt like I should be angry about this tack, but it just made me feel oddly guilty. Preemptive guilt?

"No one ever plans to." He said it so quietly, it was almost like he was saying it to himself. "I'm sorry to get maudlin. I know you don't have any plans to hurt him. It's just that he's been through so much already, I want to shelter him from anything more.

"I hope you won't be angry at me for bringing this up," he said. "I didn't even think I was going to. I guess it's just that you're the first person—the first girl—he's ever brought home. It feels like I'm going through some sort of rite of passage. I'm not sure if I'm doing it correctly."

I surprised myself by throwing my arms around him, the wet tip of the dish towel slapping against his back.

"I'll be as gentle as I can," I said.

"I know. Thanks."

We straightened up and went back to the task at hand, but now there was an awkward silence between us.

I cleared my throat. "How did he come to live with you?" I asked. Hey, things were already weird, so why not go with it?

Gene smiled at me as he pulled the drain plug and water started to gurgle out of the sink. "I think I'll leave that for him to tell. It's his story, after all."

"Okay," I said. Honestly, I was relieved that he didn't tell me. Now I had to figure out when to ask Phil.

"Well," Gene said as he surveyed our handiwork, "let's go see how much more of that god-awful show is left to go."

The show wrapped up pretty quickly after that, and Dad and I said our good-byes. Diane really did tear up as we left; she was just *so* happy we had come over. Phil and Gene both looked a little mortified. Gene gave me a hug this time instead of a handshake. Even Phil gave me a hug, albeit a really awkward one. It was more of a reach-around back pat. I'd take it.

Dad and I rushed though the rain, which seemed to come down harder than ever.

Dad started the car and got us pointed toward home.

"That was nice," he said. "And I really like Phil's art." He'd made good on his promise to check it out.

"It was nice," I said.

"Phil was nice."

"Phil is nice," I said. "Gene was nice. Diane was nice. Dinner was nice." I looked over at him. "Are we going to list every nice thing from this evening, Dad?"

"Well," he said, "things *were* nice until we started this conversation . . ."

"What is it you really want to ask me?" I asked him. This was one of Dad's pet phrases. I was always looking for a chance to parrot his own psychobabble back at him.

"Clever," he said. "I just wanted to make sure that you had a good time."

"I did," I said. "And, no bullshit, I do like Phil, if that's where this is going." He grimaced at my swear, but didn't interrupt. "But I don't know how serious it is. *If* it's serious." I looked out at the rain-slicked streets as they slid by.

I've never much cared for the rain, but I always thought that Salem looked better when it was raining. "I want to go away to school. He wants to go away to school. For now, I just want to hang out with him and have fun and stuff." The "fun and stuff" part of that sentence—zombie hunting—was likely to give Dad a heart attack.

"Okay," he said. "I knew you'd have things figured out. I'm not sure why I asked."

"You asked because you're sweet," I said. "And because you love me. And I love you for it." I slipped my shoulder out of the seat belt, leaned over, and kissed him on the cheek. He smelled of Brut aftershave.

"I'm guessing that's the tryptophan talking," he said. "But thanks."

After that, we drove on in silence. But it was the furthest thing from uncomfortable.

CHAPTER TEN
The Meaning of the Season

Dad loosened the leash after that, especially if I was going to hang out with Phil (this after a rather intense session where he grilled me about whether or not Phil had been involved with any of my shenanigans—"shenanigans" being a euphemism for me selling drugs). When I assured him Phil didn't know about it until it was all over with, Dad gave me the thumbs-up to hang with Phil after school.

It was kind of crazy to see Phil in daylight hours, and minus deadly weapons. We ate at the Bully Burger—Chacho wasn't working that day, which was a bummer. Phil took me to see a movie at the theater where he worked. His boss, a nice lady who'd owned the place for about a million years, got almost as emotional as Diane when Phil showed up with me in tow. She didn't charge us for the movie or any of our snacks; it was pretty excellent. A definite improvement over the last time I had been there when I had been attacked by a zombie in the ladies' room. I didn't mention that to his boss.

In a weird coincidence, I started to get text messages from Brandon again. I did my best to ignore them, deleting most without reading them. The few I did read were strange. He didn't ask to see me anymore, didn't suggest we get together. He just texted me non sequitur observations. "The light this time of year is so sad" was one. "What do you call it when you miss things you never had??" was another. It was like getting texts from a not very talented Beat poet. I never responded because I didn't want to encourage him. But he was on my mind a lot those days.

A couple of weeks after Thanksgiving, my dad told me he was going to have to go out of town for some conference right before Christmas. Apparently the dean of his department got in a car accident and they needed Dad to fill in.

"But!" I protested and gestured toward our Charlie Brown Christmas tree. "Presents!"

"Truly you have discovered the meaning of the season," he said in a deadpan. "Don't worry, little drummer girl, I'll be home the day before Christmas Eve. Christmas Eve eve."

"What am I supposed to do while you're gone for a week?"

"It's five days," Dad countered. "I suppose you might drive to get groceries or something. Maybe use that time to clean your room."

That wasn't even worthy of a response.

"I suppose I might throw a raging party while you're gone," I said while rubbing my chin. I hoped I looked like I was really considering it.

"If I thought you were serious," Dad said, "I'd stuff you in my carry-on and take you with me."

"Okay," I said. "No parties." Not like I had enough friends anymore for a party. I still hadn't recovered from the seismic shift in social status that dating Brandon had caused. My old clique was still being pretty standoffish. "But can I have Phil over?"

That brought him up short.

"I don't know if I like the idea of you having a boy, any boy, here while you're home alone."

"You know you can trust me," I said, thinking that he absolutely shouldn't trust me in this instance.

"I'll think about it," he said. "I might prefer you visiting him at his place."

"Think about it," I said. "Like you said. For now, I'm going to go check my chastity belt."

"You already have one?" Dad called down the hall at me. "But I got you one for Christmas, you smart-ass."

I laughed as I disappeared into my room and started to plot out what I'd be able to do with five unsupervised days. Nothing illegal, of course, but still fun. I texted Phil and told him about Dad's leaving and asking what he might like to do, then got settled in to do some homework. My Organic Chemistry wasn't going to do itself.

But I had a hard time concentrating. It felt like an idea was forming, but it refused to emerge. Okay, homework was out, but I needed to distract myself somehow if I wanted the idea to emerge. I cranked up my laptop and opened a web browser. Filling my head with random Internet garbage was always a good way to let ideas flow.

I decided to check my e-mail. I stopped as soon as I brought up the window. What was it about my e-mail? I looked at recent messages. Nothing. Then I started to look through my important e-mail, ones I'd starred to look at later. There it was. The message from Dr. Keller.

So much for not doing anything illegal while Dad was out of town.

I picked up my phone and sent another text to Phil. I told him there was one thing I definitely wanted to do with my free time.

It was a few days later, a Friday after a pretty brutal week at school—taking courses for college credit seems like a good idea in theory, but when you do that on top of having a precarious social situation, it can get downright nasty. I'd attempted to make contact with my old friends by approaching Carol Langworthy and Brandi Edwards. They were standing by their lockers chatting as I walked up to join them. Hopelessly naïve, I realized later.

As I walked up, Brandi shifted slightly so her back was to me. I thought it was an odd coincidence, but I decided to power on.

I put on my big, most sincere—I hoped—smile. "Hey, guys!"

And they kept talking as if no one had spoken to them. Was this really how things were going to be? Were we resorting to the tactics of a disgruntled three-year-old? Okay. I'd play along. I pushed my body between the two of them and took a special kind of delight in the look of shock on Carol's face.

"Oh, hey, guys," I said in mock surprise, "I didn't see you there! How are you?"

"Look," Carol said to Brandi, "it's Courtney."

"Is it?" Brandi answered. "I didn't see her."

I let that stew a minute, but I refused to give in to my anger. For now.

"Very funny," I said. "You'd think after half a year, you'd be able to cut me some slack."

Brandi wrinkled her nose. "Why don't you ask your new best friends to cut you something? That is, if you can find them."

"What's that supposed to mean?" I asked.

Brandi's eyes went all huge and Carol snorted.

"Jesus, Hart," Carol said, "you never notice anyone but yourself, do you?"

I almost asked her again what the hell she meant, not because I didn't understand her, but because there was no way I wanted to take guff from a pasty-faced bitch like her.

Rather than doing that, I looked around. Just by looking at the kids in the hall, I knew there were people missing. I'd been seeing more missing posters in the halls, hadn't I? Mostly for kids in the ruling class.

"It's the time of year people get sick," I said. It even sounded lame to me.

"Sure," Carol said. "Tell yourself that. Just be on the lookout for zombies with popped collars."

"And now," said Brandi, "if you'll excuse us, we were talking about something *important* before you came over."

"This was pleasant," I said. "It makes me remember what I liked about you guys so much. Which was nothing."

I walked away as they yelled insults at my back.

I hooked up with Phil in the parking lot. He took one look at me and frowned.

"What's wrong?" he asked.

"Nothing," I lied.

"No," he said. "Listen, I'm crap at reading people's emotions, but there's no way I'd miss the fact that you're upset."

"Pissed off."

"Pissed off, right." He opened the passenger side door for me, and that made me feel the tiniest bit better. The fact that he actually had some manners made me feel good.

He got in behind the steering wheel. "So, what?" he asked.

"I had a weird conversation with Brandi and Carol just now," I said, "that ended with us all trading insults."

"That doesn't really sound unusual," Phil said, and I couldn't tell whether or not he was joking.

"Have you noticed more kids than usual not coming to school?" I asked. I intentionally left out the word "missing."

He sat and thought about that for a minute. "Maybe," he said. "Maybe some of the rich kids?"

"That's what they said. What did it mean?" I wondered.

"I have no idea," Phil said. "Maybe they've decided that they don't need high school educations. Maybe they're all sick."

"You don't think they're missing?" I asked.

He shrugged. "Kids of wealthy folks go missing, we'd hear about it. The news would cover it, you know? Not like if kids like us disappeared."

He had a point. So, maybe they were still around, but weren't showing up to school. But why the rich kids and no one else?

"You're still frowning," Phil said.

"If me having differing emotions is too much for you right now, just say so," I said. "I can get my dad to give me a ride home."

He blinked slowly, then said, "I'm just trying to figure out how to make you feel better, Courtney."

Well, crap. Now, on top of being angry and distracted, I'd have to deal with feeling like crap because I was such a bitch. I sighed, because a good sigh can buy you five or ten seconds of time before you have to open your mouth and start backpedaling.

"I'm sorry," I said. "You're trying to be nice to me and I'm a tool."

"I think you're hard on yourself," he said.

"Yeah, well," I said, "someone needs to be, I guess."

"Maybe you should see what it'd be like if you gave that a rest," he said. "Just a suggestion."

I had nothing to say to that.

"I know what you can do to make it up to me," he said.

"What?"

"Let me buy you something to eat before I have to go to work," he said. A smile played at the corners of his mouth. He really thought he was being cute, I knew. Lucky for him he was right.

"Anywhere I want to go?" I asked.

"Anywhere you want," he said, "bearing in mind I earn minimum wage."

"Let's go to Bully Burger," I said.

Phil visibly winced at that. "I thought that's what you might say."

"If you don't really want me to make it up to you, then . . ."

"Bully Burger," he said, "that's what I was going to suggest. Let's go!" I knew that it was mock enthusiasm, but I'd take any kind of enthusiasm that came my way just then.

Before too long, the familiar, ugly hellscape that was the Bully Burger parking lot came into view. Phil pulled off onto the store's short drive and blasted his horn. A second later, an electric motor whirred to life and the gate slowly pulled open. We drove in and parked. There were just two other cars parked out there; one was the big SUV that the security guards drove. I hoped Chacho was that security guard today.

Rarely have my prayers ever been answered, but someone was smiling down on me that day. Big as shit, Chacho sat in his usual booth reading a magazine. All of his zombie-killing gear was piled on the floor beside the booth. When Phil and I walked in, Chacho looked up, did a double take, then grinned.

"It's my favorite juvenile delinquent," he said. "Finally came to see me, huh?"

"I've been here a few times," I said as I walked across the store, ignoring the glares of the girl behind the counter—either Mary-Kate or Ashley, I couldn't tell which. "But you're never around."

"Yeah," he said, "one of my boys has been sick, so I took some time off, you know?"

I searched my memory banks: Did I know that Chacho had kids? Something sparked back there, so I guess I did know it.

"I'm sorry to hear that," I said. "I hope he's okay."

"He'll be fine," Chacho said. "He just had to stay home a bunch, and you know, my wife makes more money than me, so I got to stay home with him. I got to catch up on my Bugs Bunny cartoons. Hey, Phil."

"Hi," Phil said. "She really has been here looking for you."

Chacho got this look on his face like he was suspicious. "Why?" he asked.

"Hold that thought while I go and torture Mary-Kate," I said.

"Ashley," Chacho said as Phil and I went off to order our food.

"Whoever!"

With every step closer to the counter we got, Ashley's frown deepened. It became so severe, I thought maybe her jaw might become dislocated.

"What do you want?" she asked.

"I don't believe that's how you're supposed to greet customers," I said loudly enough for the girl I pegged as shift supervisor—a new girl I'd never seen before—to stop what she was doing and check us out.

"Welcome to Bully Burger where we're bully on serving you," Ashley hissed at us. At me, really. "Now, what do you want?"

"Give me a Rough Rider meal with an RC," I said.

As she was taking Phil's order, I leaned over the counter and tried to see into the back. I wanted to see who was working the drive-through window. No dice.

As Phil forked over the cash, I asked, "Who's on the window these days?"

"Here's your change, sir," she said. "We'll call your number when the order is ready."

"I asked—"

"I heard you," Ashley said in a low voice. "I may have to serve you if you come in here, but I don't have to talk to you."

"Your customer service skills haven't improved any since I left here," I said.

"Yeah?" she asked. She looked to see if the shift supervisor was looking our way. She wasn't. "Well, you're still a piece of trash. Now get out of my line."

"Say hi to Ashley for me," I said as I walked away.

"I'm Ashley!" she yelled. "You said hi to me when you walked up!"

I put on as sweet a smile as I was able to muster. "Did I? Gosh, I'm sorry."

"Is there a problem here, Ashley?" the shift supervisor asked from behind the fry station.

"No," Ashley said, then she stripped off her apron. "I'm going on my break." And she stalked off.

Phil and I walked off to get napkins and ketchup while we waited for our order.

"There's no way our food is going to be spit-free," he said.

"We're about to eat Bully Burger food," I said. "Spit will be the least of our concerns."

When we took our possibly saliva-laden food back to the table, Chacho was grinning up at us. "Charming as ever, huh?" he asked.

"I do what I can to brighten the lives of those around me," I said with a shrug.

"And what are you doing hanging around with this creep?" he asked Phil.

"I like her," he said, "and she's the second-best zombie killer I've ever seen."

"Why aren't you dating the first best you've ever seen?" Chacho asked.

"Because I'm not gay," Phil said, "and you're already married."

That got a big laugh from Chacho, which earned us a sour look from the shift boss behind the counter. Chacho didn't seem to care, though. He doesn't work for Bully Burger; he works for a security place that contracts with the BB, so he doesn't really care what anyone other than the store's owner thinks of him. Phil was right, Chacho was the best zombie killer around. As long as that stayed true, he had job security.

We didn't talk for a while as Phil and I dug into our food. Did you know that you can develop cravings for things that are flat-out awful and just plain bad for you? That was how I felt about Bully Burgers. I knew the secrets of how they were made, so I should have been repulsed, but man, when that greasy patty and soggy bun hit my tongue, I was in heaven. I may even have moaned a little bit.

"So you took my advice?" Chacho asked after a bit.

"What advice was that?" I asked around a mouthful of edible garbage.

"You straightened your shit out," he said. "I told you you needed to do that the last time I drove you home."

Oh, right. That. That was the night I went sort of crazy and tried to kill three zombies out in the Bully Burger parking lot by myself. It wasn't the best idea, but thankfully Chacho showed up with a shotgun to lend a hand. That had been a bad time for me—my buddy Willie'd killed himself, I'd been deeply conflicted about selling drugs back then and hadn't realized it. It might have come out as an urge to kill things or self-destruct. If only I'd had access to a mental health professional to talk about all of it with. That was a joke; there was no way I would have brought any of that up with someone like my dad.

"Sure," I said. "I laid off some pretty antisocial behavior, and hooked up with a good group of friends." I shoulder-bumped Phil, who'd barely taken a bite of his sandwich. I'd give him five more minutes before I asked him if he was going to finish it.

I heard someone behind the counter shout, "Someone wants onto the lot!" but I ignored it. Just another sucker making an unwise food choice.

"So why'd you come to see me, Courtney?" Chacho asked. He eyed me warily.

I leaned forward in my hard, plastic seat.

"Why can't you believe I just wanted to see you?" I said, and I laughed when he looked even more suspicious. But that was the simple truth. I'd wanted to see him. Chacho had cared enough to try to give me some advice when I'd been at a really low point, and I'd appreciated it. I'd have been to see him sooner if I hadn't spent the summer under house arrest.

I was about to say all of that—minus the part about being grounded because it would have raised some uncomfortable questions—when the look on Chacho's face changed. He went from suspicious but slightly amused to downright disgusted. Thank God he wasn't looking at me anymore. Nope, he was looking at whoever was standing right next to our table.

At first I thought a zombie had shuffled into the store from the parking lot. Gray, ashen skin; stringy hair; a complexion that was either runaway acne, or outright rot; a unique body odor. Then he smiled.

"Hi, Brandon," I said.

"Brandon!" Phil and Chacho said it in unison.

"Hey, Courtney," Brandon said. That smile again. I remembered how dazzling it had been; before, it had almost hypnotized me. Now it was gray and dirty and I couldn't stand to look at it.

"What are you doing here?" I asked. I scooted a little closer to Phil. But not so close that Brandon might feel it was an invitation to sit down.

"I just came in to grab a bite to eat, Courtney," he said. Reasonable. It was a completely reasonable thing to say for anyone who didn't look like a member of the walking dead.

"Are you following me?" I asked him. Chacho shot me a look, then went back to staring at Brandon, but now his interest looked, I guess you'd call it "professional."

He chuckled, a low, almost coughing sound.

"Why would I be following you?"

"I don't know," I said. "Just seems like a weird coincidence you showing up here."

"And here I thought you'd be happy to see me," Brandon said.

"If you're here to eat," Chacho said, his voice flat and menacing, "maybe you can go order your food."

Brandon looked at Chacho, and it seemed like he was seeing him for the first time.

"This your dad?" he asked.

"You've met my dad before," I said. "This isn't him."

Brandon squinted, focusing on Chacho. "Right," he said finally. "Right. This is your buddy. The rent-a-cop."

"Son," Chacho started, but I put my hand on top of his and he fell silent.

"Brandon," I said, "I'm trying to have a talk with my friends. If there's something you have to say to me, say it. Otherwise, I think we're done."

Anger and hurt flashed in his eyes. "I just thought you'd be happy to see me," he repeated.

He stood there a moment without saying anything, just

sort of swaying back and forth. Then he nodded, like he'd come to a decision, and said, "Okay. Well, it was still good to see you." Then he turned and walked toward the exit. I wished I'd stopped watching him. If I had, I'd have missed it when he stopped at the door, turned, and looked at me. He gave me a weird look I wasn't able to decipher, then opened the door and went outside. He climbed into the passenger side of a beat-up, old car and drove off.

"That was Brandon?" Phil said.

"That was the jock?" Chacho joined in.

"Yeah," I said. "That was Brandon. He's looked better."

"What the hell happened to him?" Chacho asked.

"Vitamin Z, I think," I said. I didn't think it. I knew it for a fact, but it made me feel better to throw in a hint of doubt for some reason.

Phil still hadn't eaten his burger, but suddenly I didn't want it anymore. I started to wonder if I'd keep down what I'd already eaten.

"That's too bad," Chacho said. "Messing with that shit'll kill you for sure." Then he looked a whole lot less sympathetic. "Is he hassling you? Like, since you two broke up?"

"Not really," I said, and I wasn't sure whether or not that was the truth. "He's texted me a couple of times, but he's never just shown up like that before." Except for that one time at the coffee shop that I didn't mention.

"Well," Chacho said, "if he keeps showing up where he's not wanted, you let me know. Okay?"

"Okay," I said. "Thanks."

"No worries."

"Hey, Chacho!" a kid I didn't recognize called from behind the counter. "Mr. Washington called and says he's coming over."

"Thanks, Gabe," Chacho said. He turned to us. "You know what that means," he said.

Mr. Washington owned the Bully Burger, and if he was

there, he wanted Chacho outside in his gear making customers feel safe.

Chacho climbed out of the booth, put away his magazine, and started putting on his gear.

I took that as my cue to leave. I got up out of the bench.

"I'm glad you came over to see me," Chacho said. "When the weather's good, you can come over and meet my wife and boys. I'll grill. I guarantee the food will be better than this place."

"No way is it worse," Phil said.

"Thanks, Chacho," I said. "I might take you up on that." And I meant it.

Not knowing what else to do, but feeling really self-conscious about it, I threw my arms around him and gave him a hug. After a second, he returned it.

"You're a good kid," he said to me. "And I'm glad you're working things out. You help her keep on the straight and narrow, right?" he said to Phil.

"I can only do so much," Phil said.

Chacho shot him a look, because he'd said it with no emotion, so there was no way to tell if it was a joke or not. After a second, Chacho's face broke into a smile.

"Yeah," he said, "well, just do what you can." He went back to putting on his gear.

We said our final good-byes and Chacho told us not to be such strangers.

When we got outside, it was colder than I'd expected, and dark. It felt like rain was coming soon. We rushed to the car. Phil got it started and cranked the heater. The car might have been a piece of shit, but the heater worked pretty well.

"Let's get you home," Phil said.

"Yeah," I said. "I'll text my dad and let him know I'm on the way."

"Well," Phil said as the gate slid open for us to leave the parking lot, "that was almost a nice visit."

I made an agreement sound. I was thinking about things and didn't want to lose the trail.

"One good thing about Brandon showing up," I said.

"What's that?" Phil asked.

"I figured out why all those jocks are missing school," I said.

"Why's that?" Phil asked.

"Brandon's got them all hooked on Vitamin Z."

Phil didn't have a response to that, but then, really, what response might he have had?

CHAPTER ELEVEN
Of Course He Is

A few days before Christmas, Dad woke me by knocking on my door. I must have made a "come in" noise because that's what he did.

"Come on, Courtney," he said.

I opened one eye. There was no hint of light outside the drawn window shades. "Is the sun up?" I asked. "I don't think the sun is up yet."

"Come on," he repeated.

"Where?"

"You're driving me to the airport," he said.

That made me open both eyes. I sat up and tried to assess the seriousness of his previous statement. "You want me? To drive?"

"You have your license, yes?" he asked.

"I do?" I said. It came out more of a question than I'd meant it to. "But I don't. Don't drive. Much."

"Well, you can do some today," Dad said. I felt like I should be irritated by how amused he seemed right now. "And you'll need to get from place to place while I'm gone."

Now he was going to let me use the car while he was gone?

"Is this some sort of trick?" I asked.

"Yes," Dad said, "me displaying trust in you and your judgment is definitely a trick. We talked about this."

So, yes, it *was* a trick.

"Okay," I said. "Let me get dressed."

"Okay, we need to leave in about fifteen minutes," he said as he turned away. "I brewed a pot of coffee!"

"God, you're the best," I said. I made sure to pitch my voice so there was no possible way for him to hear me.

"I *am* the best," he said.

Neither of us had any idea how great he really was.

Fifteen minutes later, we were on the road, my hands at ten and two, my head constantly swiveling to check all mirrors at once. It wasn't that I was a bad driver, it was that I was a very timid driver. Everything on the road, including me, scared the living crap out of me.

"It's best if you sort of relax," Dad said.

"I think relaxing behind the wheel of a two-ton piece of machinery will lead to death," I countered.

"Fair enough," Dad said and went back to gripping the oh-shit bar above his seat.

Back before the dead returned, the Salem airport was a pretty rinky-dink affair. It was tiny—two landing strips—and serviced no commercial flights. Since the Portland airport had been knocked out of commission by an army of shufflers, Salem's had grown to about ten times its original size. Now it was a pretty major hub. It also took forever to get through security. On top of the Homeland Security guys checking your shoes for explosives, there were also CDC people looking for the slightest signs of illness. Woe unto you if you showed up for a flight with so much as a sniffle.

There were three or four cordoned areas you had to get through to reach the airport itself. Dad had me stop just outside the first one. Several guards in reflective face masks watched us, their weapons at the ready.

"I'll walk in from here," he said. "No reason for you to drive all the way in just to have to drive out again."

"Makes sense," I said.

"I don't have to tell you what a big responsibility it is to have access to the car, right?" he asked.

"Nope," I said. "I get that this is a big deal."

"Okay," he said. He leaned over and kissed me on the cheek.

"All the info about where I'm at is on the fridge," he said, "along with some cash. It'd be nice if there was some left over when I got back."

"I make no promises," I said.

"I'll be back the day before Christmas Eve," he said. "I'll text you my arrival time. Pick me up here, okay?"

"Okay," I said.

He gave me another kiss and then he left. I pulled away from the curb and found the closest taqueria. While I sat behind the wheel and ate my breakfast burrito—being very careful not to spill anything—I contemplated what to do with my free access to a motor vehicle. Actually my first thought bummed me out. I thought, *I need to call Sherri!* This was followed by the almost immediate realization that my best friend was dead—and had been dead for about six months now. Then I thought about calling Phil, but something kept me from doing that.

Instead, I threw the car in drive, found some not-too-offensive music on the radio, and just drove by myself around the city. The sun was starting to come up by then, and the clouds had opened up enough so you were able to see it. For more than an hour, I drove around the city, singing along with the radio when I knew enough words, and feeling reasonably free. Since there were hardly any cars on the road, I wasn't even too worried about dying in a fiery crash. It was nice. At some point I started to think the city looked sort of pretty in the early morning light. I shook my head and decided I'd had enough.

I headed for home, planning to do the homework I'd been assigned over the Christmas break. I felt so good, I was sure nothing could spoil the day.

Stupid, right?

It was dark out again before I poked my head up from my homework. I'd finished nearly all of it, though, so I wouldn't have it hanging over me for the rest of the break. I checked in with Phil and he was adequately impressed with me having the car while Dad was out of town. "Good, now you can haul my butt around town for a change," may have been his exact words.

I also decided to do something I'd sort of been dreading, but that needed doing. Especially while I had the car.

I picked up my phone and dialed Buddha.

Buddha, the guy who used to supply me with Vitamin Z to sell. That Buddha.

I'd never had his number in the contacts on my phone—he wouldn't allow it—and I still remembered it. My heart pounded as I hit the send button.

I thought it was going to go to voice mail and started to feel relieved, when a connection was made.

"Courtney?" said Buddha's deep voice.

"Hi," I said.

"I have to admit, I was never expecting to see a call come in from this number again."

"Yeah," I said. "I was never expecting to call you, to be honest."

"Well," he said, "now that you have, what can I do for you?"

I paused as I heard a siren outside. For a paranoid second, I thought that the cops had tapped the call or something and the SWAT team was descending down on me. Then the sound receded in the distance.

"Courtney?" Buddha asked.

"I'm calling because," I said and paused. How much was safe to say over the phone? "Because of what you sell."

"What specifically about what I sell?" he asked. A reasonable question.

"Getting my hands on some."

"For personal use?" he asked.

"Not the sort you think," I said. It seemed important to let him know I wasn't using.

"Well," he said, "I have a new sales associate in your area, Courtney."

"And I think you might know why I'd be reluctant to go to him," I said.

There was a moment of silence, then a big sigh. "I understand. Give me a few days. Come up Tuesday or Wednesday."

"Can it be Tuesday?" I asked. Wednesday was the day Dad came back home.

"Sure," he said. "I'll call the roadblocks. Same deal as always to get past them."

"I remember," I said. "Thanks, Buddha."

"My pleasure," he said. "I have to admit, I'm glad you called. I'll see you Tuesday."

I told him to count on it, then hung up. My heart had stopped beating so fast, but now I had this weird queasy feeling in my stomach. Whatever, stomach. I'd visit Buddha, and then Dr. Keller would have the Vitamin Z sample I'd promised him so long ago. I didn't know what there was to feel bad about.

I fell asleep after that, and I might have slept through the whole night except that I'd forgotten to turn off the ringer on my phone.

I woke up disoriented. A dream full of teeth and the smell of rotten meat still wrapped around me.

"Who the hell is this?" I asked. I didn't really care who I pissed off.

"Hey, Courtney." Brandon. Of course it was Brandon.

"What time is it?" I asked. "What do you want?"

"I wondered if I could come over and visit for a little while," he said.

I had to take a moment and let that sink in. I kicked the covers off my legs and sat up.

"I don't think that's a good idea, Brandon."

"Why not?" he asked.

"Ooh, boy," I said. "Where to start." I leaned over and switched on my bedside table lamp. "We barely dated and we broke up six months ago. You should have moved on, you know?"

"This isn't about us getting back together," he said.

"Then what?"

"Things have gone downhill a little for me," he said. "The last time they were good was when we were together—"

"See," I interrupted, "this is why it's a bad idea."

"Let me finish, please," he said. "I don't want to get together again with you. I just thought that maybe if we were friends again, then it might help things."

This was getting pathetic. I tried to feel zero sympathy for him, but I was failing. I finally decided that I needed to lay down the hammer, call on my inner bitch, and end this.

"Listen, Brandon," I said.

"Let me come over," he said over me. "And if it doesn't work out, I'll leave and I'll never bother you again."

"What do you mean?" I asked.

"No more calls, no more texts, no more showing up at random places," he said.

So you did do that, you little shit! I wanted to shout at him. "I don't know," I said.

"I promise, Courtney."

I stood up and started pacing. I didn't know what to do. Take him at his word and maybe be rid of him forever? Tell him to go screw himself and have him continue hounding me? Why was I even having to deal with this? I broke up with him half a year ago and he was still obsessing about me. It made no sense.

"Courtney?"

"Fine," I said. "Come over, but I'm not making any promises."

He might have started to say something, but I killed the line.

There were a couple of things I wanted to do before Brandon got there—like call Phil and dig my pistol out of my bag, but first I had to pee. I figured I had plenty of time for all of those things before Brandon got there.

Then the doorbell rang as I walked down the hall toward the bathroom.

"This is a joke," I said to no one at all. I went into the living room and looked out the window at the front porch. Big as shit, there was Brandon. Okay, then.

I opened the door and he turned on that smile.

"Were you on the curb when you called?" I asked.

"Yeah," he said. He stepped inside, then stopped and turned. He waved at the same crappy car I'd seen him get into at the Bully Burger earlier. When he waved, the car pulled away from the house.

"That your ride?" I asked.

"Yeah," he said. He stepped into the living room, gawking at everything like it was his first time inside a shelter of any kind.

"Where's your truck?" I asked.

He laughed at that, though I didn't get the joke. "I sold that thing months ago."

So, now he was having someone haul his ass all over town. I didn't want to ask how he paid the person for the privilege. Then another question came to me that I did want to ask.

"And how are you going to leave when it's time for you to go?"

He held up his cell phone. "He'll just be a few minutes away."

"Okay," I said. "I guess." I closed the front door.

"Show me the rest of the house," he said.

"Why don't we just sit out here and talk," I said. "If that's what you want to do."

"Sure," he said. He grinned like it was a joke. "You can give me the grand tour later."

He sat down on the couch, leaving plenty of room for me to sit next to him. I flopped down on the armchair. He grimaced, but hid it quickly.

"So, how you been?" he asked.

"Crappy to good," I said.

"How are classes?"

"Classes are always good," I said.

"I'm picking up on some hostility," he said.

"I wonder why."

A really uncomfortable silence settled on us like, I don't know, a really overweight stripper's butt or something. If Brandon had been anyone else, I might have offered him something to drink, or a snack, but this really didn't feel like a refreshment type of visit.

"How's business?" I asked.

"What business?"

I gave him a please don't screw with me look.

"It's good," he said, throwing up his hands. "I started selling for Buddha a couple of weeks after you stopped."

"Selling to your friends."

"Not *just* to them," he said. "I, uh, what do you call it, expanded my customer base. I knew they had the cash, and they trust me, so . . ."

"I don't think we're going to bond over work stories," I said.

He threw up his hands. "I'm not sure why you invited me over if you're not going to give me a chance," he said.

I'd been wondering the same thing. I felt mean and unfair, but the more I looked at Brandon sitting there—with his stringy muscles where he'd once had fleshy arms; his ratty clothes; his gray smile; and, worst, his dead eyes—the more I felt sick to my stomach. Sick with guilt and anger. I'd caused this. I was the reason this kid had gone to the dark side. I was the Emperor Palpatine to his Anakin Skywalker and I didn't like it one little bit. Mostly because there was nothing I could think of to make it better.

"Maybe let's call it a night," I said.

"Maybe we can get high," Brandon said as if that were a completely logical counterargument.

"Get out," I said.

"C'mon," he said. "You know it was fun the last time we did it," he said. "That's part of the reason it scares you so much." He dug into his pocket and pulled out a tiny plastic baggie full of black powder. *Son of a bitch,* he'd actually brought Vitamin Z into my house.

"You need to go," I said, standing up and pointing toward the door. "My dad'll be home soon and you don't want to be here when he gets back."

"Your dad?" he asked. "Is this the same dad I saw you drop off at the airport this morning?"

My jaw flopped open. Of course he'd been spying on me. Knowing for sure that Dad was out of the house was probably the whole reason Brandon had decided to come over tonight.

"Or maybe your new boyfriend is headed over," he said. "Phil, really? That kid's half-queer if you ask me."

"I didn't ask you, you homophobic ass," I screamed at him. "And if you think I need someone's help to throw your skanky butt out of this house, then you are delusional!"

His jaw muscles bulged; it looked like he might be grinding his teeth. Then he relaxed. Gave up. It looked like he gave up.

"Okay," he said. "Fine. This was obviously a terrible idea and I'm . . . I'm sorry."

The deflation was crazy. He'd gone from angry, preening attack animal to a little ball of self-pity in two seconds flat. I was having a hard time keeping up with the emotional hairpin turns of this conversation. I felt like I was trapped in one of those crappy reality shows Phil and his aunt loved so much.

He stood up. "I'll call my friend." He looked around. "I'm sorry, but first can I use the bathroom?"

I was so relieved that he'd agreed to leave that I pointed down the hall.

He nodded and went that way. I turned my back on him. I felt like I couldn't look at him anymore.

Once I heard the bathroom door close, I sat back down in the seat—fell back, really. Jesus, all of it seemed unreal.

I got up quickly and went to the kitchen. I poured myself a glass of water and drank it. I wished it was a beer or something harder, but Dad doesn't keep liquor in the house. I kept replaying the scene. Brandon reaching into his pocket and pulling out a baggie of Z, a huge smile plastered on his stupid junkie face.

I stopped and set the glass down. The baggie. I couldn't believe I was thinking this, but now that it'd popped into my noggin, the thought refused to just go away. If I got

Brandon to sell me that baggie, there'd be no need for me to go up and see Buddha. I asked myself if that was completely evil. Was there a chance Brandon might interpret it as renewed interest? Shit, I might just need to chance it. I'd just wait for him to come out of the bathroom and then I'd ask him to sell it to me.

It occurred to me he'd been in the bathroom for a while already. Did taking Vitamin Z affect your ability to go to the toilet? I didn't know, and I wasn't keen to learn the answer, but I decided it was time to get this little show on the road.

I walked down the hall and knocked on the bathroom door. No answer. I knocked again.

"Brandon," I asked. "Is everything okay?"

I heard a soft thud, like something falling onto carpet. It sounded like it came from my dad's bedroom. I knocked on the bathroom door again.

"Brandon," I yelled. When I got no answer, I pushed the door open. Of course he wasn't in there.

I took a deep breath and stepped down the hall to my dad's room.

"I swear to God," I said, "if you have your pants off, I'm going to kick your balls into your throat!"

I threw open the door.

Brandon lay facedown on the floor, his face toward me so I got a good view of his glassy eyes and the black foam coming out of his mouth. The empty baggie, a lighter, and a spoon sat on top of the bed. A syringe stuck out of his arm. A scene from a bad after school special was playing out in my dad's bedroom.

I ran to him and knelt down. I tried to remember everything I'd learned about overdosing. How did I check if he was breathing? Where was his pulse? Mostly, why the hell did they spend so much time teaching us how to avoid becoming zombies and so little on more important topics?

I got him turned over and more of that black foam dribbled out of his mouth. I gagged a little, then rested my head on his chest. I couldn't hear a heartbeat. His chest wasn't rising and falling.

I called his name, shouted it right in his face. I shook him with all my pathetic strength. Nothing. Holy shit, Brandon Ikaros was dead in my house.

I scooted away and dug my phone out of my pocket. I speed-dialed Phil.

"Hi, Courtney," he said. Then, "Why are you crying?"

"What?" I said. Oh, God, I really was crying. When had that started?

"Phil, I need you to come to my house," I said as calmly as I could. Which wasn't very.

"What happened?" he asked. "Is it your dad?"

"Brandon," I said. "He's dead. Here at my house."

I think most anyone else would have had a long set of questions about how Brandon came to be there, dead or alive. Phil just said, "I'll be there in fifteen minutes." Relief welled up in me. I started crying again. "Do you need me to stay on the line?" he asked.

"No," I was finally able to say. "Just get here." And the line went dead.

So I just sat there for a while and cried it out. I kept thinking it was about to stop, then I'd look at Brandon's corpse again, and it would start up all over again. It just seemed so stupid, all of the events that had brought us to this exact moment. If he'd never smoked Vitamin Z. If he'd never been interested in me. If he'd never come into the Bully Burger that first time. If neither of us had ever been born. If. If. If.

And the tears stopped. Playing the "if" game was stupid. I'd have plenty of time to regret everything after I'd dealt with the body in my house. I got up and I meant to get a sheet or something to cover Brandon. I stopped cold when I saw his hand twitch. My heart started to race. Maybe it was just some weird dead body thing, but maybe it meant that I was crap at determining whether or not someone was dead.

I ran over and knelt down next to him. "Brandon," I said. "Brandon, please be alive. If you're alive, we can be best buds and braid each others' hair." I shook him, but not as hard as before.

A moan escaped his lips, along with more of that awful black foam. I started to laugh. He was still alive. In my relief, I nearly hugged him.

Then he opened his eyes, and I knew I was wrong. I thought his eyes had been dull before; now they were lifeless. Somehow they still locked on me. There was a beat where we stared at one another, then he opened his mouth and hissed at me, black spittle spraying in my face.

I was up and running to my room, my gun. I heard him doing the same, and I blocked out the sound. All that mattered was finding the pistol. My bag lay open on the desk. I ripped it open and the gun was right there, thank God. I grabbed the holster, yanked the pistol free, and turned toward the door.

Brandon stood in the doorway. He looked at me hungrily. There was something else in that look, too, but I couldn't tell what. Didn't matter. I raised the pistol in a two-handed grip.

The moment he saw it, Brandon whirled around and ran. About two seconds later I heard breaking glass. My dad's bedroom window.

I glanced into the room as I ran down the hall; a gaping hole stood in the center of the glass. I pounded down the hall and out the front door. Careful not to get too close to the corners of the house where Brandon might try to ambush me, I raced around to the backyard. The grass was cold and wet on my bare feet.

I spotted him vaulting over the chain-link fence—four feet tall and he took it like an Olympic athlete. I stopped, got the pistol in a two-hand stance again, and aimed.

I squeezed off a shot and Brandon stumbled, but kept running. Before I was able to draw a bead on him again, he turned a corner out of sight. Somewhere nearby a dog started to bark, probably startled by the shot. Other dogs took up the chorus.

"Courtney?"

Phil stood back by the front of the house. Even in the light of the streetlights, I knew he was afraid.

"What the hell, Courtney?" he said.

"Brandon's a zombie," I said.

And to his credit, Phil didn't freak out, and he didn't start asking a million questions. Hell, he didn't even curse. He just nodded, then said, "Of course he is."

CHAPTER TWELVE

A Sexless Friendbot

I gave Phil the bullet-points version of what had happened. When I was all done, we stood in Dad's bedroom, and Phil's only response was to ask, "Do you have any plywood?"

Turned out we did have some in the garage. Phil used it to cover the gaping hole in the window.

"Tomorrow we'll call Cody," he said as he got it in place. "His dad works for Cherry City Glass. He'll give us a deal on replacing this."

"Okay," I said. For some reason, I felt weird about all of this. I thought that Phil needed to be having a bigger reaction to Brandon coming over, but I also didn't want to push it. Basically, I was worried that it meant he didn't care enough to be jealous, which was stupid because I knew that jealousy was a toxic emotion (thanks, Dad!). Still, I felt distant from him.

"We'll keep this door closed," he said. "That way the rest of the house won't get too cold, okay? You said you thought you shot him. Should we go outside and see if we can find a blood trail?"

That seemed like a good idea, especially the "we" part, but when we opened the door to go outside, it was raining again. Thanks a lot, Oregon. Any blood would have been washed away. Phil said not to worry about it.

"I'll be back in just a sec, okay?" he said. Before I could say anything, he ran out to his car and popped the trunk. He rummaged around, got something out, and closed the trunk again.

I almost asked him what the hell he was doing, but then he brandished his baseball bat—the one with the nails pounded through it.

"What's that for?" I asked when he came running back in.

"In case he comes back," Phil said.

My blank stare must have prompted him to elaborate.

"I'm going to stay the night," he said.

"To help protect me," I said.

"Safety in numbers."

I wondered briefly if this was some sort of attempt to get into my pants, but decided no, he wanted to stay the night out of concern for my safety. Sweet. Sort of annoying, but sweet.

He called his aunt and uncle and I got to hear one side of what must have been a very peculiar conversation. For me, the most interesting part was that he didn't ask if it'd be okay for him to stay over; he just told them. He said I'd had some trouble with an ex-boyfriend and he'd feel better about things if he stayed there with me. He stressed several times that he didn't think it was necessary to call the police. That was a relief.

I left the room before he was done and went to clean up the black shit Brandon had spewed on my dad's floor. Luckily, the room was covered in this thick, 1970s-era shag carpeting that was sort of brown, but not really any color at all. Like camouflage. I used to think that a unicorn might vomit a rainbow in Dad's room and you'd never be able to tell. Blotting it with damp paper towels seemed to do the trick. After that, I carefully picked up shards of glass. Phil came in while I was doing that and helped.

"Thanks," I said when we were finished.

"You're welcome," he said. "Sorry it took so long on the phone. I'd have helped you clean up sooner."

"I mean, thanks for coming over," I said. "Thanks for not being freaked out. Thanks for everything."

"Okay," he said. "I'm happy to do it. You know that, right?"

"I'm starting to get it," I said. He smiled—just for a second, but I saw it.

"I just thought of something," I said as I put more glass in the wastebasket.

"What's that?" Phil asked.

"Brandon ran away from me."

"Sure," Phil said.

"Have you ever known a zombie to run away once it catches sight of a living person?" I took Phil's silence as an answer in the negative. "And yet, when he saw the gun, he ran. Like he was concerned for his life."

"That is weird," Phil said, "but sort of consistent with all of the other zombie weirdness we've been experiencing lately."

I couldn't argue with that. I picked the last of the visible glass up out of the carpet. I'd vacuum in the morning.

"Well," I said, "I'm pretty wired. Don't think I could sleep right now. What should we do?"

"Want to watch a movie?"

No, Phil, that wasn't really what I wanted to do. "Sure," I said.

I asked him what he wanted to watch and he named a couple of things I wasn't even sure were movies. Like what is *Tokyo Gore Police* or *Karate-Robo Zaborgar*? I told him I'd pick something. Turns out he'd never seen *Animal House,* so I put that in the DVD player. That one was a big hit in our house. It was filmed down the road in Eugene at the University of Oregon, which was where my dad went to college.

Watching the movie with him was really interesting. He sat forward and took it all in, very intense. At the parts where most people might laugh, he just sort of made grunting noises. The physical stuff made him laugh way more often than any of the word play or situational stuff. He also got caught up on factual stuff, or lapses in continuity or logic.

When it was done, I asked him what he thought.

"I get why people like it," he said. "Comedies are hard for me to track. I don't get a lot of the jokes. I guess that's why I like action movies." He shrugged.

"What now?" he asked.

"Let's just sit here, okay?" I said. I pushed him back a little so he'd actually relax, or at least recline, on the couch. Then I had him wrap his arm around my shoulders so I could cuddle with him. His body was stiff and unyielding for a while, then he eased up.

"Tell me if this isn't all right," I said.

"No," he said. "It's fine."

Good, I thought.

After we got settled, I said, "Guess who e-mailed me?"

"No idea," he said and I knew he was done with that game.

"Dr. Keller," I said, keeping any trace of pout out of my voice.

He thought for a moment. "The TV professor guy!"

"That's right, Einstein, the TV professor guy." I went on to recap what the e-mails said, ending with the good doctor's suggestion that I might get my hands on a sample of Vitamin Z.

"That seems like an odd request," Phil said.

"I think he was just throwing it out there," I said. "Not

that he was assuming I was some sort of drug kingpin. Anyway, I was wondering if it was okay to ask you a favor."

"You can ask," he said.

"Cute," I said and pinched his side. He slapped me away. "Any chance you'll come up with me to visit Buddha?" I asked. "I already called him—I'm going up Tuesday."

"And if I don't go with you, you'll go up alone?"

"Yes," I said. "But don't make that the reason you come. If you're coming."

He scratched his chin. "I think I can make room in my schedule on Tuesday," he said.

"Only if it's not too much bother," I said. "I know how many demands there are on your time." I looked up at him and he craned his neck to look back. "I do appreciate it. Thanks."

We talked for a while. I asked him to tell me about the cartooning school he wanted to go to. Turns out it was in New Jersey, not far from NYC. We'd be able to see each other while I was going to Columbia.

While we talked, I snuggled in closer. I started, you know, rubbing his chest with my free hand. He shifted and cleared his throat, but he didn't say anything. We kept talking about future plans and I decided to go for it—I let my hand travel south to see what it might find.

Phil jumped like I'd electrocuted him. He pushed me away.

"What are you doing, Courtney?"

I sat up and scooted farther away from him.

"Isn't it obvious?" I asked. "I'm trying to seduce you."

"Is that what that was?" he asked. "Because I thought maybe you were checking me for a hernia."

"Jesus Christ, Phil." How repulsive did he find me that even the direct approach didn't work on him?

"Jesus Christ what?" he asked.

I put my head in my hands. I couldn't believe this was happening. I was having to explain to Phil why I was upset that he found me to be some sort of monster or, worse, he considered me a sexless friendbot.

"Most guys would like that," I said.

"Is that why you like me?" he asked. "Because I'm like most other guys."

Him making a valid point made me angry.

I stood up and slumped into the armchair. "We've been hanging out all summer, all school year," I said, "and you haven't expressed any interest in me." I paused and took a deep breath. Then I closed my eyes and said, "You know . . . sexually."

"And that's a problem?" he asked.

"Right now it feels like it," I said.

He didn't say anything for a bit, but his jaw was working like he had a piece of gum in his mouth.

"First," he said, "that's not true. I think it's more accurate to say that I haven't tried to get physical with you, right?"

"Well, why haven't you?" I asked.

"Courtney," he said. He said it slow and careful, like he was talking to a kid. Or like he was angry that he had to be saying any of this at all. "Courtney, I like you, but there's no way I want to rush into something physical. I didn't know if you were ready, hell, I don't know if I'm ready."

"I think me grabbing your junk is a clear sign that I'm ready," I said. I was trying to make a joke to lighten the mood. The look on his face told me I'd failed.

"You realize that the only reason I'm here tonight," he said, "is because you invited over your ex, he OD'd and became a zombie, and now we need to keep watch for him, right? Forgive me if I find that to be something of a boner-killer."

"Oh, Jesus," I said. "I've really screwed this up."

"Courtney, listen," Phil said and he sat forward. "I have a lot of anxieties. About everything. About sex. I've never been with anyone, I've never kissed anyone, okay?"

"Me, neither," I said.

He stopped and I know he kept himself from asking, "Really?" Which was good. That question would have derailed the progress we'd been making in the last couple of minutes.

"Okay," he said. "So you get where I'm coming from. I'm sorry if you've mistaken my, um, hesitancy as disinterest. It's not that. I have trouble reading people and I honestly couldn't tell if you liked me, too."

"Me probing your crotch wasn't a good indicator of interest," I said. This time he did laugh.

"It was subtle," he said, "but I think I got it. Now you know that I have anxieties, and now I know you have them, too. That will make things easier in the future."

Or much more awkward. But I didn't say it out loud.

"But nothing's going to happen tonight," he said. "Not under the circumstances. I'm sorry if that upsets you."

"Not upset," I said, and I stood up. "Maybe a little sad, but I can't knock you for telling me what you're thinking. Maybe I should have tried it myself a little."

He stood up, too. There we were, facing each other, close in that little space between the chair and the couch. I was willing to stand there a long time. He gave me a half smile.

"How about we go to sleep?" he asked. "I can take the couch."

And there were my hopes, raised up and dashed in the space of two sentences.

"Let me get you some blankets and stuff," I said.

As I turned to go, he reached out and stopped me with a hand on my shoulder. He put his other hand on my chin and lifted my startled face up to meet his own. He kissed me. His lips were soft. I remember that. Then I realized I didn't really know what to do with my own lips. I was never one of those girls who practiced kissing with a teddy bear or a mirror. Mostly I resisted the urge to grab his head and eat his face in a good way. So, I just kind of probed his lips with my own. He smelled good, like mint gum, and faintly of some aftershave.

When I felt him breaking the kiss, when I knew it was almost over, I darted my tongue out of my mouth, just the tip, and tasted him. I always expected French kissing to be weird. Like, you're licking another person; won't they taste just like you? No, I learned the moment my tongue touched his receding lips, no, they don't taste just like you. They taste electric, they taste like magic, they taste like them, they taste like not-you.

I can't remember whether or not I whimpered when he broke the kiss.

He smiled at me. "There, we've both had our first kiss. It'll take some of the pressure off, right?"

Take the pressure off? The sensations I was feeling south of my waistband told me that Phil had no idea what the hell he was talking about, but I didn't want to spoil the moment.

"It was nice," I said.

"Yeah," he said. "It was."

"Let me go get those blankets," I said.

Jesus, I was going to need to take a cold shower before I went to bed. If the tent in Phil's pants was any indication, so would he. Well, I guess I was happy I wasn't the only one going to bed frustrated.

The next day, Phil called Cody. Then Cody showed up with his dad in a big panel van. His dad was squat and barrel-chested. He had Popeye forearms, complete with an anchor tattoo, which I barely made out through the thick, black hair that covered him. There was something chimp-like about Cody's dad, and I didn't think that as an insult, but I also kept it to myself.

He and Cody pulled the plywood down and assessed the situation.

"Oh, yeah," he said. "I got some scraps in the van'll fix that up. Give me half an hour and it'll be better than new."

I hoped it didn't look so much better that Dad might notice when he got home, but I wasn't in a position to argue.

"How much will it cost, sir?" I asked.

He looked at me like I was some sort of talking dog.

"Sir?" he asked, then barked out a laugh. "You could learn something from her about manners." This was directed at Cody, who just rolled his eyes. "Naw, for a friend of this one, no charge. Like I said, I'll use scraps."

"Thank you, sir," I said. "I appreciate that."

It took him a lot less than half an hour. I was impressed by how efficient he was. Competency is always impressive.

"You never told me your dad was so cool," I said to Cody. We sat in the kitchen while his dad did his thing in the bedroom. Everyone had an off-brand soda in front of them.

"Yeah," said Cody, "you caught him in a good mood. Calling him 'sir' was a good move. Smart."

"I wasn't gaming him," I said. "I really was being polite."

"Aren't they different names for the same thing?" he asked. Phil laughed and Cody smiled at his own little joke. Very little.

His dad called to us from the room and we all went to see his handiwork. I made a big deal of how great it all was. A bigger deal than I normally would have since he was doing the job for free. I figured I'd pay him with appreciation.

He cleaned up and when he left, Cody asked him if he might stay with us.

"Sure," his dad said. "Just be home for dinner."

Cody agreed to this and we all went back to sit at the table.

"Tell me again what happened," he said.

I rolled my eyes and told the story for what felt like the umpteenth time.

"You're sure he overdosed?" Cody asked when I was done. "You're sure he turned into a zombie."

"Yes to both," I said.

"Wild!" he said. "This is just so crazy."

"But not in a good, Gnarls Barkley sort of way," Phil said.

"So, what are you gonna do about it?" Cody asked.

"Do about it?"

"Your ex-squeeze is running around out there," he said, "one of the undead. What are you gonna do about it?"

I grabbed their empty cans and carried them over to the sink to rinse them out.

"I don't know if there's anything *to* do," I said over the running water. "He's another zombie now. If we come across him on one of our hunts, I'll deal with him." I turned off the water. "But I wouldn't even know how to go about hunting for an individual zombie. It's not like we have a tracer collar on him."

"We need to tell his dad, don't we?" Phil asked.

That stopped me short. I hadn't thought about his dad. I wondered what their relationship had been like there at the end, after Brandon's becoming a junkie was impossible to ignore. I'd never even met his dad. All I'd ever known about him was that he had a somewhat lackadaisical take on parental responsibility.

"Courtney?"

"I'm trying to think of a way to get out of that," I said.

I leaned against the kitchen counter and crossed my arms. Both the boys looked at me expectantly. I felt resentment welling up inside me. "Part of me thinks I should be the one to do it. Part of me wonders why the hell it's my responsibility."

Phil shrugged. "He died here. After coming to visit you."

Right, *that*.

"Want me to do it?" Phil asked.

Oh, God, I didn't even want to imagine how that might go.

"No," I said. "I'll do it."

"Well," Phil said, "if you don't, I won't hold it against you."

"Yeah, it's not like you owe him anything," Cody said. "I mean, isn't he the guy who set us up as a zombie buffet last year?"

We all fell silent. The mood hadn't been exactly festive, but now it was positively goddamn morose.

"I hate to leave like this," Phil said, "but I need to make an appearance at home." He stood up and Cody did the same.

"And I ought to leave because you probably don't want me to hang out here," Cody said.

"Want to come over to my place?" Phil asked.

"No," I said. "I have something I need to do."

We made tentative plans to get together later. I wanted so bad to give Phil another kiss as he left, but Cody was there like a five-and-a-half-foot-tall cockblock. Phil told me to call if I needed to after talking to Mr. Ikaros. I promised to do that.

And then I set about putting off the phone call. I'd never wanted less to make a particular call ever. The only instance that came close was when I got caught shoplifting when I was fourteen and the store manager made me call

Dad while we sat in this crappy little office. That was a pleasant chat compared to what this talk was going to be like.

Luckily, I'm pretty good at procrastinating. First, I had to look up Mr. Ikaros's number. While I was doing that, there was a whole World Wide Web to look at. The Army announced that January 2 was the day they'd start to reclaim NYC. This prompted me to update my Facebook status, which I knew from recent experience would be ignored unless Phil happened to log on to the site in the next day or two.

Then I found some cleaning around the house that needed to be done. I was about to put on rubber gloves and attack the hallway bathroom when the ludicrousness of the situation hit me. In the great scheme of things, calling Brandon's dad was more important than scrubbing a toilet that didn't really need it.

I sat at the kitchen table and stared at my phone for a long time before picking it up and punching in the numbers I'd found online.

"Marcus and Welles Law Offices," a woman answered on the first ring. "How may I direct your call?"

"May I speak to . . ." I didn't know his first name. "Mr. Ikaros?"

A pause, then, "Mr. Ikaros is busy at the moment, may I—"

"It's about his son," I said.

Her tone was different when she answered. "Just a moment," she said and then I was on hold.

It wasn't long before a gruff man's voice came on the line.

"If this is someone that my son owes money," he said and I held the phone away from my ear because he was yelling so loud, "you need to know that I am no longer legally responsible for his debts!"

"Mr. Ikaros?" I said.

"Who is this?" he asked.

"My name is Courtney," I said. "I used to be a friend of Brandon's."

"And this is about my son?" he asked. I found I wasn't able to speak all of a sudden. "Well?" he prompted.

"Sir," I said, and my throat caught. I bit my lower lip until it passed. "Brandon is dead, sir."

Silence on the other end.

"He died of a drug overdose last night."

"And how do you know this, Courtney?" he asked.

"I . . . I . . ."

"You were with him when he died. Is that it?" His voice was gentle now. Maybe not gentle, maybe just tired.

"Do you know what hospital he's in, Courtney?" Mr. Ikaros asked.

"He's not," I said. "He died of a Vitamin Z overdose and, uh, and he . . ." My vision suddenly refracted like I was looking through a kaleidoscope. I blinked away tears.

"I see," he said. "Thank you for calling me, Courtney, but you have to understand that my son hasn't been in my life for several months."

I bit my lip again, worried that I'd draw blood.

"Brandon has been dead to me for a while, Courtney," Mr. Ikaros went on. "I've just been waiting for the call to confirm it. Thank you for calling."

And then the line went as dead as Mr. Ikaros's son.

I put the phone down on the table, lay my head beside it, and cried. I cried like it was a wild beast that needed to get out of me. At some point, I don't remember when, I ended up on the floor. It was him saying, "Thank you for calling," that did it. I kept hearing that line again and again, delivered like Mr. Ikaros was dead himself, but still remembered the finer points of etiquette.

I stopped again and dragged myself into the shower,

where I cried some more. Eventually, I stopped for good and took myself to the movies. I picked the dumbest-looking comedy that was available, anything to take my mind off what I'd just done. I craved something funny, needed it.

I ended up crying through it anyway.

CHAPTER THIRTEEN
Nemesis

Saturday I hung out with Phil and Cody at Phil's house. His aunt was in a real tizzy since Phil had *two* friends over. She kept plying us with food and sodas. And not the off-brand crap, either, but actual brands that you might see in a national television ad campaign. It was great.

We all commiserated about the horribleness that was my phone call with Mr. Ikaros. I even told them about my crying jag at the movies.

"How many people were in there with you?" Cody asked.

"Three," I said. "They left after a while. Which was nice, I guess. They might have gotten the manager to kick me out."

"Rough," Cody said.

"Sorry I wasn't there," Phil said.

"It's okay," I said. "I'm sort of glad you didn't see me. It was a pretty ugly cry."

Phil spent the rest of the afternoon before he had to go to work drawing. Cody and I sat on the floor reading comics and arguing points of nerd minutia like who would win in a fight between Superman and Thor, and who was the lamest superhero of all time. (The answer is Aquaman, by the way.)

Later, Phil drove us home. Cody brought up going on a zombie hunt later, but I still wasn't feeling up to it.

"How about tomorrow?" he asked.

"Tomorrow might work," I said. I knew I needed to get my mind off the Brandon thing, and killing shufflers was guaranteed to do it.

"Want to invite Warren along?" Phil asked.

Cody groaned. He rubbed the spot behind his ear where the doctors had just removed his stitches.

"We need to give him another chance," Phil said.

"Do we?" Cody asked. "Do we really?"

"I think so," I said. More groans from Cody. "Listen, if he takes a swing at you with his sword again, I'll help you kick his ass, okay?"

"Now I sort of hope it happens again," he said.

"Okay," Phil said. "You want to invite him along?" he asked me.

"Uh, sure," I said. I wasn't sure why I'd been designated the official contactor of Warren, but there it was. I dug out my phone and wrote him a quick text. I got back a reply almost instantly: YES.

"He's in," I said.

We dropped off Cody, then Phil took me home. He idled out front for a second.

"Want me to come over after I'm done at the cinema?" he asked.

"That's okay," I said. "I think I'll just eat some dinner and go to bed. I'm still feeling pretty wrung out."

"Okay," Phil said. "Let me know if you change your mind."

"I will," I said, "but I'll be fine."

I climbed out. Before I shut the door, I leaned into the car and kissed Phil's startled face. It felt just as good as the first one.

"Have a good night," I said.

"I think that pretty much guaranteed it'll be good," he said. He wore an honest-to-God smile as he put the car in gear and drove away.

I know I'd told Phil I'd be okay, but I spent the whole night feeling like someone was watching me. I know we've all had that feeling before, but this time it was so strong I kept getting up to open the front door and look out at the street, half-expecting someone to be standing out there watching the house. Even after I closed every drape and curtain in the house, I still felt it. I started to become certain that I'd turn a corner, or open a door *inside,* and find someone waiting for me there. It was freaky, and I almost called Phil several times. But I told myself he'd laugh at me. I think I knew, deep down, that this was untrue, but it kept me from calling him.

That night, I slept with my pistol right on my bedside table.

I woke up in the middle of the night because I heard furniture dragging out in the kitchen. Like, a chair scraping across linoleum. Were floors still made of linoleum? I shook my head to try to clear it. I grabbed my pistol and slowly opened the door to the hall. My vision dimmed until I was nearly blind, but the kitchen light was on. I distinctly remembered turning it off when I went to bed.

As silently as I was able, I crept down the hall, the pistol in two hands. I imagined I looked like the heroine in a TV cop show. A show I'm sure would have been canceled before the first season was done.

I got to the corner of the hall that opened up into the kitchen and paused. I quickly put my head around the corner, but didn't see anything. Whoever was in there must have been behind the opened fridge door. I pulled my head back and took several deep breaths—preparing myself.

Before I decided just to head back to the room to call the cops, I jumped into the kitchen and raised the pistol. I aimed it right at the fridge door.

"Come out of there, asshole!" I screamed.

Sherri screamed in return and popped up from behind the door. In one hand she held a jar of pickles. With her free hand, she covered her heart like she was the world's youngest heart attack victim.

"Jesus, Courtney!" she yelled at me. "I'm just here getting a snack. Put the gun away, Hopalong."

"Hey, Sherri," I said, like it was the most natural thing in the world for her to be there in the middle of the night. Considering she was dead and all. I flopped into one of the kitchen chairs and set the gun on the table in front of me. My heart still raced, but it was starting to settle down.

"You scared the crap out of me," I said. "I thought you were a burglar."

"Sorry," she said around a mouthful of something. "I've just been starving."

"Not feeding you where you are?" I asked.

She shrugged. "You know," she said, "the diet of worms and all."

And there it was again, that feeling of being watched. I looked across the living room at the front door. I knew—knew!—that if I got up and opened it, I'd find someone or something there waiting for me.

"Goddammit, Sherri," I said.

"Yeah," she said, "I brought a friend. But you invited him along."

"What's that supposed to mean?" I asked. I couldn't see too well again. I knew the lights were still up, but I had a hard time keeping my eyes open, and I wasn't really able to maneuver my head to look at Sherri when she spoke.

"Did you know," Sherri said somewhere near the fridge, "that the definition of *nemesis* is, 'the inescapable agent of one's own downfall'?" Her eating sounds were really getting to me. They seemed too loud, too close. I couldn't see her no matter how I tried.

"What is this, Sherri?" I asked. "You usually try to give me advice. What's going on this time?" My eyes wouldn't open properly, and I couldn't move my head. I felt like I was a quadriplegic because of how little control I had over my body.

"In tragedies, the hero almost always creates the circumstances of their own downfall," Sherri went on lecturing.

"Is this about Brandon?" I asked.

At the mention of his name, the scene changed. I no longer sat in the kitchen chair; now I sat under a fat, full moon on a huge throne of some sort. Or a stump or tree root that was shaped like a throne. I was tied to it somehow. A stiff breeze threw my hair into my face, and leaves fell through the air in a complicated dance.

Sherri stood in front of me, looking like the last time I'd seen her—freshly zombified, minus the gaping head wound.

"Let me go, Sherri," I said. "You delivered your message. I've been properly Scrooged. Now, let me go!"

No matter how I fought, I wasn't able to break whatever bonds held me. The rough seat beneath me dug into my skin every time I shifted. I imagined all of these tiny abrasions all over my backside. The smell of blood traveled far on the night air.

And then everything stopped. The leaves froze in midair, the swaying branches stopped, and the world was filled with a huge silence.

"He's here," Sherri said in her graveyard voice. "I know he's been waiting a long time for this. He won't be disappointed."

A hand snaked around my body from behind. A withered, desiccated hand. It settled on my breast and gave it a cruel squeeze.

"I mean," Sherri said, "you make such a delicious bride."

Thin light crept in around the edges of my blinds when my eyes fluttered open. I brought my hand up to wipe my eyes and hit myself in the nose with my pistol. Great, I'd been gripping a deadly weapon in my sleep; no way that might have gone badly.

I sat up and put the gun back in its holster, then put it in the drawer of my bedside table. When it was safely away where I couldn't hurt myself with it, I lay back in bed.

Those freaking dreams. If there was an afterlife, I'd have to find Sherri and apologize for giving her the starring role in them. She deserved better.

The clock said it wasn't even seven in the morning yet. I checked my internal freak-out-o-meter, and it told me there was no chance I was going back to sleep anytime soon. Great.

Well, that was what crappy basic cable was made for, right?

A full day of sleep-deprived awful TV left me in the mood to really kill something.

I'd been dozing on the couch when my cell phone started to buzz on my chest. I opened one eye and looked at the screen.

"Phil," I said after I hit the accept button. "Please tell me you're here."

"We are here," he said. "Are you ready to go?"

"I have been dressed and ready for hours," I said.

I killed the call and went outside. Warren's ninja-mobile waited on the corner. Seldom have I been so relieved to see a carload of teenage boys.

We spent a couple of hours driving around looking for any signs of zombies and came up empty. We even went back to a couple of spots where we'd seen some Zs in the past, but none had returned.

"If we don't find any walkers soon, let's call it a night," Warren said. "Walkers" was apparently what they called shufflers where he'd come from. It was definitely not catching on with us, but he kept using it. I felt like Regina in *Mean Girls*. "Gretchen, stop trying to make 'fetch' happen!"

"My folks had a Christmas party this weekend," he went on.

"And you didn't invite us?" Cody asked. He did a good job of pretending to be hurt.

"And I swiped some beer from there," Warren continued as if no one had spoken. "Let's go somewhere and chill out."

This plan had a lot of appeal for me, personally. It had been a long time since I'd done anything like that—just sitting around with friends, talking smack, and drinking. It used to be how I spent every weekend. You know, back when my friends were still alive.

"Let's do it," I said.

"Yeah, maybe," Cody said.

Phil didn't say anything. That surprised me because even though he misses some social cues, he usually isn't rude.

"Hey, Rain Man," I said and nudged him.

"What's that?" he said and sort of pointed with his chin out into the darkness.

Warren slowed the car to a crawl, and we all stared out the window. We were on a residential street. We'd been driving around so long, I honestly had no idea where we were. This part of town was a lot more run down than we were used to. A lot of yards didn't even have fences, just makeshift barriers around the front doors.

Huddled underneath the shadow of a tree, we saw two or three figures. As the car went past, the figures stepped farther into the darkness.

"Suspicious," said Warren.

"Definitely," said Phil.

"Are we thinking zombies?" Cody asked.

"I hope to God you aren't serious," I said.

"What?" Cody asked. "What did I say?"

Warren turned the corner, then the next, and parked the car.

"Let's grab our gear out of the trunk and investigate," Warren said.

Investigate, like we were some sort of league of junior detectives. Like we were the Scooby gang. I claimed dibs on Velma. But we did like he said.

When we all had our weapons in hand, Phil asked Warren, "What are you thinking?"

"We head up this street, 'cause it's farther away from the walkers," Warren said. "Less chance of being seen. Then we just try to sneak up on them. Which means we need to be *quiet.*"

"Why are you looking at me when you say that?" Cody asked.

"No reason."

In just the couple of minutes it had taken us to hear the plan, I'd already started going numb from the cold. I didn't know how ninja-like I could be with arms and legs that were numb. The zombies would probably see our breath as we approached. I didn't mention any of this out loud because I was trying to be positive.

Warren took point and we headed off up the street. As we got to the intersection, he had us stop for him to check where we'd seen the zombies. They were still there. Warren waved us on, and as fast and quiet as possible, we ran across the street and grabbed a dark shadow of our own to squat in.

We regrouped behind an SUV parked in a driveway. Phil poked his head up and checked out the situation.

"I don't think they heard us," he said. "I think they're still there."

So we made our slow way from driveway to driveway, hiding behind cars and old washing machines and whatever other junk we found in the yards. Finally we were in front of the same house as them. I really just wanted a chance to kill something because the exercise might warm me up.

"On three," Warren said. He held up three fingers. When he hit "one," we all jumped out from behind the old pickup where we'd been hiding and rushed the zombies under the tree. I gave my war whoop as I ran, and raised my wrecking tool.

"What the hell is that?" yelled a very human voice. The one who hadn't spoken started backpedaling away from us and then tripped and fell on his ass.

We pulled up short, and the four of us stood face-to-face with two dudes who were definitely not zombies. I didn't think so, anyway. Both of them looked like they were well on their way to being undead even if they still had pulses. Sunken eyes; broken-out skin; dirty, stringy hair; clothes that hadn't seen soap in a while? Check, check, check, and check. It was like looking at Brandon in the last days when he was alive. So, yeah, they were junkies.

"What are you guys doing?" asked the one on the ground. He was scratching his cheek. Like, really digging at it. I thought he was going to draw blood any second.

"Sorry, guys," I said. "We thought you were someone else." Phil and Cody shot me a look and I shrugged. Sorry that I wasn't the master of improvisation.

"Courtney?" The guy who was still standing squinted at me. "Courtney, right?"

"Yes . . ." I said, dubious. How'd this guy know my name?

"You're that chick that Brandon Ikaros was doing last year, aren't you?" he asked. Like that was a completely reasonable and not-at-all rude thing to say to someone.

Also, it garnered more looks from the boys. Even Phil looked to see how I'd react.

The dude who'd fallen down, call him Scratchy, pushed himself up and dusted off his butt. Then he went right back to scratching at his cheek.

"She knows Brandon?" he asked.

"Yeah," the first one said. "Remember her from the party at the cabin?"

Scratchy stared at me hard.

I tried desperately to make this make sense. These guys had been jocks. They'd been friends of Brandon's. He'd gone and got them hooked on Vitamin Z, and now that they were jonesing, he wasn't around to sell to them anymore.

"I don't remember you," I said.

"Gary," the first guy said. "Gary Howard." He pointed to Scratchy. "Bryce McNair."

"And you guys are looking for Brandon," I said.

"Yeah," Gary said. "He's been crashing here, but he's not around now. We were trying to think of where to look for him next. You don't know where he is, do you?" He started to sort of hop from foot to foot, like he had to pee.

"I don't think Brandon's coming back here," I said.

Gary's face sort of collapsed, like I'd just told him his puppy had died. I noticed that Scratchy—Bryce—was staring at me.

"Brandon told me you used to, uh, sell Vitamin Z," he said.

Oh, brother.

"I don't do that anymore. Sorry."

I started to back away. "I think we should be going," I said to the boys. They joined me in my strategic withdrawal.

"Sorry to bother you two," I said. "Uh, good luck in your . . . Yeah."

"Why don't you think Brandon will be back here?" Bryce asked. His face scratching had become even more furious. I really needed not to see that anymore.

They both continued to yell after us once we'd turned and walked away. I felt sick to my stomach. It turned out Carol and Brandi had been right about the Case of the Missing Seniors. Fantastic. I wondered how long it'd be before Buddha found a new dealer for the Salem area. How long before those two and all the people like them took a little too much Z and joined the population of the differently-living.

We got back in the car, which Warren started so he could crank the heat, and we just sat in silence for a while. We let the events of the last few minutes sink in.

"So," Warren said, "beer?"

"Oh, God, yes," I said.

"Not for me," Phil said.

Cody shot Phil a look and then said, "Yeah, not for me, either."

"You can drink beer if you want to, Cody," Phil said. "You don't have to hold back just because of me."

"Such ego," Cody said. "No, it's just that I have to be up early to help my dad tomorrow. If he figures out I have a hangover, he'll never let me live it down."

"Why don't you guys still come hang out with us," I said.

Cody shook his head. "Like I said, Cody get up early. Him go to sleep now."

I looked at Phil. I was willing him to say he'd come over.

"I need to get to bed, too," he said.

"So it's just you and me," Warren said.

I stared out the window for a second. Anger flared to

life inside my chest. Why the hell couldn't Phil just come hang out with us? I know from personal experience that I was highly entertaining when I'd been drinking. That finding was based on a survey of other people who'd also been drinking, but still . . .

"Yeah," I said to Warren, "I guess it's just us."

Cody shot Phil a look from the front seat, but Phil seemed not to see it, seemed not even to hear my answer.

"I guess you'd better take me and Cody home," he said finally.

And all of a sudden I wanted to cry again. I couldn't believe that Phil cared so little about me that he wasn't going to come with us, or, at the very least, ask me not to do this. I understood trying not to feel jealous, but dammit, why wasn't he at least a little jealous! I was about to go off drinking with a really gorgeous boy, and Phil should be mad and want to stop it.

Fine. Screw it, I thought. If he doesn't care, then I don't care. We'll just go and have fun, and he'll regret not coming with us.

All of these thoughts sloshed around in my mind like a tidal wave of toxic sludge as we drove first Cody, then Phil home. When we got to Phil's house, I climbed out of the car at the same time he did.

"What are you doing?" he asked. There was something in his eyes, and in his voice, when he asked that, like maybe he hoped I was going to come in with him instead of run off with Warren. But I was still feeling angry. And petty.

"I'm just getting in the front seat," I said.

He stood there blinking slowly, not saying anything. After a second, I climbed in next to Warren.

"See you later, man," Warren said through a crack in the window. He drove away.

I didn't say good-bye.

What I did was pout while Warren drove to my place. I was angry in that way you can only be angry when you know you're wrong. One way to think about this was that Phil let me go because he didn't care about me, but he'd told me he cared for me just a few nights ago. So maybe he let me go because I was a big girl and he trusted me to make responsible decisions.

"How stupid can you get?" I said to the passenger side window, my breath making a foggy patch on the glass.

"Come again?" Warren said.

"Nothing," I said. "Just talking to myself."

"Okay," he said.

We drove without talking after that. Warren played something nice on the stereo, but it was too low for me to really catch it. I looked out at the passing houses and I felt bad about going into that crappy neighborhood earlier looking for zombies. I wasn't sure why that made me feel guilty exactly. Maybe *everything* was making me feel guilty. Maybe guilt was my superpower.

We got to my place and Warren parked in front and turned off the car. I didn't make any move to get out of the car.

"Are we gonna go in?" he asked. "It'll start getting cold soon."

"I don't know," I said. I looked at my little house. I'd let Brandon in a few nights ago and that had ended in a bad way. Then I'd let Phil in and it had ended up pretty good. What might happen if I let Warren in?

"Is this because of Phil?" Warren asked.

"What's that mean?"

"I'm not dumb, Courtney," he said. "I can see there's something going on between the two of you. God, I hope you two don't think you were hiding it."

"We weren't hiding it," I said, "but I didn't think we were broadcasting it, either."

"Well," he said, "I'm sure Cody has no idea there's anything going on."

I put my head in my hands. "Oh, God, is that the bar we've cleared? Amazing. I bet those two junkies we saw earlier tonight are talking about how Phil and I have something going on."

"I don't know why you're upset," Warren said. "I think it's cool that you two like each other too much to hide it."

"Yeah?"

"Yeah," he said. "Phil's a cool guy. A little intense, but cool."

I let that sink in. Phil *was* a cool guy.

"How serious are you two?" Warren asked.

"How do you mean?"

"Is it a complicated question?"

"Sort of," I said. I suddenly felt too close to Warren, too confined inside the car. I wanted distance from him. Physical distance. If it hadn't been freezing outside, I'd have climbed out of the car. There was no way we were going in the house now, so the car it was.

"Sort of," Warren repeated. "Well, how physical have you two gotten?"

"Jesus, what is this, a locker room?" I asked.

Warren laughed. "I don't want details," he said. "I'm just trying to establish what we're talking about here."

He leaned in a little closer to me, and I retreated, but I only got so far because of the car door.

"I know you two have been an item since the summer," Warren said. His voice was pitched low like we were telling secrets and it wasn't just the two of us. "Have you had sex?"

I was so glad we were sitting in the dark because I felt my cheeks grow hot. No way did I want him to see me blushing.

"No, huh?" he asked. "Well, tell me this: Have you two at least kissed?"

"We have," I said, and I hated how small and timid my voice came out. "Twice now."

"Twice?" Warren said, incredulous. He leaned forward again, and there was nowhere for me to get away. He reached out his hand and touched my chin very softly. "Courtney, if I was your boyfriend, there's no way I'd be able to keep from kissing you." Then he leaned forward some more and all of a sudden we were kissing.

Okay. I realize that was lame. It was also using the passive voice, which four years' worth of English teachers had taught me to avoid, but it was also accurate. I knew that I was responsible for the kiss, but I felt powerless to control it. It was a force of nature, a tornado, and I was a double-wide trailer home.

There was no tentativeness in Warren's kiss like there had been with Phil. His mouth was right there, right on mine, and then, a second later, his tongue parted my lips and started dancing around inside my mouth. I just sort of melted into it. It just felt so good, so comforting, to know that I was desirable, and to have the proof on display like this. To have this gorgeous boy think that I was worthy of this kind of attention. It all just made me lose my mind for a few minutes.

Why had I wanted to get away from him? Now I just wanted to be close. I cursed the gear shift and brake lever. I wrapped one arm around his neck and snaked the other around his body. Warren responded by wrapping one arm around me, his hand on my back. The other hand went to my breast. He started to squeeze and knead it. It was too rough, almost painful, and I was about to tell him to stop when he moved his hand. Thank God. I went back to enjoying the feel of his lips and tongue.

And then his free hand was in the front of my pants, and a million warning buzzers went off in my head.

I got both hands on his shoulders and pushed, but he barely moved.

"Stop it, Warren," I said.

He tried to pull me to him again with the one arm.

"No," I said, and I shoved again, this time getting him off me. "Stop it," I said.

"What the hell, Courtney?" he asked. His voice was somewhere between bewildered and angry.

"Just stop," I said. "Which means get your hand out of my pants!"

"Oh, c'mon," he said. "I thought you wanted to do this." At least he did as I asked and moved his hand.

"I thought you were just talking about what a great guy Phil is?" I said.

"Don't throw that at me," he said from his side of the car. "I'm not the one going out with him."

"But you're supposed to be his friend," I said.

"I don't care how good a friend he is," Warren said. "Not when you're throwing off signals like you were."

"Now it's my fault," I said.

"You wanted it," he said. "You can't deny it."

"Well, now I don't."

"Just like that?" he asked.

"Just like that," I said.

I tried to open the door, but it was locked. "Oh, Jesus, I cannot believe I did this. Phil's never going to forgive me." I tried the door again. "Will you please unlock the car?"

"What if I don't?" Warren asked.

"What?" I asked.

"You heard me."

"Perfect," I said. "Just perfect." I faced him. "If you're thinking about forcing me to do something I don't want to do, it would be a huge mistake."

"I don't believe that you don't want it," he said. Shit. He was angry. How had I ever let myself get in a situation like this? My whole life I'd been taught to avoid situations exactly like this. Well, I'd been trained in other things my whole life, too.

As fast as I was able, I drew my pistol and shoved the barrel into his crotch. Hard.

"I think this might tell you how much I disagree with you," I said. It was so satisfying to see his eyes go wide, to see his mouth form this little O of terror. I gave the barrel another shove just to emphasize my point.

"Okay," he yelled. "I get it, I get it. I'm sorry!"

"Sorry for which?" I asked. "Sorry for kissing me when I was vulnerable, or sorry for threatening to rape me?"

"Rape? Jesus, Courtney!"

"That's what I'd call it," I said. "But right now, I don't want to have a semantic argument with you. Right now I just want you to unlock my damn door before I blow your pecker off."

Unable to take his eyes off the pistol in his groin, Warren reached toward the control panel and fumbled around until I heard the doors unlock.

I reached behind me, found the handle, and opened the door. Cold night air flooded the car and covered me in gooseflesh. Keeping the pistol trained on him, I got out of the car. He kept his arms up like he was being robbed. Good, him being scared was exactly what I wanted.

"Now go home, Warren," I said. "And I doubt we'll be calling you to go on any more zombie hunts."

He put his arms down. His mouth was a tight line of anger. As he keyed the car to life, he said, "Fine. Whatever, you stupid—"

I thumbed the hammer on the pistol. It was an obviously deadly sound.

"Whatever word follows that is probably bad for your health," I said. "Just shut up and leave."

I reached out with my foot and kicked the door closed.

He immediately put it in drive and slammed on the gas. The car fishtailed as it screeched away from the curb. As he rounded the corner, the window rolled down and he screamed, "Bitch!" I considered running and trying to put a couple of shots in his rear window, but I was too tired. Honestly, I felt like I deserved it. Although his lack of creativity in name calling was somewhat disappointing.

And then I was left all alone, and suddenly I felt exhausted. I'd never been so tired. I wasn't even sure I'd be able to make it back into my house. I considered just lying down on the sidewalk and letting zombies find me. But I knew that was defeatist thinking. So, I got into the yard and made my slow way up to the house. It felt like I was lifting concrete blocks every time I took a step.

When I got inside and locked the door behind me, I let myself sort of melt onto the couch.

I took my phone out of my pocket and started to compose a text to Phil. Which I deleted. I must have written a hundred texts to him that night, each one explaining what had happened and how sorry I was. I'd violated his trust in me, and now I was no longer worthy of it, or of him and his affections. I deleted every single one.

Oh, God, I was like the character in a Brontë novel. I threw the phone away. I heard it clatter along the kitchen floor with its maybe-linoleum flooring.

Why did I want to tell Phil anyway? To relieve my own guilt? Well, screw that. I was going to feel guilty for a while. I deserved it. I welcomed it.

I wanted to cry. I felt like a big, emotional release would have done me a world of good. But either I was all cried out or I was further punishing myself on a subconscious level. There was no way to force tears to come. It reminded me of that Johnny Cash song about a man who couldn't cry. If I'd had the strength, I'd have gotten up and put that song on. Instead, I just closed my eyes and fell asleep.

CHAPTER FOURTEEN

A Pretty Jittery Place

There's this line in a Hemingway novel, I can't remember which one. I can't even remember the line, exactly, but it's about how the character lay in bed for a long time before he remembered that his heart was broken. I wish I'd had the luxury of forgetfulness the next day, because the moment my eyes opened, I remembered that I'd broken Phil's heart. He just didn't know it yet.

I decided for the sake of the rest of humanity that I needed to hide away by myself. I spent that day finishing the last bit of my holiday homework and moping, with occasional bouts of guilt-induced napping thrown in. People underestimate how much you can sleep when you're depressed, but if you really work at it, you can doze through fifteen or sixteen hours in a day.

Phil texted and asked how I was doing at one point. I wrote back that I was feeling under the weather. Then it occurred to me that he probably thought I was hung over, so I immediately wrote and told him that Warren and I hadn't ended up drinking.

A few minutes later, he texted back:

Okay. Hope you feel better. Let me know if you're still up for tomorrow.

Man, I'd forgotten about going up to see Buddha the next day. I wrote that I'd still be up for it, but he didn't have to come along if he had better things to do.

Better than hang with you? Don't think so, he texted back, and I felt the guilt knife twist in my gut.

Okay, I texted back, I'm going to try and get some more rest. See you tomorrow.

Which was the actual truth, because the next thing I did was climb into my Bed of Remorse and mope my way back to sleep for the night.

I woke up early the next day, my heart pounding, my body drenched in sweat. I'd been having some sort of nightmare, but the moment I opened my eyes, it evaporated. I lay there long enough for my heart rate to get back to normal, then got out of my nest and showered and dressed.

The next thing I did was difficult. I had a mini-war over whether or not I even wanted to consider it. If I'd been in a cartoon, a little angel and devil would have appeared on my shoulders. I'm not really sure which of them won the argument, but in the end I marched into my dad's room and broke into the huge bag of cash he'd been keeping in there ever since he took it from me after I admitted how I'd earned it.

I really didn't feel good about it. I knew I was violating my dad's trust by doing that, but I also knew I needed two hundred dollars to make it past the checkpoints along the highway. I also knew that Dad would never even know the money was missing just by glancing at it. He'd have to count it all. I wondered if he ever had. I sure had. Somewhere in my room, I had a notebook with the figure down to the dollar. I tried not to think about it. This money was supposed to be my go-away-to-college fund, but it had all been earned by selling Vitamin Z. I understood why Dad had taken it from me. But I still regretted it.

I counted out ten twenty-dollar bills and folded them into two little bundles for easy bribing. Those went into the front pocket of the flannel shirt I wore over a black T-shirt. I did my best to put everything back in the drawer the way it had been. Let's see, I'd replaced one broken window in here, now I'd taken out cash I didn't want him to know about. What else might I do in that room that I'd have to hide from him? It was best not to think about it.

I then went into my room, strapped on my pistol, and I was ready. I really wished I had something more badass to climb into than a Subaru wagon, but you can't have everything. I sent a quick text to let Phil know I was on my way and then I was off.

He was waiting for me on his front porch when I got there, and I barely had to stop the car and wait for him to climb in before I was off again.

He gave me a meek smile after he got his seat belt done up.

"How are you?" he asked.

I almost asked him what he meant when I remembered I'd told him I was feeling sick.

"Better," I said. "Just a little tired. What'd you tell your aunt and uncle you were doing today? I'm sure you didn't tell them what you were doing for real. Did you?" I worried that Phil being Phil, there was at least an outside chance he'd told them the truth.

"I just said we'd be hanging out," he said.

He reached into his backpack and started rummaging around in it.

"I brought road goodies," he said. Pulled out Red Vines and cans of Pepsi.

"You may road-trip with me anytime, Phil," I said.

"These are sort of a way to apologize," he said. I started to get a weird feeling in my gut, but didn't say anything.

"I acted like sort of a tool last night. I shouldn't have. So"—he held up a can of soda—"sorry."

"Thanks," I said. "And there's really no reason to be sorry. You should be able to say you don't want to do something without me acting like a bitch about it."

"So you didn't end up drinking with Warren," he said. "What did you do?"

I squashed the urge to get defensive—*What do you mean, what did we do?* Defensiveness was a dead giveaway.

"We just talked for a little in his car, then I went in to bed." This was factually accurate with just one tiny omission. Namely, the fact that Warren and I had made out for a good five minutes. But I figured life might be better for everyone if I kept that detail to myself.

"What'd you guys talk about?" Phil asked in a sort of distracted way. I was crossing some lanes of traffic just then, and he seemed to take issue with my traffic etiquette. I wasn't sure what he was so worried about, our conversation had me so distracted that I was unable to obsess about the road, and I thought I was driving better than ever.

"We talked a little about you," I said. "And me and you." Again, this was true.

"Good things, I hope," he said.

"Of course!" Okay, this was veering toward lying territory again.

Thankfully, we were coming up on the freeway on-ramp and I slowed the car. The conversation would have to wait.

"Just sit back and don't say anything," I said.

I pulled to a stop and a soldier walked up to the window, which I rolled down. I didn't recognize this guy. Of course, after six months, the dude I used to deal with had probably been transferred or had gone back home or something.

The soldier, a Latino kid not much older than me, leaned over to look in the car.

"May I ask the nature of your business, ma'am?" he said. *Ma'am?*

"I'm headed up to East Portland to visit a friend," I said. "His name is Buddha."

At the mention of the name, the kid looked at me sharply. "License, please," he said.

I dug my license out of my shirt pocket and brought one bundle of twenties with it.

"Here you go," he said.

The soldier barely glanced at my license, but he made sure to count the money. He smiled as he handed the ID back and stuffed the money in his pocket.

"You're a lot nicer on the eyes than the kid who usually goes on this run," the guy said. Phil stiffened in the seat beside me, but he didn't say anything. "Just head north to Exit—"

"I know the routine," I said to the kid. "Thanks."

"Okay, then," he said and he motioned to a Humvee that blocked access to the road. The huge vehicle backed up just enough for us to squeeze past, and then we were back on our way. This time on the freeway with only a few freight trucks for company.

"That was interesting," Phil said.

"Yeah," I said. "They're always like that."

"Well, he got one thing right," Phil said. "You're pretty easy on the eyes."

Joy won out over guilt, and I flashed Phil a smile. "Are you flirting with me, sir?" I asked. "Because it might just work."

"Easier on the eyes than Brandon, anyway," Phil said.

I laughed pretty hard because the joke had been so unexpected. Then I started to slap at him with my free hand.

He was laughing, too, then a truck honked at us because I was weaving all over the road. That sobered us up.

"Punk," I said as I regained control of the Subaru.

"That reminds me," Phil said and he went back to his backpack. He brought out a big stack of CDs. "Travel music!" he said.

"It's only a forty-five-minute trip," I said eying the mountain of tunes.

"True," he said, "but I don't know what you like, so I brought a little of everything. This is music that I listen to as I draw."

Turns out that Phil had angry taste in music. It was all punk bands. The Ramones, The Clash, Black Flag, Misfits. I thought about giving him some guff by asking if he had any Green Day, but I didn't want to push things. We ended up listening to The Cramps. I don't know if I really liked it, but it was so loud that there was no way for us to talk, so that was a plus.

Phil was about to throw another CD into the player when I told him to hold up.

"There's Portland," I said as we negotiated the weird freeway interchange that took us to the 405. The city is split in two by the Willamette River. The west side is completely shut off to humans—well, humans who are sane or aren't running criminal empires. Folks still get into the east side sometimes, mostly to shoot at zombies across the river, but there were no people out that day.

Phil pressed his face against the window as we drove.

"My aunt and uncle talk all the time about how they used to come up here," he said. "They'd go to restaurants, shows, parks . . ."

"My dad does that, too," I said. "Portland sounds like it used to be pretty cool."

"I've only ever seen it from the freeway," he said.

"Well," I said, "you'll get a lot closer look today."

I found the exit and drove past another Humvee. The soldier behind the wheel gave us a mock salute, and then we were in the city: two of maybe a couple dozen humans among all those walking dead.

It took me a minute to remember how to get to Buddha's place, but then things started to look familiar again and I got us where we were going. We parked up the hill from him, at a dilapidated baseball stadium visible just over the horizon. When we got out of the car, I checked my pistol and pulled my flannel closer to my body. I wished I'd brought a coat. Even though the sun was out, it was still pretty cold.

"We'll leave the doors unlocked," I said to Phil. I whispered. Just because we didn't see any zombies didn't mean there were none around. They more or less owned the city after all.

"Makes sense to me," he said.

Phil joined me on the street. "We're going to walk down this hill," I told him. "When we get down there, you'll see a big brick apartment building to the right. That's Buddha's building. Last time I was here, there was a big mob of zombies we had to get through. I hope that's not the case this time."

"Me, too," Phil said. He looked a little queasy.

"Let's go," I said, "and let's be quiet."

As we walked down the middle of the road, I realized that Phil wasn't carrying his nail-studded baseball bat. That was why he looked uneasy when I mentioned zombies. He hadn't expected to encounter any. Well, I hoped he was right.

We paused at the top of the hill to look down at the apartment building below. No sign of shufflers. Excellent. I waved Phil on, and in just a few minutes we stood in front of the building's entrance—a door equipped with a keypad and an electronic lock. The last time I'd been here, with Brandon and Sherri, this door had been ajar and the lobby full of Zs. That was not the case this time, thank God.

"I hope he hasn't changed the code," I said as I punched in numbers. There was a very satisfying *click* as I hit the last number. I held the door open for Phil and made sure to close it behind me.

I stood for a moment, looking out at the trees that lined the opposite side of the street. I thought I'd seen something over there. Actually, it'd be more accurate to say that I felt like I'd seen something. But no matter how hard I stared, I didn't see anything more.

"Is there a problem?" Phil asked.

"Nope," I said. "Just jitters."

"This is a pretty jittery place," he said.

The elevator doors slid open when I pushed the up button and we climbed inside. Buddha told me once that he'd disabled the Muzak system in here as soon as he became the building's sole occupant. I thought about that every time I rode in that elevator.

We got off when the doors opened on the sixth floor.

"There's only one door in the hallway?" Phil asked.

"Yeah," I said. There used to be a few apartments, but after everyone left, Buddha had all the walls knocked down and turned it into one huge space.

"You ready for this?" I asked as we stood in front of that one door.

"Doesn't really matter," he said. "We're here now."

"Phil," I said, "you're a philosopher."

I knocked. We heard something going on on the other side of the door. Someone walking around, maybe people talking, and something else I couldn't quite make out.

The door opened, and I was surprised that a girl was the one opening it. I'd been let in by some of Buddha's thugs before, guys with mean eyes who never smiled, and of course Buddha had let me in plenty, but this was the first time I'd ever seen another female. When I called her a girl, I wasn't exaggerating. I don't think she was much older than me and Phil. She was gorgeous—tall and thin, with brown skin and dark eyes. I blushed when I realized she was wearing a man's button-up shirt and nothing else.

I wondered what Phil was thinking beside me.

"We're here to see Buddha," I said.

"Well, who else *would* you be here to see," she said.

Everything mostly looked the same as I remembered it. He'd gotten a new couch, and I'd never figure out how he got new things delivered to a city that was officially quarantined. Other than that, this girl was the only thing new in the apartment. Same stereo system, same bar, same art on the walls. Maybe the TV was new, it was hard to tell.

Buddha came out of one of the back rooms, all smiles. All he wore was a pair of jeans and a smile. His *chica* must have been wearing his only shirt. He looked the same, too. Long silver hair, pirate mustache—good-looking for someone older than my dad.

"There you are," he said to me. "I've missed that face. I see you met Precious."

The girl rolled her eyes and flopped onto the couch without speaking.

"Yes," I said. "We're great friends now."

"Speaking of friends . . ." Buddha said.

"Oh, right," I said. "This is Phil."

Phil stepped forward and reached out his hand. "Hello, sir," he said.

Buddha looked at his outstretched hand like it was some undiscovered species of slug, then he broke into a huge grin. He gripped Phil's hand with both of his.

"Hello, son," Buddha said. "This fella has much better manners than the last one you brought over here."

Phil shot me a raised eyebrow.

"Brandon," I said, and the eyebrow sank back into the depths of Phil's forehead.

Buddha sat on the couch next to Precious and she wrapped herself around him like a friendly cat.

"Grab something out of the fridge if you want," Buddha told me.

I went behind the bar to the dorm fridge he kept there. "Want anything?" I asked Phil.

"Is there juice?"

"Orange or pineapple?"

"Pineapple, please," he said.

Buddha laughed. "Where'd you find someone with such good manners, Courtney?"

"He followed me home one day, and Dad said I could keep him." I winked at Phil to let him know I was just playing.

"Phil, right?" Buddha asked him. "Have a seat."

Phil sat on the love seat across from Buddha and Precious. Brandon and Sherri had sat there the last time we'd all come here. The time we smoked Vitamin Z and Sherri ended up dying.

"How are those drinks coming?" Buddha asked. "Want to bring me a Dos Equis?"

"Sure," I said. "Anything for you?" I asked Precious. I refused to actually speak a name that dumb out loud.

"No, I'm fine," she said.

"She's fine," Buddha repeated and he ran his hand up and down her thigh. Gag.

I got our drinks and came back to the living room. I gave Buddha his beer, then flopped onto the love seat next to Phil and handed him his juice.

"Before I forget," Buddha said. He dug into the front pocket of his jeans and pulled out a little baggie full of Z. "Don't do anything stupid with that."

"Thanks," I said.

"And that's on the house," he said. Precious shot him a look like he'd just said he was giving up the drug business to become a missionary.

I thanked him again, and then something popped into my head and I just had to ask him.

"Have you been changing the formula on this?" I asked. "Like, since I stopped selling it?"

He gave me a weird look, then said, "My chemists are always tinkering with the makeup of Z. We're always looking to maximize our customers' experience. Why do you ask?"

"Just wondering," I said. I didn't know how to tell him I suspected that zombies were getting faster and smarter because he'd been altering his formula from the original recipe. Anyway, since it was just a suspicion, I thought I'd keep it to myself for now. I'd just tell Dr. Keller when I got him the sample.

"So, what's new in the real world?" Buddha asked.

"Here's something," I said. "You're going to have to hang out a Help Wanted sign again."

Phil shot me a look.

"How's that?" Buddha asked.

"Brandon," I said. "He's dead."

His face clouded over, got red, and then returned to the same placid state it almost always exhibited. I had a feeling that looking so serene took a lot of work for him.

"How'd that happen?" he asked.

"He overdosed," I said. "I was there, unfortunately."

Buddha rubbed a hand through his hair. "That's too bad," he said. "I liked that kid. But I had told him to lay off the product. You were there when it happened, huh?"

"Yeah," I said. "It was at my house."

There was that same weird look he'd given me when I asked about the Vitamin Z formula.

"And . . . ?" he asked.

"And what?"

"Courtney," he said, "you know what I'm asking."

"I do," I said. "No, he didn't stay dead. Or, at least, he didn't stay down."

"Did you put him back down?" Buddha asked. "I know your reputation in that department."

"No," I said. "He got away from me, but I'll be keeping an eye out for him."

"Well, I wouldn't want to be him," Buddha said. He turned his attention to Phil. "How about you? Are you a badass zombie killer, too?"

Precious smirked at that. I bit my tongue before I said something I'd regret.

"I do what I can," Phil said. "Mostly I try to stay out of the way."

"Sure," Buddha said. "Say, let me ask you something."

I'd never find out what he wanted to know. Just then the phone in the other room began to ring. Buddha rose to answer it, shedding Precious like a sexy lap blanket. Then the lights went out and the phone stopped ringing.

"What the hell?" Buddha said.

Phil and I exchanged a look. Buddha was supposed to have a generator in the basement that was meant to keep the lights running no matter what.

A cell phone started to buzz. Buddha reached into his pocket and pulled out the phone. He thumbed it to life.

"What?" he said. He listened, shooting a look at me and Phil. "How many?" he asked. "Uh-huh. Get everyone down to the lobby," he said. "I'll be there in a minute."

He killed the call and tossed the phone to Precious. "Hold that for me," he said. He stalked over to the window at the far end of the apartment. "Sounds like we have more guests," he said. He threw open the curtains, exposing floor-to-ceiling windows. "Son of a bitch."

Phil and I jumped up and ran to the window.

"What is it, baby?" Precious asked from the couch, her voice small like she was crawling inside herself.

It looked like every zipper in Portland was converging on Buddha's apartment. Leaning over and trying to look straight down, I saw that there was already a mass of them smashing against the windows down there.

"What are they doing?" Phil asked.

"Do you still use the basement as a warehouse?" I asked.

"What do a bunch of zombies want with some barrels of Vitamin Z?" Buddha asked. He wasn't trying to maintain the serene mask anymore, and it was a little scary.

"I don't know," I said, "except that a lot of them probably died of drug overdoses. Maybe they still crave it?"

Buddha laughed. "Junkie shufflers? Is that what you're saying?" He laughed some more, but I didn't think he found it too funny.

"We need to get out of here," I said.

"You take your friend and get out," Buddha said. "No way am I leaving my home and my business to these assholes. We'll hold them on the first floor, no problem."

"Some of the new ones are fast," I said. "Some can open doors and climb stairs."

"Well, ain't that something?" he asked. "Okay. You two get, and you take Precious with you."

"I'm not going," she said. I jumped because she was standing right behind us. When did she get up and come over? "I'm staying here with you. No matter what."

Buddha smiled and wrapped his arms around her. "Oh, baby," he whispered and he gave her a deep kiss. "You're so stupid, you remind me of me at your age." He nodded to me and Phil. "Avoid the elevator. There's a stairway access on the far side of this room, I'll show you. I'd avoid the ground floor, too. Make your way down to the basement. There's a tunnel in the northeast corner that leads out to Twentieth."

"Uh," said Phil.

"What is it, son?" Buddha asked.

"I don't have a weapon," he said. "I didn't think I'd need one."

Buddha thought on that for a moment. "I think I can get you kitted out. How are you fixed, Courtney?"

I showed him my pistol. "And I have some ammo in speed loaders," I told him.

He disappeared into his bedroom and I heard him rummaging around. He emerged a few moments later. He held a matte black shotgun in his hands.

"It's a Remington .12 gauge," he said as he handed it to Phil. "Nothing fancy, but it will do the trick. It's carrying a full load now, and there are fifteen extra shells on the strap. Okay?"

"Yes, sir," Phil said. "This should be fine."

"Manners," Buddha said with a smile. "You two be safe. I gotta get dressed and help my boys downstairs."

With that, he turned back into the room. Precious followed him a second later. That left me and Phil standing there looking dumb.

"Let's go," I said. My mouth was so dry I had trouble talking. I hadn't drunk any of my Pepsi.

We walked to the far end of the living space and rounded a corner. This was a part of the apartment I'd never seen before. Buddha had a mini-arcade back here. Pool table, dartboard, and several video games—one of which was a zombie hunter type. There was also a doorway with a red EXIT sign hanging above it.

"Let me go first," Phil said.

"Why, because you're a strong man and I can't take care of myself?"

"No, you idiot," he said. "Because if I try to shoot past you with this, I'll probably blow your head off."

"Oh," I said. "Right. You go first."

He pushed open the door and poked his head inside. A second later, he pulled his head out and looked at me.

"Clear as far as I can tell," he said. "Come on."

He pulled the door open all the way and stepped through. I took a deep breath and followed him.

CHAPTER FIFTEEN
I Need the Room

As quietly as we were able, we raced down the concrete steps. Since the power had been cut, eerie red emergency light filled the space. At each landing, Phil paused to look and listen. How he was able to hear anything over the sound of our ragged breathing, I had no idea. Eventually he'd decide everything was okay and we'd move on.

As we descended the stairs, the sound of gunfire coming up from the lobby got louder and louder. It sounded like World War III down there. When we reached the ground floor landing, we heard men shouting—and screaming—on the other side of the door. The smell of cordite nearly made me gag.

"Should we try to help them?" Phil asked.

"No," I said as something thudded against the stairwell door. "We need to get out now," I said.

Without another word on the topic, Phil continued down the stairs. We got to the bottom and stood before a door marked with a huge *B*. Phil pressed his ear against the door and listened. "I don't hear anything," he said.

"That might be either good or bad," I said. "I don't think there are ever many guys in the basement. Anyone who was in there probably went up to the lobby to join the fight."

"So we just go and hope for the best?" Phil asked.

"Isn't that the plan we've been following our whole lives?" I asked him. "Why change things up now?"

He nodded, not looking very comforted by my version of the Saint Crispin's Day speech. He put his hand on the doorknob and took several deep breaths—trying to psych himself up. Then he threw the door open and ran through.

I followed and nearly ran into him. He stood in the darkened basement, shotgun up on his shoulder and at the ready. More red emergency lights were the only thing throwing off any illumination down here, too, but the space was so cavernous—the same footprint as the building above—that it might as well have been full dark. All the support pillars down there threw what little light there was into all sorts of weird shadows that might hide a whole army of zombies.

"Which way is northeast?" Phil whispered.

Shit, why ask me about direction? I thought about it. What direction had we been traveling when we parked the car? Where was that in relationship to the building's entrance, and where were we now? Ugh.

"Over there, I think," I said and pointed in what I hoped wasn't just a random direction.

"Stick right behind me," Phil said. "And watch for anything behind us."

"This isn't the first time I've done something like this," I said. But I did as he suggested.

We crept along the darkened space, every footfall sounding like a hammer blow on the concrete. We swept our guns toward the slightest noise or perceived movement. It felt like it took us a half hour just to cover ten yards.

"We need to be moving faster," I hissed in Phil's ear.

"I'd rather take my time than blunder into some unseen zombies, Courtney," he said. He wiped sweat away from his eyes.

"One of Buddha's goons told me that this place is rigged

to blow," I said. "Apparently, Buddha's paranoid about cops or another gang taking over the place. I don't know if it's true, but I don't want to stick around and find out."

"Well, shit," Phil said. "Okay, here we go."

He took off at something halfway between a fast walk and a run. A jog? A trot? My much-loved vocabulary was failing me. Keeping up with him was taking too much effort to use my brain properly.

We cleared some pillars and then we were staring at the far wall. A door stood there, but it wasn't marked. Anything might have been on the other side of its pitted white surface.

"Is this it?" Phil asked.

"I don't know," I said. "I've never seen it before."

"One way to find out, I guess," he said. He stepped forward and threw the door open. All we saw was blackness. No lights of any kind, not even red emergency ones. But there was something.

"Feel that?" I asked Phil.

"What?"

"A breeze." I felt it against my face. Not strong, but it was there, and the smell it carried was dirt and rain and trees. Outside.

"This is it," Phil said.

"This is it," I agreed. "Let's go."

We stepped into the tunnel and for a few seconds, red light filtered into the space. Then the door closed and we stood in utter black.

Phil took point again and we moved as fast as we could in the complete dark—sort of a fast walk. As we went, I did my best to keep my brain from screwing with me. It kept wanting to serve up images of hands reaching for my face, like I was a little kid afraid of the dark all over again.

Every once in a while, one or the other of us would call to stop and we'd listen. Each time we heard nothing, but the breeze was getting stronger. We'd run on again after catching our breath.

I had no idea how long we'd been running when Phil called for us to stop.

"See that?" he said. "Ahead of us?"

I was about to tell him no when it came to me that I really did see something. If I squinted, I just made out a light.

"Let's go," Phil said.

Before we took off, we heard something in the tunnel behind us. The door to the basement opened and after a few seconds, closed again.

"Hello?" I yelled. "Buddha?" No answer. "Buddha's goons?" Still nothing.

"What the . . . ?" Phil said.

"Know what I don't like?" I asked. "This. I don't like this. Let's keep moving."

And we ran on. We kept our eyes on the growing patch of light, but behind us we heard something moving. At first it was the sound of walking, then it grew until I knew there was something running to catch up with us.

"Keep running," Phil said. "We're almost there!"

And then something stepped into the light from outside the tunnel. Phil's steps faltered, but I grabbed him by the arm and kept running. "Don't stop," I said.

So we ran right at the zombies that were waiting for us at the end of the tunnel. I fell back as Phil let loose with a blast from his shotgun. I whirled around and assumed a two-hand stance. The moment a runner came into view, I pulled the trigger. The thing's head flew backward and its feet kept running. It looked like it ran into a clothesline.

More shotgun blasts and I squeezed off another round as a zombie, a girl, came into view. I hit her shoulder and she stumbled, but she kept coming. Dammit.

I took a deep breath and squeezed off another round. A

small dot appeared on her forehead and she looked sort of surprised as she fell over.

My ears rang because the shots were so loud in the confined space. Phil grabbed me by the shoulder and motioned for me to get out of the tunnel. He slammed new shells into the shotgun. I took off. Just as I cleared the mouth of the tunnel, a zombie jumped at me from the underbrush. I screamed and swung at the thing. The barrel of my pistol gouged a huge gash in its face, but that hardly slowed it down. It was on top of me in a flash.

As I lay on my back, I looked up an embankment and saw the street. I almost called for help before I remembered that there were no people up there, just shufflers and runners.

I did my best to hold the zombie at arms' length, but the damn thing moved like a monkey or something. I had time to notice it wore a letterman's jacket, but not from any high school I recognized.

"Phil!" I shouted.

I heard two more shotgun blasts. How many shots was that? I hoped Phil was keeping count.

I kept trying to get the pistol in position to do some good, but the monster on top of me refused to hold still. Just when I thought my arms were about to give out, a foot lashed out and connected with the thing's head and it flew off me. Phil stood over me, then aimed his riot gun at the thing thrashing on the ground. Its thrashing days came to an abrupt end.

Phil gave me his hand and helped me up. "We have to get out of here," he said. I agreed.

We ran up Twentieth for a few yards, then ducked behind an overgrown shrub. Looking back down the street, I realized that unless you knew what you were looking for, you'd never see the entrance for the tunnel. No way the zombies just happened to be standing there.

"I got two more that had been behind us," Phil said. "Sorry about the one that jumped you. I thought I'd cleared the entrance."

"It was waiting for me," I said. "It was trying to trap me. The whole thing in the tunnel was a trap, you get that, right?"

"I guess I do," he said. "There's no way it could have been anything else."

That was the very first time someone had ever agreed with me when I talked about zombies laying traps. Usually people looked at me like I needed some new medications. I felt a strong urge to kiss him right then, but I put it in check.

"We need to keep moving," I said. "I think we need to work our way up past the apartment complex, then up the street where we left the car." God, I hoped they hadn't found the car.

We moved off as fast as our feet were able, stopping whenever we thought we heard something that wasn't us. It took us a good fifteen minutes to make it around the apartments. Somewhere in there it started to rain and we were soaked and freezing. I was worried I'd be unable to squeeze the trigger anymore as cold as my hands felt.

Pretty soon we were running up a street that ran parallel to the one the car was on. We just needed to find a cross street, then we'd be able to cut over. The sun was starting to go behind the Portland hills and it'd be dark soon. I wanted us on the freeway before that happened.

We found a connecting street and ran for all we were worth. There it was. God, never had I been so relieved to see a stupid Subaru. Phil climbed in and I was about to follow suit when I stopped.

"What is it, Courtney?" Phil asked. "What's going on?"

I looked down the street, the way we'd originally walked to get to the apartment building, and I saw a lone figure standing there watching the carnage at the bottom of the hill. Brandon. Brandon stood there like some sort of slack-jawed general watching his troops.

I walked away from the car and from Phil, and walked calmly down the hill toward Brandon. As I walked, I raised my pistol and fired a round. It didn't hit him, but it got his attention. He turned and looked at me. For a second, I thought he was about to wave or something, then he hissed at me. I fired again. And missed.

"Come here, you shit!" I yelled at him.

A handful of zombies, boys and girls, but all young, came running up the hill toward me. I stopped walking and started aiming more carefully and picked off three of the things. Then there was a pair of strong arms around my waist and Phil was carrying me back to the car whether or not I wanted to go.

"Put me down," I shouted and thrashed in his arms.

"We need to get the hell out of here," he shot back.

I slammed my head back in frustration, and through the back of my skull, I felt something give way on Phil's face. It wasn't enough to get him to let go. We got to the car and he threw me in the front seat. When he leaned in to make sure my legs didn't get shut in the door, I saw that blood streamed out of his nose and down his face. That calmed me down. I'd done that to him. Hell.

He turned and unslung the shotgun from across his back. He let off three or four volleys from the scatter gun and the rest of the zombie pack fell down dead, or near enough. He walked around the front of the car and climbed in.

"Go," he said.

I did as he said. I swung the car in a tight U-turn and got us headed in the opposite direction.

"I think the rumor about the building being rigged to blow was bullshit," he said.

Just then from behind us a huge fireball filled the darkening sky. It felt like someone shoved the rear end of the car, and I fought to keep it under control. I slammed on the brakes and we turned in our seats to look. Orange flames threw everything into shadow. Brandon stood down the street, silhouetted by the explosion. I couldn't tell for sure, but I thought he was still watching us—me—rather than the destruction of his zombie army.

We sat forward in our seats, both of us too tired and freaked out to say anything about what we'd just seen. I put the car back in drive and got us the hell out of there.

The guard who let us back on the freeway asked if we knew what had happened.

"We seen a big ol' fireball," he said, "but we're not sure where it come from." He might have asked us because both Phil and I looked like we'd been in a war. The hundred dollars I slipped the soldier shut him up, though.

We'd been on the road for a while when I said to Phil, "Sorry about your nose. Is it broken?"

"Don't think so," he said, touching it gingerly.

"I wasn't really thinking straight," I said.

"I gathered."

"You saw who I was shooting at, right?" I asked.

"Yeah," Phil said. He wiped his nose with his sleeve and grimaced. "And before you ask, yes, I know just who orchestrated that little surprise party at Buddha's."

I didn't know what to say. Again, I'd expected some push back for thinking that zombies planned and orchestrated anything more complex than walking.

"I guess the question," Phil went on, "is, what do we do?"

"You're asking me that?" I asked.

"Yep," he said. "You've been thinking about this longer than anyone, Courtney. So, I'm going to look to you for some sort of answer."

It was one thing to go from being a lone nut whom no

one believes to being looked at like some sort of expert whom folks look to for leadership.

"I'll have to get back to you on that," I said.

"Great," Phil said. "Until then, I'm going to close my eyes and hope this pain in my face goes away."

He dropped off to sleep, and I still didn't have any answers by the time he woke up.

We went to my place as soon as we hit Salem to let Phil wash his face. While he was in the bathroom, I started to cook an actual meal. Sure, most of it was frozen stuff that just needed to be opened and thrown in the oven, but it was better than calling for takeout.

When Phil came into the kitchen, the blood was all gone, but that just made it easy to see how swollen his nose was.

"God," I said, "I'm so sorry."

He waved it off and went to call his aunt and uncle and tell them he'd be having dinner at my place that night.

Later we sat down to a dinner of chicken strips, tater tots, and formerly frozen peas. It felt very domestic and grown-up. We talked about a few things, school and Cody's goofiness, but we kept coming back to what had happened earlier that day.

"Do you think Buddha made it out of the building?" Phil asked.

"No," I said. "I just hope he let it fill up with as many zombies as possible before pushing the button."

"I keep thinking about that girl," Phil said.

"Precious."

"What a stupid damn name," he said.

"She should have gotten out with us," I said.

"She didn't know us," he said. "She wanted to be with someone who made her feel safe."

"I know what you mean," I said. "That's why leaving with you was the only choice for me."

Phil put down his fork and leaned across the table. I met him halfway and we kissed. After so much death and destruction, it felt like a jolt of life. I felt just the barest twinge of guilt about having kissed Warren a couple of nights ago.

"That was nice," I said.

"It was," he said.

"I wish you'd stay the night," I said. I covered my mouth with my hand. I hadn't expected that to come out of me. I'd just been thinking it.

"I don't know," Phil said.

"No funny stuff," I said. "I swear. It's just that after today, I need some closeness, you know?"

He seemed to really consider that. "Yeah, I do know what you mean." He got up to call his aunt and uncle again.

"Thank God my uncle answered," he said when he came back into the kitchen. I'd started cleaning up and he joined me. It reminded me of cleaning the dishes with Gene, his uncle.

"What did you tell him?" I asked.

"What do you mean?" he asked as he took a dish from me and started to dry it.

"Did you tell him you were staying over at Cody's or something?"

"Why would I do that?" he asked. "No, I told him I was staying here for the night."

My mouth fell open and I nearly dropped the plate I was holding. "Phil!"

"What? My aunt and uncle trust me," he said. "I'm not going to lie to them about what I'm doing."

"Do you tell them everything you do?" I asked.

He thought about that for a moment. "No," he finally said, "but I don't actively lie to them unless I have to."

"So you just said, 'Hey, Uncle Gene, I'm going to shack up with Courtney tonight,' and he was okay with that?" I asked. I couldn't wrap my head around this.

"I would never say 'shack up,' " he said. "Otherwise, yeah. He grilled me about protection and stuff." He had the good grace to blush at that, and I did, too. "I told him nothing was going to happen." He gave me a significant look.

Fine, dammit. Though to be honest, I wasn't sure why I wanted something to happen so badly. Sure, Phil made me think impure thoughts, but things were more complicated than that. Part of it felt like it might make up for what I did with Warren. Maybe that was reason enough to just let it go if Phil wasn't ready.

"Nothing will happen," I said. "Scout's honor."

"You were never a scout," Phil said.

"True," I said, "but I always thought I'd look good in the uniform."

We decided to watch a movie, and I let Phil choose the DVD this time. Watching him go through the process of picking something was sort of terrifying and fascinating at the same time. He dug out literally every film we had and started making piles. First by genre. Some genres got discarded immediately—good-bye, comedies; farewell, musicals. Then he went through the piles that were left and made discard and keep sub-piles. On and on it went until he'd finally settled on something he wanted to watch.

"Black Hawk Down," he said. "I get war movies, you know? The motivations and objectives all make sense to me."

"I knew you were going to choose that the moment you laid your hand on it," I said. "The look you got in your eyes."

"Maybe," he said. "I still needed to go through the process."

I didn't have the heart to point out that it had taken almost as long to pick something to watch as it would take to actually watch it. We put it in and snuggled together and I fell asleep almost immediately. When it was all over, he woke me up and I tried my best to dry the huge drool spot that I'd left on his chest.

"Ready to hit the hay?" I asked.

"Yeah," he said. "I'll take the couch again."

"Nope," I said. "You'll sleep with me in the big bed." When he started to protest, I put up my hand and stopped him. "Listen," I said, "I promised you no funny business, and I meant it. But after the day we had, I want some snuggle time, and I'm not going to argue about it."

He heaved a sigh, but didn't argue anymore.

He got ready in the bathroom in the hall, and I used the one in the master bedroom. I thought about trying to sexy up my nightwear, but decided that might be 1) unfair, and 2) impossible. There was only so much you could do with a T-shirt and boy's boxers.

I slipped into the big bed in Dad's room since there was no way my bed could fit the both of us. Phil came in a few minutes later. He wore nothing but plaid boxers. We'd never been swimming or anything, so I'd never seen his body before. It was a good body. Not like six-pack abs or anything, but not flabby or scrawny, either. Just nice. I wondered how I was going to keep my "no funny business" promise.

"You're staring," Phil said.

"There's a lot to stare at," I said. "I didn't take you for a boxers kind of guy."

"Well," he said, "I need the room."

I saw that for myself.

I pulled the covers back for him to slide in. Which he did. Then he lay back like a corpse in a coffin.

I snapped off the lamp and lay on my back, too, for a while.

"Screw this," I finally said. I turned on my side away from him and said, "Snuggle with me."

He did as he was told. He wrapped his arm around me and pulled me close. Something poked me in the back. That was surprising.

"What are you thinking about, Phil?" I asked.

"Courtney," he said. His voice had a warning tone that I chose to ignore.

"I can help you with that," I said.

"Right," he said and turned over. "You snuggle me."

I rolled my eyes, which was wasted since it was completely dark and he was faced away from me, but I did it. We settled down and it felt nice to be pressed up against him, my face in the back of his neck, my body wrapped around him.

"I'm glad you were with me today," I said. "Not that it all happened, but if it had to, I'm glad you were there."

"Thanks," he said. "And I know what you mean."

"I never want to do anything to drive you away," I said, worried that I already had.

"I'm not going anywhere, Courtney," he said. "You can forget that particular worry."

"Okay," I said. "I'll hold you to that."

Then we fell silent and a few minutes later we were asleep.

CHAPTER SIXTEEN
A Custom Among My People

I took Phil home the next day before driving to the airport. I pulled up to our agreed-upon meeting place, and there was Dad. I felt big with love for him. He was so frumpy and potbellied and sweet. How could I not love him?

And of course he immediately asked me if anything had happened while he had been gone, to which I replied, "Not really." Because the love I had for him meant that I tried to shield him from the shit storm that was my life. As we drove home, he told me all about his conference in exhaustive detail. Or exhausting, whichever.

He eyed the house carefully when we got home. Looking for evidence of a Hollywood-style kegger, I'm sure. I'd tell him that I didn't have enough friends for an actual party to reassure him, but it might have made him sad.

"Did you cook an actual meal here?" he said when he saw the kitchen.

"Yes," I said. "Phil came over last night and I made him dinner."

"Did you now?" he asked.

"Don't make it into a thing," I said.

"Far be it from me to express interest in my daughter's life."

"I just like him, that's all," I said, "and if you make a big deal out of it, it'll be weird. So don't."

He raised his hands in surrender. "As far as you know, I don't care at all about this."

"Good," I said. "Keep it that way."

He took his things down the hall into his room. "Hey," he yelled and I wondered what he'd found. What had Phil or I left in there that gave us away? "Did you clean my windows?"

Oh, God, the new window glass was too clean. I needed to take the time to have smudged it up.

"Yeah," I yelled. "I thought it'd be nice to allow sunshine to actually, you know, come into the house."

"I need to leave town more often," he said.

We chilled the rest of that day, mostly watching TV and getting takeout for dinner. Surprising absolutely no one, Christmas Eve the next day was more of the same. Neither of us were big on Christmas, so it didn't seem weird to spend the day before Jesus' birthday watching horrible basic cable.

We went to sleep after binge-watching *A Charlie Brown Christmas, A Christmas Story,* and *It's a Wonderful Life.* You know, life might have moved on after the dead came back, but no one had made a really good Christmas movie since then, either, so maybe we weren't as okay as everyone pretended to be.

We got up early the next day and opened our few presents. Dad gave me lots of gift certificates, which some might see as an admission that he didn't know me very well, but I took it as a sign that he was pretty freaking savvy. I gave him some new clothes in the form of socks, underwear, pants, and shirts. Since he never shopped for himself, it was up to me to keep him clothed.

After that, it was all about drinking eggnog and watching more Christmas specials.

That was the plan anyway. A little after noon, my cell phone rang. Dad and I both looked at it suspiciously. I finally picked it up. Phil.

"Hey," I said when I answered it.

"Merry Christmas," he said.

"Yeah, merry Christmas," I said. "What's up?"

"What are you doing later?"

I thought of all the glorious, terrible TV watching I had in front of me.

"Nothing," I said. Dad raised his eyebrows at that, even though he didn't know the question to which I was responding. I got up off the couch and moved the phone call into my bedroom.

"What are you thinking?" I asked.

"Want to go to the movies?" he asked. "I love to go to the movies on Christmas because there's no one else in the theater."

"Maybe," I said. "I'd have to ask my dad."

"You should definitely ask him," Phil said. He almost sounded chipper.

I assured him I'd do that.

"Also," Phil said, "I got you something."

"What?"

"I got you something," he repeated. "A gift on Christmas. It's a custom among my people."

"Oh," I said. "I didn't get you anything, Phil. We didn't talk about gifts."

"That's fine," he said. "You didn't have to get me anything. Going to the movies is all the present I need."

I grinned. For someone who claimed not to understand human interactions, he was hitting it out of the park on this one.

"Let me talk to Dad," I said. "I'll call you back."

Of course Dad said yes. He said he'd be able to drink all the eggnog and watch all the TV by himself if he had to. The sacrifices that man was willing to make for me.

Phil picked me up later and we saw some action thing. I honestly couldn't tell you what it was about or who the good guys were or what they were trying to keep the bad guys from doing, but Phil seemed to enjoy it. After the movie, he suggested we get dinner.

"Not at the Bully Burger," he said.

I agreed to eat a non-fast-food meal, and we went to a little place called the Spaghetti Warehouse, which was as charming as you might imagine from the name. It was the kind of place that used a Chianti bottle as a candle holder. Okay, I'll say no more.

After we ordered our food, Phil produced a manilla envelope seemingly from nowhere and handed it over.

"This is a really beautiful wrapping job you've done here, Phil."

He didn't say anything to defend himself, so I just went ahead and opened it.

I ripped off the top of the envelope and reached inside. I pulled out a comic book. I didn't understand at first. Had Phil bought me a single issue of a comic? Maybe money was tight in his house this year. Then I looked at the cover: *Zombie Hunter* it said in blood-dripping type across the top, and there in lurid color was a portrait of a girl who looked a lot like me facing off against a horde of the undead. *FIRST PULSE-POUNDING ISSUE,* it said in a burst.

"Oh, my God," I said. "It's your comic!"

"I just photocopied it at OfficeMax," he said. "But it is the very first copy, and it's yours."

"This is the best Christmas present I've gotten in years!" I squealed. God help me, I actually squealed. "Thank you. You need to sign it." That made him blush, but he smiled, too. I knew I was making a proper big deal out of this.

"Well," he said, "I hope you like it."

"You're about to watch me read it," I said, "so you'll be the first to know if I like it or not."

He started to protest that I shouldn't read it now, but I

ignored him. I didn't even stop when the waitress brought my lasagna.

It was all about a girl named Coral and her sidekicks, Bill and Brody, as they hunted zombies around Cherry City. They had an occasional ally, a good-looking black kid named Willis. Though it was revealed at the end that Willis was really a bad guy who mind-controlled zombies and only pretended to be on the good guys' side. I loved it from start to finish and told Phil so when I was done.

"Good," he said, and smiled. "I'm glad you liked it. I used it as part of my admissions package to the cartooning school."

This got more squeals from me. I was so happy he'd actually applied.

"It feels like everything is falling into place," I said. "You're going to go to school and learn comics, and I'm going to get into Columbia. It'll be perfect."

"It seems like it, huh?" Phil asked.

I'd been sitting across from him, and I scooted over to the chair right next to him.

"I hope you don't mind public displays of affection," I said. Before he answered, I laid a huge kiss on him. He returned it right away. I heard someone at a table whistle at us, but I didn't care.

When we broke, the waitress stood beside the table smiling down at us.

"Any dessert for you two," she said, "or did you just have it?"

Phil blushed a deep shade of red, which I thought was adorable. But, honestly, I still wanted dessert.

"May I have the tiramisu?" I asked. Phil ordered the spumoni and we ate our desserts sitting side by side, holding hands under the table. It must have been nauseating to witness, but I didn't care. Actually, it might have been the first time ever that at least half my brain wasn't taken up with wondering what other people were thinking of me. It was a feeling I wanted to get used to.

It was getting late after that, so Phil drove me home. I was eager to repeat this date, so I asked Phil, "What are you doing tomorrow?"

"Oh," he said. He looked embarrassed. "I didn't tell you? My aunt and uncle always rent a place on the beach, and we get together with some family friends the week after Christmas."

"No," I said. "You didn't tell me that."

"I'm sorry," he said. "I meant to."

I tried really hard not to get mad. I didn't want to spoil the evening. But man, I was pissed. How could he forget to tell me something like that? How does that just slip your mind?

"When will you be back?"

"We always come back the day after New Year's," he said.

Great, so I had to go a whole week without seeing him. "We can do something that day," he said. "And we'll have that whole weekend before school starts again."

I knew he was trying to make me feel better, and I let him believe he'd succeeded. I smiled, and laughed at his jokes, and let him kiss me good night, but inside I was in a deep funk. Part of me was angry at myself for taking it this way. This was Jane Austen territory—the mooning heroine, pining for her wayward paramour. Screw that.

I just wished my resolve matched my mood. I moped through the whole week. I wasn't really sure how Dad put up with me. Actually, toward the end of the week, he stopped putting up with it and went into the office to take care of "something."

Phil called a couple of times from the coast, but I let it

go to voice mail. After the third or fourth attempt to get me, he just left a message that said I should call him if I wanted to talk. Now I was caught in a spiral where it was up to me to act like an adult. Every time I picked up the phone, though, I'd find some reason not to punch in his number.

I did text him once, though, because texting is the passive-aggressive enabler that humanity had been waiting centuries for.

Sorry I haven't called. We'll talk when you get back.

I looked at that message for a long time before I hit send. Was it possible to compose a lamer message? I didn't think so. It might actually win some sort of award . . .

I finally overcame my pettiness and called him on New Year's Eve.

He answered on the first ring.

"If you wanted to get back at me," I said, "you would have let it go to voice mail."

"If I wanted to get back at you," he said. "Mostly I wanted to talk to you."

I heard party sounds in the background—laughing, music, drinking. I swear I heard drinking.

"I don't want to keep you," I said.

"Bullshit," Phil said. "I've been waiting to talk to you for a week. I'm not going to let you go so easily."

I'd called him a few minutes after ten, and we were on the phone for hours. He told me everything he'd been up to with his family and their friends since the moment they'd arrived in Seaside, and I told him about my many adventures moping around the house.

"Jesus, Phil," I said, "I drove my dad away. The most understanding man I know had to leave the house because of my crappy attitude!"

At one point, there was a burst of cheering in the background.

"Oh, man," I said. "I made you miss the New Year."

"I've always thought," he said, "that you need to spend the turning of the year doing what you want to do for the rest of the year. So I'm glad I spent it talking with you."

It was so corny, and yet I felt a lump form in my throat and tears well up in my eyes.

"Why are you so nice to me?" I asked.

"Must be because I like you," he said. "Go figure."

We talked a bit longer, but really that was the end of the conversation because with those six words, Phil had managed to kill me. Must be because he liked me. Yep. I was done.

We made vague plans to go kill zombies the night he got back. I'd have agreed to do anything with him then. Then we said good night and I went to bed and slept better than I had since I'd started acting like an idiot. Oh, I was still an idiot, but at least I knew I hadn't ruined things with Phil.

Two nights later, I sneaked out of the house and ran to Phil's car waiting at the curb. I wore a heavy jacket and thick wool socks inside my Dr. Martens because it was freezing. They'd actually predicted snow, which was pretty rare for Salem despite how much it rained.

I slid into the front passenger seat. I wanted to throw my arms around Phil's neck and start making out with him, but Cody sat in the backseat.

"Hey, Courtney," he said. "How was Christmas and New Year's?"

"Good," I said. "How about you?"

He shrugged. "You know what I got for Christmas?

Oh, it was a banner year at the old Bender family. I got a carton of cigarettes. The old man grabbed me and said, 'Hey, smoke up, Johnny.' "

Phil looked confused. "What?"

"You know," I said, "I never liked that movie. I know that's sacrilegious or whatever, but there it is."

"Oh, a movie," Phil said. That meant he felt safe to dismiss it. He pulled the car away from the curb. "Did you get ahold of Warren?"

"I thought it would just be us tonight," I said.

Cody broke into a huge grin at that. "Okay!"

"If that's what you want," Phil said.

"It's what I want," I assured him.

So we spent a while cruising around town looking for signs of zombies. It seemed like they were still on vacation somewhere. Didn't they realize we were ready to get back to work?

"Maybe we're sticking too close to town," Phil said. "Let's go a little farther out." No one else had a better idea, or any idea at all, so we headed out for the sticks.

We were somewhere on the far north edge of town when Cody got all jacked up in the backseat.

"Hold up," he said. "I think I saw someone. A few someones."

"What?" Phil asked. He'd idled the car in front of a little farmhouse.

"Kill the lights and back up," Cody said. Phil did. "Okay, stop!"

I couldn't see what Cody was talking about because the house blocked most of my view of the backyard, where the action seemed to be.

"Yes," Cody said. "Three, no four of them. They're in the back, milling around some sort of pen. Chickens or something."

"You're sure they're zombies?" Phil asked. "I don't want to roll up on some farmhands. Seems like a good way to get shot."

"Well," said Cody, "one of them is naked, and one seems to be missing an arm."

"That doesn't sound like farmhands," I said, "but I know country ways are mysterious to us city folk."

"Okay," Phil said, excitement creeping into his voice, "everyone grab their stuff out of the trunk. Let's do this."

A bitterly cold wind cut through me as I climbed out of the car. I speed-walked to the back of the car and grabbed my trusty wrecking tool from the trunk.

"Jesus," I said. The thing was freezing. How did I remember a coat, but forget gloves? "Let's start killing things so I can warm up."

"Is there a plan?" Cody asked.

"We run around the house and kill everything we see," Phil said. "As long as it's a zombie."

"You have the best plans," Cody said.

Phil led the way. As quietly as he was able, he opened the gate that let us into the yard. We ran across a big expanse of lawn and stopped at the corner. Cody looked quickly around the side of the house into the backyard.

"I think they're going after the chickens," he said. I heard birds squawking, so I was sure he was right. "We've gotta save those poor chickens."

"On three," Phil said. "One, two . . ."

We all started running, weapons at the ready. The zombies were trying to negotiate the chicken-wire fence that enclosed the coop. They looked up at us, as surprised as they could be since they were dead and all.

Phil was in the lead, and he swung his bat at the naked dude Cody had seen. Even though that one went down, he had to hit it a few more time before it stayed. I ran past him and took out the next zombie in line, a beefy jock type with half his face gone. Luckily my tool didn't get stuck in the dude's cranium like the last time I'd used it.

Cody ran past me and squared off against the third zombie. This one was a girl. She didn't look like much, short and skinny, but she was a fast zombie, so you never knew.

"You got her?" I asked Cody.

"Yeah," he said, "go get the last one."

The last one, another dude, was wrapped up in chicken wire so I thought he'd be easy pickings. He was a little older than the others we'd already taken on, maybe twenty or so, and he was another fast one.

He hissed as I approached him.

"Easy there, boy," I said like he was a dog or something. "I don't want to hurt you. I just want to bash your head in!" I lunged at him and he scooted away, chicken wire trailing behind him.

"Are you kidding me?" I said to no one in particular.

I heard squishy noises behind me and assumed that was Cody dealing with the chick. Phil came up and checked out the situation.

"Try to get around him," he said. "Cody, get up here. We'll play pickle with him."

I had no clue what that meant, but I got the general idea. I ran as hard as I could toward the back fence and swung at him when he came near. The zombie veered away from me and turned toward Cody. It was like a deadly version of reverse tag as we chased him all across the yard. At one point, the thing stopped running and I thought that maybe it was finally tired. All three of us converged on it, weapons at the ready.

At the last minute, it sprang at Phil, knocking him down, then ran past us and toward the front of the house. It was going to get away.

Just as the thing reached the corner, a black-clad figure stepped out, sword drawn, and sliced the top of the runner's head off. The thing actually ran for a few more steps before it realized it was a goner, then it just fell right on its face.

Cody and I helped Phil to his feet. We warily approached the guy who'd come to our rescue.

"Hey, Warren," Phil said.

Warren laughed as he pulled off his balaclava. "Guys," he said, "that was truly pathetic. The three of you couldn't handle one little ol' shuffler."

"He was a runner," Cody said. "And what are you doing here?"

"I picked you up back in town," Warren said. "I followed you for miles. I'm surprised you didn't figure out someone was on your tail."

"We weren't expecting to be followed," Phil said.

"Well," said Warren as he sheathed his sword, "you ought to be glad I did. That 'runner' was about to embarrass you all."

"Forgive me if I'm not too happy about that," I said. "Forgive me if I've had enough with boys showing up where they aren't wanted."

Warren looked at me like he was surprised to see me there. "Is that you, Courtney?" he asked. "I have to admit I'm surprised to see you and Phil hanging out."

I thought I was going to vomit. Warren wasn't really going to do this, was he?

"What's that supposed to mean?" Phil asked.

Warren looked at all of us, and he started laughing all over again. He actually doubled over. The son of a bitch. I thought about drawing my pistol and wiping the smile right off his face.

"You didn't tell him, Courtney?" Warren asked. "Well, why would you, I guess."

"Courtney?" Cody said.

Phil refused to look at anyone but Warren. "I asked what you're talking about."

"Phil," I said, "I was going to tell you."

"I didn't ask you," Phil said, his voice deadly calm. "I asked him."

Warren stopped laughing and took on a look of mock solemnity. "The last time we went out on a hunt," he said as I placed my hand on the butt of my pistol. Warren saw this and shook his head. "You won't do that," he said. Then he turned back to Phil. "Me and her had a nice little makeout session."

Everyone stood frozen. If it hadn't been for the wind, I'd have thought that time had stopped.

"We'd have gone further," Warren said. "But she suddenly got an attack of conscience."

"Why are you telling me this?" Phil asked.

Warren put his hand over his heart. "I knew she wouldn't, and I thought, as your friend, you had a right to know."

Phil's hand tightened on his baseball bat. "Make fun of me or Courtney again and I'll kill you, understand?" he asked.

Quicker than I thought possible, Warren drew his sword and brandished it at Phil.

"You really think you'd be able to manage that?" he asked.

"I bet the two of us could," Cody said and hefted his bat.

Christ, this was all getting out of hand. Someone was going to get hurt or killed, and all because I had poor impulse control.

"Everyone just stop," I said.

"Keep out of this, Courtney," Warren said. "I think this is between me and them."

"It's between you and your ass, you douche," I said. I stepped between him and the boys.

"I screwed up," I said to Phil. "I was going to tell you, I swear, but there was never a good time." A chirping sound started up, but I ignored it. "Please believe me when I tell you it was a mistake and I felt terrible about what I'd done."

"Courtney," Phil said, as the chirping sound continued.

"Please let me finish," I said. "I wish I'd said all of this a long time ago."

"Courtney," Phil said again, "answer your phone."

My phone? It rang in my pocket, but everyone who might call me was right here.

"My dad," I said. Dad had discovered I'd sneaked out. Oh, God, on top of everything, now I'd have to deal with being grounded again. I walked away from the boys—let them kill each other. I swallowed hard, thumbed the answer button, and brought the phone to my ear.

"Dad?" I said.

"Courtney?" Dad said. There was something wrong with his voice. "Thank God, are you with Phil, are you safe?"

That was a relative term, but I knew what he meant.

"Yeah, Dad," I said. "I'm safe, I'm with Phil. What's going on, Dad?"

"I'm not sure," Dad said. "Something outside woke me up. There are a lot of zombies outside the house. They're just milling around out there, I'm not sure why."

Him saying that triggered something, some deep memory, but I wasn't quite able to dredge it up, not that it was important now.

"Dad, did you call the police?" I asked. At that, Phil took a step or two toward me, then stopped.

"I did," he said. "Nine-one-one is on the landline. I told

them I needed to call you to make sure you were safe." I heard him rummaging around.

"What's that noise?" I asked.

"Digging the shotgun out of the closet," Dad said. "I doubt I'll need it, but you never know." He chuckled like he was trying to make me feel better.

"How long until the cops get there?" I asked. I realized I was crying.

"Oh, pumpkin," Dad said. "I didn't call you to upset you."

"Get me home!" I yelled at the boys. "Please just get me home!"

A floodlight sprang to life, plunging us into false day. Someone stepped out into the backyard from the house, and there was the sound of a shell being racked into a shotgun.

"Who's out there?" a voice demanded. "Did you get into my chickens?"

"What's going on there?" Dad asked. Those were the last words he ever said to me.

I heard Phil's voice cut in as he stepped up and guided me to the car. "Warren, explain what's going on. I need to get Courtney home. Cody, come on."

Without Phil's help, I'd have never found the car, the tears were falling so furiously. On the phone I heard Dad curse, then the sound of splintering wood and shattering glass. A *thud,* maybe the phone dropping. Dad cursed and there was a shotgun blast. And another.

Cody helped me into the front seat and closed the door. Phil already had the car started, and he sped off the moment Cody's butt was in the seat.

"What's going on, Courtney?" Cody asked. I ignored him.

I heard more shotgun blasts, but they weren't as loud,

like they were farther away. Had Dad moved down the hall?

More shots. Was that eight or nine? I'd lost count. He'd have to reload soon. Muffled shouting, thudding, then the sound of splintering wood again. And one last shotgun blast. There was nothing for a moment, then I heard my dad's anguished scream as the zombies fell on him.

I let out an animal wail that made Phil swerve the car. After that, I collapsed into the seat and sobbed. At some point the phone slipped from my hand and fell to the floor of the car.

As I wept, I was aware that Phil's hand rested on my leg. He didn't say anything, didn't try to soothe me, just let me be aware of his presence. Somehow that made me sob even harder.

I'd settled down some by the time Phil pulled the car in front of the house. The whole front section of the chain-link fence had been pushed down and the lawn had obviously been churned up by dozens of pairs of feet. The front door was split in half, part of it lying on the ground, the other barely still on the hinges.

I opened the gate and started walking across the lawn. Phil shouted after me to wait for the cops. I didn't listen.

Two zombies lay dead in the doorway. Another three were sprawled on the muddy, gore-soaked carpet in the living room. As soon as I entered the house, I smelled rotten meat and decay, and crap. I heard the phone making that screeching noise you get when you forget to hang up. I ignored it. I felt like I was in a dream as I walked down the hallway and drew my pistol from its holster. I stepped over another body to reach the bedroom at the end of the hall.

"Courtney?" Phil was back by the front door, taking in the scene I'd just walked through.

The door to Dad's bedroom looked like it had been

blown up; fragments lay all over. One more zombie was crumpled at the foot of the bed. When I saw what lay on top of the bed, I let out a strangled cry.

Dad had been laid out on top of the covers, and he'd been gutted—his insides all around him on the bed.

"Oh, Dad." I knew I'd have plenty of weeping ahead of me, but not then. Not yet.

I walked over to the bed and sat down next to my dad, careful not to sit in the blood that soaked into the covers. I put my hand on his cheek.

"Courtney." Phil stood in the doorway.

"Six of them," I said. Phil looked confused. "He had nine shots in that shotgun, and he got six of them." I caressed his cheek, felt the rough stubble on the palm of my hand. "This is your badass zombie hunter," I said.

Phil stood over the bed, unsure what to say or do.

"We need to go, maybe," he said. "They left him like this. He might . . ."

"I know," I said. He might turn. I also knew that he'd been left like this deliberately. They left him for me to deal with. Not they, him. Brandon.

I took my pistol in my hand and placed the barrel under his chin.

"I'd never let him have you twice," I said, and I pulled the trigger.

The shot was loud inside the room. It rang in my ears and the smell of cordite filled my nose. I stared up at the ceiling, refusing to look at what had become of my dad. Not that I would have seen anything; tears filled my eyes, refracting the light and making me blind.

"Get some things together," Phil said. "You can't stay here."

"Where am I supposed to go?"

"With me," he said. "You'll stay with me and my aunt and uncle."

I hung my head. "God, after what you just learned tonight?"

"I'm not happy with you right now," he said, "but I'm not going to abandon you after this. Please, get some things and let's go out and wait for the cops."

I let him help me up. We went into my bedroom and saw that it had been trashed. Everything had been up-ended, shattered glass crunched under our feet, and it looked like the mattress and bedding had been ripped to shreds.

"Looks like Brandon was upset to find you not at home," Phil said.

"I'm going to kill him," I said. "I mean it, that's not just something I'm saying."

"I know," Phil said.

He helped me find my backpack. I picked out a few pieces of clothing that weren't ripped or too covered in glass. Phil helped me get my desk upright and I found my laptop in the drawer where I kept it. It looked like it had made it through unscathed. That went into the bag, too.

All of the drawers had been pulled out of my dresser. I finally found the one with a false bottom—the false bottom Willie had made for me before he was killed by zombies last year. I removed the baggie of Vitamin Z and then threw the drawer down on the floor.

"I still need to get this to Dr. Keller," I said.

After that, I gathered some stuff from the bathroom.

"Is that everything?" Phil asked.

I thought for a minute. "Nearly," I said.

I went back into Dad's bedroom, careful not to look at him on top of the bed.

I went to his chest of drawers and opened the one that contained all the stuff he wanted to keep away from me. Underneath a pile of old *Playboys*, I found the gallon-sized Ziploc full of cash I'd earned in my time selling Vitamin Z for Buddha. Phil's eyes went wide when he saw the money. I put it into my bag.

We walked back into the living room. I didn't hear the screeching sound anymore. Phil must have hung up the phone.

By this time we heard sirens. The cops were finally on the way.

"Okay," I said, "now I'm done."

I had just enough time to stash my things in Phil's trunk before the cops arrived. They had surprisingly few questions. Turns out they'd heard most everything I did over the landline phone. Mostly they wanted to know where I'd been at the time of the attack. I told them I was out with friends. Then they wanted to know if I needed a place to stay. I looked over at Phil, who was answering his own questions.

"I have a place," I said.

The policeman gave me a couple of cards after that. One was for a crisis center that helped people out after losing loved ones to zombies, and another was a service that cleaned up houses after violent instances. That was what he called it, a "violent instance."

I thanked him and sat in the car to wait for Phil.

When he was done, he climbed in and got us going.

"The police will get Cody home," he said.

I didn't answer. It didn't seem like anything needed to be said.

Phil drove us to his place, and we didn't speak the entire way.

CHAPTER SEVENTEEN
Pretending to Be a Grown-up

I thought that losing my two best friends at the end of the previous school year might be some sort of preparation for losing my dad. I mean, years of school had taught me that anything could be dealt with if you just prepared and studied enough, right? Well, that was just stupid. There was literally no way you could prepare for so much loss.

I woke up every morning in the guest bedroom that Phil's aunt and uncle had been nice enough to provide for me, and I experienced the same crushing realization that Dad was gone. Every morning. God, that was the time I really should have learned that Hemingway quote.

The hardest thing I had to do in those first few days, maybe the hardest thing I had to do ever, was to attend the memorial service for my dad. Gene arranged it for me, for which I was super grateful. Since it was standard operating procedure to cremate folks in those days, I didn't have to worry about paying for a burial plot. We just had a little metal urn full of Dad's ashes on a stand up by the lectern, where a priest stood and told everyone how great my dad was even though they'd never met. Yes, we had a priest. Give me a break, I was looking for comfort wherever I could find it.

A whole ton of Dad's coworkers showed up, and a few of our neighbors. Dad didn't seem to have many friends

outside of work, but it was still nice to see how many people showed up. It was less nice when I realized that they
might all want to talk to me, to express their condolences.
That was just one long, sad parade that I barely made it
through.

My mom didn't come, but that might have been because I hadn't invited her. Must have slipped my mind.

Phil's aunt and uncle tried to make things as easy for me
as possible. I mean, they opened their home up to me and
told me to stay as long as I needed. They knew about my
mom, but they also knew there was some complicated history there. I really had no interest in moving to Seattle
halfway through my senior year of high school. I was
guessing that they didn't know that I'd messed up and
complicated my history with their nephew, too. I wonder
how openly they'd have welcomed me if they did. I guess
I was just lucky that Phil wasn't petty. It felt like he and I
were starting from scratch, sure, but he didn't denounce
me like I was the junior version of Hester Prynn.

Maybe things would have been easier somehow if he
had been as hard on me as I was on myself those days. I
blamed myself for everything—my rocky relationship
with Phil, my dad's death, the rise of a new zombie breed.
Man, that was a lot of blame for one girl to shoulder.

Even though things were bad in the months following
Dad's murder, there were some good things, too. Things
that are easier to point out in hindsight than they were at
the time. I mailed the Vitamin Z sample off to Dr. Keller,
along with a note asking that he please not ask me where
I got it—so I felt like I was helping in the anti-zombie effort. I hated like hell that I wasn't going to see him up in
Portland, but there was no way I could have done it just
then with everything that was going on.

The Army actually started reclaiming New York City.
This basically meant they had to go building by building

and door to door in a city that used to hold eight million or so people. I followed the news a lot in those days, and I took every bit of it personally. If the Army had a good day, I'd think it was a sign that things in my own life were getting better. If they experienced a setback of some sort, like when they lost a whole company of soldiers to a nest of zombies, then I believed that meant I'd never be able to make amends for all the things I'd done. It was crazy, but that was where I was.

The school insisted that if I didn't go to a support group, I'd have to at least visit with the school counselor. Ms. Bjorn and I had a history. When I was caught smoking Vitamin Z at the end of the previous year, I'd been ordered to visit with her about it. She was nice enough and I got that she meant well, but she'd told me right up front that she was required by law to disclose any criminal activities I might talk about. That made it difficult to talk at all, since criminal activities were the only kind I'd been involved in back then.

But after my dad died, it was different. I still had to avoid talking about selling drugs, but since I wasn't doing it on a daily basis, it was easier to talk. Boy, did I talk. I told her everything I could. Once a week, I found myself in her cramped little office, sitting across from her, a desk piled high with student files between us. She was really interested in my zombie-hunting exploits and why I felt compelled to do it.

"Well," I said, "zombies are pretty evil. I mean, look, they killed my dad." Also, I felt responsible because I had gotten a lot of people hooked on a drug that created new zombies. That part I didn't say.

"I know they killed your father, Courtney," she said. "But they hadn't killed him when you started hunting them. There must have been some motivator before that.

How about if you journal about what that might have been?"

I actually took the journaling seriously—given that there were certain subjects I didn't dare write about—and it did help me figure some things out. Whenever I found myself reluctant to sit down and write, I'd hear my dad's voice telling me that someone who wanted to get better had to trust in the process of healing, and then I'd get to work. Even in my imagination, Dad was full of psychobabble.

Something else that helped ease the pressure—really, two something elses—were that Crystal Beals and Elsa Roberts each approached me at different times to tell me how sorry they were that my dad had died. It was nice to have her talking to me again. She even told me she was sorry for getting so mad at me about Brandon and Vitamin Z.

The whole time she talked, I remembered Brandon talking about her, and I wondered if they were a thing. Somehow, I just couldn't bring myself to believe it.

"It was terrible of you to sell it," she said, bringing us back to the subject of my moral shortcomings, "but it was his stupid decision to smoke it and get hooked, you know?"

Gee, thanks, I thought.

"Anyway, he was the one making decisions," she said. "It was wrong of me to take it out on you."

And Elsa was a friend of a more recent vintage. She'd stopped talking to me when I experienced a temporary bump in social status as a result of dating Brandon last year. But both of them suggested we should get together sometime, and that made me feel good. Or at least it made me feel better. Good was probably a long way off.

It took the police about a month to wrap up their investigation. They decided that Dad had died by misadventure. I thought that was an interesting term for being ripped apart in a coordinated zombie attack.

The day after the case was closed, I got a call from a lawyer. Dad had left everything to me, and this lawyer, Rudy Alvarez, would handle all of it until I turned eighteen. I had to go to his office downtown and sign a bunch of papers. Alvarez had a slick smile and equally slicked-back hair. He looked like he'd just gotten back from his bus-stop-bench photo shoot. Gene went with me, which I really appreciated. Signing everything, I felt like I was pretending to be a grown-up. I expected someone to pull off my mask any moment, like on an episode of *Scooby-Doo*. Gene and the lawyer talked a lot about finance stuff. The lawyer was going to take care of getting the house cleaned, and he recommended hiring a management company to take care of it and to rent it out. He figured that there were always college kids looking for housing.

Gene told me that was a good idea—it would be a good monthly income. Not that I'd need it. Apparently, Dad had a rider on his insurance that paid out a crapload of money if he was killed in a zombie attack. I guess lots of people had that in those days.

The two of them decided to set up a bank account for me. They'd put a certain amount into it every month, and if I needed more than that, I had to contact the lawyer. I didn't know what to say for a minute—it wasn't every day you figured out you're a trust-fund baby profiting off your dad's untimely death.

"Is there anything else I can do for you?" Alvarez asked.

"Yeah," I said, "help me convince this guy to take money from me every month for rent." I hooked my thumb at Gene. "Because I know he'll say no."

Which he did. The lawyer finally brought him around by telling him that I could more than afford to help with household expenses. "Especially because she's asking to," Alvarez said. "She wants to contribute, it seems to me."

Gene agreed and I walked out of the office feeling better than when I'd walked in. At least now I knew I wasn't freeloading.

One night, about a month later, as I helped Gene clean up after dinner, the phone rang. Diane came into the kitchen and answered it.

"Hello," she said. She listened for a while without speaking. At one point she turned and looked at me and I got a chill. Finally, she said, "Just a moment, please." And she held the phone out.

"It's for you, Courtney," she said. "It's your mother."

I swallowed hard. I hadn't really expected her to call for some reason.

I took the phone and stood there staring at the receiver as Diane hustled Gene out of the kitchen.

Finally, I took a deep breath and put the phone to my ear. "Hello?" I said.

"Oh, baby," said a woman on the other end. She sounded like she'd been crying. "Courtney, I just heard about your dad. I'm so sorry, sweetie!" I didn't bother to point out that nearly two months had gone by since Dad's death.

"Thanks," I said. That felt sort of lame, so I added, "Thanks for calling."

"Of course, baby," she said. "I'd have called sooner, but I just found out. You know your dad and I weren't really close anymore."

You hadn't called in five years and you're reminding me that you weren't close with Dad? You don't say?

"Is there anything you need?" she asked.

I honestly couldn't think of anything I wanted from her.

"No," I said. "I'm fine. I'm staying with the family of a friend."

"Oh," she said, "that's great! I would have offered to have you come up here, but it's not a good time right now."

"No, that's fine," I said.

"You know, Bill and I are moving into the bigger house," she pressed on, talking to me like I knew all of this garbage she was spewing. "And then we need to get the nursery ready."

"The nursery?" I asked, and I immediately regretted it.

"Oh, you haven't heard," she said, breathless with excitement. "You're going to be a sister, Courtney! Isn't that exciting? I'm due in June."

I wondered if she remembered that *my* birthday was in June.

She blathered on for a while longer, but I had stopped talking. I don't think she noticed. I kept coming back to the fact that she was relieved when I told her I wouldn't be moving up to Seattle with her. Probably glad I wasn't going to be spoiling her nice new family.

I managed to hold it together while I was on the phone with her, but the moment I grunted good-bye and hung up, the tears welled up and spilled down my cheeks. I sat on the floor and just wept. For years I'd imagined finally talking to my mom, telling her very calmly how upset I was with her, cataloging her sins against me, Dad, and the world. Instead, I'd sat there and let her tell me all about her perfect little life. She probably thought I was excited for her!

I felt so dumb and small and useless.

At some point I heard someone walk into the kitchen and stand over me. After a second, he got down on the floor with me and wrapped an arm around my shoulder. Phil. He didn't try to comfort me by telling me it was going to be okay. That would have been a lie anyway. Instead, he just let me know he was there. He waited to hear what I needed from him.

"She didn't even want me," I finally choked out.

"We want you," he said. We. Not *I* want you, but "we." I'd take it for the time being.

He stayed there until I stopped, then he squeezed me one last time and let me go.

"I'm sorry about your mom," Phil said. "If she doesn't want you around, then she's an idiot. I can't believe you think she might have saved the world."

"I'm sorry," I said.

"Sorry for crying?" he asked.

"No, Phil," I said. "I'm not sorry for crying in front of you. I'm sure I'll be doing more of it." I took a deep breath. "I cannot believe you're making me say this," I then said. "I'm sorry about what happened with Warren."

He nodded, but didn't say anything.

"I was just frustrated and angry and hurt," I said, "and stupid. Can't forget that."

"Does seem kind of dumb," Phil said.

"And I've regretted it ever since it happened." I wiped my nose on the sleeve of my sweatshirt, which I'm guessing wasn't super attractive. "I know it hurt you, and I didn't ever want to do that."

"I know," Phil said.

"Can you forgive me?" I asked. I was so afraid of what his answer might be.

"Forgiving is easy," Phil said. "All you had to do was ask."

"I hear a 'but' coming."

"But," Phil said, "I'm still trying to trust you again. That's going to take a while longer."

"Anything I can do to speed up the process?"

"Just keep doing what you're doing," he said. "And don't make out with Warren anymore."

It took me a second to realize he was joking. I smiled at him and he returned it.

"I'll try," I said, "but sometimes it just happens. Like tripping. . . .

"Okay," I finally said when he didn't rise to my bait. "No more of that."

"Good," he said. He gave me another hug. "Let's go watch some TV or something. I'm sure my aunt and uncle are wondering what's going on in here."

I said that sounded like a good idea. Phil stood up. I was sort of bummed that he hadn't just forgiven me outright, but I understood where he was coming from. It was a huge relief to have apologized. I imagined it would have been easy to get addicted to it—apologizing, I mean. I pictured a life where I went around doing terrible crap and then basically got high from saying how sorry I was.

"What's so funny?" Phil asked.

"Just my brain," I said.

He held his hand out to me and helped me up.

"Well," he said, "it's nice to see you smile."

Seemed like someone else had told me that before. I decided to try to do it more often. Which was probably what I thought the last time I'd heard it.

Things became nicely uneventful for a few months after that. I hung out with Crystal a few times, and Elsa, too, so that was nice. I hunkered down and got serious about school. My plan was to take a year off after graduation and wait for Columbia to start accepting applications again. I knew that I was setting myself up for a possible disappointment by pinning all my dreams to just one college—a college that might never open again—but there was no way I'd be able to do anything differently. It had been the plan for so long, I couldn't imagine changing it.

The biggest thing that happened during that time was that we celebrated Phil's birthday. Gene and Diane sprang for all of us, including Cody, to go to Phil's favorite restaurant, a Vietnamese place that looked like it was one health-code violation away from being closed, but which actually had really awesome food. I got Phil some really nice pens and some art board—the guy at the art supply shop said it was the kind of paper that comics professionals use. Phil said he was super-excited to try it out.

And a couple of weeks later, we got to take Cody out for his birthday. It was just the three of us; I wasn't sure where his folks were. We went to a pirate-themed pizza place that was filled with really little kids running and screaming all over the place. It was crazy, but that was where he wanted to go. They also had a pretty decent arcade, including black-light laser tag. Phil bought him a collection of *X-Men* comics and I got him a gift certificate to a local record shop—which was exactly what Phil had told me to get him. Cody was so knocked out by all of it that it was a little sad, but I refused to get bummed out thinking about it and just had fun. This included lots of rounds of laser tag where I let Cody "kill" me.

Phil, Cody, and I kept going out on patrol, but we never saw any zombies. Phil thought that maybe a lot of them had been killed in the assault on Buddha's place. He forgot that they were still able to muster enough forces to attack my house and kill my dad. I didn't bring that up, because there was nowhere good it might have led.

"I think they're lying low," I said. "You know, biding their time, waiting for us to put down our guard. Saving their strength until just the right time."

It was early May by this time, and we had the windows rolled down as we drove. The sky was cloudless and I thought that the city looked nice right then. In darkness. No way would I ever think that in the full light of day.

"Jeez, Courtney," Cody said. "They're the undead, not a division of Nazi tanks or something."

"I don't know," Phil chimed in. "She's been right about most everything else zombie-related."

"Thank you," I said to Phil. Then I flipped Cody the bird and blew him a raspberry.

"I love you, too, Courtney," he said.

"What do you think they might be planning?" Phil asked.

That was the question, and I had no idea what the answer was. I'd applied all of my power to channel Nancy Drew, but I wasn't able to think of a single damn thing. We'd all noticed that kids at our school had stopped disappearing—something I attributed to the explosion at Buddha's and the fact that Vitamin Z had dried up overnight. Drug dealers in other towns hadn't rushed in to fill the vacuum, either. I think the fact that the Army patrolled the highway made that pretty difficult. At least until these theoretical drug dealers figured out who to bribe, anyway.

I threw up my hands. "I have no idea what they're thinking. But we need to figure it out—they're not going to stay quiet forever."

And I had a really bad feeling that whatever they did, at least part of it would be aimed at me personally. Brandon apparently held a grudge. Even in the afterlife, he didn't accept that I'd dumped him. He was like the undead version of Billy Zane in *Titanic*.

"We're not going to see any shufflers tonight," I said. "Let's go to the Safeway and get a soda. The one on Center has one of those magic fountains where you can combine all the flavors."

No one had any objections, so a few minutes later, we pulled into the parking lot. Off in the far corner of the lot, four or five cars were grouped together, and a bunch of kids stood in the beams of their headlights, just talking and laughing. I never really understood hanging out in parking lots, but I know it was a major pastime for a lot of my classmates. We heard kids laughing as we pulled to a stop.

"Have you noticed people seem happier or something at school?" Phil asked.

"Everyone's getting squirrelly for the end of the year," Cody said. "Finals are in three weeks, graduation is a week after that. We're almost done!"

"If we survive that long," I said.

"You are always such a ray of sunshine," Cody said.

We climbed out of the car and headed toward the store.

"Courtney?" someone, a girl, called out. "Is that you?"

This same someone waved at me from the group at the far end of the lot. I had to squint against the brightness of the headlights.

"Courtney, come on over," she called.

"Crystal?" I yelled.

"Yeah," she said. "Come say hi!"

"We're going inside to get sodas," I said. "We'll be right back."

"Bring a bag of Doritos!" she yelled at me as we went into the store. We all got our drinks—lime Vanilla Coke for me, thanks!—and I grabbed a bag of Doritos. The boys went off in search of Twinkies and I loitered near the front of the store as they completed their quest. As I studied the covers of the magazines at the checkout stand—I'd never lower myself to actually touching one of them—I heard a man call my name.

I turned and saw a middle-aged Latino guy standing there in shorts, flip-flops, and a Western Oregon University sweatshirt. He had a cart piled high with food, and a little boy in the kid's seat. I sort of smiled, not sure if I knew the guy.

I took in his Fu Manchu mustache. Then my mouth fell open. "Chacho?"

"Took you long enough," he said. "Do I look that different out of my uniform?"

"Yes!" I said. You look like a human dad, not a killing machine.

I walked over to where he was, and his little boy—a beautiful little kid with huge brown eyes and an unruly mop of brown hair—tracked my every move.

"Is this your boy?" I asked, even though there was no one else who could have fathered the kid.

"My youngest," Chacho said. "Say 'hi,' Anthony."

"Hi," the boy said, and I nearly wet my pants from cuteness overload.

I kept wanting to stare at Chacho. The reality of the situation was a function my brain refused to compute. Running into him out in the real world was like seeing one of your teachers outside of school, but times one million because I'd never seen any of my teachers wearing riot gear and smashing in zombie skulls.

"What are you up to tonight?" Chacho asked.

"Just hanging out," I said. "Wasting my youth, stuff like that."

"Good for you," he said. "Waste it while you got it." He raised his hands to indicate the cart and all its contents and, by implication, all the responsibilities of adulthood. It was a very eloquent gesture.

"Well, I gotta go," he said. "Gotta get this one to bed." Anthony started shaking his head. "Yes," Chacho said to him in mock seriousness, "it's bedtime when we get home." The kid giggled like that was the funniest thing he'd ever heard.

"Yeah," I said. "I'll see you around."

"Sure," Chacho said. "Oh, that reminds me. I'm having a barbeque next Saturday. You should come. Bring your little boyfriend."

My little boyfriend. "Um, maybe, sure."

"You still have the same number as when you worked at the Bully?"

"I do," I said.

"Okay, I'll text you the address," he said. "I'm gonna grill up a tri-tip. My wife is making potato salad, a pot of beans. We'll start fattening you up."

I touched my belly. I didn't know if I liked the sound of that.

"Have a good one, Courtney," he said as he pushed the cart away. "Don't get into too much trouble tonight."

"I already tried and it didn't take," I said. "See you later."

Phil and Cody walked up, Cody slurping on his soda. Phil watched Chacho walking away.

"Who were you talking to?" he asked.

"That was Chacho," I said.

Phil did a double-take that made my whole night.

"That's not Chacho," he said. "That guy's wearing flip-flops. Chacho would never wear flip-flops!" He sounded offended at the thought.

"And yet," I said.

"Who's Chacho?" Cody asked.

"He's like the Terminator's cool older brother," I said.

"Which variety?" Cody asked skeptically.

"T-100," Phil said, "obviously."

Cody seemed suitably impressed, and we went to the ten-items-or-less—which really needs to be the ten-items-or-fewer—line to pay for our stuff. My treat, since I suddenly found myself in a much higher income bracket than anyone else I knew.

After we made our purchases, we headed for the exit.

"You guys ready for this?" I asked the boys.

"Sure," Phil said. "Why not?"

"Ready like Freddy," Cody said.

"If you say anything else that dumb when we're with those people," I said, "I *will* make you wait for us in the car."

He had the gall to look hurt.

"Let's do this," I said.

Crystal whooped when she saw us emerge from the store, and she ran toward us as we got close. I thought she was just super-excited about the Doritos I'd bought her, but she actually threw her arms around me and gave me a huge bear hug. Or the closest thing to it she was able—a cub hug? That close, I smelled her breath. She'd been drinking. That explained a lot.

"It's so great to see you," she said as she tore herself away. "Come say hi to everyone!"

"Everyone" turned out to be a bunch of people I vaguely knew from school. There were a few folks I knew going all the way back to grade school. To those people, I said hi. Everyone else got the standard chin nod by way of greeting.

"This is my friend Phil," I said, indicating the person standing next to me.

"Oh, I know Phil," Crystal said. "We're in English together."

"That is true," Phil said. "Hi, Crystal."

"And who's your other friend?" Crystal asked. "What school do you go to?" That last question was directed at Cody.

"Are you kidding?" he asked. "I go to school with you. I was in History with you all last year."

She squinted at him in a really exaggerated way, but I knew that she wasn't picking up any hits from her memory.

"Are you sure?" she asked.

Before he exploded, Phil guided Cody away to another pod of people. Phil apparently knew them. As they walked away, I heard Phil say, "She's drunk, Cody." He sounded like that cop who talks to Jack Nicholson at the end of *Chinatown*: "Forget it, Jake. It's Chinatown."

"Courtney, do you know Gabe Toye?" Crystal asked me.

Gabe was one of those kids I'd gone to school with since first grade, something Crystal might have remembered if she was sober. He was a good-looking kid, in a beefy all-American way. He stood there grinning at me in a way that I immediately disliked. It was patronizing or condescending or something.

"I think we've met," I said, and that patronizing smile grew bigger.

"Gabe just found out today that he got accepted to . . . Where was it, Gabe?"

"University of Montana," he said. I did not roll my eyes.

"He's going to study making movies," Crystal said.

"Media theory," Gabe corrected her.

"Wow," I said. I sipped on my soda so I wouldn't be expected to say anything else.

"Gabe was just telling me about his application essay," Crystal said. "Tell Courtney what you wrote about."

"*Scooby-Doo*," Gabe said.

The answer was so unexpected that I burst out laughing. That patronizing smile faltered a little bit.

"What about *Scooby-Doo*, exactly?" I asked.

"I wrote about how the show is a rationalist anti-fairy tale," he said. "It basically teaches children that there are no such things as monsters or the supernatural."

I waited to see if there'd be more, but he just crossed his arms and leaned back. His trademark smile was back.

"That's interesting," I said. It wasn't. It also wasn't very original or deep. "But I think you missed the point of the show." Crystal giggled and Gabe looked at me like I was speaking a foreign language. I was sure he wasn't used to people disagreeing with him or challenging him in any way. How boy-like.

"*Scooby-Doo* is a horror story," I said, "just not the kind you expect it to be. It's actually an existential horror story where the kids learn again and again that the true monsters are people. All someone needs is some distancing technique, like, you know, a mask, to feel comfortable committing a crime.

"I mean, it's got more in common with *Crime and Punishment* than it does with *Tom and Jerry.* You know?"

Crystal's smile got bigger and bigger as I spoke, and Gabe's frown deepened.

"I mean, that's just off the top of my head," I said. "I'm sure I'd be able to flesh it out a bit more if I was going to write an essay about it."

"Oh, Gabe," Crystal said as she laid a hand on his chest, "don't be mad that Courtney is smarter than you. She's smarter than *everyone.*"

"Yeah, cute," Gabe said. "I'm going to go talk to some guys over there." He pointed his chin in a vague direction and then stalked away.

"I don't think he liked my theory," I said.

"Oh, God," she said. "*Scooby-Doo.* He just wouldn't shut up about it. I knew you'd put him in his place."

"You could have just told him to leave you alone," I said.

"Oh, God," she said. "I'd never do that! That's so rude."

That made me laugh because she didn't think that using me like some kind of smarty-pants guided missile was rude at all.

"So, how about you? Have you heard back from any of your colleges yet?" she asked me. "I'm still waiting on the Evergreen State College and Beloit. I got into U of O, but that's my safety school."

"I didn't apply anywhere," I said.

She looked at me like I'd farted in church or proclaimed my hatred for UGGs.

"I want to go to Columbia," I said. "I've had my heart set on it forever, and I'm willing to wait until they re-open it."

"So what are you going to do next year?" she asked. "Work?"

"Maybe," I said. "Or I might volunteer somewhere. I haven't given it too much thought."

"Wow," she said. "My dad would blow his top if I didn't go directly to college."

Worse than what she said was the look on her face as it slowly dawned on her what she had said. She clasped her hand to her mouth like she was holding back a scream.

"Oh, God, Courtney," she said. "I am so sorry."

"It's okay," I said. "You don't have to police everything you say around me. And the truth is, my dad and I talked about it a few times before he died. He wasn't crazy about the idea of me taking a year off, but he also didn't think it'd be good for me to rush into school if I wasn't fully committed."

"Well," said Crystal. "I'm still sorry. I feel like a douche."

"You are probably the least douchey person I know," I told her.

"You know," she said, and she frowned as she said it, "I wish we'd stayed close like we were before high school. I really miss you sometimes—and the stupid crap we used to do, you know?"

I took another sip of my drink to cover the fact that I didn't know what to say. I was not prepared for Crystal to enter the maudlin phase of drunkenness, especially not with me as the target for her tears. Thankfully, this was Crystal Beals, and her being depressed lasted about five seconds.

"Oh! Have you heard?" she exclaimed, all hints of sadness evaporated like a drop of dew in the face of a nuclear blast.

"Um, I don't know," I said.

High-pitched laughter and the sound of breaking glass came from somewhere in the depths of the group. I saw that it was time to wrap this up soon.

"They announced the details of the senior kegger!"

"That's great," I said.

"You're going, right?" She grasped my arm like my answer was the most important thing she was able to imagine.

The senior kegger was a tradition going back at least to the 1970s—so, *ancient*. It was interrupted for a couple of years right after the dead came back, but nothing could keep teenage kids from drinking, so it came back. It's a yearly party, a huge blowout for all of the seniors. *All* of the seniors, no one excluded. It's one of the few democratic social events on the high school calendar. It's also highly illegal. The cops shut down about 75 percent of the parties before they even start, despite the fact that the seniors who plan it bring an eye for detail to the task that made Dwight Eisenhower look like he just threw together D-day at the last minute.

Of course Crystal was among the first to know where the party was going to be.

I looked at her smiling, hopeful face, and I felt my heart sink. I really hadn't planned to go, but how could I disappoint that face?

"I'm not sure," I said. "They always get raided, and then everyone gets a minor-in-possession. Not sure if that's the best way to kick off the summer."

"It will totally not be busted this year," she said. "Michael and Dillon and Tyler have a foolproof plan for keeping the location a secret." I recognized those names; they were all members of the ruling Jocktocracy. I didn't think those knuckleheads could come up with a foolproof plan for picking their noses, but I thought I'd humor Crystal.

"Yeah," I said. "I'll think about it. Where's it going to be?"

"Can't tell you," she said with a grin.

"How am I going to get there if I don't know where it is?" I asked.

"That's just it," she said. "They won't tell anyone until the day of the kegger. You'll have to text a number and they'll text back with the location."

I was able to see several flaws in this well-thought-out plot. The first one was that all it might take to bust the party was one fat-mouthed kid telling their parents or the cops what the number was to text. I didn't point this out.

"Okay," I said. "Like I said, I'll think about it."

I looked around for Phil and Cody. I spotted them on the far side of the group talking to some girls.

"It was good to see you, Crystal," I said. "I'm going to go find Phil."

"I really hope you'll come," she said. "It might be our last time to hang out before we all go off to real life."

She didn't let me leave before I assured her several times that I really meant to think about it. Okay, I might have lied and said I would be there for sure, which I hated to do, but man, I needed to get out of there. The crowd was getting rowdier and louder. There was more breaking glass. As I skirted the crowd to get to Phil and Cody, a shoving match broke out between two meatheads. It was pure play yard stuff, but it was a general indicator that we needed to scoot.

"Hey, Courtney," Phil said as I approached. "I think it's time to go."

"I was just thinking the same thing," I said. A beer can, hopefully empty, sailed past us to punctuate the point.

"Go?" Cody said. "Why would we go?" He'd obviously been talking with a girl, a pretty, somewhat chubby girl who looked sort of familiar to me, but I wasn't able to place her. She had apparently been talking back to him. I understood his reluctance.

"Have you been paying attention to what's going on around you?" I asked. I saw him looking at the girl and realized that, no, he hadn't been paying attention to anything else.

"The cops are going to be here any minute, Casanova," I said. "Say good-bye to your new friend if you don't want to end up with an MIP." I pointed at the red Solo cup he held in his hand.

"Really?" he asked.

Phil just nodded.

"Okay," he said. But he said it in the same way he might ask us to punch him in the junk.

"I have your number," he said to the girl. "I'll call you, okay?"

"Sure," she said. "We need to get out of here, too." She indicated her posse of bored-looking girlfriends.

Even though he'd agreed to go, Phil still had to grab Cody's arm and drag him away.

As we pulled out of the parking lot and toward home, I heard sirens in the distance. I wondered how many kids would have a bummer of a story to tell come Monday.

"Who was your friend?" I asked Cody. "She seemed nice."

"Didn't she?" he asked. "Her name is . . ." He dug a folded piece of paper out of his pocket and consulted it. "Hannah."

I started laughing at that, which just made Cody mad, which just made me laugh more.

"Stay gold, Ponyboy," I said when I was finally able to breathe again. "Stay gold."

"I swear I don't understand half the crap that comes out of your mouth," Cody said in a huff.

That just made me laugh even harder.

And that was a pretty good wrap-up to the day.

CHAPTER EIGHTEEN
Areas of Concentration

Mondays were one of the days that I spent the afternoon at the community college for my Organic Chemistry and Biology classes. This was the college where my dad taught, so people, mostly teachers and administrators, were always seeking me out to give me their condolences, offer help, and such. I knew they meant well, but sometimes the last thing you want is to be confronted with the fact that your dad is dead. Especially when you already woke up every morning thinking about him.

By the time I got home, I was always exhausted—emotionally if not physically. That following Monday was no exception.

I mumbled something incoherent when Diane asked how my day had been, then I told her I was going to rest for a little bit before I helped her with dinner.

I closed the door to my room and lay down. Then I figured I'd surf online at the same time. Just because I was resting didn't mean I couldn't multitask.

I dragged my laptop out of my bag and onto the bed beside me. I fired it up and closed my eyes while I waited for it to come to life.

I opened one eye when an alert sounded telling me I had some unread e-mail.

I brought up the e-mail tab and gasped. I'd gotten a note from Dr. Keller. I sat up and clicked on the message.

Subject: Thank you

Dear Miss Hart (Courtney hereafter),

Thank you very much for sending me the sample of Vitamin Z. As you requested, I won't ask how you got it, but hope someday we might be close enough that you'll share. I'm sure it's quite a story.

My colleagues have been studying the sample, and while they have made no great discoveries as of yet, it has given them several avenues to explore which they had not previously considered. Again, we owe you a debt of thanks.

Speaking of debts, I recall from one of your earlier e-mails (actually, I don't need to recall it, I simply looked up our past correspondence) that you were interested in attending Columbia University. As I'm sure you know, the Army has begun the process of reclaiming the city from the hordes of zombies that currently occupy it. What you may not know is that there is a plan in the works to reopen Columbia as soon as possible once that is accomplished. The administration-in-exile is optimistic that they can be opened to students as soon as the beginning of next school year.

Why might I bring this up? A number of instructors and researchers from every field taught at Columbia have already pledged to return once classes resume. We have been asked to reach out to prospective students to help fill the ranks for that first year. If you are still interested in attending Columbia, Courtney, I would be happy, honored, to offer you my highest recommendation to the admissions board.

There was more, but that was the point where I started whooping in joy.

About two seconds later, my bedroom door burst openand Phil stood there, wild-eyed, looking for signs of danger.

I sprang up and nearly tackled him in a hug. He looked at me, a complete lack of understanding all over his face. Suddenly I couldn't stop myself. No matter what, there was no way to keep my lips off that face for another moment.

I kissed him, a huge, wet, openmouthed kiss, and after a second, he joined me.

I don't know how long we kissed, but we only stopped when Phil's aunt cleared her throat behind us.

"Is everything all right, Courtney?" she asked.

"I'm going to Columbia," I said. They both looked surprised and I laughed. I felt so buoyed, so high. I let go of Phil and grabbed my laptop off the bed. I read the e-mail aloud to them (minus the opening paragraphs about obtaining the sample of Vitamin Z) and by the time I was done, Diane was hopping up and down, clapping her hands. All thoughts of me violating her nephew were long gone. She took the two of us in a group hug.

"This is amazing news, Courtney," she said. "And I can't think of anyone who deserves it more than you. Oh, I need to call Gene. We'll have to celebrate tonight!"

She went off to make plans and left Phil standing in my room somewhat awkwardly.

"Sorry about the kiss," I said. "I was caught up in the moment, you know?"

"Yeah," he said. "You deserve to be. It's great news. I'm really happy for you."

"Thanks," I said. "And I know you're going to get into the comics school. We'll both head out there together."

"I hope so," he said. "If it happens like that, it might lead to more kissing . . ."

I smiled so big I thought my cheeks were in danger of splitting.

"Oh, I don't think we have to wait for that."

I wrapped my arms around his neck.

"No," he said, "but we do have to wait until my aunt isn't in the next room."

Killjoy.

"Fine," I said, and gave him one quick peck as an act of defiance. "I'll behave. Now I need to finish reading this," I said. I sat back on the bed and put the computer in my lap.

Phil watched me for a second before going back to his room and his homework.

The rest of Dr. Keller's e-mail detailed how to go about applying, if I was still interested. Yes, sir! I wrote him a quick response, telling him that I was most definitely still interested, and to thank him.

My only regret right then was that my dad wasn't around for me to talk to. I'm pretty sure he'd have been happy for me.

So, thinking about Dad, I got to work on the application materials.

Working on the application kept me occupied for a while. I had to track down my transcripts and have them forwarded to the university's admissions department. I needed to get people to write letters of recommendation (besides the one Dr. Keller was writing)—I asked my Organic Chem instructor, Professor Kassovitz, and the high school's counselor, Ms. Bjorn. I figured she knew me better than most of the staff at school, and I thought she'd be sympathetic. I also needed to write a couple of essays.

Normally writing an essay was something I'd be able to do in my sleep, but these were supposed to be about me and why I wanted into Columbia. I agonized over every word. For the first time since I was a freshman, I went to the school's writing center and got several people to critique what I'd written.

Finally, after about a hundred drafts—I'm not kidding—I gathered everything together in one e-mail and shipped it off to Dr. Keller for him to look over and forward to admissions.

I collapsed on my bed and thought I'd sleep for a million years.

Phil came in and sat on the edge of my bed.

"Go away," I said. "I'm not here."

He rubbed my leg.

"You can stay if you keep doing that," I said.

"Did you send it off?" he asked.

"Yes."

"Then you're ready to blow off a little steam?" he asked.

"What sort of steam-blowing were you thinking about?" I asked. If it had anything to do with the leg rubbing, I was in. I tried to remember if Gene and Diane were in the house.

"It's Saturday," Phil said, like that was an explanation.

"I'm not following you," I said.

"Chacho's party is today," he said. "Did you forget?"

"Of course not," I said. But I totally had. "Do I have time for a nap?"

"No," he said.

I wanted to mount a brilliant verbal defense that would make him leave me alone to sleep. What came out of my mouth was, "Blargh."

"Exactly," Phil said. He stood up. "Let's go. We have to stop at the store on the way. Can't arrive empty-handed."

It took more effort to get out of that bed than it had

ever taken for me to do anything, but I got up, put on clothes that a human person might wear, and followed Phil out to the car.

In the end, of course, I was really glad I went.

Chacho had texted me the address, and he lived not too far from Phil's place. His house was tiny and immaculate. So was the yard. It looked like something out of a magazine photo essay. Like, Martha Stewart would have been proud to claim it as her own. The only thing spoiling the effect was the fence that surrounded the yard. It was to other chain-link fences what a Sherman tank is to a VW Bug. Easily six feet tall with heavy metal support beams, it looked more secure than the fence at our school. I bet the supports were nice and deep. It'd probably repel a whole army of zombies. Well, I knew where I was heading during the next undead uprising.

The gate stood open, which seemed bad from a security standpoint, but there were a lot of people, mostly kids, hanging out in the front yard, so they'd have been able to close it in case of shufflers, I guess. The kids all openly stared at us as we walked past. I waved, feeling self-conscious. Phil seemed not to notice.

"He must be in the back," he said. "You can smell the barbecue."

It was a good guess. We went around the side of the house and as soon as we turned the corner, we saw Chacho. He was dressed even more casually than the last time I saw him. I knew he wasn't going to be wearing his security outfit to grill for family and friends, but I just wasn't ready for him to be shirtless and wearing cut-off jeans.

"Hey, you made it!" he hollered from behind a very complicated-looking piece of machinery, which I assumed was a grill of some sort.

We walked over, Phil handing over the gallon of store-bought fruit salad we'd brought.

"You didn't have to do that," Chacho said, "but thanks." He set the salad on a table already groaning under the weight of all the food it held.

"Hey, love," he called in the general direction of a group of women who stood a ways off talking and laughing. "Come over here. Someone I want you to meet."

A pretty, tall blond woman detached herself and walked over. I don't know why, but I'd expected Chacho's wife to be Mexican, too. Mexican or Latina or I wasn't sure of the politically correct term. I'd just not mention ethnicity.

"This is my wife, Karla," Chacho said, and she shook our hands and said hello. "Karla, this is Phil and Courtney."

At the mention of my name, she stopped for a second and really looked at me. I felt like I wanted to shrink. What the hell had he said about me?

"Hi, Courtney," she said. "I've heard a lot about you from Michael."

"Michael?" I asked. "That's your name?"

Chacho frowned and looked at his wife, hurt. "Karla."

"I'm sorry," she said. "Were you trying to keep up the tough-guy act? It doesn't work so well when you're dressed like that."

"It gets hot behind the grill," Chacho said.

I knew that I was going to like Karla just as much as I liked her husband.

"My boys are running around over there somewhere," Chacho pointed to a big group of kids who were tearing it up back along the fence. "At this point, I couldn't tell you which ones are mine."

"Maybe if they sit still long enough to eat, we can introduce you," Karla said.

"Courtney, you should ask my wife about her job," Chacho said. "Karla's a nurse. Courtney wants to be a doctor or something, right?" he asked me.

She and I walked off and talked while Phil stayed behind and pretended to help Chacho with the grill. Turns out Karla was a registered nurse who now worked almost exclusively as a nurse/midwife. She had to work with doctors all the time, which was why Chacho thought we needed to talk.

I explained that I really wanted to be an epidemiologist and not the kind of doctor that saw patients and stuff. Despite that, she had some interesting things to say about the schooling and what you needed to do to get through it.

She asked where I planned to go to school and I told her about the deal with Columbia and Dr. Keller. She stopped and appraised me again.

"Michael said you were a sharp one," she said. She seemed to approve.

"Okay, everyone," Chacho called. "The tri-tip is ready. Paul, go get the folks from the front yard. Make sure the gate gets closed, okay?" A teenage boy said okay and ran around the house.

A long line of people with paper plates formed up on either side of the table. I hadn't thought I was that hungry, but as soon as I saw—and, more importantly, smelled—all that food, I was starving. I took just a little of everything, which still meant my plate was overflowing. Phil and I sat on the grass underneath a big shade tree with Chacho and his family. They managed to wrangle their boys over. Anthony I'd met at the store, and he recognized me enough to sit right down next to me and peer into my face until I smiled at him. Chacho's older boy, Tomas, barely looked at me before he ate a few bites and then ran off again. Anthony followed him because I guess that's what little brothers did.

"I'm sure they'll be hungry later," Karla said as she watched them run off.

"Yeah," Chacho said, "right before bedtime."

They grinned at each other and it made me feel warm inside to see the two of them happy. It was sort of a weird feeling since I barely knew either of them.

"You two make beautiful babies," I said. They both smiled at me. "No, seriously, you two could breed, like, an army of super handsome children."

"We'll take that under advisement, Courtney," Karla said. She turned to Chacho. "Did she tell you her news, Michael?"

"What news is that?" he asked around a mouthful of food.

I repeated the story about Columbia and Dr. Keller. Chacho looked impressed.

"No shit," he said, and when Karla gave him a disapproving look, he didn't miss a beat and said, "No kidding. Well, that's great, Courtney. I'll be sorry to see you go, but I knew there was no way you'd be stuck in this town forever."

"It's not a for-sure thing yet," I said. I felt I needed to hedge my emotional bet just in case I didn't get in.

"It'll happen," Chacho said.

"And what's wrong with this town?" Karla asked.

"It's fine for us old fogeys," Chacho said, "but not for kids who want to go out and save the world."

Karla harrumphed and turned to Phil. "And what about you, Phil? What do you plan to do next year?"

He told them how he'd applied to the cartooning school. That really got Chacho excited.

"You're gonna draw comics?" he asked. "That's great. I'll tell the kids, they'll love that. Maybe you could draw them some pictures."

"Sure," Phil said, "that'd be fun . . ." He looked at me uncertainly. I just shrugged. There was no way he'd say no after the meal we'd just had, and how nice Chacho and Karla had been.

"Only if you want to," Karla said. She smiled at him to let him know he could say no.

"No," Phil said. "I'd love to. It'll be fun."

So after everyone had eaten and everything had been put away, and quite a few folks had left, Phil sat down with the kids who were left and started drawing. At first he drew whatever came to mind, but pretty soon the kids called out requests and he did his best to satisfy them. "Vampire T-Rex" was the most interesting.

Chacho and I sat at the table, which had been cleared of food. We watched Phil for a while.

"He's a good one," Chacho said.

"He is," I agreed.

"Not like your last one."

The last one definitely turned out to be no good, that was for sure.

"Let me run something crazy by you," I said.

He sat forward and squinted at me. "Is this about zombies?"

"It is," I said.

"Okay," he said. "I had a feeling this was coming."

"Why?" I asked.

"Because you're more absorbed with zombies than anyone I know."

I think he meant obsessed, but I let it go. Instead, I told him everything that had happened in the last few months. Everything, which meant letting him in on my less-than-legal activities when I worked at the Bully Burger.

"How long did you do that and no one caught on?" he asked.

"A long time," I said. "Like, a year."

He shook his head, but let me go on. I reminded him how last year I'd felt that zombies were getting smarter, that I'd been ambushed a couple of times. Then there was the zombie attack out at Brandon's cabin. That definitely felt coordinated. This year there was the assault on Buddha's place and then the group that killed my dad.

"I didn't know about that," Chacho said. "I'm sorry."

"Thanks," I said, "but what do you think of my theory?"

He scratched his chin and thought for a while before answering. I sipped on my lime-flavored Jarritos. The sky was starting to turn the color of an old bruise and soon it was going to be too dark for Phil to keep drawing.

"I think two things," Chacho finally said. "One is that I don't know if I believe you. Just stop." He held up his hand to keep me from arguing with him. "Let me finish. I don't know if I believe you because I haven't seen any change myself in the zombies. The ones I see at the Bully Burger seem the same to me.

"But, okay, saying that, I don't know if I need to believe you." He rubbed his bald head and took a drink of the beer that sat in front of him. "I know you believe it, and that's enough."

My heart beat faster. I could live with him not believing if it meant he didn't outright dismiss me believing it.

"So, an enemy that uses coordinated attacks, right?" he asked, and I nodded. "When I was in Iraq, the Taliban, they would target areas of concentration."

"How do you mean?" I asked.

"Markets," Chacho said, "mosques, army barracks, police stations. Anywhere the numbers of people concentrated. That's where they sent in suicide bombers.

"Once I got home, it took me years to feel comfortable in a crowd of more than three or four people."

"Then where does that mean they might attack?" I said. "Because it feels like something's coming down the road."

"I don't know, Courtney," he said. "You're gonna have to figure that out on your own."

"Thanks for not thinking I'm crazy," I said.

Chacho grinned. "I never said that."

Karla came out and sat in Chacho's lap. She sipped off his beer while we all watched Phil with the kids for a while.

"We really need to get those boys off to bed," she finally said.

"Yeah," Chacho agreed. "It's getting late."

"It was very nice to meet you, Courtney," Karla told me and she gave me a hug. "I hope you'll come by again before you leave for New York."

I told her I'd like that and she went over to gather her kids, and to say good night to the last few partygoers.

"You should come back for sure," Chacho said. "Bring Phil. He's good with kids."

"Okay," I said. "I'd like that."

I heard the boys both proclaim, "Aw!" when Karla told them it was time for bed. Phil gathered up the drawings and held them out to Tomas.

"You have to keep those safe, okay?" he said. Tomas took them and looked so solemn, I almost laughed.

"Yeah," Chacho said. "He's much better than the last one."

On the way home, I turned to Phil and said, "You have the Chacho stamp of approval."

"Really," he said. "I don't know why, but that makes me feel oddly happy."

"It probably ought to," I said. "Minus the 'oddly' part."

"What else did you two talk about?"

"Lots of stuff," I said. "You know?"

Phil nodded and I watched the city roll by past the window. The last bit of light was about to disappear over the West Hills.

"I figured something out, though," I said.

"Oh, yeah?" Phil asked. "What's that?"

"I know where Brandon and his zombies are going to attack."

I turned back to the window and the light was completely gone.

CHAPTER NINETEEN
A Lot of Spiritual Questions

I felt like there was a lot to do, but I needed to talk to Crystal Beals first, and the next day was Sunday.

"What time do people get out of church?" I asked Phil. We sat in my room, me on the bed, Phil at my desk. The door was open, which was the house policy if we were in one another's rooms, so we whispered.

"I'm not sure about Crystal," he said. "But I can usually get a hold of Cody around one on Sundays."

"I forgot," I said. "His family goes to church. Seems kind of weird to me."

"Not sure why that is," Phil said. "Seems like a lot of people are religious nowadays. I mean, c'mon, the dead rose up and walk the earth. Don't you think that's going to lead people to have a lot of spiritual questions?"

"I'm not going to keep talking to you," I said, "if you're going to insist on being logical."

"I know it's annoying," he said. "I've been told that a lot."

"Well," I said, "it's twelve thirty now. I'm going to try her."

I punched in her number and pressed send.

They picked up on the third ring. "Beals residence," a man's voice said.

"Good afternoon, sir," I said. "I was wondering if I might

be able to talk to Crystal." There, Phil wasn't the only one who was able to turn on the politeness.

"May I ask who's calling?" he asked.

"Please tell her it's Courtney," I said.

There was a pause.

"Courtney Hart?" the man asked. I said yes. "Courtney, I remember you. This is Rob, Crystal's dad. Gosh, it used to seem like you lived here with us. We haven't seen much of you lately."

"No, sir," I said. "I haven't been around much." Like, for the last four or five years.

"Well," he said, "let me go get her. It was nice to talk with you, Courtney. I hope we can see you soon." He set the phone down and called for Crystal.

Phil gave me a look, wondering what was going on.

"I used to hang out over there a lot," I said to him. "He remembered me."

Over the phone, I heard Crystal come into the room and ask what was up. Her dad told her I was on the line for her.

"Courtney!" she said. "How are you?" She pitched her voice lower. "You were smart to leave Safeway when you did. Me and Gabe barely made it out of there when the police showed up."

"I'm glad you got away," I said. "Listen, the reason I called, Crystal . . . It's about the senior kegger. Are you somewhere you can talk?"

"I can't tell you anything about that," she said. "You know that." Her tone was scolding, like I was a little kid she'd caught being naughty.

"Okay," I said. "Just let me ask you a question. Not about the location."

"I guess that'd be okay," she said, dubious.

"When he was still alive," I said, "was Brandon helping to plan the thing?"

Silence on the other end of the phone.

"I mean, he was friends with those guys, right? With Mike and Tyler and Dillon?"

"It's Michael," she said.

"Right," I said. "He was friends with them, though, right?"

"Yeah."

"And was he helping to plan the kegger?" I asked.

"I think so," she said. "What's this about, Courtney?"

"One more question, Crystal," I said. "I'm just going to ask a yes or no question. All you have to do is answer it, okay?"

"Maybe," she said.

"The kegger is going to be out at Brandon's cabin, isn't it?" I asked.

She gasped. Then she said, "I still can't tell you, Courtney. I don't even know why it's so important for you to know."

"Okay," I said. "I'll stop pressing you. Sorry. I was just trying to figure out if a hunch I had was correct. You know how much I love to be right."

Phil cocked an eyebrow at me over that. I waved away his look.

"Yeah, I guess I've noticed that," Crystal said.

"We should get together this week," I said. "We can grab something to eat, or coffee. My treat. And I won't bring up the kegger, I promise."

"I'd like that," Crystal said. "Yeah, let's keep in touch and do that."

We exchanged a few more pleasantries and then we hung up.

"The kegger is definitely at the cabin," I said.

"And Brandon was planning it when he was alive," Phil said, "so we can guess that he'll remember that now that he's a zombie."

"I think so," I said. "If we can call what he does 're-membering.' "

"How many seniors will be there?" Phil asked.

"I don't know," I said. "A lot. Like ninety percent of the seniors show up, right? What's ninety percent of a lot?"

He sat back in the chair, arms crossed over his chest, and stared at the ceiling.

"What do we do now?" he asked finally.

"I'm not sure," I said. "Well, that's not true. I know what we have to do, I'm just not sure how to do it."

He stopped staring at the ceiling. "What do we have to do?"

"We have to convince everyone that there's going to be a zombie attack at the senior kegger. And then . . ." I trailed off because the next part seemed crazy even to me.

"And then what?" Phil asked.

"And then we have to convince them all to go anyway," I said.

Having such a monumental task ahead of us, we did what any other people in our situation might do. We waited for it to get dark, then we sneaked out of the house to go hunt zombies.

I mean, sometimes there's just nothing like ripping into a bunch of the undead to clear your head. If we were able to find any, anyway. So we treated it like a Sunday drive— windows down, music on. Pleasant. We'd just happened to bring some deadly weapons along just in case.

I asked Phil to lay off the punk music, so we listened to this British guy named Billy Bragg. Phil said he was a punk folk singer. I was dubious until he popped in the CD, and then I was won over pretty quickly.

We headed right for the outskirts of town since that was the last place we'd run into any Zs. We were in Phil's car with him behind the wheel. I was seriously thinking I needed to sell the Subaru that Dad left me since I didn't really drive it. Or maybe I'd give it to Phil to make up for how often he'd had to taxi me around to different places. As we drove, I did my best to peer into every shadow as we drove slowly down the rural roads. I was seriously thinking about paying for one of those super-bright lights that can be controlled from inside the car. The kind the police have. I would definitely be able to afford it. It wasn't like I was spending my money on much else.

I sat up a little straighter when a thought popped into my head.

"We didn't call Cody," I said. "We've never gone out hunting without him."

Phil grimaced. "We can't tell him about this," he said. "Especially if we find something."

"I can't believe we forgot."

We drove on for a while, stopping from time to time to study a yard where maybe we'd seen movement. The moon was only half full, but it seemed like it was bright enough for what we were doing. There didn't seem to be any shufflers around.

"Did he tell you he took that girl out?" Phil asked. "Hannah?"

"No," I said. "What did he tell you?"

He got a sort of pained look. "Maybe I shouldn't have said anything. If he'd wanted you to know . . ."

"Too late now, mister," I said. "You brought it up. Besides boyfriends and girlfriends don't keep things from one another."

As soon as it was out of my mouth, I realized what I'd said.

"Not that we're, you know," I said. "I wasn't trying to imply . . ." I didn't know how to finish.

"You're funny," Phil said. "One minute, you're like Wonder Woman—kicking ass, taking no prisoners. Then sometimes I almost swear you stepped out of some sort of, I don't know, Victorian novel where none of the characters are allowed to actually talk about what they're feeling."

"You and I both know that I can talk about my feelings," I said.

"Sometimes," he said. "Sure, but sometimes, the most obvious times, it's like you try to pretend you don't have feelings at all."

"The most obvious?" I asked.

"Yes."

I didn't believe it. My superpower used to be the ability to hide any emotion—that and Reed Richards–level intelligence, of course—and now the boy who couldn't comprehend human interactions was able to read me like an insecure book. Fantastic.

"Can other people see these feelings?" I asked. "Or is it just you?"

"What's that?" he asked, pointing up the road.

From where we were, it looked like a house up the road was having a party. The front door was open, light spilled out into the yard, and a bunch of people were crowded around the front door.

"Get closer," I said.

Phil gunned the gas, the acceleration pushing me back into my seat.

When we got up to the house, I saw it wasn't a party at all.

A one-level farmhouse was under attack by zombies. They were crowding into the front door, creating a bottleneck. I counted at least a dozen of the creeps.

There was a sturdy metal rail fence all around the place, its gate twisted and open with the effort the zombies used to push it in until the chain keeping it closed snapped. A zombie lay on the ground just past the gate—it must have been semi-crushed by the crowd that charged the gate. It was down, but still trying to crawl to meet up with its buddies.

Phil pulled the car into the drive and made sure to park the car's front tire right on the prone zombie.

"Phil," I said. "There are too many of them for us to handle. We need to call the cops."

He killed the engine, and we heard a scream coming from inside the house. High-pitched, it was either a woman or a kid.

"You stay and call the cops," he said.

He climbed out, slammed his door, then went to the back of the car, where he keyed open the trunk. He came back into view a second later carrying the shotgun Buddha had given him. He racked a shell into the chamber as he walked to the house.

Dammit. I climbed out and ran to the trunk, which he'd left open. I grabbed my wrecking tool. Then I checked to make sure I had my pistol and speed loaders.

As I ran to the house, I saw Phil approach the group of zombies who were re-creating a Three Stooges routine in the front door. They never even saw him as he walked right up, stopped, and raised the shotgun to his shoulder.

His first shot took out two of the things. He racked another round and fired. Then he ran a little ways back toward me, turned, and waited.

I caught up with him and drew my revolver.

The runners figured out that something new was happening outside. A group of them peeled away from the house and ran right for us. Phil took the time to load a few more shells into the shotgun's magazine. His face was completely blank. I could take lessons from him on how to hide my emotions.

As the first runners got to us, Phil raised his gun and fired, and kept firing. He didn't need to tell me to do the same.

I pulled the trigger six times pretty quickly. I wasn't sure how many I got, but more were coming. There wasn't time to reload, not even with the speed loaders. I holstered the pistol and raised the wrecking tool. Phil got off a couple of shots, then he was empty. He raised the shotgun like a club.

They were on us in seconds. A guy with a mangled eye and a JUST DO IT shirt ran at me, and I buried the blade of the tool in his skull. He kept going for a few steps before falling. I used his momentum to wrench the tool out of his noggin. I heard Phil crack open a zombie's head next to me, but didn't check on him. By the time I stood up, another runner was right on top of me. I fell backward and swung at the thing's legs as it ran past. It went sprawling into the grass, its right leg a few feet behind it. I'd have to deal with that one later; more were coming.

A shotgun blast came from the house, then I heard yelling in some language I didn't recognize.

I barely had time to react as the next zombie, a girl in a miniskirt and UGGs—very fashionable—came at me. The best I was able to manage was to club her on the shoulder and knock her down. I jumped down on her chest, raised the wrecking tool, and brought the spike down right on the center of her forehead.

"Courtney!" Phil called. He struggled with a huge biker-looking dude with no lower jaw, using the shotgun to keep the guy at bay. At least biting seemed like less of a danger. The biker must have been the last zombie—I didn't see any others.

I tried to pull the wrecking tool out of the skull of the chick, but it didn't budge. How deep had I sunk it in? Did it go all the way into the ground? Screw it, I thought. I stood and drew my pistol. I popped the cylinder and ejected the empty shells. As quick as I was able, I got out

one of the speed loaders and fumbled with it. I watched it
tumble into the grass.

"Shit," I said.

"Courtney!" Phil and the biker zombie went down.

I couldn't see the loader I'd dropped. I went to get the
one that was still in its pouch on my belt.

A shotgun roared right next to us, and the biker zombie flew off of Phil.

A guy who looked like he'd just stepped out of a high
school production of *Fiddler on the Roof* stood there with a
double-barrel shotgun. He had a huge, bushy beard and
wore something that looked like a peasant's shirt. He
cracked the thing open and ejected the spent shells. He
then reloaded it and snapped the barrels back into place.
The whole time he did that, he kept up a steady stream of
muttering in what I thought was Russian. I wasn't able to
understand any of it, but I'd know a steady stream of cursing in any language.

The biker zombie lay on his back and was trying to
right himself like a turtle. The Russian dude walked up to
him, put the barrel of the shotgun right up to his face, and
pulled the trigger.

The Russian then noticed the zombie whose leg I'd
chopped off. He walked over to it and gave it the same
treatment he'd given its biker friend.

Phil and I hadn't moved since the shotgun-toting Russian had come out and made his presence known. I think
we were too shocked to do anything, but now we'd recovered. Phil slowly stood, and I found the speed loader I'd
dropped.

"You okay?" the Russian asked us. He walked over to
me and gave me a once-over. "You hurt? Scratched?"

"I'm okay," I said.

"And you?" he asked Phil.

Phil kind of patted himself down. "I'm all right," he said.

Instead of saying anything else, the dude rushed up and took Phil in a huge hug. He actually lifted Phil's feet off the ground. When he set Phil down, he turned and smiled at me.

"Thank you so much," he said. I thought he'd be happy with that, but then he charged me and gave me the same kind of hug he'd given Phil. All the air rushed out of my lungs. Jesus, he might have just hugged the zombies to death.

A woman called something in Russian from inside the house, and the guy answered back in the same language. Right in my ear.

He set me down as a woman wearing a long peasant dress and white head covering came out into the yard. She carried a baby, maybe a year old, and two little girls stood tentatively in the doorway looking out at us.

"I don't know where you come from," the Russian said to us, "but I thought my family was dead. Thank you."

"You're all okay?" Phil asked.

"Yes, all," the guy said. "All of us. I got us into cellar when the zombies attack." When he said it, it sounded like "zumbias." "They were breaking down cellar door when you come."

"Well," I said, "we're glad everyone is fine."

"You come in," he said to us. "You come in and clean up." He yelled at his wife in Russian again. "We have food, drink. Please."

"We can't," Phil said. "We were just passing by when we . . . when we saw. We need to be going."

The guy's face fell, sad we'd rejected his offer. Then a look of wonder came over him.

"You just passing by?" he asked. "And you stop to help? You are sent by God."

We really weren't, I almost said.

"Maybe we were," Phil said. "I've heard he works in mysterious ways."

The Russian laughed at that, then hugged Phil again. Then hugged me. He had tears coming down his face by then, and they fell into his beard and made it glisten like dew in a thick, shaggy bush.

He finally let us go, following us to the car, singing our praises and telling us God smiled on us. He kept shaking Phil's hand as Phil tried to get in the car. The moaning of the zombie underneath the car's wheels finally tore his attention away from us.

"You go now," he said to us. "I clean up here." He reloaded his shotgun.

Phil started the car and backed up onto the road. He waved one last time at the Russian and then at the guy's little family back up at the house. The two girls in the doorway waved back shy little waves.

We heard the *pop pop* of two shotgun blasts as we drove away.

"I knew there were a lot of Russian Orthodox who lived out here," Phil said, "but I've never met any of them. They mostly homeschool their kids."

"That's very interesting," I said. "You know what else is interesting?"

"What's that?" Phil asked.

"You running into a huge crowd of zombies and not waiting for any kind of help whatsoever!" I yelled at him. "That was super-interesting."

I was so angry, I pounded on the dashboard and yelled. It felt dramatic and petty, but I also needed that right then.

"You came and helped out eventually," Phil said. "I knew you would."

"Not the point," I shouted. My heart pounded, and I heard my blood rushing in my ears.

"The point is, you could have been hurt or killed and . . . and what the hell would I do then?" I asked.

He didn't answer. What answer was there to give? He just continued driving on for a few minutes.

Then, very abruptly, he pulled the car off the road and threw it into park. I was jerked back and forth by all the sudden movements.

"What the hell, Phil?" I asked.

"I was seven years old," he said. He turned in his seat to face me, his left arm draped over the steering wheel.

"What are you talking about?"

"I was seven years old," he repeated and something about the flat way he said it, a flatness masking anger or something scarier, made me shut up. "This was a couple of months after the dead came back. Do you remember what it was like back then?"

I nodded.

"People either thought it was the end of the world," he said, "or they thought it was all going to blow over any day. That was before everyone had fences and gates. Hell, some people, like my family, hadn't even gone out to buy guns yet.

"My family—my mom and dad, my two older sisters, and me—we were all going to go up to a cabin that we had out in Eastern Oregon."

"Phil," I said. "You don't have to do this."

"You asked, Courtney," he said. "I told you I didn't know if I'd ever be ready to tell you. Guess what? I'm ready."

I shrank away from him a little. I didn't think I was ready for this.

"We'd loaded up the car," he went on. "We were just about ready to go. I got away from my parents, the way kids do. You know what I mean, right?"

I thought about the couple of times my parents had lost

me when I was little. I never even noticed that we'd become separated, and then they'd be in my face, angry and scared and telling me to never wander off ever again. I nodded.

"I'd actually gotten outside, was waiting by the car.

"And then I noticed that there were a bunch of zombies shuffling down the street toward me. So I did what any little kid might do, I started screaming.

"My mom ran out and saw what was happening. She told me to get in the car and I did. Then she ran after me. I don't know why she did that. If she'd just gone back inside, I think everything might have been okay."

He took his arm off the steering wheel and sat back in the seat. He stared out the windshield and started talking again.

"She ran after me. Maybe she meant to get in the car with me." He shrugged. "She didn't make it. The zombies were on her before she reached the car. My dad saw what was happening, and he ran out to help my mom.

"And he didn't close the door behind him."

He turned his attention from whatever was outside back to me. "Do you understand what I'm talking about?" he asked.

"Yes," I said. I had to say it twice because the first time no sound escaped my throat.

"I sat in the car and I watched those monsters tear apart my family. Then they surrounded the car and tried to get at me. For hours I sat in the back of the car and watched those things pound on the windows. I can still see the bloody hand and fist prints they left on the glass. My family's blood.

"I passed out from the heat at some point," he said. "I would have died from exposure—you know, like how dogs sometimes die if they're locked in a car? But some neighbors called the police to report the zombies. After the cops cleared out the shufflers, someone thought to look in the car and they found me. I was almost dead of dehydration and, what do they call it? Hyperthermia? Heat stroke?"

He took a deep, shaky breath. I bit my lower lip to keep from crying. For some reason it felt important not to cry about this in front of him, like he wouldn't have liked it. Oh, later, when I was alone, I'd become Weepy, the eighth dwarf, but for the moment, I intended to keep it together.

Phil shrugged again, as if there was so much to communicate that only moving his shoulders up and down might do it.

"I used to wonder if I was happy that I was saved," he said. "Then, a few years ago, I figured out I was saved so that I could do things like we just did. There was no way. No. Way. I'd have just sat there and watched that family be attacked. Even if it meant I got killed in the process. Okay?"

"Okay," I said. "But that won't stop me from trying to keep you alive."

"I appreciate that," he said, and gave me a grin. "Now, let's go home. I think we've done enough damage for one night."

"Speaking of damage," I said, "I still can't feel my body since that guy hugged me."

"You're young," Phil said. "You'll grow a new spine."

We headed for home. We didn't talk much on the way. I'm not sure why Phil was quiet, but I could have ventured some guesses. I kept my lips zipped because I had a ton of stuff to think about. I understood now what Gene had talked to me about at Thanksgiving. I wondered if I got Chacho and Phil together to talk about their experiences, would they find them to be similar? I wondered if the term post-traumatic stress might come up?

And I have to admit, even though I told Phil I wouldn't

try to stop him from joining a fight in the future, I was scared. Scared of what it might mean that he saw himself as some sort of anti-zombie crusader. What was the difference between being a zealous monster hunter and having a death wish? I wasn't sure, but I knew I didn't want to find out.

CHAPTER TWENTY

My Uncle Benjamin

Time was growing short on the whole "preventing a mini zombie apocalypse" front. Finals were a week away and the senior kegger always happened the weekend after finals. So, call it two weeks. I refused to give up any study time, either. I mean, what good might it do me to survive a mass attack of flesh-eating ghouls if it meant I screwed the pooch on my grades? No thanks, I'd rather go down as zombie chow.

During the run-up to finals, Phil, Cody, and I had a lot of discussions about how to convince others to believe us about the coming attack. Or to at least prepare for it even if they didn't quite believe us. Nothing seemed like it might work. The most common thing any of us thought of was some variation of, "Trick them?" But that wasn't realistic, you know?

We also talked a bit about the zombie attack we foiled without Cody. He did act hurt—okay, he wasn't just acting, he really was hurt—but he eventually got into trying to dissect what had happened and why.

"Maybe Brandon is losing control of the other zombies?" he asked.

"Or maybe he sent them out on a foraging mission," I said. "It's hard to know."

"Well, I'm just glad there's, like, a dozen less zombies for us to fight later," Cody said.

"Fewer," I hissed, but Cody seemed to miss it. Phil put his hand on top of mine to help calm me down.

It was during a combination study-slash-strategy session at Denny's one night that Cody sat back and rubbed his face. We'd already been talking for hours about it, going round and round the same few crappy ideas.

"I have a thought," he said. Phil and I waited. I might be able to add that I waited dubiously, but that would make me sound like a bitch.

"What if we told them what we thought?" he said. "We keep thinking of ways to try to trick them or something. Why don't we treat them like fellow human beings we respect and walk up and talk to them?"

I thought of a lot of reasons not to do that. Being laughed at, getting stuck in a nuthouse. Getting further ostracized at school. Those were all pretty good reasons not to try the honest, direct approach.

"I mean, it's like me and girls," Cody said. "I spent so long trying to think of a way to game some girl—any girl—into liking me. Maybe if I dressed a certain way, did certain things, wore the right clothes.

"Then I decided to forget all of that and just be myself and tell a girl that I liked that I liked her. And now? Now I'm getting my wick dipped on the regular. Know what I mean?"

"Yes, Cody," I said. "Despite your subtlety, I do think I know what you meant."

"Jesus," Phil said and rubbed his eyes. "I didn't want to know that."

"You're gonna think about it later," Cody said with an evil grin. "You are welcome."

After I swallowed down some vomit, I asked, "What do you suggest, Mister Darcy?"

"I don't get that," Cody said, "but it's simple. Start with one person. One person that you know and like, and that you think, you know, trusts you. Tell them. See how it goes over."

"I can't think of a single person not already at this table who might trust me," I said. I took a bite of my Moons over My Hammy.

"I can think of two," Phil said. "Crystal and Elsa. And all the kids who were at Brandon's party last year? The ones you helped save? I bet they'd listen to you."

"Right," Cody said. "Start with one or two, get them to be a, what did you call it? An advocate, right? They'll help convince others, and so on."

I forked more cold, chewy potatoes into my mouth to buy some time. I was really going to have to do this, wasn't I? Stake whatever little reputation I still had on trying to convince one or two people to believe me.

"Screw it," I said. "I'm leaving town the moment I can anyway. What do I care if people think I'm even weirder than they already do?"

"That's a good attitude," Phil said. "It works for you."

"I'm only going to do it if you give me the rest of your chocolate shake," I told Cody. He picked up the glass of ice cream goodness and started sucking it down for all he was worth.

"Fine," I said. "I'll do it anyway. Are there any people you two can talk to?"

They both thought there might be.

I figured it would be easiest to talk to Elsa first for a couple of reasons. One, Crystal seemed way invested in the success of the kegger and she'd likely resist any suggestion that it might not go off according to plan. Two, Elsa had a relatively low social standing and if she laughed in my face and started talking smack about me around school, very few people would listen. A fairly brutal assessment, I know, but I needed to go into all of this with my eyes wide open.

I was glad that she seemed excited when I asked her to go to coffee with me that Friday.

We met up at the Starbucks in downtown where we'd had coffee the last time we hung out. Elsa ordered some blended monstrosity that claimed to be a coffee drink. I figured, what the hell, and ordered the same thing. It was like a milk shake that got you buzzed. Why had no one ever told me about them before? I resisted getting a second one after I sucked down the first.

We caught up on what had been going on this past year. Elsa was careful not to bring up my dad. That was a relief, actually. While I liked to remember Dad, I sort of hated talking about him. It felt like talking about him would make me stop remembering how he was when he was alive, and start remembering him like he was in the stories I told. I wasn't even sure if that made sense.

Elsa got accepted to Smith College and was getting ready to move to Massachusetts in a few weeks. I congratulated her and she smiled demurely, but I knew she was proud. I got hung up on the fact that I thought Smith had originally been founded as a religious college. Was Elsa religious? Not that it mattered.

"What about you?" she asked.

Am I religious? I thought, but thank God, I didn't say it out loud.

"What are your plans for school next year?" she clarified when I gave her a totally confused look. I told her about the Columbia thing.

"Damn, Courtney," she said. "You've always got to top everyone on everything, don't you?"

"That was the main reason I wanted to go to Columbia, yes," I said. "The other reason is their bitching football team. It just worked out this way, Elsa."

"I know," she said. "It's just frustrating."

We fell into a somewhat uncomfortable silence then.

She sipped at her coffee drink and I wished I had one to sip on some more.

"Let me ask you something," I said. That was not the stealthy and elegant conversational opener I'd been planning to use.

"What's that?" she asked.

"It's about zombies," I said.

"A favorite topic, if I remember correctly," she said.

"Did I talk about them a lot?" I asked.

"Only all the time," she said, but she smiled, which made me think she might be teasing me. "What about zombies?" she asked.

I leaned forward, my arms on the table, and laced my fingers together. I cleared my throat. All of these were stalling tactics, of course.

"What, Courtney?" she asked.

"What if I told you that I thought zombies were acting differently?" I asked.

"You mean, how they seem to be smarter?" she asked. My jaw came unhinged. "And they seem to be able to plan? And they move faster now, too, right?"

I closed my mouth before something fell into it. Well, the bit about them being faster was easy to figure out. All you had to do was look at them, but how did she know about their being smarter?

"How did you . . . ?" my voice trailed off.

"Brandi Edwards," Elsa said. Brandi? "She told us a few months ago about getting attacked at her job—she works at the bookstore downtown. One night she had to take the recycling out to the alley. She got ambushed by three speedsters who were working together.

"If she hadn't been carrying the store's shotgun, she'd have been toast."

Months? Speedsters? They'd known for months and

they had their own lingo for the new zombies. I felt totally out of the loop and useless.

"Well," I said, "why didn't you tell anyone?"

"Tell who?" she asked. "Who would believe us? About anything. If we walked inside soaking wet and said it was raining outside, people would look outside to double-check."

"That's true," I said. "That's the same reason I haven't really brought it up to anyone other than Phil and Cody until recently. Listen, if you vouched for me with Brandi and Carol and them, do you think they'd be willing to talk about how to maybe stop the new zombies?"

"I think so," Elsa said. "Honestly? I think they've missed you. They'll probably act like bitches, but that's just what they do. It won't last."

"They miss me?" I asked. I got a little choked up.

"Yeah, but if you mention it to them, they'll deny it all," she said.

"That's what I'd do," I said.

"You don't say," she said. "Let me talk to them over the weekend. I'll get back to you Sunday or Monday, okay?"

I told her that would be great.

She finished up her coffee drink. "What do you want to do now?"

"Want to catch a movie or go hang at the comics shop?" I asked. I knew I was on a mission to stop the zombie hordes, but I figured I had time to hang out with my newly discovered friend.

"Let's hit the comics shop," she said. "I ought to have new stuff in my pull box. Besides, it's been a while since any strange boys have said inappropriate sexual comments to me. The comics shop is always good for that."

I couldn't argue with that, so we headed off.

★　★　★

The next day, Saturday, Phil, Cody, and I got together and compared our progress. We sat in Phil's room, him at his desk, me on his bed, and Cody on the floor. We all had surprising successes. Phil talked with Ray Simmons, the unofficial head of the goths at school.

"Ray was really open to the idea of the new types of zombies," Phil said. "He said he'd been hearing rumors for a while. And I was surprised how willing he was to start killing zombies," Phil went on. "I always thought that they were sort of on the side of the shufflers."

"I think that's vampires," Cody said.

"Oh," Phil said. "Then I'm glad it's not bloodsuckers we're facing."

Phil had also talked to the art school and drama department kids. He basically had an in with all the artistic types. They were on board.

Next, we moved on to Cody. He'd talked to the vo-tech crowd and got buy-in from them. He'd also talked to his girlfriend's clique. They were sort of middling popular, maybe two steps up the social ladder from those of us down on the bottom.

"They seemed happy just to be invited to play with everyone else," Cody said. "They're like the Ringo Starr of the high school groups."

"We all did pretty well," I said.

"Yeah," Phil said. "There's really only a couple of groups left to talk to."

"The jocks and rich kids," Cody said. "Lots of overlap there."

"Yeah," said Phil. "Seems like you'd be able to talk to one person and touch both groups."

I stared at him and my heart sank. I knew what he was getting at. And even though I'd already said I'd do what he was suggesting, I still didn't want to.

"I can talk to Crystal," I said finally, "but I don't know how open she'll be to any of this."

"She was with you when you got attacked at the cabin," Phil said. "Twice. Remind her of that."

"I doubt I'll have to remind her," I said.

"When will you talk to her?" Cody asked.

I got my phone out of my pocket and texted her. Can you meet with me soon? I wrote.

"As soon as she answers this," I said. "If she'll see me."

Phil went back to drawing and Cody looked through his collection of comics. Phil had a better selection of comics than the local library.

"Say," I said, "does this house have a basement?" I didn't think it did since there weren't any doors that led to a basement, but I thought I'd ask.

"Not a basement, really," Phil said without looking up from his drawing board. "But it has a root cellar, crawl space thing."

"How do you get into it?" I asked.

"There's a trapdoor in the kitchen. It's under a rug." He stopped and looked up at me. "What's up?"

"I was just wondering," I said. I felt a plan circling somewhere outside of my ability to grab it. If I didn't think about it too hard, it'd come to me.

Phil had just gone back to drawing when my phone chimed. We all sort of jumped. Before I looked at the screen, it beeped again.

"It's Crystal," I said.

"What'd she say?" Phil asked.

"She said to call her tomorrow afternoon, we can get coffee or something. And she said she doesn't want to talk about zombies."

"Well," said Cody, "that sounds promising."

"Is there anyone else you can talk to?" Phil asked. "Or

maybe one of the folks we've talked to recently can approach someone?"

I thought about that. "Do you trust anyone else to do it?"

"No," Phil said.

"Right," I said. "If it's going to be me, there's no one else I can talk to. No one else that I know as well as Crystal, at least. I just need to try to figure out how to bring her around."

"I just want to tell you good luck," Cody said. "We're all counting on you."

Phil looked at Cody, confused.

"It's a quote from a movie," I said. "A comedy. You probably haven't seen it."

Phil accepted this and went back to drawing. Cody went back to his comic. I wished I could have done the same, but now I needed to figure out a way to convince Crystal of something she didn't even want to hear about. Whee!

The next day, I still hadn't decided what I was going to say to Crystal, but I knew I wasn't going to lie to her to get her to meet me. I figured I'd lay it all out while I had her on the phone. If she hung up on me, we'd have to figure out a plan B, but at least I'd keep from wasting a bunch of her time.

I took my phone out to the backyard with me and sat on the grass in the sun. I punched in her number, hit send, and waited.

Someone picked up on the first ring.

"Hi, Courtney!" Crystal said. "How are you?"

"I'm great, Crystal," I said. "How are you?"

"I'm great, too," she said. "What do you want to do today?"

I took a deep breath, completely unsure how this was going to go.

"Crystal, I know you said you didn't want to talk about zombies," I said, "but we have to."

"Courtney," she said in a flat tone. She sounded angry. It was the same tone she'd had after we were attacked by some zombies out at Brandon's cabin the first time. "We really don't."

"We used to be really good friends," I said. "We used to be super close and we told one another everything. Remember that?"

Silence on the other end, but at least she hadn't hung up. That was something.

"I miss those days," I said. "And if you miss those days, if those days meant anything to you, you'll give me five minutes to talk this through."

"I don't know, Courtney," she said, and I heard the uncertainty in her voice.

"Two minutes," I said. "Just give me two minutes!"

Again, silence. I took that as the go-ahead to press on. My mind whirled. I honestly hadn't expected to get this far.

"You know that Brandon was using drugs, right?" I asked, but I didn't wait for an answer. "It was Vitamin Z, Crystal, you know that—a drug made out of zombie brains. When people die of an overdose from it, they can turn into zombies. I know because I've seen it. I was with Brandon when he died, Crystal."

"Oh, God," she whispered.

"And when he came back, he wasn't like any zombies you've ever seen. He was fast; he was, I don't know, aware."

"He was a roadrunner," Crystal said.

"Have you seen them?" I asked.

"No, but some of the boys claimed to," she said. "I didn't believe them."

Others had told her. That was the wedge I needed.

"Believe them, Crystal," I said. I stood up and started pacing back and forth across the lawn. "I've seen a couple of big, organized attacks. My dad died in one."

I let that hang in the air. I hadn't expected to say it; it just popped out of my mouth.

"I'm sorry, Courtney," Crystal said.

"Don't be," I said. "It had nothing to do with you, but this does. Listen, now that you know what's going on, you can't ignore it."

"I don't know," she said.

"If you don't trust me," I said, "that's fine, but what about the other people who've told you the same kinds of things? Do you trust them?"

"It's not that I don't trust you," Crystal said.

"All I want is to talk to some of these guys who've seen what I've seen," I said. "Something big is coming. I think I know where and when."

"The kegger," she said.

"The kegger," I agreed.

"These guys, Courtney," she said. "No matter what you say, they won't want to cancel the kegger. They've been looking forward to it all year long. If you ask them to cancel it, they'll pretend they don't believe you."

"Crystal," I said, "I'd never dream of canceling it, or of asking folks to stay away. I want as many people there as possible."

We talked a few more minutes, but she'd already made up her mind and I knew it. She rung off saying she'd make some calls and get back to me.

I went back into the house. I walked into the kitchen and poured myself a big glass of water. My mouth was completely dry and I was sweating. I couldn't believe that I'd convinced Crystal, but part of me thought she must have wanted to be convinced on some level, even if it was sub-consciously. For the millionth time, I wished my dad was around so I was able to talk to him about all of this. I gulped down the water and went off to find Phil and Cody.

They sat on the floor on opposite sides of Phil's room. They were tossing a ball back and forth and talking. They fell silent when I walked in.

"Well?" Cody asked.

"How'd it go?" Phil asked.

"I convinced her," I said. I climbed up onto the bed and curled up. I thought about closing my eyes, but there was still stuff to do.

"How'd you do that?" Cody asked.

"Turns out she'd already been hearing some stuff from people she knows," I said. "Hearing the stuff from me just reinforced what she'd been thinking."

"What's next?" Phil asked.

"Wait for her to call," I said. "I don't think it'll be too long. In the meantime . . ."

"What?" Phil asked.

"Let's take a trip to a gun store," I said. "I want to buy you both another late birthday gift. I want one for myself, too."

Cody grinned and Phil just said, "Okay."

We were driving over to a gun shop on Twelfth Street that was open on Sundays when my phone rang. It was Crystal.

"Hi," I said. "What's up?"

Phil looked at me in the rearview mirror. I mouthed Crystal's name and he nodded, then went back to concentrating on the road.

"I talked to those guys," she said. "They want to hear what you have to say."

"Okay," I said, "that's good. Thank you. I'll figure out a place to meet sometime this week. Soon, I hope, okay?"

"Okay," she said.

"And, hey, listen," I said. "I'd still like it if we got together sometime. Maybe after all of this bullshit is done and we won't mention zombies once."

"I'd like that," she said. "Let me know when and where to meet."

We said our good-byes and I hung up. I lay my head back and closed my eyes. I was exhausted. I liked it so much better when people either did what I told them to or when I just went off and did my own thing without worrying about anyone else. I was not cut out to be a negotiator.

"Sounds like that went well," Phil said.

"Yeah," I said. "They want in. We need to talk to everyone and figure out a time we can all get together."

"Sure," Phil said.

He turned left and the bumping of the car told me we'd pulled into a parking lot.

"We're here," he said.

"Okay," I said. "Give me a second."

I opened my eyes and sat up. I pulled my backpack up off the floor and unzipped it. I pulled out the bag of drug money. I could have used the debit card that was tied to my bank account for this shopping trip, but I didn't really want the lawyer, Alvarez, to know about it.

When he saw the money, Cody's eyes grew about ten times larger than usual.

"What the hell, Courtney?" he asked.

"Just some walking around cash," I said.

I counted out more than I thought I'd need, then I counted out some more. I really had no idea how much high-quality weaponry cost.

"So what exactly are we doing here?" Phil asked.

"We're all going to pick out the finest firearms we can find," I said. "And it's my treat. Come next Saturday, I want us all coming away from our little reenactment of the gunfight at the OK Corral. How are your aunt and uncle fixed for guns?" I asked Phil.

I counted out some more money.

The inside of the Gun Wrack—yeah, it was misspelled, I have no idea why—was so brightly lit that I had to shield my eyes even after having been outside in the full sunlight. Maybe being temporarily blinded discouraged shoplifting.

Every square foot of the place was crammed with deadly weapons. Rifles, both for hunting and the automatic kind that are only meant for killing humans and the formerly human; all sorts of shotguns; bows and crossbows. It was like a candy shop for Second Amendment aficionados.

"How can I help you kids?" the guy behind the counter asked. He was a big, beefy guy. Bald and red like he spent all day in the sun rather than under fluorescent lights. Behind him on the wall hung some less conventional weapons: AK-47s, assault rifles, something that looked like a grenade launcher.

"Well, sir," I said, "my friends and I were thinking of buying some shotguns. Some top-of-the-line stuff."

"I already have a shotgun," Phil said.

"That thing Buddha gave you?" I asked.

I held up a Benelli M4. It looked like a shogun that was created by the same evolutionary process that produced the wasp.

"Wouldn't you rather have one of these?" I asked.

"Well . . ." he said.

"And did you kids bring your folks along with you?" the guy asked.

"No," I said. "But I did bring my uncle Benjamin." I took a huge wad of cash out of my pocket. "And a bunch of his friends, too."

"Was that supposed to be clever?" the guy asked.

"I had hoped yes," I said.

"Listen," he said, "do you know how much trouble I'd get into, selling weapons to minors? I'd lose my license. Now run on home and come back with a grown-up."

I decided to stop acting like an idiot and go the polite route. I wished I'd done that to begin with, but I had poor impulse control.

"Actually, sir," I said. "I'm an emancipated minor. I can make decisions and purchases on my own."

"What about them?" he asked.

"We're both eighteen," Phil said. "We can show you our driver's licenses."

"And I'm sure they're not fakes," the guy said.

"Who gets a fake ID to show that they're eighteen?" Cody asked. "Wouldn't we have some that say we're twenty-one so we could drink?"

"Right," the guy said. "That makes a lot of sense. Well, let's see what we can kit you out with today."

Cody had made a convincing argument. This was turning into a really interesting day.

After he got over being annoyed with me, the clerk really got into helping us. He loved talking about guns and showing off how much he knew.

In the end, I got the Benelli that I'd shown Phil. It was similar to the one I'd used during the zombie attack last year and I knew I'd been happy with it. The boys both bought nice Remingtons. Phil went with a more traditional model, but Cody chose a tactical model with a pistol grip and folding stock. I got the clerk to put shoulder straps on all of them, then sprang for ammo belts that strapped across our chests, and enough shotgun shells to sustain a small war. Which was probably what we were walking into.

"How are you all fixed for handguns?" the guy asked. He showed a glass case filled with any kind of pistol you might have wanted.

"I've got this already," I said and showed him my revolver. He made noises like he approved.

"How about you boys?" he asked Phil and Cody.

"The shotgun will be enough for me," Phil said. Cody looked like he was on the verge of asking to look at something from the case. Phil nudged him in the ribs. "Isn't the shotgun enough?"

"Yeah, right," Cody said. "That's plenty. Thanks."

"If you say so," the guy said.

He totaled everything and even threw us a volume discount. Still, the total was pretty impressive. Cody whistled low when he heard the figure. I counted out bills and laid them on the counter as I went. When I was done, the clerk shuffled the stack into a neat pile.

"You kids aren't gonna use those to rob banks now, are you?" he asked.

"Don't worry," I said. "We won't tell the police where we got them."

Big piles of cash seemed to improve the guy's sense of humor because he laughed pretty heartily at that.

He threw in some soft gun cases for us to carry our purchases out in and he showed us the door.

"I do believe I may close early today," he said. "You kids have a good day!"

We all thanked him and stepped outside. Phil opened the trunk and we stowed our new arsenal in it.

"Where to now?" he asked.

"Let's go break in these bad boys," Cody said. "We can go out into the hills and shoot some stuff."

"I think I need to go home," I said, and Cody immediately grew a pouty bottom lip.

"Finals start tomorrow," I told him. "I don't know about you, but I want to study a little more. I mean, we may actually have a future beyond Saturday."

"Maybe Friday after our last final we can go out and shoot these," Phil said. "We'll want to be at least a little bit familiar with them before we use them to, you know . . ."

We all knew. If we wanted to live to see graduation the following week, we'd all need to be ready to kill a lot of zombies. A lot of our former classmates, I was guessing.

"Yeah, fine," Cody said. "We can go shooting later in the week. But I don't even know why you're worried about it," he said to me. "As if you'd ever fail a test."

I smiled at him. "That is the sweetest thing you've ever said to me, Cody. Thanks."

"You're welcome?" he said.

We all piled into the car and headed back home.

I thought about all of the firepower in the trunk and I hoped it might be enough to get us past next Saturday alive.

CHAPTER TWENTY-ONE
A Common Cause

I only had one final on Monday, and that was for Organic Chemistry later in the afternoon at the community college. The boys and I spent the morning talking to people, arranging a time to meet. We gathered phone numbers for everyone and sent out group texts.

After several rounds of texting, we decided on Wednesday night after school.

"Where do you want to meet?" Phil asked me after that was settled.

I thought about it for a few minutes. We needed a public space; parents might get suspicious if all of us showed up at someone's house. But we needed to be able to have privacy, too.

"Oh, I know," I said. "The IKE Box." That was a local coffee shop. The location had originally been a funeral home, believe it or not, and there were lots of rooms on the main floor that people used for meetings. The owners just asked that everyone coming in for a meeting buy something.

When we sent that suggestion out to the group, the response was almost immediate, and everyone said yes.

I stared at the screen of my phone for a minute, not quite believing we'd actually pulled off arranging a meeting of all the various cliques at school. It was like we'd put together a UN summit for the Middle East or something, only a lot more of the delegates would be wearing Axe body spray than at the real UN. I hoped.

"We did it," I said. "Unbelievable."

"Yeah," Phil said. "Great job."

"You, too," I said and bumped him with my shoulder.

"Now we can concentrate on our finals," he said. "So, you know, yay?"

It was a relief to have it all planned out and to be able to concentrate on something as mundane as standardized testing. So that's what we did for the next couple of days.

I think Phil's aunt and uncle suspected there was something going on, but they must have chalked it up to us being nervous about finals. I mean, there was no way they'd have suspected what it really was.

Wednesday rolled around, and the four of us went over to the Ike Box to claim a room and wait for everyone else to show up. Yes, there were four of us. Cody's girlfriend, Hannah, insisted on coming with us. Now, I didn't really have anything against her, but I didn't know her very well, either, so I wasn't too comfortable around her. Then there was the fact that she'd had sex with Cody and every time I looked at her, I imagined it. It wasn't pleasant.

People started to trickle in not too long after we settled in, all of them with cups of coffee. We made several attempts at small talk, but really, there was nothing for us to talk about except for the one thing that had brought us together. And there was no point in talking about that until everyone showed up.

Elsa and Brandi and a few others from my former peer group showed up. Elsa was the only one to make a point of coming over to say hi. Everyone else settled on giving me the stink-eye. It was very neighborly.

The last folks to show up were Crystal and the jock delegation. I recognized a couple of the guys. Michael and Dillon, two of the dudes who were organizing the kegger; Zander Matthews, the captain of the football team; and Gabe, the guy who thought he was so clever writing about *Scooby-Doo,* and the one I'd made look pretty dumb in front of Crystal. He didn't look too happy to see me. I hoped he wouldn't be a problem.

"I think that's everyone," Phil said, and he got up to close the door to the room.

As he swung the door shut, a hand reached in and stopped him. The door swung out again and Warren stepped in, looking cool in all black Chucks, jeans, and a T-shirt. He grinned at us, then found a seat. I noticed that he hadn't bought a drink.

Phil recovered. "Thanks for coming, everyone," he said as he sat down. "I think it's pretty cool that we can all come together like this and, you know, have a common cause. Seems like we don't all see eye to eye about many things." He shrugged. "That's all I had to say. Now I think Courtney ought to talk."

I cleared my throat, but before I said anything, Dillon spoke up.

"Before you talk," he said, "I need to say something. I already told Crystal this, but I'll say it to you." He looked right at me. "Any talk of shutting down the kegger, and I'm out of here."

If this was the UN, Dillon had just proclaimed himself China. Okay, I'd find a way to work with that.

"I don't want to shut down the kegger," I said. "Believe me. I think we need to encourage as many people as possible to be there, in fact."

"That's what I'm talking about," Dillon said, and he bumped fists with Michael. Charming.

"Okay," I said. "I think you all know, or have heard

about, what the three of us did last year when Brandon's party got attacked, right?" Everyone looked at Phil, Cody, and me, and they nodded. "And some of you were there." I looked at the jock contingent. "You know, you saw it. We were able to organize a counterattack and then start moving folks out of the house and to the cars and safety."

"Not everyone made it out of that house alive," Zander said.

"Yeah, but that had nothing to do with us," Phil said. "They'd been sent into the room at the back of the cabin before we ever showed up with extra guns and ammo."

Zander considered that for a minute, then his body language relaxed.

"That's true," he said.

"Over the last school year," I went on, "you've all either seen or heard about a new kind of zombie. A smarter, faster zombie. Right?" Everyone agreed. "We think these zombies are smart enough to organize and give and follow orders. Phil and I saw them—saw maybe a hundred of them—attack an apartment building up in Portland."

"What were you doing up in Portland?" someone asked.

"Yeah, how'd you get past the Army roadblocks?" Gabe asked.

"That might be a topic for later," I said, "or for never, since the answer might get us into hot water with the police. But please believe us that we were there and that we saw this. Can you do that?"

Everyone agreed they could. They were all a lot more reluctant, but they still agreed.

"Good," I said. "It's important that you believe us about that attack. Because we think we know where they plan to attack next."

"The senior kegger," Dillon said.

"Right," Phil said.

"But you don't want us to cancel it?" he asked.

"We don't want to cancel it," I said. "We don't want people to stay away from it. In fact, our plan depends on as many people coming to the kegger as possible. Hell, we may even want to invite the juniors and sophomores to come."

"But not the freshmen," Phil said.

"No, probably not the freshmen," I agreed.

"Okay," Ray, the king of the goths, said. "So, what is this plan?"

"The plan is really simple," I said. Then I laid it out for them.

It was just about fifteen minutes later before everyone got up and started filing out of the room. That had included time for questions and answers.

"I think that went pretty well," I said to Phil. I noticed he wasn't looking at me.

Warren still sat at the table grinning at us. I really wanted to slap that grin off his face.

"You didn't ask, but I thought it went good," he said.

"Well," I said.

I took a lot of joy in watching his grin go down a notch.

"What the hell do you want?" Cody asked.

"I heard about this little powwow," he said. "And I thought I'd see what it was all about. I thought I'd get invited, but I guess that got lost in the mail."

"Why would we invite you?" Cody asked.

"Why would you invite me?" Warren parroted back. He looked totally offended.

"Cody's right," I said, "which is something I never expected to say."

"Thanks," Cody said.

"We invited people who'd be able turn around and get

other people to join in and help us with the plan," I said. "Last I checked, the only person you could get to follow you anywhere is . . . Who exactly?"

He leaned his chair back and crossed his arms. "You seemed ready to follow me some interesting places."

Phil started to stand up, but I put my hand on his arm and he sat down.

Warren chuckled like he thought it was funny. Like he wasn't threatened at all by Phil. Maybe he didn't realize that if he started something with Phil, he'd have to deal with me and Cody, too.

"That's another thing," I said. "You are absolutely the biggest douche I know. Maybe the biggest douche I have ever met."

"Hey," he said, "I wasn't the one who kissed you."

"This doesn't have anything to do with the kissing," I said. "I accept full responsibility for that. No, what makes you a tool is that you then tried to use that to drive a wedge between me and Phil. What made you do that?"

"Maybe I did it because—"

"You're an ass," I said. "We've established that. Listen, you want to show up at the kegger, we're not going to stop you. Heck, we can use you there, but don't think you're somehow going to become our best buddy or something."

He rocked his chair forward and stood up. I thought he was going to say something, but he just turned and walked out of the room.

We all sat there for a while to recover.

"I'm sorry," I said to Phil.

"Why?" he shot back.

"Because I gave that guy the ammunition he's been us-ing against us."

"If it hadn't been"—he stopped and cleared his throat—"if it hadn't been you kissing him, it would have been something else eventually. Some people are only happy when they're creating chaos in everyone else's lives."

"Yeah, well," I said, "I'd still rather it had been one of you two doing something rather than me."

"I don't think either of us would make out with him," Cody said.

"Speak for yourself," Phil said, his face deadpan. "He may be a jerk, but he's still pretty dreamy."

"You guys are a regular comedy duo," I said. "Like Martin and Lame-Ass."

"I'm Martin," they both said at the same time. Then they cracked up. Okay, that had been sort of funny.

"All right, smart-asses," I said. "Let's get home. Some of us still have some finals to study for."

"How can you study knowing what's coming up on Saturday night?" Cody asked as we got up.

We gathered the cups and plates that people had left behind.

"I can study because I know that I'm going to be alive on Sunday," I said. "And those test results are going to be important."

"Makes sense," Cody said. "But I still don't think I'm going to study too much."

I guess we all dealt with the impending apocalypse in our own ways.

Over the next two days, I had three finals—including one out at the community college. I was pretty sure that I did okay. I was more or less done with school after I put my pencil down on that last test. Sure, we'd all still be coming to campus next week, but all we'd be doing was a bunch of looking-back-on-your-school-career type stuff. There were assemblies planned, a field day—a field day, like we were in elementary school! We'd get our last yearbooks. All of this pseudo-nostalgic bullshit. As if most of us couldn't wait to get the hell away from the place and never come back. The worst part was that if we skipped, they might withhold our diplomas come graduation on Friday night.

It just felt like one last opportunity for the school district to bully us.

Fine, whatever, I'd take another week of this place if it meant I got to escape at the end of it.

That Thursday, we took Cody out to shoot our guns like we'd promised. He brought along a bunch of over-sized stuffed animals that he'd bought at Goodwill.

"What are those for?" I asked.

"Target practice," he said, plainly disgusted that he'd had to actually say out loud something so obvious.

We drove out north and found a large field that wasn't fenced in. We walked into it a ways, each of us carrying a couple of ridiculous novelty animals. Once we got far enough away from the road, we arranged the animals and stepped back away from them.

"I feel weird about shooting Mr. Cuddles," I said.

"It's your fault for naming him," Cody said. Then he raised his shotgun, quickly aimed, and pulled the trigger. A giant blue cat tumbled through the air, spewing stuffing as it went. Cody howled and danced around.

Then it was my turn.

I felt bad about how good it felt to shoot Mr. Cuddles. We didn't stop shooting until all that was left of the animals was some brightly colored fur and our memories of them.

I saw Ms. Bjorn, the counselor, one last time the next day.

I sat across from her, the desk between us, and she stared at me for a while.

"What have you been up to?" she asked.

I got suddenly paranoid. What did she suspect? Worse, what did she know?

"I'm not sure what you mean," I said.

"You just seem different," she said, and I relaxed. She was just saying the same thing Chacho had said a while ago; it had just taken her a lot longer to notice it. I guess that was one reason she was stuck here in a high school rather than a real psychologist's practice.

God, that seemed bitchy even to me.

"Just taking charge of my life, you know?" I said.

"How so?" she asked.

"I'd messed up a while ago," I said and she raised an eyebrow but didn't interrupt. "I hurt someone close to me and I finally owned up to it and apologized. Things have gotten a lot better."

"Care to elaborate?" she asked.

"Not really," I said.

"Okay," she said reluctantly. "Have you heard back from Columbia yet?"

"Not yet."

"I'm sure you will soon," she said. "And I know what the answer will be." She opened up a drawer in the desk and pulled out a gift-wrapped package. A small one. She set it on the desk in front of me.

"For me?" I asked.

"No wonder everyone thinks you're so smart," she said.

Ms. Bjorn was sassing me. I liked it.

"Go ahead," she said. "Open it."

I picked it up—it was obviously a book—and tore open the paper.

"It's hopelessly out of date," Ms Bjorn said. "I mean, the last year they printed an updated guide was back in 2005, after all."

I held a battered copy of *The Rough Guide to New York*

in my hands. It looked like it had spent a lot of time in someone's backpack.

"That was the copy I used when I went to New York," Ms. Bjorn said. "The maps will still be good, at least. God knows what businesses will be open when you head back East."

I didn't know what to say. No one had ever given me such a thoughtful gift before. The only thing that came close was when my dad bought me my first revolver.

I felt tears welling up in my eyes, but I blinked them back. I stood up and went around the desk. Ms. Bjorn, not being fresh off the turnip truck, knew what was coming and she stood up to receive my hug.

"Thank you," I said.

"I know you're going to do great there," she said. "You're one of the most interesting and unique students I've ever met with."

Most unique? I let it slide.

She pulled away from the hug and smiled at me.

"Even if half of the things you've told me have been bull," she said.

My face must have fallen because she laughed. For a long time.

"Don't worry about it, Courtney," she said. "No one who comes in here ever tells me everything. God, I'd probably run screaming for the hills if they did. I figure that the important things will come out eventually."

"Okay," I said. She'd known all along that I was hiding stuff from her, and she hadn't called me on it or let on she knew at all. Crazy. My opinion of her grew by an order of magnitude.

I went back around to the other side of the room and put the book in my backpack. Our time was just about up.

"I wrote my e-mail address on the inside front cover," she said. "I'd love to hear how you make out."

"I'll write you," I promised. "Thanks."

"You're welcome," she said. "It's just an old book."

"Not for that," I said. "For everything. For caring."

"I think a lot more people care than you know, Courtney," she said. "Or are willing to acknowledge."

We hugged one more time, and then I left her office for the last time.

Phil waited for me at my locker.

"Are you okay?" he asked. "Were you crying?"

"It's Ms. Bjorn's fault," I said. "She waited until the last possible moment to reveal that she's cool."

"By making you cry?" he asked. "That is pretty cool."

For someone who claimed not to understand how comedy worked, he was funny when he wanted to be. Not that I'd ever let him know I thought that.

"What do you want to do tonight?" Phil asked.

"Let's get something to eat," I said.

"Let me guess," he said. "Bully Burger."

"This may be the last time I ever see Chacho," I said. I knew I'd been acting all confident about how the kegger was going to go, but I guess I still wanted to be prepared in case something went wrong.

"Okay," Phil said. "As long as you let me buy. It's been kind of weird having you pay for everything lately."

"Don't you like having a sugar mama?" I asked.

"Ugh. Please promise never to say that ever again."

"No can do," I said. "I never know when I'll need to gross you out."

We headed out of the school and to Phil's car. God, I wouldn't miss looking up at guard towers and seeing the sunlight glint off rifle scopes.

"Hey, can we stop at a hardware store on the way?" I asked.

"Sure," Phil said. "What do you need there?"

"I've just been thinking of a little project," I said.

He didn't ask any more questions, and we climbed into the car and drove off through the security cordon.

The old dudes at the hardware store were super helpful. I love that about old guys, actually. What I could live without was their condescension. I've never been called "hon," "sweetie," and "little lady" so much in my whole life. But at least we walked out of there with everything I thought we'd need for my task.

After that, we headed to Bully Burger, which was a little disappointing. Mr. Washington, the owner, was there, which meant Chacho had to stand outside and do his guard thing. Mr. Washington was happy to see Phil and me, though. So happy that he bought both our dinners.

"I still get credit for wanting to pay for your meal," Phil said.

"Whatever," I said, "cheapskate."

We only got to talk to Chacho for fifteen minutes when he took his state-mandated break. Well, less than that because it took him a while to get his armor off and use the bathroom.

He knew something was up, but he didn't press it. He thanked us again for coming to his barbecue, and told us the next one was going to be on the Fourth of July.

"We'll be done in time for you to go see some fireworks somewhere," he said, "and whatever other trouble you kids get up to." He even told Phil he ought to bring his aunt and uncle.

We talked about not much at all, but when we all stood up—me and Phil to leave, and Chacho to get back to work—I surprised him by giving him a huge hug.

"You're making me worried," he said. "Tell me you're not going to do anything stupid any time soon."

"Nothing more stupid than the usual," I said.

"Oh, boy," he said. "Well, be careful."

"Always," I said.

"And you take care of her," he said to Phil.

Phil took my hand in his and squeezed it. "Always," he said.

He held my hand so rarely. I'd be damned if it was going to be the last time.

CHAPTER TWENTY-TWO
I Guess It's Time

I slept in late the next day. I figured that later I'd appreciate all the rest I could get.

I found Phil in his room, at his drawing board, of course. A large white envelope sat on the table next to him.

"What's that?" I asked as I sat on the floor. I didn't have the energy to climb up onto his bunk bed.

"What's what?"

"Don't," I said. "You know what I mean."

He finished up whatever he was drawing and then set his pencil down. He looked down at the envelope.

"That came today in the mail," he said. "It's from the Kubert school, the comics school."

I sat up on the bed, the last bit of sleepiness chased away by excitement.

"What's it say?" I asked.

"No idea."

"What the hell does that mean?" I asked. " 'No idea.' "

"Just what I said." He turned and looked at me. "I'm not going to open it until tomorrow. Whatever it says might not matter after tonight."

"Oh, my God," I said. "I can't believe you're doing this to me!"

"I'm pretty sure I'm doing it to myself," he said.

"You only think that because you're so incredibly self-ish," I said.

I really didn't understand what he was doing. If I got a letter like that from Columbia, no force on earth could stop me from opening it.

"What did your aunt and uncle say when it came?" I asked.

"They weren't here," he said. "They still aren't. They went to the nursery and some other places, I think. They'll be gone for hours."

"Oh," I said. "You know what we should do while they're out?"

He turned his swivel chair around to face me and grinned.

"What?" he asked.

"We should work on the project," I said.

"Oh," he said. "That. Sure."

"Why?" I asked innocently. "What were you thinking?"

"Funny." He stood up and stretched. I heard his spine crack. "Go get dressed. I'll get the tools."

It only took about an hour to install the hardware I'd bought to the crawl space's trapdoor. We tried it out a few times and it seemed to work perfectly.

After that, I showered and ate. Then came the long, fidgety wait for it to be time to leave for the party. I tried reading, listening to music, watching TV, surfing the web. None of it held my interest. Phil was no help, either. I eventually decided to leave him alone because he was in some sort of Zen trance with his drawing. I knew it annoyed him every time I interrupted him.

Gene and Diane finally came home, and I leaped up to help them unload the car. Anything to take my mind off the waiting. They'd bought a small forest's worth of plants, along with potting soil and fertilizer. It was very domestic.

"Thanks, Courtney," Diane said. "If only we might get someone else to be helpful."

"Don't be hard on Phil," I said. "He's lost in his drawings." I declined to mention anything about the letter he'd gotten.

When we got back into the house, I pointed to the rug that covered the trapdoor and said, "I did something to the crawl space door, and I hope you won't mind."

"What'd you do?" Gene asked. He craned his neck to look, even though I hadn't pulled the rug back.

I bent down to do that, then stopped.

"I hope you won't think I'm weird or paranoid," I said, "but I've been thinking about how my dad died, and I don't want the same thing to, you know . . ."

They looked at each other, then turned back at me with identical strained smiles.

"Oh, sweetie, we'd never think that of you!" Diane said, and Gene nodded vigorously.

"Okay," I said. I pulled back the rug. They looked underwhelmed.

To be honest, there wasn't much to see. Just the tops of three flush-head bolts.

"Give me a second," I said.

A small ring was screwed into the top of the trapdoor and sat in a little recess. I pried the ring up, and pulled up the door—which was made of plywood a couple of inches thick. On the underside of the door, each bolt attached to a short length of chain secured by a big washer and nut. The three chains were joined together with another bolt and nut. It formed a sort of cradle that you were able to slip your hand through to hold the door closed from inside the crawl space.

I explained all of this, then got into the space. Standing on the hard-packed dirt floor, the floor of the kitchen was still at waist level. "Try and open the door," I said to Gene, then I closed the door behind me, sat on the ground, and grabbed on to the chain.

After a few seconds, I felt resistance on the chain, but the door barely budged at all. All I had to do was let my weight hang from the chain and there was no way Gene was able to open the door without using tools. No matter how smart and coordinated zombies got, I doubted they'd ever become little undead handymen.

I felt the individual links biting into the flesh of my palm.

"Okay," I yelled at Gene. "I'm going to let go now."

I waited a second, then did like I said. I pushed the door open and stood up.

"You couldn't open it, right?" I asked even though I knew the answer.

"There was no way to get leverage," Gene said. He was smiling at me like I was a kid who had just spelled her first word.

"Right now," I said, "the only problem I can see is that holding on to the chain hurts your hand. I can rig something else up, but for now, you might try to keep some work gloves handy. You know, just in case."

"I think it's great just like it is, Courtney," Gene said. "I only hope we never have to use it."

"Me, too," I said. There was no way I wanted to tell them they might be using it sooner than they'd like without sounding like a loon.

"It's very thoughtful of you," Diane said, and she gave me a hug.

"Thanks," I said. "It was nothing." I suddenly felt really tired. Maybe it was from having installed the hardware onto the door, but it felt more emotional somehow.

"I think I'm going to go take a nap or something," I said.

"You want to be fresh for tonight," Diane said as I started walking out of the kitchen. I stopped, startled.

"Phil said you two were going to some sort of party," she said. "Have a good rest."

"Thanks," I said. "I will.

I closed the bedroom door behind me, closed the drapes, and lay down on top of the covers. After a few seconds, I stripped off my socks and jeans, then lay back down again. Finally, I got under the covers. I just couldn't get comfortable. Wasn't that the worst? You have the chance to take a nap and your body just rebels. I was just about to admit defeat and get up when sleep finally crashed down on me like an iron anvil in a Warner Brothers cartoon.

I stood on the shore of the lake where the kegger was going to be several hours from now. It was night, and moonless. The only light came from the cabin behind me, which was burning out of control. Water lapped up on the beach even though there was no wind. Was something out in the lake?

I heard footsteps behind me on the sand.

"Hi, Sherri," I said. I pulled my sweatshirt closer around myself, even though it was a warm night.

"You realize it was a year ago?" she asked. She stepped up beside me. "Exactly one year ago that you were here before. Of course, I never got to be here in person."

"What are you here to tell me this time?" I asked. "'Cause I have to tell you, I'm getting really tired of the Ghost of Zombies Future thing."

"Technically," she said, "I'd be the Ghost of Zombies Past." She grinned at me.

I refused to play along.

"Fine, be that way," she said and rolled her eyes. "You could always get so pissy. No, Courtney," she went on, "I think I'm just here to be here. To see you. No matter what happens tonight, I don't think I'm coming back for any more visits."

I didn't know how I felt about that. On the one hand, scary dreams starring your dead best friend kind of sucked. On the other, I'd miss her if she was truly going to be gone forever.

"You're just part of my imagination, right?" I asked her. "Or my subconscious?"

She shrugged. "Would you believe me if I said anything different?"

"No," I said.

"Then let's just say that."

We stood watching the water for a while. I knew it was only a dream, but it felt so comforting just to stand with my friend on the beach. The house burning behind us gave the scene a lot of atmosphere.

"Say," I said, "I've been wondering. How come Willie never came back to say hi?"

"I don't think he was smart enough to find a way back," she said. Then she covered her mouth and looked both horrified and really pleased with herself. "Oh, God, that was terrible!"

We both laughed.

"God," she said, "I loved that kid, but, you know."

"I've missed this," I said. "Standing around, bullshitting."

"Me, too," she said. "Hey, maybe tonight you'll screw the pooch and we'll get to hang together more often!"

"Bitch," I said, but I wasn't mad. It was just her way. What I did do was reach over and grab her hand. She didn't pull hers away or accuse me of being gay or anything; she just let me hold on to her.

"No offense," I said, "but I don't plan on seeing you again for a long time."

"That's cool, too," she said. "I can wait."

And we just stood like that as the house fire behind us started to wind down.

A knock on my door brought me back to the real world.

"Yes?" I asked.

Phil's voice came through the door. "It's time to get ready to go."

"Okay," I said. "Give me a minute."

I heard him walk away and I burrowed my face into my pillow. It was wet with tears.

A half hour later, we had Cody in the car and we were driving through Silverton on the way to the kegger. We didn't say much; everyone seemed wrapped up in their own heads. I was trying to shake the feeling that there was something I hadn't thought of. That I was going to get a lot of people killed—myself included. Well, I told myself, if I died, I wouldn't have to deal with the guilt of knowing I'd been wrong. I didn't really believe it, though.

Phil suggested we listen to music.

"Oh, yeah!" I said. "I forgot that I brought this to listen to." I pulled a CD out of my sweatshirt pocket and handed it over.

"Lucinda Williams?" he asked.

"Put it in," I said. "You'll like it. And if you don't, don't say anything."

Lucinda's desperate voice sang out as we drove, and I suddenly didn't feel so worried. We lived in a world where she'd been born and been allowed to make music. Things weren't all that bad, I thought.

"So I decided I'm going to Chemeketa Community College in the fall," Cody said. "I'm going to do the Occupation Skills program, then see about maybe going to a four-year state school or just getting a job after." He shrugged his shoulders. "I don't know."

"That's good, Cody," I said.

"Yeah, I decided to sign up after you talked about making plans past the other night," he said. "I figured I'd better get on the stick and figure out what the hell I wanted to do with my life."

"It's good to have plans," I said. "And to realize that we'll probably make it past tonight."

I looked at Phil. He didn't say anything, but he shook his head slightly. So he hadn't told Cody about the letter, either. I guess tomorrow was going to be a surprise for everyone but Phil and me.

We made a few more attempts at small talk, but every time our talking died out before it even started. Eventually we gave up and drove on in silence. It was silent except for the music, anyway. I watched the trees and fields slide by outside the window.

Sherri had been right. In my dream, she'd been right. It had been exactly a year since I'd been out to the cabin and helped repel a zombie attack. It made a kind of sense that I was doing it again, but I promised myself there'd be no third time.

We eventually came to a drive cut into the surrounding forest, a steel tube gate blocking the way. A couple of kids I barely recognized, a white kid and a Latino, stood at the gate, rifles hanging off their shoulders. Phil pulled up and braked long enough for them to open the gate.

"Are you guys juniors?" he asked.

"Yeah," the Latino kid said. "Dillon said we could come to the party if we stood guard at the gate for a while."

I recognized them then. They were both on the varsity football team even though they were juniors. The fact that they were here tonight probably meant that they'd be planning the thing next year. That was how it worked, I thought. Jock kings handing down the responsibility for the kegger to their hand-chosen little princes. It made a majestic sort of sense when you thought about it.

"Just follow the drive all the way up to the cabin," the Latino kid told us. I didn't bother to tell him I'd already been here a few times.

"Thanks," Phil said. He drove on past the gate.

It took a few minutes before we came to a large clearing, maybe a couple of acres of lawn that was bordered by forests on three sides and a beach on the fourth. The cabin we'd burned down a year ago had been rebuilt, or replaced. I wasn't able to tell if it was the same as the old one. The building was dark; none of us would be going inside it tonight.

Another gun-toting junior stopped us and told us to pull the car down by the beach. We were lucky to get there early. Once the spots on the beach and by the house were taken, everyone else was going to have to park along the road and walk up.

A bunch of other cars and trucks were already parked near the beach. They were arranged in two semicircles. A couple of dozen yards separated the two lines of cars. We parked in the outer ring. We left our weapons in the car, but we also popped the trunk so we'd be able to get at everything easily.

Michael and Dillon and Zander stood in the back of a huge pickup that had been lifted to ridiculous heights. Three plastic trash cans took up most of the truck's bed, each one filled with ice and a keg. That seemed like a lot of beer to me, but I guess there'd be a few people showing up. I wondered how much time they'd have to drink before things got interesting.

"Hey, dudes," Zander called out to us. "Want a beer?"

"Actually, yes," I said. Phil gave me a look and I told him I wanted to have one now and then I'd stay dry. "I want to be completely sober later, but I also want to have a beer at my senior kegger."

He and Cody also asked for one.

The three bros in the truck took a lot of joy in pouring the beers.

"Here you go," Mike said. "Eat, drink, and be merry."

"For later we kick some zombie ass," Dillon chimed in and they all laughed.

I wondered how much they'd already had and whether or not that was going to be a problem. Seemed a little too late to worry about it now.

As we sipped our beers, we watched some kids stacking wood for a bonfire. The beer tasted good. They'd actually gotten something quality rather than just settling for Budweiser or some other crap. I approved. Not that they'd care.

"I like this place," Cody said. "It'd be cool to come here when we weren't worried about hordes of the undead, you know?"

"Yeah," said Phil. "Maybe I'll have a place like this one day and we can all hang out together."

Cody gave him a look that I wasn't able to interpret. "Sure," he said. "That'll be cool."

"Where's Hannah?" I asked.

"She'll be here soon," he said. "When we were in the car, she texted me to let me know that she and her friends were on the way. They needed to stop and buy ammo before they headed out of town."

"Well, it's good they're coming prepared," I said. "She seems like a good one."

"She is," he said.

Phil pointed down the beach. "Hey, there's Lance and Sarah. I'm going to go say hi. Want to come?"

"Nah," Cody said. "I'm going to wait for Hannah and them."

"Me, too," I said. Cody shot me a look, but he didn't say anything.

One of the cars parked near the beach started to play

some god-awful music. I think it was Kid Rock. A couple of kids gave one of those whoop/yells that's really just a cry for help.

After Phil walked away, I took a step closer to Cody.

"What's up?" I asked him.

"What's that supposed to mean?" he asked.

"Don't play dumb with me," I said. "I saw that look you had when Phil talked about hanging out in the future. He may have seen it, too, but he doesn't know to be concerned about it."

Cody sighed and took a long drink of his beer.

"Do you really think there's going to be a lot of hanging out between us in the future, Courtney?" he asked. "You guys are leaving, headed off to wherever doctors and famous freaking cartoon guys head off to. I'll be here. I'll go to Chemeketa and then, if I'm lucky, I'll get a job at some factory. The potato chip plant if I'm *really* lucky. When will we hang out?"

I didn't know what to say, but I felt sick to my stomach. Maybe the beer wasn't as good as I first thought.

"And it's cool," he said. "It's fine. I want Phil to go off and be successful. You, too. We give each other a lot of shit, but I'll be happy if you go away and become a success. Go win the doctor equivalent of the Stanley Cup, why don't you?"

We each sipped our beers.

"Well," I said, "I for one hope you do get a job at the potato chip factory. Then you can send me bags of those sea salt and pepper kind."

He laughed.

"See," he said, "you're okay. I'll be fine here." It sounded like he was trying to convince himself.

"Hey, baby!" Hannah and her crew came walking toward us. She had an assault rifle—I think it was a Smith and Wesson—tricked out with a scope strapped across her chest, but the rifle was done up in pink and black camou-flage. Pink. And black. I bit back vomit.

She walked right up to Cody, smacking her gum like a cud, and laid a big ol' kiss on him. It was like they were using their tongues to check each other for cavities. Her friends looked as disgusted as I felt.

"Hey, girl," she said to me when she finally came up for air.

"Hello, female," I said, and she laughed.

Cody looked dazed by it all. Yeah, I guessed he really was going to be okay.

"I am so buzzed about tonight," she said. "I've been waiting to put this to some use, you know?" She slapped the rifle that was doing such wonky things to her boobs.

"I'm glad you're ready," I said. I nodded my head in the general direction that my boyfriend had headed. "I'm go-ing to go find Phil."

As I walked up the stretch of sand, I noticed that the semicircles had been filled, and so had the spaces up by the cabin. A steady stream of people were now walking up. Things would be in full swing soon. Soon.

I felt all giddy with anticipation, but afraid, too. It felt like Christmas when Leatherface was handing out presents.

Phil found me watching the people arrive. He sidled up next to me and put his arm around my waist. It felt good, dispelling all thoughts of nominally religious holidays and horror movie bad guys.

"How were Lance and Sarah?" I asked.

"It's going to start getting dark soon," he said.

"Their relationship?" I asked. "Gee, and I thought they were really doing well."

"Ha," Phil said. He didn't laugh; he actually said the word "ha."

"I mean the sun will go away soon and it will become dark," he said. "Outside. Where we are now."

"I guess you're right," I said. I snuggled in closer to him for a second. "I wish the sun would never go down. Maybe that'd keep the zombies from coming."

"Maybe, but then we'd never be done with this."

"Whatever, Mr. Practical," I said.

Crystal Beals found us standing there, and I tore myself away from Phil to give her a hug. It wasn't as satisfying, but I was glad she still liked me enough to give me one. While we embraced, I looked up at the rows of cars and noticed Warren standing there all by himself just watching us. He didn't have a gun that I was able to see, but he did have his sword strapped to his back. At least he came somewhat prepared. After a second, he made eye contact with me, then slowly shook his head and wandered off. What the hell was that about?

Crystal broke away and we talked for a few minutes. She was back to her old, cheerful self. Good, I'd worried that I'd done some damage to what we seemed to be rebuilding. I was also happy to see she was sober.

Actually, I noticed that most people were taking it easy, beer-wise. Mike and the organizers might have a lot left over at the end of the night.

After Crystal moved on to talk to other people, the evening became a long parade of people coming up to say hi. Everyone who'd been at the summit meeting said hello (well, everyone but Warren). A bunch of other people, too. Elsa and that whole crew had shown up together, and while Carol and Brandi weren't exactly exuberant, they at least spoke to me and didn't spit at me even once. I chalked that up in the progress column.

It was interesting to watch all of the social groups mingling a bit. Everyone laughed and talked, and there were hugs. Awkward hugs since most everyone was packing serious firepower. It was heartwarming to see, like an after school special sponsored by the NRA.

Sooner than I'd have thought possible, it was full dark. Some of the boys started throwing gasoline on the bonfire. Everyone stopped what they were doing. Gabe reached into a box of Molotov cocktails someone had prepared, and pulled one out. He used a silver Zippo to light the rag that stuck out the top. Then he used the flaming rag to light a cigarette. It looked cool, but I wondered why he wasn't more concerned about dying in a huge ball of fire. Once his cancer stick was lit, he threw the bottle into the middle of the pile of wood.

There was the sound of breaking glass, then the whole thing went up in a mushroom cloud of flame and smoke. I felt a rush of wind as the fire sucked the surrounding oxygen into itself, and I was immediately hot.

I was glad they'd started the fire. It was going to be a couple of hours before the moon came up, and we'd need the light.

Phil seemed to be the only one who wasn't watching the fire.

"It might be time to call the cops," he said.

Calling the police was step one in the plan.

"Why?" I asked. "Is it time?"

"They seem to think it is," he said and pointed out toward the trees.

A ragged line of zombies had come out of the tree line and stood watching us.

"Yeah," I said. "I guess it's time."

CHAPTER TWENTY-THREE
I Wish We Could Kill Him Again

Someone killed the crappy music, and everyone fell silent as they watched more zombies make their way out of the trees.

No one screamed; no one flinched. Not outwardly, at least. My own heart started thudding in my chest and my mouth instantly went dry. I wanted another beer in the worst possible way.

Beside me, Phil took out his phone and dialed 911.

I worked up some spit to wet my mouth, and said, "Get in position, everyone."

A bunch of us split off from the group and ran to the outer ring of cars. We'd arranged them to use as defensive positions—something to stand behind and use for cover and as braces for aiming. Cody and I got to Phil's car at the same time. I threw the trunk open and he pulled out our shotguns and ammo.

Phil came up after a second and grabbed his gun, too. We all braced ourselves against the car. Then we sat.

"Wait until they get close," I shouted. "Don't waste your ammo! And wait for my signal before you fall back." I hoped falling back wasn't going to be necessary.

I stared down the gun barrel at the runners who just stood there. What were they waiting for? Some sort of signal? And where was Brandon? The fire cast long, disorienting shadows and made it hard to see too much detail. I didn't see Brandon, but I knew he was out there somewhere.

On some cue that I was unable to make out, the zombies hissed, and then they came running at us. Maybe the worst part was that they ran silently. Whenever you see a scene like this in a movie, the rushing army always yells as they approach, but these guys were completely silent. I heard my breath, and my pounding heart. And their pounding feet.

"Hold on," I said.

Phil's cell phone started to ring, but he ignored it.

The zombies had covered nearly half the distance to us when a figure came running up from behind us, leaped onto the trunk of the car, then launched itself toward the zombies.

Warren. He hit the ground running and sprinted toward the monsters, drawing his sword as he went.

"What the hell is he doing?" Cody shouted.

He hit the wall of runners and two fell as he swung his blade. Several of the zombies altered their course to intercept him and he kept swinging and they kept falling.

The mass of the horde kept running at us, though.

"Get ready," I said.

Warren was surrounded now. He kept up the sword work, but I heard him drawing in ragged breaths from where I stood. He must have been getting tired.

"Ready," I said. The line of runners were just yards away.

Warren screamed as one of the zombies he'd cut down but hadn't killed grabbed his leg and bit it. He plunged his sword into the thing's head.

"Fire," I screamed.

I nearly went deaf from the volley of rounds everyone let loose. It was like the whole line of zombies hit a wall as the bullets and buckshot tore through them. The monsters fell and they didn't get back up. A deafening silence came over all of us as we took in what we'd done.

A yell went up across the line. The idiots were celebrating.

Then they saw Warren and they went silent again.

He limped back toward the group, his leg bleeding freely.

"I think I may have messed up back there," he said.

"Look!" someone shouted, and they didn't mean to look at Warren.

More zombies had come out of the trees. We'd only survived their first wave.

Warren looked from the zombies back to me and Phil. Or maybe just to me. I've never been sure. He smiled.

"Saves me from having to ask you to shoot me," he said.

As fast as he was able, which wasn't fast, he ran back to get his sword, pulled it out of the zombie's head, then kept running toward the tree line.

The runners took this as their cue to attack. They roared wordlessly and came for us. The ground beneath my feet rumbled as they charged.

"Same as before," I yelled. "Hold your fire until they're right on us."

Warren collided with the line of runners. He might have taken out a couple, but then they overwhelmed him. A strangled cry was cut short. I thanked whatever deity was out there listening that the approaching line of ghouls blocked my view of what happened to him.

The zombies reached the piles of their dead buddies, and I shouted, "Fire!"

Another volley, and another. They fell, but there seemed to be more to replace them. Did Brandon plan to bury us under sheer numbers?

A couple of guys started lighting Molotovs and pitching them into the mass of runners. Setting fire to the zombies running at us didn't seem like a big improvement, but after a few seconds, the zombies who'd been set ablaze fell over and just burned.

"Keep it up," I shouted.

Too soon, the guys ran out of their homemade bombs.

Several zombies reached the car we hid behind. Kids stood and backed away; some just ran back to the next line of cars.

"They're getting through!" Phil shouted. I heard more screams, and then some of the kids were firing into our own lines. That made more gaps. I saw where this was going.

"Fall back to the next line!" I shouted, and I heard the order repeated.

I ran full-out to get behind a truck. I shouted for the people already there to start firing. Zombies started to fall. More kids came up and joined us, firing the whole time. The runners weren't able to get past the cars.

Then I heard someone shout behind us.

"They're in the water!"

Everything slowed down for a second, moving in slow motion as I turned from the charging zombies, back toward the beach. I'd felt earlier like there was something I'd forgotten, and I'd worried it might get us killed. But it wasn't something I'd forgotten; it was something I hadn't even considered in the first place.

Zombies were emerging out of the lake behind us.

How long had they been there? Hours? Days? They'd sat there patiently just waiting for the signal to attack.

Dammit, I couldn't wait to get get my hands on Brandon. Even if I was going down tonight, I wanted to take him with me.

A few kids stood on the grass near where the sand started. "Start shooting them, you jerks!" I shouted.

A few did, but not enough. They seemed stunned.

I put my hand on Phil's shoulder. "You have to hold those zombies back. I have to go deal with this other thing."

He nodded, then turned back to the task at hand.

"Keep shooting," he yelled.

I ran down the line of kids firing toward the trees, tapping shoulders as I went.

"Come on," I yelled. "Down to the beach!"

We ran and joined the few kids already there. I knelt down and started shooting. The kids I'd tapped knelt down on either side of me and did the same. I hoped the others would follow our lead.

I got why they'd been freaked out. Watching the zombies rise up out of the lake, water dripping down them, it was just plain unnatural. It was like an image out of an old EC horror comic. I wondered if Brandon had chosen that tactic partly because it was creepy as hell.

I glanced back at the few people still just standing there, gawking.

"Get down here and help if you want to get out of here alive," I shouted at them.

I went back to the task at hand and drew a bead on a zombie. I pulled the trigger and there was one less undead asshole in the world. I repeated the process again and again. I reloaded whenever I noticed I'd run empty, and I hoped each time that some speedster wouldn't choose that moment to go to town on my butt.

More shouts and screams from up by the cars. There was no way I could leave what I was doing to help or even

check on them. I had to hope that Phil had everything under control.

The line of zombies emerging from the water had slowed.
Were their numbers dwindling? Were we winning? I allowed myself to smile at the thought.

And then the shooting up by the cars stopped.

Just before I looked up to see what was going on, I noticed that the zombies down on the beach had stopped.

"Courtney?" Phil called.

He stood with his shotgun dangling from his right hand.
He looked exhausted, and he had black zombie gore
splashed across him. One of the runners must have gotten
close.

I stood, sparing another glance at the zombies near the
lake. They were still playing a creepy game of freeze tag.

I ran up the slight incline to where Phil stood.

"What is it?" I asked. "Why's everyone stopped shooting?"

Phil was the only one looking at me. Everyone else
faced the woods and whatever was out there. More zombies was my guess.

"What is it?" I asked again when I reached him. His response was to turn and look where everyone else was.

A single zombie stood alone in the middle of the grass,
an army of runners standing well back from him. Of
course it was Brandon.

"What the F?"

"Right," Phil said. "It's an interesting development."

I stepped out from behind the line of cars. The space
between the first and second line was filled with bodies.
Most of them zombies, but a few were my classmates. I
turned away from them. When this was all over, I'd make
sure and look at all of them, study their faces, and memo-
rize their names, but for right now, there was still a job to
finish.

When he spotted me, Brandon roared, a horrible, animal sound. Spittle flew from his lips.

"Hi, shithead," I whispered.

He roared again like he'd heard me. It was a sound that reached way deep inside of me and touched something old—something that remembered the roar of ancient predators that hunted us humans. I wished he'd stop that; I'd probably pee my pants if he did it again.

I looked at the kids gathered around and found a girl a little bit bigger than me.

"Give me your sweatshirt," I said to her.

"You're already wearing one."

"I didn't ask for a report on my clothes, Tim Gunn," I said. "Just give me the sweatshirt. Please."

She didn't look happy, but she started to strip it off.

Phil walked up next to me. "What are you doing?" he asked.

"This is all about me and him," I said. "He thinks we have unresolved issues. Fine, I'm about to resolve them."

"Why don't we just kill him?" he asked. "One well-placed shot ends this thing."

"Who knows what he's told his army to do if anyone interferes," I said. "I think the safest thing to do will be to face him." I smiled up at him. "You know I can take him, right?"

"How is that even a question?" he asked.

The girl held out her sweatshirt to me. God, it was pink.

"Thanks," I said. "I'll buy you a new one. You won't want this one back."

I pulled the sweatshirt on over my own, doing my best to keep the sleeves from bunching up. I needed some protection. If Brandon wasn't able to bite or scratch me through my clothes, then he couldn't turn me into a zombie. I thought that two layers of shirts and a pair of jeans ought to do the trick.

"Open the trunk for me," I said to Phil. He followed me to the car. Its windows had been blown out, gaping holes were torn in the quarter panels and doors, and the tires on the passenger side were flat. All of the cars in the outer ring looked like that.

"Sorry," I said. "I hadn't thought of that. You can have my Subaru."

"Sweet," he said. "I've been jonesing for that."

He popped the trunk and I grabbed my trusty wrecking tool.

"Time to do something stupid," I said as I hefted the tool.

Phil snaked his arm around my waist and pulled me in for a kiss. It was a real stunner. Like, I saw stars.

"Kill him once for me," he said.

"I'll do my best," I said. "More of that when I get back, okay?"

"I'll be here."

I stepped past that first line of cars, and then there was nothing between me and an army of the undead. Nothing but Brandon, anyway.

My heart beat too fast in my chest, and I drew breath in great gulps of air. I had seldom recognized up until that point when I was doing something truly stupid, but my whole body was yelling at me that this was really damned dumb. Single combat was something we'd left behind back when Richard the Lionhearted was kicking the crap out of Jerusalem. But here I was about to revive the grand old tradition.

Brandon roared at me again and that did it. I'd had enough. I didn't want to hear that voice ever again.

I shot back my own roar. "Go to hell!" And I started running.

He charged across the grass, snorting and grunting, black spittle flying.

I ran for all I was worth, my lungs burning, my legs pumping. When we were just a few feet apart, Brandon leaped at me. I fell on my back like I was sliding into home plate and raised my tool, and the nail-puller caught him in the belly. I held on for dear life and got a hot load of zombie guts dumped on my chest as a reward.

I bit back vomit and stood up as fast as I was able. Brandon looked down at himself and roared again. In pain, maybe. But no matter how much it hurt him, that wasn't an injury that might keep a zombie down. I brandished the tool.

"Let's go, you creep!" I yelled.

He eyeballed me, then jumped over his own intestines at me. He hit me harder than I expected and I went down on my back with him on top of me.

The stench of rot was almost unbearable. But there was nothing like fighting for your life to keep your mind off your sense of smell.

He snapped his jaws inches from my face, but I was able to hold him back with the tool, which I held across his chest with both hands. He tore at my arms and chest with his claws. If it hadn't been for the extra layer of sweatshirt, I'd have been toast. I needed him off me, fast.

As fast and as hard as I could, I turned my whole body, bringing the tool with me. The tile-ripper head caught him in the face and I kept turning. I felt the tool meet resistance, then it wrenched free of whatever had caught it. I heard a weird, strangled cry come from Brandon, then silence.

I rolled a few feet away and got to my feet. I turned to

face Brandon and found him kneeling in a pile of his own guts, his jaw half ripped off. He looked at me, his dead eyes filled with anger and betrayal.

"Sorry," I said. I took a step forward and swung the tool like a short baseball bat. It connected with his head and sent a shock wave up my arms. He fell backward.

I dropped down on his chest, my legs on either side of his body. He tried to fight me, but he had nothing left to give.

I got the chisel head up where his chin would be if his jaw had still been attached to his face, then, with all my strength, I pushed it up into his mouth, through his soft palate, and into his brain.

Brandon's body convulsed beneath me a few times, and then he was still.

I pulled the tool free and stood up to face the army of zombies. I showed them the tool, their boss's necrotic brains dripping off the end.

"You want some, too, you undead assholes?" I yelled at them. "Well, come on!"

They milled around. I swear, they looked like school-kids getting scolded by their friend's angry mom.

A few turned and walked off into the woods. Then more, then all of them were walking away. Had I just scared off a zombie horde?

Kids came running up alongside me, firing their guns into the crowd of runners. I didn't try to stop them. I turned and walked back to the cars and Phil.

I passed Warren on the way and stopped to look at him. He was surrounded by dead zombies. Zombies he'd killed.

I knelt down.

"You were a jerk," I said. "But you were pretty good at killing shufflers."

I pulled my pistol from its holster, put the barrel against

his temple, and pulled the trigger. When I stood up, I left the pistol behind. I felt done with killing anything—even something that was already technically dead—for a while. Maybe forever.

I stripped off both sweatshirts and threw them away. Phil came out from behind the cars and held me for a long time without saying anything.

As we stood there in our embrace, the sound of gunfire petered out and I heard the distant wail of sirens.

"Better late than never," I said.

Then I realized I was really thirsty. "I want another beer," I said.

"Me, too," Phil said. "I hope no one shot the kegs."

"Oh, God, don't even say that."

By the time the cops showed up in their anti-zombie armor, most of the kids had drifted back to the kegs and were drinking merrily away. We didn't even stop when the cops told us all to get down. Most of us sat like they requested, but we put just one hand over our heads. We had to use the other hand to hold our beers.

We were all going to have to face the fact that about a dozen of our classmates had been killed in the attack, and it seemed like a drink might help with that.

The cops made their way over to us, stepping gingerly through a mass of dead runners, and more than a few of our classmates. They found us all sitting there with illegal alcohol.

And you know what? Not a single kid got a minor in possession that night.

We answered questions. Lots of questions. Everyone left out the fact that we had planned for an attack. We made it sound like we'd all just been out there and it had happened. While we were being interviewed, the police sent teams out into the forest to hunt down stragglers, so we kept hearing sporadic, distant gunfire. It sounded like fireworks. You know, festive.

When I finished up being interrogated, I found Phil. He was standing there just staring at his phone, his face pale.

"What's wrong?" I asked.

"Um, nothing, really," he said.

"No, what?" I asked.

He looked up at me and smiled. "My aunt and uncle were attacked. Their house. Their house was attacked by a big group of zombies."

"Oh, my shit," I said. "Are they okay?"

"They got in the crawl space and they used your chains to keep them out."

"It worked?"

"They're alive because of you," Phil said. "They called the cops while they were down there, and the cops came and cleared out the undead." He hugged me, a tight embrace, and I felt his tears on my neck. "You saved them, Courtney."

"It worked?" I asked. I couldn't get it through my head. "And the zombies attacked? I knew they might. I knew Brandon might want to eff with my life like that."

"I wish we could kill him again," Phil said.

He broke the embrace and looked a little embarrassed at his display of emotion.

"He's dead enough," I said.

"Let's think about finding a ride home," he said.

"Maybe soon, but there's something I want to do first," I said.

"What's that?"

"I want to see if the cops will let me help with the bodies of our friends," I said. "I want to see everyone who gave up their lives, you know?"

"I'll help," Phil said.

A few others helped, too—Crystal and some folks I didn't know. It didn't take long. There were fewer than I'd feared, but still too many.

We caught a ride with Hannah and Cody and one of Hannah's friends. No one said much on the way home. I mean, what was there to say?

EPILOGUE

"Drive," She Said

Things seemed to move fast for a while after that night. Like we were living in a crappy movie and we'd come to the montage.

I woke up the next day—evening, if you want to be accurate—to find Phil standing in my doorway. Diane and Gene were somewhere else in the house whooping it up.

"Are we under attack again?" I asked.

Phil held up a sheet of paper.

"Yes?" I asked.

"I got in," he said. "The Kubert school."

I lay back down and felt a huge grin spread across my face. "I knew you'd get in," I said in a singsong voice.

"I was pretty sure I would, too," he said. "Get dressed, we're going out to celebrate."

"Where we going?" I asked.

"Olive Garden."

I groaned.

"Don't mock the ways of my people," he said. "Come on, Cody and Hannah are going to meet us there."

That made me sit up. I remembered what Cody had said the night before.

"Did you tell him?" I asked.

Phil nodded.

"How'd it go?"

"He said he was really happy for me," he said. "But . . . but there was something else to it. I didn't press him."

"He's going to lose his best friend," I said.

"He's not going to lose anyone."

Do you really think there's going to be a lot of hanging out between us in the future, Courtney? Cody had said that the night before. Maybe I shouldn't have been surprised that he was better at judging the situation than Phil was. I forced myself to smile.

"Okay," I said. "Let me get dressed."

A few days after that, I got a double-barrel shotgun blast of happy news. When I turned on my computer, my e-mail beeped at me. It was a Google alert notice I'd set up with news about New York. The Army was announcing the end of major operations in New York City and was now moving civilian contractors into the city for cleanup.

I was dancing around in my chair when my e-mail beeped at me again. I almost ignored it. I didn't need a late notice from the library or a piece of Viagra spam to bring me down. I went ahead and checked it anyway because I was compulsive like that.

From: Rjkeller@columbia.edu
Subject: Congratulations

That was all I needed to see. I screamed and ran out of the room. Diane was the first person I found. She was supervising a guy installing a new front door—the zombies had wrecked the old one. She was startled, of course, but then I told her about the e-mail I got and she joined in on my screaming and dancing and hugging. The guy hanging the door just stood there staring at us.

We all went out together that night again. I chose a place that was not Olive Garden, thanks very much. All night long, Cody kept giving me weird I-told-you-so

smiles, but he seemed genuinely happy for me and Phil.
Maybe he was smarter than I ever gave him credit for.

After dinner, Phil and I were driving home in Phil's
new-to-him Subaru.

"I could do with some dessert," I said.

"After all the Vietnamese food you packed away?" Phil
asked, but then he saw the look on my face and backed off.
"What are you in the mood for?"

"A milk shake," I said, "but one made without a trace
of real dairy products."

He thought about that for a second. "Bully Burger it is."

"Chacho will want to hear our good news," I said.

A few minutes later we came around a corner and there
was the BB parking lot. But something was wrong. Huge
high-intensity lights had been set up so that construction
workers were able to see what they were doing in the
darkness. The building itself was completely boarded up,
and it looked a lot like it might have been set on fire, too.

We parked and I was out of the car before it had even
come to a complete stop. I ran to the fence and looked in
at all the workers. Where was the security guy? There had
to be security with this many people around.

Phil joined me and gave me a confused look.

"Hey!" I shouted. "Hey, where's the security guard?"

A couple of guys stopped what they were doing and
looked at me, but then they went back to whatever tasks
they were being paid to do.

I kept shouting until I saw a black-clad dude toting a
shotgun come out of a single-wide trailer off in the corner
of the lot.

"Courtney," Chacho shouted, "what's going on?"

"Oh, thank God," I said. "What happened here, Chacho?"

He came up to the fence, took off his helmet, and
wiped sweat off his bald head.

"We got attacked the other night," he said. "A whole swarm of zombies. I haven't seen anything like it since Baghdad."

"Saturday night?" I asked.

"Yeah," he said and squinted at me. "How'd you know?"

I told him a very shorthand version of what our Saturday night had been like. Chacho shouldered his shotgun and wiped away more sweat.

"Doesn't sound like a coincidence to me," he said. "Must have been something to that theory of yours."

Of course Brandon knew that I considered Chacho a friend. So he'd sent some of his undead army out here to try to kill Chacho. God, that guy had sucked. I agreed with Phil: I wished we could kill him again.

I bit my tongue and didn't shout, "I told you so!" in Chacho's face. Instead, I asked, "What happened here?"

He looked back at the shell of the Bully Burger.

"Like I said, a big load of zombies came crashing through the fence," he said. "We called the cops and then we defended the stupid place."

"Who was here?" I hooked my fingers through the chain link.

"Me, Mr. Washington, the twins," he said, "a few people you don't know. A guy named Karl, another we all called Mullet.

"We ended up huddled behind the counter fighting off the zombies. I finally doused the dining room in oil and set a bunch of them on fire. When the fire suppression system activated, we went out the back door and made our last stand in the shelter with the garbage.

"We lasted long enough for the cops to show up."

"Did everyone make it?"

Chacho looked down at the ground and spat. He shook his head.

"Mullet got it in the first wave. Mr. Washington died saving Ashley. Stupid old man."

"Mr. Washington's dead?" Phil asked.

"Yeah," Chacho said. "Mrs. Washington is running the show now. She's having this whole place remodeled. It's going to be an 'upscale coffee boutique,' whatever that means."

"Jesus," I said.

"Yeah," said Chacho. "Hey, I'm glad to hear you two made it through okay, though. Anything good going on with you?"

"Oh, shit, yes!" I exclaimed and Chacho took an involuntary step back, then caught himself and grinned.

"Well, don't keep it to yourself, *chica*," he said.

So Phil and I got to take turns telling him our news, and Chacho listened, grinning from ear to ear the whole time.

"I knew you'd both be going places," he said. "That's really great news."

A guy in a hard hat came out of the trailer and looked around until he spotted us.

"Hey, Chacho," he yelled. "Barry wants you to do a check on the . . ." He made a circle motion with his finger.

"The perimeter, gotcha, Frank," Chacho shouted back.

"Listen, I gotta go," he said to us. "But it really is great news. Like I said, come by the house on the Fourth. We're having a big barbecue. We'll celebrate."

We told him we'd think about it.

"Bring your family, Phil," he yelled as he walked away. "And your friends. But not too many."

We spent the next month getting ready for a move across the country and for school in the fall. Gene helped me out a lot—he put me in contact with an apartment broker who found me a place to live in a rent-controlled building. The guy assured me that rental prices had never been as low as they were right now, and they never would be again. "There are a lot of advantages to being one of the first people to move back into the city," he told me via e-mail. The same broker put Phil in touch with a woman who helped him find a place in New Jersey.

The lawyer, Alvarez, got me set up with an account at an East Coast bank. He also offered to have all the accounting stuff transferred to a lawyer on that side of the country. Or I could take it all on myself since I'd just turned eighteen. I told him he was doing a great job and to please keep doing a great job.

And, yes, that's right, in all of the craziness, I forgot my own birthday. Even Gene and Diane had missed it. I didn't mention it to them, but I did bring it up with Phil.

"I forgot," he said. "Hell, I'm sorry. I'd been planning something, a new drawing, but then . . ."

"But then we were fighting the undead, getting into college, preparing to move across the country."

"What do you want to do to celebrate?" he asked.

"Hang out with you and your family," I said.

"That's what we always do," he said.

I shrugged. "And yet, that's what I want. Finish that drawing you were working on and give it to me," I said.

"Okay," he said.

I leaned in for a quick kiss. "Okay," I said.

The next time we came up for air was to go to Chacho's Fourth of July cookout thing. Gene and Diane and Cody went with us. Chacho's wife was super-excited to hear all of our news and gave us hugs. The food was amazing, and all of the adults looked the other way when Phil, Cody, and I sneaked some Mason jars full of sangria.

As the sun was setting, we had Gene and Diane drop us

off at the waterfront so we could watch the fireworks along with most of Salem and every armed policeman on the city's payroll. It was a very well-behaved crowd at events like this.

As we waited for the fireworks to start, we lay on our backs in the grass. The sky was a deep blue-black and it was going to be full dark soon. Even though I'd eaten most of a cow back at Chacho's, the smells coming from the food booths made my mouth water.

"So, when are you two leaving?" Cody asked. We'd talked about this a bunch of times, but he kept asking. It was like he wasn't able to hold it in his memory, or maybe like he couldn't accept it.

"Monday," Phil said. "We drive off on Monday. Courtney mapped out the whole route."

"I found every city that's safe to stay in between here and New York," I said.

"I want to hang with you every day between now and then," Cody said. "Even if all we're doing is packing your stuff."

"You know it," Phil said.

We fell silent as the fireworks began to burst overhead.

And somewhere in there, the local newspaper ran a story about how the Salem chapter of Narcotics Anonymous received a cash donation of nearly sixty thousand dollars. Anonymous, of course.

A few days after the Fourth, Cody, Hannah, Gene, and Diane helped us load our things into the Subaru. The bulk of our stuff was already being shipped to our apartments.

We all said our good-byes and hugged and maybe, just maybe, there were a few tears, too.

When I hugged Cody, I whispered in his ear, "Thanks for being such a great friend to Phil."

"Now it's your turn," he said. "Don't screw up all of my training."

"Never," I said.

We got into the car, Phil behind the steering wheel, and I told him I wanted to take a little drive.

"Maybe you haven't noticed, but we're about to head out on a long drive, Courtney," he said. "The car's all packed up and everything."

"A side trip," I said, "before we get going."

He blinked at me and asked where I wanted to go. When I told him, he actually looked surprised.

"Well, let's get going," he said.

He backed out of the drive and got headed in the right direction as we waved good-bye to Diane and Gene. And to Cody, of course.

Without me asking him to, Phil drove us past my old house. The new renters had painted it and had redone the landscaping, but it was still my house. I half expected my Dad to step out of the front door and wave at me as we cruised by. I don't know if he'd have been happy with me leaving, but I think he'd have been proud of me anyway.

I wiped at a tear. There must have been something in the air.

Phil sat on his rock and looked out over the city.

"I can't believe you wanted to come out here again," he said.

I shrugged. "Seemed appropriate somehow."

I sat next to him and took in the whole of Salem. It hadn't changed much at all since the last time we'd sat there, at the beginning of the school year. There was the Gold Man on top of the capitol, the banks and churches, the tree-lined streets. Somehow, though, I felt differently about it. It didn't make me angry or nauseated.

I think that since I was leaving, I wanted to be a little generous toward the place where I'd grown up. But I swore I'd seek out counseling if I ever started to miss the place.

"It feels like a lot more than a year ago that we sat up here," I said.

"It was nine months ago," Phil said. "And we remembered to bring our weapons this time."

I rested my head on his shoulder.

"If you ever tell anyone that I said this, I'll deny it," I said, "and then I'll kick you in the junk, but it's sort of pretty."

"Yeah," he said.

"And we should go before I have a full-on psychotic break."

We made our way up the embankment and to the car.

When Phil keyed the engine to life, the radio came on. But rather than music, the DJ was blathering at us.

"A lot of people are saying they jumped the gun on reopening New York," he said. "No one knows for sure if it's really safe."

"Right," said his partner. "A lot of congressmen are saying that when they retake Washington, D.C., next year, they're not leaving Fort Collins until it's proven to be one hundred percent zombie-free."

I clicked off the radio.

"Those guys can suck it," I said as if Phil had asked what I was doing. "I, for one, choose to remain positive about this move."

"That's the healthiest choice," Phil said.

I leaned over and gave him a quick kiss.

"That's for always knowing the right thing to say. Okay, 'Drive,' she said," I said.

He put the car in gear and I put my feet up on the dash as we drove off toward our futures.